KEPT FOR HER BABY

BY
KATE WALKER

Kate Walker was born in Nottinghamshire, but as she grew up in Yorkshire she has always felt that her roots are there. She met her husband at university, and originally worked as a children's librarian, but after the birth of her son she returned to her old childhood love of writing. When she's not working, she divides her time between her family, their three cats, and her interests of embroidery, antiques, film and theatre, and, of course, reading. You can visit Kate at www.kate-walker.com.

For Anne and Gerry, to celebrate
this very special Caerleon Writers' Holiday.

CHAPTER ONE

THE heat of the day was fading from the atmosphere and the warm air was slowly beginning to cool. The shadows of evening had started to gather as Lucy carefully brought the small, scruffy rowing boat up to the beach where the edge of the tiny island sloped down to the lake and jumped out.

The cool shallow water swirled around her bare feet, coming up ankle deep, just below the rolled up cuffs of her blue cargo pants, as she tugged the small craft onto the shore, biting her lip as she heard the raw, scraping sound its hull made in the sand.

Would anyone hear that? She couldn't afford to be caught now, still too far away from the house to achieve her aim. If one of the small army of security guards that Ricardo employed had heard the noise and came to investigate then she was lost before she had even started. She would be escorted off the island, taken back on to the Italian mainland and dumped back into the tiny, shabby boarding house which was the only place she could afford to stay this week.

This vital, desperately important week.

If she managed stay in Italy at all. Once Ricardo knew she was back he was far more likely to decide that he wanted her out of the country as well. Out of Italy and out of his life for good. Just as he had believed that she was already.

'Oh, help.'

Realising that she was holding her breath, she let it go again on a raw, despondent sigh, pushing a hand through the tumbled blonde hair that had escaped from the band she had fastened it back with as her clouded blue eyes flicked rapidly, urgently from side to side, trying to see if she could spot anyone approaching. If someone had been alerted by the sound of the boat on the sand then surely they should be here by now?

It had to be safe to move. Dipping into the boat, she snatched up her canvas shoes, carrying them to the edge of the beach before she sank down onto the grass to dust off her feet and pull on the footwear.

She wished she could pull the rowing boat up further on the shore. Perhaps even cover it with leaves or branches so that it was more fully concealed from view. But she didn't have the strength to move it any further and the impatient, nervous thudding of her heart urged her to take other action, move on quickly.

Now that she was here, she really couldn't delay any more. She'd waited and planned for this so long, making careful preparations, and she couldn't do so any longer. From the moment that her letter to Ricardo had been returned to her unopened, she had known that this was her only way. She had to take matters into her own hands and do the only thing possible.

She'd tried the polite way, the civilised way and had been firmly rebuffed. She'd tried to appeal to Ricardo's better nature but it seemed that he didn't have one—at least not as far as she was concerned.

And so she'd been forced to come here like this, in secret. Like a thief in the night she had come back to the island in the gathering dusk, finding her way to the one spot where she knew that, tight as Ricardo's security was, it was just possible

to sneak up close when hidden behind some bushes that
overhung the lake. Paddling rather than rowing so as to be as
silent as she could, she'd managed to get onto the shore
without being spotted and now she could only hope that her
luck would hold as she made her way to the house.

Pausing under the shady protection of a big cypress tree,
Lucy found that she was blinking back bitter tears as she
stared up at the huge neo-Gothic villa that rose up before her
at the top of the lushly green sloping gardens. Carefully
shaped terraces with ornate stone balustrades linked by flights
of steps led up to the sprawling white-painted building that
had once been a monastery and then later a palace.

The glass in the Gothic windows reflected the glow of the
setting sun, and in the south western corner a tall tower rose,
crowned by battlements sculpted in stone with floral decora-
tions. From those windows in the Villa San Felice she knew
you could look out across the calm blue waters of Lake Garda
and see the provinces of Verona to the south-east, and Brescia
to the west. Directly opposite was San Felice del Benaco,
which gave both the island and the villa its name.

This amazing place, this fantastic house had once been her
home.

But it was her home no longer. Not for many months
now. And it hadn't ever *felt* like home in all the time she'd
lived there…

Lucy shivered in spite of the mildness of the evening as
memories assailed her. Distress made her skin prickle with
cold goose bumps and she shuddered at the images that passed
through her thoughts, reminding her of how it had once felt
to be here. To live here and yet never feel that she belonged.

'I can't do this!' she muttered aloud to herself. 'I can't go
through with it. Can't face…'

Abruptly she shook her head, fighting to drive away the unhappy thoughts. She had to face things, had to go through with it. Because inside that villa, as well as the terrible memories of some of the worst months of her life, there was also the one thing that mattered most to her in the world. The one thing that made her life now worth living.

Her feet followed the indistinct path with the ease of instinct built up in her time living on San Felice. She found the small gate into the private gardens in the same way, easing it open carefully and wincing in distress as the weathered wood creaked betrayingly.

'Please don't let anyone come,' she prayed under her breath as she dashed across the soft grass and into the concealment of the lush shrubbery that grew beside the lowest level of the stone paved terraces.

'Please don't let anyone see me.'

She had barely hidden herself again when she heard the sound of a door opening above her. The patio doors that led from the big sitting room, she recalled. The same doors through which she had made her escape not quite seven months before when she had fled this house, not daring to look back, terrified of what might happen if someone realised what she was planning and stopped her.

'*Buona sera…*'

The voice from inside the house floated down to her, making her heart stop dead in her chest so that she gasped in shock. A moment later it had kick-started into action again, setting her pulse racing.

Ricardo.

She recognised that voice instantly; would know it anywhere. Only one man possessed those dark, sultry tones or had that slightly husky note in every word he spoke.

How many times had she heard him speak her name in so many different ways? In amusement, in scorn, in anger. And yet, at other times—times she could no longer bear to remember—she had heard him speak to her in burning ardour, taking the simple ordinariness of her name and turning it into magic as he called her his *Lucia*, his delight, his passion…

…*His wife.*

Her heart flinched away from the memory of that word and the way that Ricardo Emiliani had once used it with a note of pride—or so she had thought at the time.

'My wife,' he had said as he took her hand to lead her away from the altar where the priest had just declared that they were married. *'Mia moglie.'*

And for a time she had gloried in the title. She had let herself enjoy being called Signora Emiliani. She had buried the doubts that assailed her deep under the cloak of happiness that shielded her from reality. She had smiled until her jaw ached and she had played the role of the happy young bride who had all that she could dream of.

When all the time, deep down inside, she had known the truth—the only reason why Ricardo had married her in the first place.

And love had had nothing to do with it.

'If you hear anything more, then let me know…'

The once-loved voice came again, startling her because it spoke in English and not his first language of Italian.

So who was he talking to in English? And why?

A nervous shiver ran down Lucy's spine as the sudden thought struck her that perhaps she might have made a fatal mistake in coming out of hiding and getting back in touch with Ricardo after so long. By writing to him, however desperate her need, she had let him know where she was. And Ricardo, being the hugely wealthy, hugely powerful man that he was, would have no difficulty in using that information to find out more. He had only to click his fingers and he had an army of men at his disposal—private detectives, investigators, ready to do anything needed to find out more, to track her down and…

And what?

What would the man who in one last dreadful row had declared to her face that marrying her had been the biggest mistake he had ever made in his life do once he found out where she was?

'I want to see this matter sorted out and finished with.'

'I'll get on to it right away. The contracts will be ready for you to sign tomorrow.'

Somehow it was the other man's voice that brought her back to reality with such a bump that she almost laughed out loud, only just catching herself in time before she gave herself away.

Who was she trying to kid? Why would Ricardo want anything to do with her? He had let her go without a second thought, hadn't he? No one had come after her to try and drag her back to this house and all she had left behind in it. And hadn't the message of the letter returned to her been loud and clear?

Contracts and signing—of course. What else would be on Ricardo's mind other than his huge luxury car business?

Ricardo Emiliani wanted nothing to do with her. He would never forgive her for what she had done, so now he was glad that she was out of his life and he wanted it to stay that way. She was a fool if she allowed herself even to dream that it could be anything else.

She shrank back into the shadowed space between the shrubs and the stone wall of the terrace as slow, heavy footsteps brought Ricardo down the last flight of steps and into the garden. Watching him stroll away from her, Lucy felt as if something or someone had suddenly punched her hard in the chest, driving all the breath from her body and making her heart jump painfully in her throat.

Even from behind like this, he still had such a potent physical impact that it made her freeze and just stare, unable to look away.

He had been walking away from her when she had first seen him. So the first impression she had had been of that proud, black-haired head, held so arrogantly high on a strong, deeply tanned neck. Her eyes had been drawn to those broad, straight shoulders, the powerful length of his back sweeping down to narrow hips and long, long legs. Then, as now, he had been wearing denim jeans so worn and tight that they had clung to his powerful thighs like a second skin. But that day on the beach, two years before, he had been wearing no shirt, nothing to conceal the bronzed skin of his torso, stretched tight across honed muscles that flexed and tightened with every movement, making her mouth dry in sensual response as she'd watched. He'd been barefoot too, seeming nothing but the casual holidaymaker she was herself, his appearance giving no sign of the wealthy, powerful man he really was.

She had been halfway in love with him before she had found out the truth.

Today he wore a white polo shirt, untucked at the waist and hanging loose. But she knew what was under that shirt. She had let her hands slide underneath his clothing so many times, stroking hungry fingers over the warm satin of his skin, feeling his shuddering tension as he responded to her provocative caress. She had closed her palms over the tight muscles of his shoulders, digging her nails into his flesh in yearning hunger as she had ridden his passion hard and hot until it had taken her right over the edge into ecstasy.

Oh, no, no, no, no! She must not think of that! She must not let herself remember how it had been, how she had once responded to him so fast, so easily. She couldn't let herself remember that or she would be finished before she started, her plan ruined before it even began.

She had come here for one reason only and that was…

A sudden sound, new and unexpected, broke into her thoughts, stopping them dead. For a moment it was as if it was so much an echo of what was in her thoughts that she almost imagined that she had conjured it up inside her head, wishing—dreaming—that she had heard it, rather than actually catching it in reality.

But then the sound came again, a snuffling, choking sort of wail, not too far away, faintly muffled, as if being held against something soft.

The world jolted beneath her feet, swung round once, and then back again the opposite way, leaving her feeling weak and queasy. One hand went out to grab at a nearby low branch, hanging on for dear life while her thoughts swirled and her head spun sickeningly.

'No…'

It was a low-voiced moan, one she had no hope at all of holding back. It couldn't be true. It couldn't be real. She had to have been imagining it, creating it in the hungry depths of her own thoughts.

But, as her clouded eyes cleared, she blinked hard and saw the way that Ricardo's arms were bent at the elbow, held in front of him as if he was carrying something, cradling it close to his chest. And as she registered the care and concentration he was exerting to hold his small burden, the way his down-bent gaze was directed at it, concentrating only on what he held, her heart clenched once again, skipping several beats in agonizing shock.

'Hush, *caro*…'

Once more that painfully familiar voice murmured huskily, the soft note in it tearing at her vulnerable heart.

'Time to sleep, *mio figlio*…'

Oh, dear God!

Mio figlio…

Somehow the new angle of Ricardo's body gave her a better view. Now she could see. And what she saw made her heart twist inside as if some cruel hand had just reached into her chest and wrenched it savagely, threatening to tear it right out of its assigned space.

Now she could see the way that Ricardo's arms were bent at the elbow, the way they curved around the small body he held. She could see the shock of soft hair—jet-black like that of the man who held him—that was cushioned in the crook of one arm, where the small head rested, relaxed and totally at ease.

And why not? The small boy was safe in his father's arms.

In a way that she once feared he would never be safe in his mother's.

'Oh, Marco…'

Her vision blurred, the harsh, bitter tears welling up at the back of her eyes, pushing against them until they ached and burned. An ache that was echoed deep inside her heart, tearing at her cruelly.

To her shock, she found that she had reached out a hand, stretching her arm towards the man who still stood with his back to her, oblivious to the fact that she was there.

No, not towards the man but towards the child he held. The reason why she was here at all. The one and only person for whom she would have braved Ricardo's anger, the fury of hatred she knew would be in his eyes when he saw her.

She had thought that she would never see her husband

again, and she had resigned herself to that. But what she had never managed to resign herself to was the fact that she would never again see the baby boy she adored with all her heart but hadn't been strong enough to love properly.

His baby boy—and hers.

Her son.

CHAPTER TWO

HER son was no more than a few metres away from her.

And never before had the phrase 'so near and yet so far' meant so much to her. Never before had it slashed at her with the cruel truth that she was so near to Marco that all she had to do was to take a couple of steps forward and she could be close to him. She could look down at him and see how much he had grown, how he had changed—because he had to have changed, surely, in the time she had been away.

Perhaps she could even reach out and take him in her own arms…

No!

Even in her dreams that was just a step too far.

She knew that Ricardo would never let her touch their son. And deep inside she really knew that it would be just too much to bear if she did. How could she reconnect with her little boy after all this time? She knew how the world would look at her—how Ricardo would see her. What loving mother, what good mother, would abandon her baby, walk out on him, leaving him alone with his father?

It had taken her long enough to accept that she had been ill. To acknowledge that she hadn't been able to find any alternative. The doctors said that she was well again now—but she didn't *know* it, deep in her heart.

Cruel, bitter tears flooded her eyes, blurring her vision. All she knew was that she couldn't stay in this hateful, appalling, 'so near and yet so far' situation and not give herself away.

She felt as if her already wounded heart would break, splintering into tiny pieces that scattered all over the paving stones at her feet. And yet this was what she had come this far for, after all. She had crept onto this island, sneaking past the security, just for this. The chance to see her little son.

But not like this. Not when she was not ready, not prepared.

And not with Ricardo Emiliani's cold, dark eyes watching her, cruelly assessing everything she did.

Stumbling slightly, she turned away. Not looking where she was going, not caring, she headed in the vague direction of the way she had come, hoping that she would reach the shore, and the boat, before the pain got too much and she sank to the ground and howled like an animal.

The crack that came when her foot landed on a fallen branch sounded appallingly loud in the stillness of the evening. There was no way that Ricardo could not have heard it. Freezing, Lucy tensed, waiting for the inevitable.

'Who's there?' Ricardo's voice was sharp, harsh in contrast to the soft tones of just moments before.

Not daring to look back to see if he had actually spotted her, Lucy plunged on, dashing into the bushes in the hope of hiding from his sharp-eyed gaze.

'Stop!'

There was no way she was going to respond to that…

'Marissa! Here—now…'

Behind her, Lucy vaguely heard the sound of swift footsteps—female footsteps—hurrying down the stone steps to where he was in the garden.

'Take Marco…'

That was the last thing she heard as she fled headlong, pushing aside branches that got in her way as she ran. Twigs snapped back, slapped her in the face, but she didn't care. All she could think of was getting away, reaching the boat and heading back across the lake. Anything other than facing an angry and aggressive Ricardo.

'Stop!'

How had he got to be so close behind her already? He had had to hand the baby over to Marissa—the nanny?—and then come after her but still it sounded as if he had made up so much ground that she could almost imagine that he would catch up with her at any moment. Heavy footsteps pounded behind her, making her heart race even faster in fear and apprehension.

'Giuseppe…Frederico…'

Ricardo was speaking to someone else. A swift, desperate glance over her shoulder revealed that he had taken out his mobile phone and had flipped it open, speaking into it as he ran, not breaking stride or even adjusting his breathing. A string of curt, sharp commands in Italian were flung into the receiver and Lucy's thudding heart lurched in even greater fear.

He was calling security. Summoning the trained bodyguards who watched the island boundaries for him, protecting his privacy—and making sure that his baby son was safe. And now he was setting his bloodhounds on to her.

And he was not pleased. There was no mistaking that tone of voice. She'd heard it often enough when she and Ricardo had been together. That tone meant that security had failed him and he was furious. Ricardo Emiliani didn't countenance failure and heads would roll as a result of this.

A furious Ricardo was not someone she wanted to face. She had come here to try and talk to her husband, it was true, but she had planned to tackle him with the advantage of surprise on her side. Facing him now was quite a different matter. Seeing little Marco so unexpectedly had ripped away the flimsy protective shield she had built up around herself, taking with it several much needed layers of skin and leaving her raw and bleeding deep inside. She needed to get away, regroup and gather her strength again before she dared risk taking things any further.

The shore where she had left the boat was just around the corner. If she could just put on one last spurt, force her tiring and shaking legs into action, she might just do it. But whether she could get the boat onto the lake and actually get away was a very different matter.

Making a last effort, she pushed herself to breaking point, her breath coming in laboured gasps as a lack of fitness resulting from the past few months started to tell on her. She couldn't look where she was going, caught her toe on a clump of grass, missed her footing and fell headlong.

Or, rather, started to fall.

Just as she felt herself totally lose her balance, convinced that the ground was coming up to meet her, she felt a hand grab her flailing arm, clamping tight around her wrist and holding firm.

'Got you!'

With a jarring jolt she was jerked back from the fall, hauled upwards so she balanced upright for just a moment, swaying precariously, before tumbling the other way. Straight into the arms of the man behind her.

'Oh, no!'

She hit him like a ton of bricks but, although he staggered

back, he didn't fall and the punishing grip around her arm didn't loosen for a moment. If anything, it tightened bruisingly so that she had no hope of pulling away.

'So who the devil are you?'

There was no way that Lucy could answer him. Her mouth seemed to have dried so much that her tongue couldn't form a word and her throat felt as if it had tied itself into knots.

But Ricardo didn't seem to need an answer. Instead, he adjusted his hold so that he could spin her round, bringing her to a position facing him where he could see her for himself.

'I said...*you!*'

It took every nerve in Lucy's body to force herself to look him in the face, though she flinched away from meeting his eyes, terrified of the darkness she would see there. She could almost feel the cold burn of his glare on her skin, flaying it from her bones.

'Me,' she managed and the uncomfortably jagged beat of her heart made her voice sound brittle and defiant.

The stunned silence that greeted her response stretched her nerves to near breaking point. In desperation, knowing he wasn't going to be the one to break it, she pushed herself to say something—anything—to try to show that he didn't totally have control of this situation.

'*Buona sera*, Ricardo.'

The sound of Ricardo's breath hissing in between his teeth told her that she'd caught him on the raw and the way his hand tightened about her arm betrayed the struggle he was having with himself to control the burning temper that she knew was flaring inside him.

But all he said was one word—

'Lucia...'

Her name. Or rather the Italianised form of it that only he

had ever used. The low, almost whispered syllables slid off his tongue in a way that could have been a verbal caress or then again might have been the hiss of an angry snake, preparing to strike. And not knowing which brought her eyes up in a rush to clash with his glittering black gaze, the ice in their burning depths making her shiver in uncontrolled response.

'Lucia.'

He said it again and this time there was no doubting the way that he meant it. The venom injected into the syllables of her name made her quail inside, shrinking away from him as far as his cruel grip on her arm would let her.

'What the hell are you doing here?'

Don't tell him the truth.

The warning words slid into her thoughts as if spoken aloud.

Don't say a word about Marco. If you put that weapon into his hands, then he will use it against you.

'I said…'

'What do you think I'm doing?'

Somehow she found the strength to answer him, to put a note of defiance into her tone. She even managed to lift her chin in an expression of rebellion that was a million miles from what she was actually feeling. And although she actually made a pretence of looking into his eyes, of meeting their savage glare head on, the truth was something so very different. Deliberately she let her gaze slip out of focus so that all she could see was the dark blur of his face up above her. The jet-black pools of his eyes were bleak hollows where no light, no hint of feeling showed in their depths.

'I certainly haven't come to try to renew our marriage.'

'As if I'd think that was why you were here.'

Ricardo's tone was rough but laced with a deadly control that refused to allow any real emotion into the words. And although he still held her, she felt that his attention was not on what he was doing but on the thoughts that were inside his head. The thoughts that his icy command refused to let show in his face.

'Our marriage is over. It was over before it really started.'

From the moment he had accused her of trapping him into marriage. Of letting herself get pregnant purely to get her hands on some of the vast wealth he possessed.

'Well, that's something we both agree on, at least.'

Lucy tried an experimental tug to try to free her arm, recognising how much of a mistake the action was when Ricardo's grip tightened, restraining her without any real effort.

'If it's not that—*grazie a Dio*—then what is it?'

He was finally starting to recover from the shock of seeing her, Ricardo admitted privately to himself. Finally coming to terms with the fact that she was here, in front of him—the woman he had never wanted to see again for the rest of his life. The woman who had deceived him, played him like a fool. The woman he had thought was gone for good, out of his life for ever, and that had suited him to perfection.

And yet here she was, standing before him, her arm tensed against the pressure of his, her head flung back, her small chin raised, and those blue, blue eyes glaring into his in wide, determined defiance.

She hadn't changed much, he acknowledged unwillingly because he didn't want to notice anything about her. He didn't even want to look into her face, into that lying, devious face, and see the beauty that had once caught him, entrapped him—deceived him. A beauty that had once knocked him so off balance that he had forgotten all the careful rules by which he lived his life.

More than forgotten. He had ended up breaking every

single one of them and had turned his life into a form of hell from which he had been only too glad to escape. The one and only time he'd broken his self-imposed rule, he'd been caught by a scheming gold-digger in the guise of an innocent lamb. And he was not about to let that happen again.

She had lost weight, it seemed, losing some of the softness of her face and her body. He wouldn't be human—or male— if he didn't feel a pang of regret at the loss of the soft swell of her breasts, the curve of her hips. But then she had been pregnant for so much of the time they had been together that naturally her figure had been more lush, the feminine parts of her body more emphasised. If she hadn't been pregnant then he would never have married her, would never have rushed into the union that he had come to regret so badly. Would never have tied himself to a woman he had come to detest so savagely and so soon.

'If you'll let go of my arm, then maybe we can discuss this like civilised human beings!'

'*Civilised!*' Ricardo scorned. 'That's not the word that comes to mind when I think of how I'd like to be where you are concerned.'

Now there was a word he would never use to describe Lucy Mottram—Lucy Emiliani as she was now, though the thought of his family name being attached to someone like her brought a sour taste into his mouth. *Civilised* didn't describe a woman who had deliberately let herself become pregnant just to trap herself a rich husband, and then walked out on her marriage when that baby had not even been two months old.

'And it's not the way I'd want to describe your behaviour in the past.'

Had she actually winced, flinching away in response to the

taunt? If she had then she had recovered almost instantly, tossing her hair back and glaring defiance up into his face.

'Equally, it's hardly *civilised* to hold me prisoner like this—just because you're stronger than me.'

'Oh, *si*—and if I let go then you will run off again and I'll never find out just what you're up to.'

'I'm not *up to* anything! And I promise I'll stay still.'

He'd be a fool to believe that. But, all the same, he eased his grip on her arm just a little. Out of the corner of his eye he saw that Giuseppe and Frederico, his damned inefficient security guards, had finally come up behind them, each one taking an approach from a different side, and he realised that he could at least afford to relax a little.

'I'd be a fool to trust you,' he declared, letting her hand drop in a gesture of deliberate distaste. 'But there's no way you can escape three of us.'

'Three bully boys onto one little woman!' Lucy flashed at him, her eyes sparking rebelliously. 'That's really balancing the odds.'

'There will be no bullying,' Ricardo tossed back. 'And you're hardly such a little woman!'

Deliberately he let his gaze slide over her tousled blonde head, her flushed face, and down the length of her body to where her narrow feet in the battered canvas shoes betrayed her mood in the way that they moved restlessly on the dusty path.

Her height had always been one of the things that he had liked most about being with her. The fact that he only had to bend his head just a little to meet her eye to eye had been a delight. The way that her mouth was just inches away from his when he did so had been a new and enjoyable experience after having to almost stoop in order to kiss the other women he had had relationships with.

Those eyes were what he remembered most about her in the past. The clear, bright blue that had seemed to reflect the colour of the sky on a summer's day when she smiled, or sparkled in amusement like the warm waters of the lake that surrounded this private island. At other times they had flashed in deliberate provocation when she had thrown a challenge at him. And then at other, very different times darkened into cloudy sensuality, heavy lids drooping into an almost sleepy look when all the time he knew that she had never been further from sleep. That her senses were on high alert, her body warming with awakening desire, her…

No!

With a brutal mental effort he caught his thoughts back from the dangerous path they were on. They threatened to scramble his ability to think, heating his blood and sending his brain into meltdown at just the memories.

That was the way she had caught him the first time around. That was never ever going to happen again. *Never*, damn it.

'So now…' his voice was rough with the effort of control '…I've waited long enough. I want an explanation and I want it fast.'

For a couple of seconds Lucy's mind hazed over as she struggled to find the words with which to answer him. Once again that warning voice sounded in her head and she acknowledged the fact that she couldn't let Ricardo see into the real depths of her heart. To do so would be to make herself too vulnerable, too exposed and defenceless. And she knew that, hating her as he did, Ricardo would take great delight in using her deepest need against her. He would exploit the overwhelming longing to see her baby again like a weapon and he could hurt her terribly that way, wrenching her heart into so many little pieces that it would be impossible to put it back together again.

'Lucia…'

Her name was a warning, a command and a threat all rolled into one and simply hearing it made her mouth dry in panic so that she had to swallow long and hard in order to find the strength to answer him.

'I…' she began, but he had already started to speak again, too impatient, too angry to wait for her to find the words.

'Just tell me why you are here and what you want!' he snapped. 'I've wasted too long on you when I have better things to do.'

'Better things like what?' Lucy challenged, stung by his dismissive tone. 'Signing more contracts? Making more millions? Or perhaps you have some hot babe waiting for you…'

The words shrivelled on her tongue as the image that they conjured up scorched her brain. She struggled to try to force away the memory of Ricardo in bed, as she had seen him so many times during their brief marriage, his jet-black hair ruffled and his bronzed skin dark against the whiteness of the sheets. She couldn't allow herself to remember how it had been. To do so would destroy what little was left of her self control and she knew that if Ricardo spotted just the slightest chink in her carefully protective armour then he would pounce.

But she had reacted too slowly. He'd already seen it and he had no hesitation in taking advantage of it.

'What's the matter, *cara*?' he drawled cynically. 'You're not jealous, surely?'

'What would I have to be jealous about?'

'What, indeed? After all, you were the one who declared that our marriage was over, and then walked out.'

Leaving your baby behind. He didn't actually say the words but he didn't have to. It was as if they hung there between them, big and dark and carved from ice.

And she knew that she was being a coward by avoiding them but she didn't dare bring the subject out into the open. Certainly not in front of the two muscular security men who were hovering just within hearing distance, obviously waiting for Ricardo to give a command so that they could take whatever action he demanded.

'And now you're back. And I'm wondering why.'

'Why not?'

Lucy aimed for bravado and missed it by a mile. She could only wince inside as she heard how sharp and brittle her voice sounded in the stillness of the evening, with just the faint lap of the lake water against the shore to break the almost total silence.

'After all, this was my home…'

No, blustering had been a mistake. She knew it immediately from the way that those brilliant black eyes narrowed sharply, always a danger sign in this man who had once been her husband. When his face changed like that, sensual mouth clamping tight shut, eyes seeming like gleaming slits above his carved cheekbones, then she knew he was at his most ruthless, his most coldly furious.

'*My* home,' Ricardo corrected coldly. 'A home that you only had a place in as my wife. A home you said you hated—a home you couldn't wait to turn your back on.'

The coldly obdurate way that he had said *my home* seemed to sear across her skin, burning away all trace of caution and pushing her into a total change of mood. He couldn't have made it plainer that she no longer had a place in his life, that he didn't want her here. She had only been tolerated because she'd been pregnant with his child, the heir to his fortune. Once she had given birth to Marco, all the tenuous value she had possessed had vanished. After that Marco had become an Emiliani and she…she had become nobody—not needed, not wanted.

Her fingers itched to slap that coldly ruthless look from his face but she knew that any such action would be a mistake—if only because of the still watchful, wary presence of the two security guards.

But there was more than one way to skin this particular cat and a wicked imp of inspiration told her exactly what to say to have the same effect verbally if not physically.

'Ah, but I've had a rethink since then and changed my mind. After all, I am still your wife, if only in name.'

'And only in name is all you'll ever be.'

'Fine.'

Lucy forced herself to give sort of a smile, knowing very well that it brought no light to her eyes and so made her look distant and disdainful.

'And as soon as I can arrange a divorce then I'll get rid of your name with relief. But there's one thing that came out of our marriage that I do want.'

'Of course…' Ricardo's arrogant gesture seemed to throw her words back at her in savage dismissal. 'I should have known that you'd come looking for the money you think you're entitled to.'

The fact that he thought she had come for money—and only for money—incensed Lucy, making her want to lash out, hurt as she was hurting. She was glad that she hadn't even mentioned Marco. Being the cold hearted man that he was, Ricardo was capable of flinging any request to see her son back in her face and walking away. But at least he had given her the opportunity to get in a few hits of her own before she revealed the truth.

'Not think, Ricardo—know. As your wife, then legally I'm entitled to a decent settlement.'

Could those dark eyes narrow any more? Half-closed though the lids might be, they still seemed to have the burn and force of a laser as they were directed at her face.

'Didn't you spend enough when you were here? As I recall, you damaged my bank balance pretty badly just before you left.'

The cruel words slashed like a blade, slicing into her heart, into her control and destroying every bit of command she had over it.

'I wasn't myself then! I was ill!'

To her shock and horror, Ricardo's reaction to her desperate admission was to throw his proud head back and laugh out loud. The sound echoed across the open space, seeming to swirl around the small bay and come back at them, dark, eerie and frighteningly cold.

'Of course you were ill.'

Hearing the sudden quietness of his voice, the complete ebbing away of even the dark humour, Lucy felt her head spin as if someone had just slapped her hard in the face, knocking her for six.

Was it possible that he believed her? That he actually understood?

'Oh, yes, you were ill, all right—you'd have to be sick to behave as you did. Sick to walk out and leave your baby behind.'

'It wasn't like that!'

She had to try to protest, even if she knew that he wasn't listening. The deliberate way that he had changed the words around so that he had exchanged the word 'sick' for 'ill', with its very different emphasis and meaning, told her all that she needed to know.

Ricardo's mind was totally closed against her. She could try to explain all she liked. She could offer any possible explanation to exonerate herself and he wasn't going to believe her. He wasn't going to listen and that was that.

But still she had to try.

'I can explain!'

But Ricardo shook his head in total rejection of the appeal in her voice, in her eyes.

'I don't want to hear it. There is no explanation that would justify such behaviour—none at all.'

'But Rico…'

Too late she realised the mistake she had made. In her fear and panic she had slipped into the shortened, softened form of his name that she had once been able to use. And the way that his face closed up told her that, if it was possible, he hated her for it even more than before.

'Please…'

But he was already turning away. She was dismissed from his thoughts, and his mind was already on something else as he turned to head back to where the lights inside the house gleamed out through the Gothic windows, emphasising the way that dusk had fallen as they had talked.

'I don't want to hear it,' was his callous declaration, followed by an imperious flick of his hand towards the two security guards, still standing as silent, stolid observers of the scene before them.

'Giuseppe…Frederico…escort Signora Emiliani off the island. Take her to wherever she is staying—and make sure she doesn't come back.'

He paused just long enough to let the words sink in before adding with extra emphasis, 'And this time make sure that you do the job properly. If she sets foot on this island ever again then you will both lose your jobs.'

Then he strode away, climbing up the slope towards the lights of the house without so much as a single glance back to make sure that his orders were carried out. He obviously had no doubt that they would be and that he could dismiss his soon-to-be ex-wife from his mind without a second thought.

CHAPTER THREE

LUCY was back.

Ricardo paced restlessly around the elegant white and gold sitting room, the glass of wine he had poured and then forgotten about still untouched in his hand. His thoughts were too preoccupied to allow him to drink, or even to let go of the glass his hand was clenched around, almost as if it was the arm of his errant wife, which he had held so tightly a short time before.

Lucy was back and in just a short space of time she had managed to throw his life into chaos just by reappearing in it.

'Dannazione!'

He slammed the glass down ferociously onto the nearby table, watching without a flicker of reaction as some of the ruby-coloured liquid slopped over the side and landed on the polished wood.

Lucy was back and he was damned if he knew what she wanted.

She had come looking for money, she had claimed.

Well, yes, of course she wanted money. What the hell else would bring her crawling back into his life when she had flounced out of it so carelessly and selfishly just over six months before?

She had to need money because she would be missing the more than generous allowance he had given her from the moment she had agreed to become his wife. The allowance that she had gone through with such speed and almost a compulsion in the weeks after Marco had been born. Then she had thrown money away on anything and everything that took her fancy, often buying half a dozen or more of the same item, in as many different colours as were available.

And then, more often than not, she'd discarded them when she'd grown tired of them, often without even wearing them, he recalled.

She must miss that allowance now that it was no longer hers. He'd cut off the supply of money as soon as he'd known that she'd left him—and the baby. At the time he'd foolishly thought that by cutting off her income he would bring her out of hiding more quickly, force her to come back to ask for more so that he could at least try to persuade her that her child needed her. But she had disappeared completely, vanished off the face of the earth, and even the extensive enquiries he had set in motion had been unable to track her down.

But she had to have lived somewhere and, with her bank account frozen, everything she had managed to stash away would soon have been used up so that she would have to come looking for more.

'No.'

Speaking the word out loud in the silence of the empty room, Ricardo shook his head as he moved over to the huge, high window that looked out across the lake and over towards San Felice del Benaco.

No, she wanted more than money. She had declared that she wanted a divorce, that she was putting in a claim for a 'decent settlement'. But, if that was what she wanted, why had she come creeping onto the island in secret, sneaking round to where he had been in the garden, watching him walking with Marco…

Marco!

Ricardo's hands clenched into such tight fists that if he had still held the wineglass it would have shattered in his grip.

Was Marco the real reason that Lucy had come back? Was she in fact here to try to get her hands on the baby son she had abandoned so heartlessly?

He'd die rather than let her! And no court in the country would give her custody after the way she had walked out on her child before he was even old enough to know her.

I can explain!

Lucy's voice sounded inside his head and in his thoughts he could see her face, pale in the gathering dusk, as she had turned to him. What explanation could justify her behaviour?

But what if there was some explanation—some justification that she could use against him? What if she had some story that she could take to court and try to claim custody of the baby—his son?

'*Dannazione*, no!'

That was never going to happen. He'd make sure of that.

There was one way he could ensure that his troublesome wife never got her hands on the baby she had abandoned so heartlessly. Lucy needed money and she would have as much as she wanted—more money than she could ever have imagined in her dreams…

…but at a price.

Snatching up the phone, Ricardo pressed a speed dial number and waited impatiently, long fingers tapping restlessly on the table top until someone answered.

'Giuseppe…' he snapped as soon as he heard the other

man's voice at the end of the line. 'My wife—Signora
Emiliani…' His tongue curled in distaste as he made himself
say the name. 'When you escorted her home, where exactly
did you take her?'

Lucy couldn't sleep.

No, the truth was that she didn't want to sleep or even try
to. If she so much as lay down on the bed and closed her eyes
then images of the evening floated in her mind.

Images of Ricardo, tall and dark and devastating as ever.

Ricardo walking down the stone steps, along the grass. His
long lean body silhouetted against the distant lake, his voice
carrying to her on the still air of the evening.

And then that other sound, the faint, whimpering cry…

Marco.

Her baby.

Pain lanced through her, cold and cruel. A choking sob
escaped her as she wrapped her arms around her body, feeling
that she had to hold herself together or she would fall apart
completely.

'Oh, Marco…'

The little boy's name was a moan of despair. Lucy moved
to the small, high window and leaned against the wall, staring
out across the darkened lake.

'So near and yet so far.'

Out there was her baby—her little son. Her arms felt empty
and her heart ached with the longing to hold him. But if her
visit to the island this evening had told her one thing it was
that Ricardo was going to fight her every inch of the way.

*You'd have to be sick to behave as you did. Sick to walk
out and leave your baby behind.*

Her husband's voice echoed in the bleakness of her

thoughts, black with cruel contempt. She would never get to see her baby again, not if he could help it. He clearly had no intention of ever forgiving her for what she had done.

And who could blame him?

Lucy swiped the back of her hand against her eye to wipe away the single tear that had welled up there, threatening to fall.

Why should Ricardo be able to forgive her when she couldn't forgive herself? She had walked out on her baby. But she hadn't known what she was doing. And she hadn't left him alone. He had had his father and the trained nanny to care for him. The nanny that Ricardo had insisted on from the moment she had given birth, making her feel useless and inadequate in a way that must have contributed to her breakdown. In her thoughts, they had been so much better for her darling son than a mother who didn't know her own mind well enough to know if she might be able to look after him—or if she would actually harm him.

She had hoped for a chance to tell Ricardo that. But he clearly wasn't prepared to listen. He had sent her letter back to her and now he had had her escorted from the island without a chance to explain. He would never give her another opportunity. She had known that he must hate her, but until today she had never truly realised just how much.

A sudden sharp rap at the door broke into her thoughts, making her start, her head coming up and her eyes widening in surprise. No one knew she was here.

'Who…?' Her voice croaked, broke on the word. 'Who's there?'

'Lucia…'

The husky male voice with its distinctive use of her name was too familiar, too disturbing. It was as if by thinking of Ricardo and their meeting earlier this evening she had conjured him up out of the air and brought him to her door. And that thought froze her in the middle of the room, unable to move forward, unable to think.

'Lucia!'

It was louder now, more impatient, definitely Ricardo. So definitely Ricardo that, in spite of herself, it brought a wry, remembering smile to Lucy's face as she recalled the times—the many times—that she had heard just that note in his voice.

'We can't have a conversation through the door. Everyone will hear us.'

Ricardo paused, obviously waiting, and in spite of the thickness of the wood between them Lucy felt that she could almost hear the irritated hiss of his breath in between clenched teeth as he waited for her answer.

'Lucia!'

Once again his knuckles rapped hard on the door. Clearly he had no intention of leaving. Suddenly afraid that he would take his annoyance out on the door even further, or that he would disturb other guests in the boarding house, Lucy was pushed into action, hurrying to the door and unlocking it. Yanking it open, she glared at Ricardo as he stood in the corridor.

'Are you determined to disturb everyone in the house?' she flung at him. 'Some of them may be sleeping.'

'Not at this time,' Ricardo dismissed with a swift glance at his watch.

'There might be children asleep!'

'And you care about that?'

'Of course I do!'

Too late she saw his face change and knew the direction of his thoughts. How could she care about other people's children, he was obviously implying, when she had walked out on her own son when he was barely a month and a half old? Didn't he know that nothing he did or said could make her feel any worse than she already did?

'I can't afford to cause any trouble that might get me thrown out of here. I have nowhere else to go.'

'So are you going to invite me in?'

'Do I have any choice?'

Not if she wanted to keep this private and quiet, Ricardo's burning glance said. And, knowing she had no other option, Lucy unwillingly stepped back, allowing Ricardo to stroll into her room. Those deep-set dark eyes subjected their surroundings to a swift, assessing scrutiny and his black brows drew together in a quick frown.

'*This* is where you're staying?'

'It's not so bad.'

It was pretty bad really, Lucy had to admit, suddenly seeing the room from his point of view. It was at least clean but it was definitely shabby, the flooring worn and the white covers dulled and thin from repeated washing.

'Hardly what you're used to.'

'Not what *you're* used to—or what you used to provide for me, you mean!' Lucy snapped back. 'I managed with worse before we met—how do you know what I've been used to while we've been apart? You stopped all my allowance, remember.'

Seeing the expression of dark satisfaction that crossed his face, she knew that she'd played right into his hands. He was thinking that the only reason she was here was because she was after his money. But then who could blame him? It was the impression she had set out to give in those few desperate moments on the island when she had been afraid to let him know her real reason for being there.

'There is such a thing as work—paid employment.'

Ricardo's scorn lashed at her like a cruel whip, the black contempt in his eyes seeming to flay her savagely.

'Or have you decided that that's beneath you?'

'Why would I want to work when I have a filthy rich husband?'

Determined to give as good as she got, she laid a bitter emphasis on the word *filthy*, knowing that she'd stung him when she saw his mouth tighten into a thin hard line as if clamping down on some more violent expression that he didn't want to let loose.

Just for a moment she feared—or was it hoped?—that he would actually turn on his heel and march away, walk out without another word. Instead, he pushed the door to with a bang, shutting them in the small room together.

A room that suddenly seemed so much smaller than ever before. Ricardo's tall, strong form seemed to fill the confined space, his dark colouring in stark contrast to the white-painted walls. She had not been alone with him for over six months—and being here, like this, in the intimate surroundings of a bedroom made Lucy's heart kick sharply, her pulse rate beating twice as fast.

In all her time apart from him she had never forgotten the sheer physical impact that Ricardo had on her. It was, after all, what had brought them together in the first place. That intense rush of burning awareness, the deep, hungry sexual attraction that had had her in Ricardo's arms within an hour of meeting him, in his bed just a few short days later. Just being with him had seemed to lift her life on to another plane entirely. One in which every sense was heightened, every experience felt new and wonderful. And the months they had been apart had done nothing at all to diminish the way he made her feel.

Every nerve seemed to prickle with excitement. She was so sharply, stingingly aware of the height and strength of him, the burn of those deep, dark eyes, the golden tone of his skin and the gleam of his jet-black hair. In the confines of the room she could even catch the clean, totally personal scent of his skin that coiled around her like the most seductive of perfumes.

Feeling overwhelmed and unsettled, she wanted to move somewhere—anywhere—to put a bit of space between them but the size of the room made that impossible. The only place to sit was on the edge of the narrow, uncomfortable bed, and just the thought of that made her stomach twist and knot so painfully that she pushed the idea aside in a second.

'I haven't been able to work,' she managed, keeping to the far side of the room while Ricardo paced restlessly around, making her think unnervingly of some big, sleek feline predator caged in a space that was too small for its size. 'Even if I'd wanted to.'

'No,' Ricardo conceded unexpectedly. 'You said you'd been ill.'

'You believed me?'

After his response earlier, on the island, she'd assumed that he would think the story of her illness was just that—a story—with no truth behind it at all.

The look Ricardo slanted at her from those dark eyes said that he wished he didn't have to believe her but he had no alternative.

'You've changed since I saw you—lost weight. But you're well now?'

'Oh, yes.'

That, at least, she could say without fear of how he would judge her. She wouldn't be here now, like this, if that wasn't true. Having forced herself away from Marco once in her life, there was no way she was going to risk having to make that terrible decision ever again by coming back too early.

'Yes, I'm fine.'

Fine didn't really describe it, would never describe it. Not until she had her beloved baby boy back in her arms and could make reality of the assurances that the hospital had given her. But, before that could ever happen, she had to deal with his father. And, because she didn't know why he was here, she didn't know how to handle Ricardo.

But he was here—and he had accepted that she had been ill. So would she be a gullible fool to allow herself to hope for something from that?

'I'm sorry,' she said, slipping into careful politeness in the hope of steering the situation into calmer waters so that they could at least talk civilly. 'I should offer you a drink…or something. But, as you can see, I'm afraid this room doesn't even boast a kettle.'

Her hand gesture, used to indicate the lack of facilities in the room, was a little too wild, a little too expansive. It gave away too much of the uncomfortable way she was feeling inside, the struggle she was having against the need to demand to know just what he wanted from her.

'I didn't come here for a drink.'

'No? So what did you…' Abruptly the courage to ask the most important question deserted her and she rushed on instead to a different distracting topic. 'I think I could do with one…'

There was a bottle of water and a glass on her bedside table across the other side of the room, just near to where Ricardo was standing. Without thinking, she moved to reach for it, stretching out her hand in the same moment that he did just the same. Their fingers clashed at the top of the bottle,

tangling, pausing, snatched back, only to pause again, just
touching, as they froze, barely inches apart, staring deep into
each other's faces.

'Lucia…'

'Rico…'

Their voices clashed too, just for a second, then died away
into stillness as silence reached out to enclose them, hold them.

It was as if they had both been struck by lightning. An
electrical response had sizzled up her arm, fizzing along every
nerve at just the feel of the heat of his body, the burn of his
skin against hers.

Now she really did need that drink of water. Her throat was
drying out completely in the wave of heat that seared her
body, shrivelling her thoughts in its fire and setting alight the
senses that she had barely kept under control from the moment
that Ricardo had walked through the door.

'Rico…' she croaked again, unable to drag her eyes away
from the burn of his glittering gaze, unable to move, unable
to think, only able to feel.

And what she felt was the rush of awareness, of need that
she had known from the first moment this man had touched
her. A need and a hunger that had grown with each kiss, each
caress. A hunger that she had convinced herself she could learn
to live without as long as she was far away from him, never
seeing him, never speaking to him, never touching him…

And she had managed it until now.

But she had only to touch him, have him touch her, and it
had all sparked off again in the space of a single heartbeat.
Nothing had vanished; it was all still there.

He felt it too. She could read it in his eyes, sense it in the
change in his breathing, the way that a muscle jerked at his jaw
line. It was still there, as strong, as sharp and as primitively

intense as ever. Body speaking to body, sense to sense. Whatever had burned between them in the eleven months of their marriage, it was all still smouldering just below the surface, needing only a touch to make it flare into life all over again.

'Oh, Ricardo…'

Acting purely at the demand of her instincts, Lucy finally moved. Twisting her hand around, she let her fingers brush his palm, watching fascinated as his own fingers jerked just once, convulsively, as if about to close around her teasing touch, but then were abruptly forced still again. Those gleaming black eyes were suddenly hooded, hidden from her, concealing any trace of his thoughts. But Ricardo couldn't hide the way that his breath caught sharply in his throat, the deep swallow that struggled to ease the dry discomfort that matched her own.

Lucy let a small smile curl the corners of her mouth, grow until her lips curved upwards, wide and soft at the thought that at least in this one way she could still affect this hard, distant man as she had once been able to.

'It doesn't have to be like this. It really doesn't.'

'No?' Ricardo's voice was thick and rough, seeming to come from a throat that was so clogged with something raw that he could barely speak.

'No.'

Softly she let her fingertips drift over the palm of his hand, watching the strong hand quiver in uncontrolled response. Circling his thumb, she caressed her way over the powerful bones in his wrist, watching as the sinews tightened, the muscles clenched. It was impossible to control the need to touch him, impossible to fight back the urge to provoke him to react in a way that revealed that he was no more immune to her than she was to him.

To feel him close like this, scent his skin, feel the heat of him, made her mind respond as if she had slipped back to the days when she had been free to touch him, to caress him whenever she had wanted. She had loved those days, adored that freedom—adored him. And she wanted to go back there—wanted it, needed it so much…

'It never used to be this way.'

She didn't deliberately pitch her voice to sound so breathy, so husky. It just came out that way naturally. And right now she couldn't regret the way it revealed how the tiny physical contact had shaken her. How aware, how aroused it had made her. With her eyes fixed on Ricardo's taut face, she could see how, just for a moment, his tongue slid out to moisten suddenly dry lips.

Perhaps he too recalled the softer times in their relationship. The times before suspicion had changed him, darkening his opinion of her.

'It could still be…'

Moving her hand again, this time she curled it around Ricardo's, fingers lacing with his, palm pressing to palm, deepening the contact, making it more intimate.

And she knew her mistake as soon as she'd done it.

'*Inferno*—no!'

The harsh mutter was harder, more biting than if he had shouted. And the way that he froze, before deliberately, coldly uncoiling his hand from her gentle grip, pulling away almost in slow motion, was so obviously a deliberate insult that it stung like a slap in the face. With a flick of his wrist, he seemed to shake off even the last traces of her touch as he swung away from her, putting as much distance between them as it was possible to do in the small bedroom.

'It could not "still be" anything,' he declared, every word pure ice. 'There is nothing left between us, nothing I want to revive. Certainly not how it used to be. That is not what I came here for.'

'So what did you come here for?'

Determined not to show how his rejection of her had hurt, Lucy brought her head up defiantly, turning what she hoped were cold eyes on him as she injected every ounce of control possible into her voice.

'I take it it wasn't just to pass the time of day—renew an old…' she hesitated deliberately over the word '…friendship?'

'Hardly. We were never *friends*.'

'Husband and wife.'

'Legally, perhaps.' Ricardo dismissed her pointed comment with an indifferent shrug of his broad shoulders. 'But I doubt if we were ever married in the true sense of the word.'

'And just what, in your opinion, is the true sense of the word?'

'For better, for worse, to love and to cherish,' Ricardo quoted cynically, making her wince inside as the words stabbed at her.

'For richer for poorer…' she flung back, refusing to let herself think of the other words—the ones that said *in sickness and in health*.

If only she had been able to turn to Ricardo at a time when those words had meant so much, then how different things might have been. But she had known from the start that their marriage was never meant to be *as long as we both shall live*. If she had never become pregnant then he would never have married her at all. It was only because of his determination that his son would be legitimate that he had ever put a ring on her finger.

'For richer, certainly, in your case. You played your virginity like a trump card, withholding it from the poor Italian fisherman you first thought I was but only too keen to lose it to the rich man you then discovered me to be.'

'If that's the way you want to read it.'

It was the only way he'd ever read what had happened. He had never understood the very real fear that had held her back at their first meeting, forcing her away from him even though she'd feared she would never see him again. He would understand even less the bitter regret that had eaten at her for days afterwards, so that when she had met him again, in the very different circumstances of an elegant society party, she had been unable to hold back and, buoyed up on an unwise glass of champagne, had practically thrown herself into his arms.

'And I did not *play*…'

'You sure as hell did,' Ricardo tossed back at her. 'You played with both our lives—and the life of the baby we unwisely created between us. You told me…'

The temptation to put her hands over her face and hide from his anger—his justifiable anger—was almost overwhelming but Lucy forced herself to brave it out. She knew what she'd said. That she'd given him the idea that she was protected. But the truth was that she had been so wildly, blindly lost in sensation, in the heat and hunger that his kisses, his touch had aroused, that when he had muttered, 'Is this OK? Are you all right?' in a voice so thick and rough it betrayed only too clearly how close to losing control he was, she had only thought that he was considering her inexperience. She couldn't have said no if she'd tried. The only word in her head had been yes, the only need in her body, in her heart, had been to know the full reality of this man's sensual possession. And so, 'Yes, oh, yes!' had been her only possible response.

She had thought she *was* safe. The time of her cycle should have made her safe. But in that she had been stupid and naïve too.

'And richer is what you really want me to discuss. So OK,

let's get to the real point. You wanted to know why I came here. I came to ask you just one question.'

'And that is?'

'How much will it cost me to get rid of you?'

'Get…'

In the scrambled muddle of her thoughts, Lucy couldn't decide if it was shock, fury or just plain horror that kept her tongue from being able to form an answer to his question. She could only stare at him in disbelief, her eyes wide.

'It's a simple question, Lucia.' Ricardo's voice was tight with impatience and exasperation. 'Surely you can have no problem in understanding it. What I want to know is how much will you take to leave now, get out of here—and stay out of my life for good?'

CHAPTER FOUR

COMING here had been a mistake, Ricardo told himself furiously. A big mistake. A bad mistake.

And a mistake that he should have seen coming if he had any sense. Which he obviously didn't. At least not where Lucy was concerned.

But then sense had never been part of the way that he had reacted to this woman. His *senses*, yes.

Maledizione, he had always been at the mercy of his senses from the moment they had met. His mindless senses had rushed him into taking her to his bed, making her his—making her pregnant in the sort of stupid, irresponsible slip-up that he hadn't made even as a teenager.

It was those damn senses that had trapped him into a marriage that had been a mistake from start to finish.

And those same damn senses had been on red alert ever since he had walked into this room.

'How much will I take…?'

She was looking at him now as if he had suddenly sprouted horns and a tail. Those blue eyes were wide with what he would have described as shock if he hadn't known better. But of course he did know better. He knew just what his precious, greedy little wife was after, and all the pretence of shock and disbelief in the world wasn't going to make him think otherwise.

'You want to know how much it will cost you to have me leave?'

'That was the question.'

At least she had stopped the soft-voiced attempt at seductive persuasion. The *it doesn't have to be like this*…that she'd tried earlier.

She'd damn nearly had him with that. With the breathy note on the words that had made it sound as if she was totally overwhelmed at being here with him like this. Never before had he been so aware of the slender, curving shape of her in the clinging, worn jeans, the faded T-shirt. The scent of her body had seemed to surround him as he had looked down into the wide, wide eyes that had seemed almost hazy with need. And the soft touch of her hand on his skin…

Dio santo, but he had found it hard to resist that. That gentle touch had raised so many memories in his mind. Erotic memories that had had his body hardening in spite of his furious attempts to divert his thoughts onto other, less dangerous pathways. She had touched him like that on their first night together. Tentative, almost hesitant. As if she was shy and nervous.

Well, that shyness had pretty soon disappeared. It had evaporated like the mist over the lake at the first touch of the summer sun. In his arms she'd turned into a wild and seductive temptress. In his bed she had been the fulfilment of every sensual dream he could ever have imagined.

But they couldn't live out their lives in bed.

'So you're offering me a pay-off?'

'A settlement,' Ricardo amended. 'A generous settlement in return for a quick and quiet divorce—I'll even take the blame, provide you with grounds if you want it that way. And then you get out of my life for good. You go and you stay away. I never want to see you again.'

How could he ever want to see a woman who was capable of walking out on her own child, leaving behind just a frivolous, careless note that told him the marriage was over and the baby—Marco—was his responsibility now?

She was considering the proposition. Considering it seriously. That much was obvious from the way that her expression had changed, the softness vanishing from her eyes just before she let her pale eyelids drop down to cover them, concealing her thoughts from him.

'You really must want to be rid of me.' Her tone was flat, no emotion showing in it at all.

'Oh, I do,' he confirmed, his tone deep with harsh sincerity. 'Believe me, I do.'

'And you'd pay anything I asked?'

Her jaw had tightened so much that it drew in her cheeks, narrowing the whole look of her face and making the words come out as stiffly and as jerkily as if they had come from the carved wooden mouth of a painted marionette. Blue eyes lifted briefly to look into his face in a swift glance that was coolly assessing.

'In English law I'd be entitled to half your fortune. You should have thought about getting me to sign a pre-nup.'

If he'd had any sense then he would have done just that. But at the time the only thing that he'd been thinking of was the child they had created between them. The child that had to be born in wedlock and with his name as the father on the birth certificate. No child of his was ever going to grow up illegitimate, with all the snubs and the social exclusion that he had endured. The barriers to belonging that had blighted his mother's life as well as his own.

He had known that it was only his money that had convinced her to marry him in the end. But, if he was honest, then at that point he really hadn't cared. All that had mattered was getting the ring on Lucy's finger and ensuring that her name—and her child's—were the same as his.

He had thought that he would have longer to see if the relationship between the two of them would grow into something so much stronger than the wild, fiery passion that had brought them together in the first place and had resulted in the creation of the tiny life that Lucy had carried within her.

'And would you have signed one?'

At the time she would have done anything, Lucy acknowledged. Ricardo had only to ask and she would have said yes. She had been in so deep, so totally besotted so that she had been unable to think straight. She hadn't even hesitated over his proposal, though common sense should have told her that he didn't want her. All he had wanted was the child in her womb.

'I don't want marriage, Lucia,' he'd said. 'Never have. No woman has ever even made me think of it. But your news changes everything. We have a baby to consider and my child is not going to grow up illegitimate. That's all that matters to me right now.'

'It would have made sense—on your part, at least,' Lucy answered now, covering the lacerations on her heart with an armour of control. 'After all, neither of us was going into that marriage with any romantic stars in our eyes. We both knew it was just a business and legal arrangement.'

'And now?'

'Now? I wouldn't sign anything you asked me to without having it thoroughly checked out first.'

'Not even if it gave you everything you'd ever wanted—more than you ever dreamed of?'

'I don't think that's possible.'

If she could have Marco in her life, then she would feel as if she had been given the world and would want nothing more. But, without her son, there was no amount of money or possessions that could compensate for the emptiness his loss would leave in her life. And she knew, deep in her soul, that Ricardo would never let her have Marco.

'Try me.'

For the life of her, Lucy couldn't bring her numbed, bruised brain to recognise whether there was pure challenge or invitation in the two words that Ricardo tossed at her. And she didn't really dare to hope for the latter. Any invitation from Ricardo Emiliani came hung about with so many chains of doubt and risk, so many conditions, that it was like putting your head into a noose just to consider it. And a challenge was something she dreaded.

'Tell me what you really want—and you can have it. Anything, so long as you get out of my life and never come back.'

'You'll never give me what I want so there's no need to even ask.'

'Why not? I—' Ricardo broke off abruptly as a buzzing sound from his pocket drew his attention to his mobile phone. '*Momento*…'

Pulling it out, he checked the screen, frowning as he did so. 'I have to take this.'

With the phone clamped to his ear, he swung away again, listening hard and then firing sharp, incisive questions into the receiver in rapid-fire Italian that was too fast for Lucy's schoolgirl grasp of the language to allow her to keep up.

But she caught one word, clearly and distinctly, and that fastened onto her nerves, twisting and tugging with every second that passed.

'Marco...' he'd said. And, again, 'Marco...'

Whoever was at the other end of the phone had rung him because of something that was happening with Marco and just to think of that pressed Lucy's personal panic button, sending her thoughts into overdrive. Her heart was pounding, her breathing harsh and shallow. Something had happened to her little boy and she didn't know what.

She couldn't stand still, finding that only by pacing rest-lessly around the room could she keep herself from grabbing that phone from Ricardo and demanding to know what was happening. But the dimensions of the small space were re-stricted so that she found she had barely started before she was forced to turn and head back in the opposite direction. And still the conversation went on until she was ready to scream, only keeping a grip on herself by clenching her fists tight, digging her nails into the palms of her hands.

But then, at last, Ricardo thumbed off the phone and turned to her again.

'What's happened...?'

'My apologies...'

Their voices clashed, froze, then, because Lucy couldn't manage anything more, it was Ricardo who continued, his tone rough with impatience. 'I have to go. My son...'

Catching the look she gave him, he at least had the grace to pause in faint acknowledgement but only for a second. Immediately he continued, emphasising that possessive claim once again. 'My son has woken and is upset. I need to get back.'

'Is he all right?'

The concern wouldn't be held down. She didn't care what Ricardo thought of her, how he might interpret her enquiry. She only knew that if Marco was distressed then she had to know more.

'He will be when I can get to him.'

Once more the exclusion of her was deliberate, pointed. The words stung cruelly; as she was sure they were meant to.

'You left him in that big house—out there on the island—on his own…'

'Never on his own!' Ricardo cut in furiously and Lucy flinched from the fire that flared in his eyes. 'Of course he was well looked after. His nanny was with him.'

Of course, the nanny. How could she forget the nanny?

'He was asleep when I left…but he woke and she thought he was too upset to settle. She felt he needed his papa.'

His papa. Another vicious put down, slapping her in the face with the fact that he was Marco's father, the parent who cared for the little boy. While she was just an outsider. The woman who had given up her claim on her child when she had run out on him. For reasons she could explain if only she got the chance.

But now was not the time. Already Ricardo was turning towards the door.

'I have to get back to him.'

'Of course.'

But if she let him walk out of the door, let him walk away, would she ever get the chance to talk to him again? Would she ever even see his face again? And, much, much more important, how could she let him walk away when she knew that, back in the Villa San Felice, his baby son—*their* baby son—was awake and miserable and in need of comfort?

Not pausing to think, she snatched up the bag that was lying on the bed, stuffed her feet hastily into flat pumps and hurried after him. The speed and length of his strides had taken him out of the door and along the landing already and she had to push herself to follow him. She caught up just as Ricardo was about to let the main door swing to behind him.

'What the…?' The question was pushed from him as her hand clashed with his, catching the door before it slammed.

'I'm coming with you.'

'No way…'

'Yes.' She didn't know how she managed to get such strength into her voice. Determination perhaps, or just plain desperation.

What she would do if he refused point-blank to let her go with him, she didn't know. She could stamp her feet and demand that he let her—stand in the middle of the street and threaten to scream until he agreed. The problem was that, knowing Ricardo, he was more than capable of getting into his car and driving away, leaving her behind.

So she tried the opposite approach instead. She had nothing to lose, after all.

'Please,' she said. 'Please, Ricardo, let me come with you.'

And watched his head go back in shock, his eyes narrowing sharply as he studied her face.

Please…

Ricardo felt as if he'd had a knock to his head, jarring his brain so that he couldn't think straight.

Please. It was the last thing he had expected Lucy to say, at least in these circumstances and in that tone of voice. Correction, Lucy asking to go with him at all was the last thing that he had expected.

And she was *asking*. Making it sound as if it mattered to her. Making it sound as if she was actually concerned about Marco.

'Ricardo…' she said now, bringing his eyes to her face again.

In the light from the open door of the boarding house, she looked pale and drawn, forcing him to remember that she had said she'd been ill. What the hell had been wrong with her?

But he didn't have time to hang about here any longer. He

was needed back at the villa where, if the experience of the past few nights was anything to go by—and the sound of the nanny's voice on the phone had certainly seemed to indicate that it was—at this moment Marco was wide awake and roaring his head off in protest at the discomfort of having another tooth come through.

Oh, yes, Donna Lucia would just love that…

And that was the thought that made up his mind for him.

'OK,' he said abruptly, expecting and seeing the shock and blank confusion that crossed Lucy's face. 'You can come. Get in the car.'

A wave of his hand indicated the vehicle parked at the roadside.

'I…do you mean that?'

'Lucy—' his tone made his fierce impatience plain '—if you're coming with me, get in the car or I'll leave you behind.'

She moved then, hurrying to the car door and sliding into the seat as soon as he opened it for her.

Did she know what was ahead of her? Ricardo wondered. He doubted it. When Marco got into one of his crying jags then he made certain that the whole world knew that he wasn't happy. And, as far as his father could see, a baby boy in a bad mood didn't come with a volume control.

One thing was sure, if she hadn't already had enough of being a mother, as she had declared in the cold-blooded note she had left behind when she'd walked out, then the next couple of hours were going to push her as far as she could go. For even the least reluctant mother, Marco's screams could be positively the last straw.

And that was why he had finally agreed to let Lucy come back to the house with him.

If she needed any encouragement to persuade her to go, get

out of his life and stay out of it for good, then the sight and sound of his baby son in a tantrum was probably the most likely thing to provide it.

Which suited him perfectly, Ricardo told himself, slanting a swift glance at the woman beside him as she fastened her seat belt and sat back. A faint cynical smile curled the corners of his mouth as he started the engine, put the car into gear and set off down the road.

This was going to be interesting.

CHAPTER FIVE

THE noise hit Lucy's ears as soon as she stepped through the main door of the villa and into the huge tiled hallway from where the big marble staircase curved upwards towards the first floor. Even in a place the size of the Villa San Felice, the furious, distressed baby yells could be heard right through the house. And, hearing them, Lucy had a terrible fight with herself not to just forget everything that had happened, forget her ambiguous position in this house and run up the stairs as fast as she could, her arms outstretched to take her little son into them.

She had even moved part way to the foot of the staircase when Ricardo came past her, taking the steps two at a time, long legs covering the ground so fast that Lucy had to put on a burst of speed as she reached the wide landing in an attempt to catch up with him.

She only made it just in time as her husband pushed open the door to the nursery and strode inside.

'Marco…*mio figlio*…'

The soft words should have been drowned out by Marco's wails but somehow the quiet tones cut through his distress and had him pausing in the middle of his sobs to look up and see his father.

'Marco…' Ricardo said again, crooning the name, and immediately the baby recognised his father. The wailing paused and from his nanny's arms Marco held out his hands.

Reaching for *Ricardo*, Lucy suddenly understood, knowing an appalling, terribly cruel sense of loss as she realised that she had been about to step forward. Only to recognise, painfully and belatedly, that she didn't have the right to hold her son. Not here, not now.

And besides—wasn't she fooling herself to imagine that there might be any chance that Marco would recognise her? She had been away from him for so long. And he had been just a tiny infant when she had left.

She had to force herself to stand back, putting her hands behind her on the wall as both a source of support and a way of keeping herself from reaching out as she watched Ricardo take on the responsibility of comforting their child.

Her heart was thudding violently, just as it had done from the moment that the call had come through that Marco was refusing to settle. Although Ricardo had made it plain that he didn't think there was anything more seriously wrong with Marco than a bad night and cutting some teeth, she had still found herself imagining every possible worst thing that could happen as the car had made its way down to the shore where the boat was moored.

Luckily the speedy motorboat that Ricardo used to cross the lake made the trip in a tenth of the time that it had taken her earlier that evening in the heavy old-fashioned rowing boat that was all she had been able to hire for herself. But, all the same, the short journey had seemed endless as Lucy stood at the prow of the boat, hands clenched tightly together, watching the lights of the big house coming closer, willing it to move faster—*faster*—so that she could be sure.

And now she was sure. Although miserable and irritable,

Marco was clearly not seriously unwell. But somehow, knowing that didn't make her feel any better. Seeing him safe in Ricardo's arms, the tones of a familiar voice reaching to him as his sobs eased, only made everything so much worse. She couldn't help but imagine how many other times this had happened, as the result of a banged knee or a miserable cold. How many times had Marco woken in need of a cuddle and she—his mother—hadn't been there? The doctors had said that she should forgive herself for that, but how could she forgive what she couldn't bear to think of?

'*Calma, tesoro,*' Ricardo soothed, pacing slowly up and down the room, the little boy in his arms. '*Calma…*'

At last the wails stopped, the sobs subsiding to a low murmur and then a snuffling silence, broken occasionally by a faint hiccup, a slightly gasping breath. A small hand came out and patted Ricardo's cheek, gently, lovingly. Seeing the gesture, Lucy caught back a moan of longing and loss.

She would barely have recognised him. He was not the tiny, hairless little doll she had last seen but a small boy. So clearly his father's son, with the Emiliani jet-black hair and wide dark eyes. Eyes that stared up into his father's face with total confidence, total devotion.

Another shaft of pain ripped through her, tearing at her heart. She couldn't hold back a small choking sound as she struggled with her distress.

The noise brought the child's head round towards her. From the safety of his father's arms, his head pillowed on the man's strong shoulder, the little boy regarded her with wide-eyed curiosity, his soft brown gaze focused directly on her face.

'Oh, Marco…' It was just a whisper.

Did he recognise her? Was it possible? She longed to be

able to believe it, prayed he might show some sign—
however small…

But then those heavy eyelids drooped, his head lowered,
the small cheek, flushed with the effects of teething and his
crying jag, pressed against Ricardo's shirt. A small thumb was
pushed into his mouth and sucked on hard.

It was the last thing that Lucy saw with any clarity. The
tension that had been all that had been holding her upright
suddenly seemed to evaporate, leaving her whole body sag-
ging weakly. Her vision blurred as the stinging tears filmed
her eyes and all the fierce blinking in the world wouldn't clear
it for her. Her head was swimming, there was a buzzing sound
in her ears and she had to put a hand to the wall for support.

'Excuse me…'

She didn't know if Ricardo heard her, but the truth was that
she was past caring. If she stayed she would be a problem.
She had to get out of the room, get some air. She didn't dare
to look back at Marco for fear that seeing him would finish
her completely and she would collapse in an abject, miserable
heap right at Ricardo's feet.

She doubted if anyone saw her go.

At the far end of the corridor was a sliding glass door that
she remembered led to a balcony that looked out over the lake.
A place where on a fine day you could see the shore so clearly
that it almost seemed as if there was no lake. As if you could
simply step off the balcony and walk straight into the village
without getting your feet wet. It was all in darkness now, of
course, and as she leaned on the carved stone balustrade and
gulped in much-needed breaths of the cool evening air the
lights of the houses seemed to dance before her eyes.

The silence behind her told her that Marco was no longer
crying, that he had calmed, perhaps even now was falling asleep.

Falling asleep in Ricardo's arms.

A sobbing gasp escaped her as she wrapped her arms around her body, feeling the need to stop her heart from breaking apart. She had longed for this day, had dreamed of it for so many weeks. And yet, when it had happened, it had been almost more than she could bear.

She had so wanted to come back here, had so needed to see her baby. And yet now, when she was here, the only thing she could think was—did she really have the right to come back into her little boy's world? Did she have the right to stay, to disturb the routine he had obviously settled into with his father?

Ricardo was so good with him. She couldn't doubt the evidence of her eyes on that. It was so clear that this was not the first time he had comforted the baby through a disturbed night, soothed the little boy's distress when something hurt or he didn't feel well. Every movement, every touch, every caressing sound of his husky voice, carefully gentled to calm and reassure, made it clear that he had done this so many times before.

She didn't have a place here. She had given it up when she had fled from the villa, abandoning her baby. And wouldn't it be kinder, fairer…?

'So this is where you're hiding.'

Ricardo's voice came from behind her, making her jump. Clenching her hands tightly over the edge of the stone balcony, she tried to suppress the betraying start, only managing it by continuing to stare fixedly out across the bay rather than turning to respond.

'I'm not hiding! I just had to get out of the room.'

'Couldn't take it, hmm?' The cynicism in his voice had deepened. 'Who would have thought that such a small person could make so much noise? He has a strong pair of lungs.'

Lucy could only nod, not trusting her voice to say anything

about Marco. A mist seemed to have descended over the lake and it was only when she blinked her eyes firmly that she realised her vision was again blurred by the film of tears that she was determined not to let fall.

'Not quite your image of a pretty little baby lying sweetly in a crib?'

That brought Lucy swinging round, her eyes going to Ricardo's face as he stood in the opening of the door out onto the balcony. The unwise movement made her head spin sickeningly and it was a moment or two before she could focus properly. When she did, her heart lurched to see his dark and shuttered expression, the tightness in his jaw that drew his beautiful mouth into a thin, hard line.

'I knew he was not going to be totally quiet—you said he was unsettled. So I thought I'd better leave you to it. I'd have gone back to the boarding house but there isn't any way I can get a boat.'

'So you were running away again.' Ricardo's cynicism stung like a whip.

Moving suddenly, he strolled across the terrace to stand beside her, his back to the lake, lean hips propped against the stonework. Positioned like this, his face was in shadow and all she could see was the cold gleam of his eyes in the moonlight.

'I was not *running*…'

'Only because you could not find someone to take you over the lake.'

'I didn't know who to ask.'

'And it would not have done you any good if you'd tried.'

He leaned even more negligently against the wall and folded his arms across his chest. Lucy supposed that the position was meant to make him look more relaxed, totally at his ease. Instead, it had exactly the opposite impression. A shiver ran down her spine at the feeling that he was watching her intently, waiting for her to take a false step, make some mistake that she had no idea would actually be a mistake.

Or perhaps she had already made it and didn't even realise it. With Ricardo standing there in the darkness, looking like judge and jury all rolled into one, she had the terrible feeling that she had been tried and found guilty and she didn't know quite what she had done.

'No one would have taken you. My staff have been told not to take you anywhere. Not unless I give them specific instructions.'

Not just tried and found guilty, but tried, condemned—and *imprisoned*. The shiver at Lucy's spine turned into a full blown shudder and she grabbed at the balcony as her legs felt suddenly unsteady beneath her.

'Are you saying I can't leave?'

'That is exactly what I'm saying. Until I give permission for you to go, then you stay here.'

'I thought you wanted me out of your life.'

She might be worried—definitely on the verge of nervous—but she was damned if she was going to let it show. So she put the note of challenge back into her voice, lifted her chin as high as it would go and made herself meet the cold darkness of his eyes.

'After all, wasn't that the reason why you came to find me in the first place? "Tell me what you really want—and you can have it."' She quoted his own words back at him. '"Anything, so long as you get out of my life".'

'...and never come back,' Ricardo completed, making her wince inwardly at the sound of the words. 'Remember? That was the important bit. This time I want you gone—out of my life for good.'

He really must hate her, Lucy reflected miserably. And it was shockingly disturbing to find such revulsion directed at her, spiced with bitter venom.

'Hate you?' Ricardo echoed and, to her horror, she realised that she had actually spoken her thoughts out loud.

'Hate you?' he repeated. 'No, *cara*, not hate. I don't care enough about you to do that. But I do know a mistake when I see one and you—'

He unfolded his arms and one long finger came up, gesturing to indicate her slender form with a controlled savagery that made a nonsense of his denial of hatred.

'You are one of the biggest mistakes of my life. If not my absolute worst.'

The shaking in Lucy's legs was growing worse. Surreptitiously, she pressed her hand down harder on the rough stone of the balcony, needing the extra support to keep her upright. After a day of emotional shocks and changes, it seemed that her strength had been drained away, leaving her fuzzy-headed and unsteady on her feet.

'You know, that really doesn't make any sense,' she managed.

'No?' Ricardo scorned. 'And why not?'

'If I'm—' she had to drag in a gasping breath in order to give herself the strength to speak the hurtful words. '—the biggest mistake of your life. One you want out of here for good. Then why—*why*—are you keeping me a prisoner here?'

'Hardly a prisoner…'

'But you're making sure that I can't leave! Which amounts to the same thing. And why would you do that if you feel I was such a mistake in your life?'

It was the question he'd been asking himself all day long, Ricardo acknowledged privately. And the fact that she was asking it now too didn't make it any easier to answer.

He had never seen his relationship with Lucy as going anything beyond the hot, passionate nights they'd shared in his bed. But once he had found out she was pregnant then everything had changed. Their marriage had been for the baby and nothing more.

No, correction, their marriage had been for the baby and the hot blazing sex that had led them to create that baby. The hot, passionate sex that was the glue that had held them together in the place of anything else. And that he had thought would hold them together until they could put something else in its place.

Because, OK, they had rushed into marriage purely for convenience and to ensure that Marco was legitimate. But surely, when the baby was born, they could have taken some time to get to know each other properly. To find out if there was anything more than that blazing passion that had yoked them together from the start.

But Lucy hadn't stayed around long enough to find out if that was the case. No sooner had Marco been safely delivered than she had launched herself into a lifestyle from which he—and the baby—were totally excluded. She had been out on the town every day, spending money like water, bringing home innumerable carrier bags of clothes, shoes, make-up. Most of which she had never worn or used. She had moved into a separate room, had had to be cajoled into seeing her son, was blatantly reluctant to care for him, leaving him instead to the care of his nanny almost twenty-four hours a day.

Then, within six weeks, she had simply walked out. Leaving a heartless note that made it plain just what she had wanted out of the marriage. It hadn't been Marco—and it most definitely hadn't been a life with Ricardo. All she had wanted was the lifestyle, the luxury, that his wealth had brought.

I gave you the son you wanted and almost a year of my life. Think that's quite long enough. You can have Marco—after all, he's the only reason we went through this farce of a marriage—and I'll have my freedom. I'll be in touch about the divorce.

And now here she was. Just as she had promised. She had come back into his life for the sole purpose of doing just that—talking about the divorce. And, of course, just how much she was going to get in her settlement.

He detested her. He hated who she was, what she'd done. So why in the devil's name would he try to keep her with him any longer than he had to?

'We haven't talked about the divorce. About what you want out of it.'

Had he actually touched a nerve there? Was it possible that she could be affected by what he had said? Certainly it looked as if some sort of a light—the light of challenge and defiance had gone out of her eyes. Or was it merely some trick of the moon that had taken that from her gaze in the same way that it seemed to have drained the colour from her face?

'When we have an agreement, then you can go. I'll have Enzo bring the launch around and you can be back on the shore in less than fifteen minutes. I'll even give you an advance on your settlement so that you can book yourself into a decent hotel—providing you get the first plane from Verona Airport tomorrow morning.'

Once again it seemed that he had caught her on the raw. She actually flinched, wincing away from his words. A frown creased the space between his brows but, just as he was leaning forward in some concern, her head came back up again, blue eyes flashing defiance.

'No!'

Just for a moment she looked almost as if the force of her refusal had taken her by surprise as much as him. Those clear, bright eyes seemed to go out of focus for a second, then came back to clarity again as she blinked hard. She swayed suddenly as if buffeted by an unexpectedly strong wind that had blown up out of nowhere but then straightened again, fixing her furious gaze on his face once more.

'That isn't going to happen! I won't go!'

'Won't?'

Ricardo frowned his deep confusion, trying to read just what sort of mood she was in.

'Now you're the one who's not making sense. A moment ago you couldn't wait to get away.'

'Yes…but…I can't go like this.'

'Yes. you can. It's quite simple—all you have to do is to tell me what you want and I'll give…'

'But you won't!' Lucy cut in, her voice sharp and shaking, her hands coming up in a wild gesture to emphasise her words. 'You won't give it to me.'

'I gave my word.'

She was shaking her head violently, sending her hair flying out around her in a crazily flurried halo.

'But you won't keep it!'

'I will—damn it, Lucia—I promise…'

'Don't promise what you can't…won't…'

It was as she shook her head again, clearly on the edge of losing things completely, that Ricardo felt his own control crack. That swirling hair had brushed against his face, the feel, the scent of it bringing so many memories rushing to the surface of his mind.

How could he ever forget the fresh, clean scent of it,

perfumed by some herbal shampoo that tantalised his senses? Or how it had felt to know the silken slither of that long blonde hair over his skin as she knelt above him, his body sheathed in hers? As his groin tightened in instant response he almost felt again the slow, sensual movements that had driven him to the edge of his control, keeping him there in subtle torture until he could take no more.

'Lucia—stop…' he growled, reaching for her flailing hands. 'Stop it, now! This isn't doing you any good.'

The rough little shake was just meant to force her to rethink, to come back to herself. But when she threw back her head, drawing in a ragged breath, ready to speak again, he knew that touching her had been a mistake. A big mistake.

A mistake he had been heading towards all evening. Ever since that moment when she had touched his arm earlier in the shabby little room in the boarding house. No—earlier than that, when she had been about to fall and he had caught her, yanking her upright so that she had slammed hard against him. Her body pulled into close and intimate contact with his.

Just recalling that made his heart kick up a pace, his breath coming raw and uneven into his lungs. His hands tightened even more about her arms, moving upwards, towards her shoulder, stilling her, holding her…

And, in that moment, she looked up into his face, her soft pink mouth half open, her breath coming as unevenly as his. Their eyes caught and clashed, held and…

And all control left him as he saw her eyes widen, saw the shocked response and then the sensual awareness that clouded them. It clouded his mind too, leaving him no ability to think. He could only feel.

And hunger.

And that hunger drove him into mindless action, pushing

him into hauling her hard up against him, wrenching her chin up towards him and clamping his mouth down hard on hers. Letting loose a rough grunt of satisfaction as he felt her lips give, opening instinctively under the hard, fierce pressure of his kiss.

A small murmur of distress got through to him, ripping apart the clouds of burning sensuality that clouded his mind, bringing a flash of rational clarity to his heated brain. Immediately he gentled his kiss, easing the pressure on her mouth, using softness, enticement, seduction to counter the brute force he had subjected her to just moments before.

It started out hard to silence her, control her. He had snatched at her lips, trying to crush back the cries of distress, stop them from pouring from her mouth. He didn't understand why she should be so upset, why she was in such a state, but there would be no talking to her until she had calmed down.

'Hush, Lucia, hush… There's no need for this. Whatever you need—whatever you want—whatever trouble you've got yourself into—I'll deal with it.'

That stopped her, froze her. She could only stare mutely into his face, her expression white and strained, huge eyes colourless in the moonlight. With a devastating sense of shock, Ricardo realised that the strange glitter on their surface was not the effect of the pale, cold moonlight but the glisten of unshed tears.

'Lucia?' It was a shocked whisper. And his next kiss was soft, gentle, wanting to wipe the upset from her lips. He took her mouth slowly, carefully, and his heart seemed to stop dead, then start up again in double-quick time, ragged and uneven as he felt the tiny, involuntary, almost automatic softening of her lips in response, the gentle pressure of her mouth against his.

The scent of her skin was all around him. The slide of her hair was against his hands. The softness of her body was in his arms, tight against him. And deep inside the hunger was waking, starting to grow.

But, even as he slid his hands down her back, he knew that something had changed. Lucy had hesitated, drawn back faintly, then a little more strongly, putting her hands on his chest to push him away from her.

'You mustn't do this. You shouldn't.'

'Why not?' Trying to make light of it, he even tried a rough laugh deep down in his throat. 'You were becoming hysterical. Something had to be done—and there are only two traditional ways to calm a hysterical woman. You surely wouldn't have wanted me to slap you.'

Numbly she shook her head, her eyes glazed with something that looked close to despair. 'You might wish you'd done that when I tell you.'

'When you tell me what? Damnation, Lucia, what the hell are you talking about? What is it that you want? And why are you so sure that I won't give it to you?'

Her hesitation caught him on the raw, tugging on nerves that suddenly felt painfully exposed, desperately vulnerable. A terrible sense of oppression shot through him, a prediction of something that was coming that he wasn't going to like at all.

'Because you won't give me Marco. And that's what… who I want…nothing else. The only thing in the world that I want is my son.'

If she had spat right in his face he couldn't have been more appalled. As it was, he felt the sense of dark shock reverberate through him so that he released her at once, almost dropping her to the ground as if she had turned into a poisonous snake in his arms. From wanting to hold her so close, he jumped to the sense that holding her would contaminate him in the space of a single devastated heartbeat.

'Marco? You came here for *Marco*? To take him…'

Unable to find the words, Lucy just nodded, then immediately realised that that was just what she should not have done. She hadn't come to *take* Marco, not in the way that Ricardo meant. But it was already too late. She had nodded and she watched Ricardo's face close down, the tightness of his jaw and the darkness in his eyes making her shiver.

'Never,' he said and the word was disgust, an ultimatum, a warning and a threat all rolled into one. 'After what you did? Not in my lifetime.'

'But—' Lucy's voice broke on the word. 'I can explain…'

'You can try. But I cannot imagine that anything you say will ever convince me.'

He paused, waited, head slightly tilted to one side, giving her such a pointed look that she practically felt it scrape over her skin like the sharp end of a needle, raising a raw, red weal.

He would listen, that look said, but he would not believe. He was already armoured against her. Even if she mentally beat her fists hard against his unyielding defences until they were raw and bleeding, he would not let her reach him.

'So…' he goaded when she still didn't speak, couldn't find a way to start '…explain.'

She wished she could. But how could she say anything when those cold black eyes seemed to probe her skull as her brain frantically tried different ways of beginning and discarded each one as unusable? At least that was what she thought she was doing but her thoughts seemed so completely unfocused that she found that nothing she tried made sense. And nothing would form clearly so that she could follow it through for herself, let alone explain it to Ricardo so that he would understand and believe her.

Because he had to believe her.

'You can't, can you? Because there isn't an explanation. Not one that would satisfy anyone else. And certainly not someone who loves Marco.'

'*I* love him…'

Her voice sounded frail, just a thin thread of sound—what she could hear of it over the buzzing inside her skull. It was as if a swarm of bees had suddenly invaded her head and were swirling round and round inside it.

'Love him!' Ricardo scorned 'How can you say that? How dare you say that? You left him! Abandoned him…'

'I know and that was wrong—but I was ill. I'm back now. And I want…'

'You want?' Ricardo echoed, his voice a vicious snarl. 'You *want*—always what you want! Well, let me tell you, *cara*, that what you want is not going to happen—never. Not while I live. Not while I can stop you. And if "I love him" is the best damn explanation that you can come up with then, to be honest, lady, I don't want to hear it.'

He was turning away as he spoke, using his body as well as his face, which was set hard and cold against her, to express the way he felt.

'Ricardo, please…'

She had to stop him; had to make him listen. Lurching forward, she tried to grab at his arm, to hold him back, but missed. Her hand, aiming for the hard strength of his arm, found instead only empty air and waved wildly, frantically. The awkward movement threw her right off balance, jarring her head nastily.

The buzzing in her head grew louder, wilder and a burning haze seemed to rise before her eyes, blinding her completely.

'Ricardo!' she cried on a very different note as the world swung round her, lurching violently. Her hand groped for support, found it for a moment in the feel of muscle under warm, hair-hazed skin.

Then she lost it again as her grip loosened completely. A wave of darkness broke over her and she slid to the ground in a total faint.

CHAPTER SIX

'ARE you awake?'

The voice, huskily male and disturbingly familiar, broke through the clouds of sleep that filled Lucy's head, making her stir in the bed, frowning slightly as her head moved on the pillows.

Softer pillows than she remembered. She must have got used to the conditions in the boarding house. The first night they had felt so rough and lumpy, but now...

'Lucy! It is time to wake up.'

The voice came again, rough and impatient now. It broke into the wonderful oblivion of much needed sleep that had hidden everything from her, almost wiping her memory clear of all that had happened.

Until the sound of Ricardo's voice brought it all back in a way that had her bolting upright in the bed, staring wide-eyed at the figure standing in the middle of the room.

'What has happened? Where am I?'

'*Buon giorno, bella* Lucia,' Ricardo drawled lazily, strolling across the room to lounge at the end of the bed.

Propping one hip against the ornately carved wooden bed frame, he pushed his hands deep into the pockets of the jeans he wore with a deep red polo shirt, open at the throat.

'You have no need to panic; you are quite safe. You are in the Villa San Felice, just as you were last night. So one might say that in fact you have come home.'

'*Home* is not a word I associate with this place!' Lucy tossed at him as she tried to collect her scrambled thoughts, feeling that panicking was exactly what she *should* be doing. 'Nowhere where you are could ever be home to me.'

She was more aware of her surroundings now. Aware enough to recognise and be thankful for the fact that at least this was just one of the smaller bedrooms in the east wing of the villa. To her intense relief, the heavy wooden furniture and the soft blue curtains and carpet were not the ones she remembered from the room she had shared with Ricardo in her time as his wife. She didn't feel that she would have been able to hold herself together if she had woken to find herself in their suite.

'So how did I get here? What happened?'

Ricardo pushed a long hand through the darkness of his hair, disturbing its sleek black strands and his piercing eyes never left her flushed face as he observed every change of expression, every fleeting emotion that crossed it.

'You were taken ill—you passed out. Do you not recall?'

'No...I...'

But then she did remember everything in a rush. From the moment she had set out on her attempt to get onto the island, to see Marco...

Marco...

'I fainted,' she managed, piecing the events back together in her thoughts. 'And you...'

The memory of Ricardo's voice, his cruel words, swirled inside her head, making her feel dizzy just from the thought of it.

You are one of the biggest mistakes of my life. If not my absolute worst.

'How did I get to be here? Who brought me…'

'I brought you here,' Ricardo inserted calmly, the smooth tones of his voice sliding into the rising hysteria of hers. 'And yes—before you ask, I put you to bed.'

'You…'

If he had slapped her across the face he couldn't have brought her up sharp any more forcefully than that. Suddenly she became aware of the fact that she was sitting upright against the pillows with the soft comfort of the downy quilt slipping down to fall around her waist, exposing the top half of her body.

The top half of her body that was now wearing only the thin, plain bra that cupped her breasts.

'You undressed me!'

Hot blood rushed into her cheeks, then ebbed away again almost at once as she snatched at the coverings, yanking them up to her neck to conceal herself, protect her body from those probing eyes. But just too late to erase the sensation of his searching gaze raking over her skin, flaying off a much-needed protective layer. It was impossible not to remember how he had once used to undress her—undress her so softly, so gently, or at other times almost ripping the clothes from her with such a wild urgency that her heart threatened to burst with just the memory of it.

'I undressed you,' Ricardo confirmed.

His beautiful mouth twitched, just once, in an expression that could have been anything—amusement, annoyance, contempt or just plain triumph. Lucy had no idea which, and the hot embarrassment that was flooding her thoughts left her incapable of even trying.

'And why should that disturb you? Surely it was better…'

'Better!' Lucy interrupted, still struggling with the uncomfortable feeling of being…violated was the only word that came to mind. She knew that Ricardo would dismiss it as being exaggerated and overblown, and deep down she knew that it was. But it was how she felt all the same at just the thought of those long tanned hands unbuttoning her shirt, sliding it from her, taking her jeans…

'And tell me just why it's better to have you manhandle me…'

'I did not manhandle you!'

She'd caught him on the raw there, sending sparks into the darkness of his eyes and making him bite out the words in a tone of barely controlled fury that had her flinching back against the pillows and pulling the duvet even more tightly around her in spite of the warmth of the sun that was coming in through the narrow arched window. Beyond that window she could hear the calm blue waters of the lake lapping lazily against the stony shore and then ebbing back again with a faint sucking sound as they pulled against the tiny pebbles. It seemed unnaturally loud in the dangerous silence that descended before Ricardo drew in a long harsh breath.

'I have never 'manhandled' a woman in my life and I do not intend to start with my wife. Because surely that is the point here—that I—as your husband—performed this duty for you myself rather than leave it to a stranger.'

'You are not my husband!'

Lucy wouldn't have believed that it was possible for Ricardo's expression to grow any more glacial or for the cold anger in his eyes to burn any more savagely but clearly her words had provoked him into darker fury as he flung a glance of bitter recrimination in her direction.

'We took the vows,' he declared icily. 'We were married.'

'But only to make sure that our son was born legitimate with two married parents to be named on his birth certificate. Beyond that, the whole thing meant nothing—and the vows less than nothing. I didn't want to marry you and you…'

'I wanted you as my wife.'

'Because I was Marco's mother. Oh, come on, Ricardo, are you telling me that if I hadn't got pregnant you would still have asked me to marry you?'

'No…'

'No.' She tried to make it sound as if his answer satisfied her, but the truth was that there was no satisfaction to be found in the single word. 'I thought not.'

'I wanted you…'

'Oh, I know…' She couldn't keep the bleakness, the bitterness from her voice. 'You made that only too plain. But you could have had me in your bed without tying yourself— without tying both of us—down to marriage. But I got pregnant and that trapped us, Ricardo. Trapped us in a marriage that neither of us wanted.'

It was weak, it was foolish—it was downright masochistic—but all the same she couldn't stop herself from pausing, waiting just a second, just long enough for her stupidly vulnerable heart to give a couple of unsteady, jerky beats just in case Ricardo actually thought about *denying* that statement.

Well, if she'd hoped it might happen then she was destined for disappointment. He remained stubbornly silent, forcing her to go on.

'And now I want to get out of it. We both want to get out of it. Which is why it's not…appropriate…for you to…'

'For me to do what?' Ricardo cut in, satire burning in the words. 'Not appropriate for me to help a woman who is evidently unwell and who has fainted at my feet? Not appropriate to pick her up and carry her inside, put her into a comfortable bed—and perhaps remove her outer clothing so that she may sleep more comfortably? I think that only you would assign some sort of sexual motive to that.'

His cynicism lashed at her, making her flinch inwardly. Her face was burning once more but this time with a very different sort of embarrassment. Hearing it like that, it did sound so perfectly innocent. Did she really think that she was so sexually irresistible that he was unable to keep his hands off her?

If she had been foolish enough to even consider any such thought then his tone and the blazing fury in his eyes would have very soon disillusioned her. Ricardo might have once been so determined and so hungry to get her into his bed that he had broken what he had told her was normally an indestructible rule and made love to her without using a condom, but it clearly was not the case any more. He had seen her as nothing more than some woman who needed help and he had acted accordingly.

'You did that?' Her whole body was burning with embarrassment so that the words quavered on her tongue. 'Thank you—and I'm sorry.'

A swift, curt nod was Ricardo's only acknowledgement of her response and almost immediately it seemed that his mind had moved on to something else.

'Someone had to take care of you. You obviously weren't taking care of yourself. Tell me, Lucia—when did you last eat?'

The question was unexpected, catching her off guard and forcing her to consider.

'Yesterday…' she said slowly, still thinking about it.

'Are you sure?'

No, she wasn't sure. Yesterday morning she had known that she was going to try to get onto the island. That she was going to try to see Marco. And that had left her nerves so tightly strung that her stomach had clenched painfully from the moment that she had woken up, and it had stayed like that all day. And the day before...

'You told me that you had been ill.'

She'd told him but, if he was honest, he hadn't considered that it was serious, Ricardo admitted to himself. But when she had collapsed at his feet then he had had to take notice. And picking her up to carry her indoors had sent a sensation like a brutal kick straight to his guts.

She had lost so much more weight than he had realised. In his arms she had felt as fragile and vulnerable as a lost bird, one that had fallen from the nest before it had quite learned how to fly. Beneath the protection of her clothing, she was skin and bone, and the way that stabbed at his conscience was uncomfortable and disturbing.

'But you didn't say what was wrong with you.'

He'd touched on a raw nerve there. Those concealing eyelids flickered up, fast but hesitant, and the blue eyes flashed one swift, wary and defensive look in his direction before she stared down again, focusing on where her hands were twisting in the protection of the quilt, revealing an uncertainty she didn't want him to know about.

Yesterday he had wanted to hate her. It had been *easy* to hate her when she had come sneaking onto the island like a thief in the night, invading the world he had built around Marco since she had walked out on them. He hadn't wanted to listen then.

And hatred—hatred and rejection—had been uppermost in his mind when she had declared to his face the truth of why she was here. That she had come to try to claim Marco. Then his rage had been like a red mist in front of his eyes and he had had to turn away from her rather than give in to the murderous fury that boiled inside him.

He wished he still felt like that. To stay feeling that way would have been so much simpler. It would have made things so much more easy and straightforward. This woman had walked out on their marriage, their child so carelessly and selfishly, without even a backward look. Now she was back, walking into the life he had made without her.

And demanding her son.

No!

Even now the roar of rejection was wild and savage inside his head. It obliterated every other consideration in a storm of savage feeling. It felt wonderful, simple, strong—and right.

But then she had fainted. She had turned white, all the blood draining from her face, had just seemed to shrivel up at his feet. She had lain there unconscious and he had had to kneel beside her, checking her pulse, her breathing, her temperature. Knowing that he had to take her somewhere more comfortable, he had had to bend to lift her up...

And that was when everything had changed.

'No, I didn't say,' Lucy flung at him now. 'Are *you* saying you want to know what happened? Do you really...'

She had to break off the question as a knock came at the door. Of course—Tonia with the food he had told her to prepare for Lucy. Food it was obvious she needed.

'Eat your breakfast,' he commanded gruffly. 'Then we'll talk.'

'I want to talk now...' Lucy protested, struggling to sit up enough to take the tray on her knees without letting the covers fall down at the same time.

The sudden pretence of modesty set his teeth on edge so that with a muttered imprecation under his breath, he strode to the wardrobe and wrenched open the door. Snatching a white robe from a hanger inside, he tossed it in Lucy's direction, gesturing to the maid to leave at the same time.

'You need to eat.'

Now she was trying to pull on the robe while still balancing the tray.

'Dio santo!'

Clamping his jaw tight shut against the irritation that almost escaped him, he lifted the tray again, carrying it to the small table set in the bay window and dumping it down. Then he moved back to the bed, taking the robe from her while she still struggled with it and holding it open for her to get into it.

'If it will speed up the process, I assure you I am not looking,' he told her satirically when she still hesitated.

He didn't have to look—the memory of every inch of her body was etched onto his brain. And not just from last night, when he had taken the shirt and jeans from her unconscious body. No, the memories he had were from the time when they had been together. When her warm, smooth skin and long slender limbs had been a source of endless delight. When he had known the scent of her, the taste of her, every intimate inch of her.

Six months had not been long enough to erase the memories that could still torment him. And last night just knowing that she was back in his life had badly disturbed his sleep, making him twist and turn in the grip of erotic dreams. Eventually he had woken in a tangle of bedclothes, soaked in sweat and breathing as hard as if he had run a marathon.

So now, even with his closed lids concealing his eyes, he could still see her in his thoughts, still feel the heat of her body as she slipped into the robe he held for her. And the soft slide of her hair over his fingers as she flicked it back, the clean, deeply personal scent of her skin, intensified by the warmth of the bed she had just left, was a sensual torment, hardening his body into tight and aching demand in an instant. He couldn't stay in the room a moment longer and not give in to the hot demands of his body.

As soon as Lucy had shrugged the robe up over her shoulders and was reaching for the belt he seized the opportunity to head back to the table, pulling out the chair with an unnecessary flourish.

'Eat,' he commanded. 'And then get dressed.'

He knew that he had stunned her, could feel the focus of her eyes on the back of his neck as he headed for the door.

'But you said that we have to talk.'

'Later,' he tossed over his shoulder at her. 'Get some food inside you and get dressed, then we'll take things from there.'

'Dressed?'

Her voice was sharp in a way that was disturbingly close to the edge on his own tongue, shaking him right to the core with the suspicion that she too might have felt the fiercely heated tug on her senses that he had experienced just a few moments before.

'Dressed in what? At least have the courtesy to tell me where you've put my clothes.'

'You'll find all you need in there…'

A wave of his hand indicated the large, carved wooden wardrobe set against the far wall but he still did not let himself pause, didn't even glance back to see if she had registered his response. He needed to get out of here, get himself back under control. Giving in to his most primitive male urges right now would be the worst possible mistake he could make.

But, *madre di Dio,* he was tempted…

'I'll be back in twenty minutes,' he warned on his way out of the door. 'Be ready.'

CHAPTER SEVEN

I'LL be back in twenty minutes, Ricardo had said. *Be ready.*

And the *be ready* had been a command, one that his tone had told her that he expected to have obeyed without question.

A swift glance at the clock told Lucy that well over half of that time was already up and she was no nearer to obeying that autocratic command to be ready than she had been in the moment that Ricardo had strode from the room, obviously not wanting to spend a moment longer in her company than he had to.

At first she'd done as she was told and eaten her breakfast—rather mutinously perhaps, but she'd been really hungry and the savoury frittata had looked and smelled wonderful, as had the coffee and freshly baked bread. It had been too long since she had eaten and after just one bite even the concern over just what Ricardo had planned for her faded in the face of her appetite and she'd wolfed down everything that was on her plate.

She would have liked to have lingered over a second cup of coffee, but already the time was passing and she still had to shower and dress. Just the thought of Ricardo arriving while she was still in the shower was enough to send her rushing into the bathroom and switching on the water.

She felt so much better when she was washed and refreshed, her hair clean and combed clear of the knotty tangles that the wind on the lake yesterday had whipped it into.

She must have looked a real sight, she reflected as she fastened a towel around her and padded back into the bedroom, glaring at her reflection in the big mirror on the door of the wardrobe. With her tangled hair and too pale face without even a trace of make-up, it was no wonder that Ricardo had barely spared her a glance.

She looked nothing like the woman he had married. The woman who, well aware of the fact that she was not the sort of woman that Ricardo Emiliani was usually seen with in the gossip columns of the celebrity magazines, had made sure that she always looked her best for him.

And, if she had needed any extra push in that direction, then the conversation she had overheard in the Ladies at a party shortly after her wedding had made certain that she stuck to her resolve. Hidden in one of the cubicles, she had heard the sneering tones of one of the female guests.

'Not his usual type, is she?'

'Not at all,' another woman had answered. 'But she's been clever. She trapped him by getting pregnant. He'd never have married her otherwise.'

'Not clever enough. Everyone knows he's just waiting till the baby's born and then he'll divorce her. I mean—what does she have to offer a man like Ricardo? She's too plain, too unsophisticated, way too clingy. I give her a year max after she's delivered before he's back playing the field.'

Lucy had made a vow right then and there that she wouldn't cling—ever. She had also vowed that she would always be as groomed and glamorous as the women Ricardo was usually seen with. She…

But that was where her thoughts stopped dead, dying in the

moment that she flung open the wardrobe door. Her hands shook, her heart seemed to stop beating as she stared at the contents in horror, her whole body trembling in the rush of bitter memories.

'You'll find all you need in there…' Ricardo had said, and all she had expected to find inside the wardrobe was the clothing he had taken off her. Just the cotton shirt and jeans, looking lost inside the vast space of the cupboard.

But nothing looked lost. On the contrary, the wardrobe was stuffed full of clothing—skirts, trousers, dresses, tops, even shoes, all crammed into the available space without an inch to spare. So many—most—of the items were still in their cellophane wrapping or the plastic bags that had protected them in the shop, the shoes in their boxes. And all still with the price labels attached, just as they had been brought home after a wild spending spree.

A wild, crazy, mindless speeding spree.

'Oh, my—'

Lucy clamped her hands hard over her mouth to hold back the choking cry of despair that almost escaped her, stinging tears burning at the back of her eyes. But the truth was that she was beyond crying, beyond thinking. She could only stare in horror at the evidence of just how out of her mind she had been.

The shopping expeditions were a blur in her mind. She knew she'd been on them, of course; she hadn't completely lost her memory of that appalling time—she only wished she could. But the details had been gently hazed by the passage of time until now, when she was confronted with the physical evidence of the truth.

Had she really bought all these clothes—hundreds, *thousands* of pounds' worth of clothes? More clothing than she could ever wear in a year—a decade! Some of the items were almost identical—the same style, the same shape—except that they were in a wide variety of colours, one of each in the whole range the shop would have stocked. And not even everything had been unpacked. There were still bags and carriers stuffed in at the bottom of the cupboard, bearing the names of the exclusive stores in which they had been bought, brought home—and left unopened and untouched.

'Oh, dear heaven…'

What had she really been like in those dark, desperate days? And what had it been like for Ricardo, living with her, watching her crazy behaviour? He had already thought she wanted his money—these wild spending sprees could only have confirmed his darkest suspicions.

She slumped against the door, shaking her head in despair.

If she needed any proof of the fact that she had been right to go, to leave when she had done, then it was here before her, with no room for doubt. She had been out of her mind, totally incapable of managing her own life, let alone taking care of her precious baby son.

And did she have any right to stay here now? To come back into Marco's life and turn it upside down when he was so obviously settled and happy with Ricardo? She knew what it was like to be at the centre of a parental custody battle, to be torn and unsettled, tugged this way and that between her father and her mother like a bone between two dogs when they had been going through a bitter divorce. She couldn't do that to her little boy.

Still half-blinded by tears, she reached out and grabbed the first clothes that came to hand, pulling on underwear, a deep pink skirt and a pink and white top without even noticing what she was wearing. If she could get out of here before Ricardo came back…

She was at the door when it swung open in her face, forcing her to step back hastily.

'So you're ready—good…'

Ricardo's dark eyes swept over her assessingly, and she knew the moment that something of the truth hit him from the way that his black brows snapped together in an angry frown and his whole expression changed from approval to forbidding in the space of a single heartbeat.

'Leaving, *cara*?' he questioned sharply, the tone of his voice and the icy glare that accompanied it sending a shiver down her spine. 'I think not.'

'And why not?' Lucy was determined not to let him see how much he was getting to her. 'You can't keep me here.'

'I think you'll find I can.'

'So you're still determined to keep me a prisoner?'

'Not a prisoner, *tesoro*…'

Ricardo's wickedly sensual mouth curled over the word in a way that took it to a point light-years from the term of affection it was supposed to be.

'You'll find no locked doors here, no bolts—no chains.'

To Lucy's amazement he actually stood back, pushing the door wide open and leaving it that way so that she could get past him—and out—if she wanted to.

'I just think you would find it very difficult to get off the island. But, if you want to try, then be my guest. You were always a strong swimmer, as I recall.'

Coming to an abrupt halt, Lucy had a nasty little fight with herself not to sink back against the wall in admission of defeat. She couldn't quite believe it herself, but she had genuinely forgotten that the villa was set on its own little island. The distance between here and the shore was far too great for her to want to risk trying to swim it.

'All right,' she said, her lips and throat stiff with tension. 'You've made your point. But I still don't see why you want me here when earlier you were so keen to get rid of me. Oh, of course…' Realisation dawned as she remembered. 'You're waiting for that explanation. No?' she questioned when Ricardo shook his head.

'No,' he confirmed. 'There is something we have to see first.'

'Something you've decided I must see, you mean,' Lucy shot back and watched as he sighed his exasperation.

'Do not look at me like that. I promise you that this is important.'

'Important in what way?'

'Lucia!' Ricardo raked both his hands through the black silk of his hair, shaking his head in disbelief. 'Must you argue with *everything*? Can you not trust me on this?'

'Trust you?' Lucy scorned. 'So tell me why I should trust you when you have trapped me here, made sure I can't leave unless I swim for it and…'

Her voice trailed off as she suddenly looked into Ricardo's deep dark eyes and caught something there. Something that stilled and held her frozen.

'Trust me,' he said again and the words tugged on something deep inside, twisting around Lucy's heart just when she was least expecting it.

It wasn't rational, it was totally unwise, probably very naïve, but just in that moment she did trust him. So much so that when he took her arm and turned her in the opposite direction, she didn't pull away from his grasp but allowed herself to be directed down the corridor again, towards the other side of the house.

The part of the villa where their suite had been when they had lived here as man and wife.

That set her nerves tingling in apprehension. Not at the thought of what Ricardo might do but the fear of just how she might react if she was forced to go back to that part of the Villa San Felice where she had lived with him as his wife. The part of the villa where she had been at her happiest, she admitted to herself, fighting against the slash of pain that the memories brought. How would she feel if she had to look into the room where she and Ricardo had spent so many wonderful, blissful nights?

Only *physically* blissful, stern reality forced her to remind herself. Any emotional contentment she had felt had been based on a lie. A lie she had told herself just to keep from facing up to the truth. She might have fallen head over heels for her husband, but for Ricardo the marriage had just been one of pure convenience. The fact that it had also put a willing and passionate sexual partner into his bed every night had just been a bonus in his eyes.

'Ricardo…' she tried but he either didn't hear her or refused to acknowledge that he had.

But the twisting nerves in her stomach eased as they rounded a corner and Ricardo took the opposite direction to the one she had been anticipating with dread. The next moment he stopped before a closed door, turned the handle and pushed it open.

Immediately Lucy knew what he was doing and, if she had felt fearful before, now a terrible sense of panic rushed at her with the emotional force of a tsunami. She froze in the doorway, unable to move back or forwards, though she knew from the way that Ricardo's hand gripped her elbow that he was not going to let her escape.

The room was decorated with all the bright pictures, the blue and white carpet and curtains that she had chosen with such joyful anticipation before the birth of her baby. The same huge soft cushions were set on the floor, the same mobile with the cheerful painted animals hung from the ceiling. All this Lucy took in in a single glance. But then her gaze went to the big cot standing against the far wall and every other thought left her head.

'Marco…'

It was just a whisper, barely a thread of sound, and she was amazed that she could get that out past the knot in her throat. Her heart, which had stopped dead in the moment she had recognised the room as the nursery, was now beating so fast and so wildly that she couldn't catch her breath. If it got any worse, then she feared that it might actually burst out of her chest in the rush of emotion that made her head swim viciously.

At her side she was barely aware of Ricardo making a silent gesture with one hand. In response a young woman in a neat uniform, clearly the nanny hired to look after the baby, slipped silently from the room, leaving them alone. And all the time Lucy couldn't move, couldn't speak, couldn't think. She could only stare wide-eyed at the small person lying under the quilt in the cot, his black hair startling against the white sheet.

Marco's eyes were closed and he was fast asleep. One small hand was flung up outside the coverings and his deep breathing made soft snuffling noises as he exhaled.

'Marco…'

It was all that she could manage and she swayed towards him where she stood but didn't dare to try to make a move towards the cot. It was what she wanted most in all the world and yet what she feared in the same moment as she longed for it. Tears blurred her eyes but they were too hot and too bitter to give release to them. She almost felt as if they would burn down her cheeks like acid if she actually let them fall and flow.

And all the time she was so desperately aware of Ricardo standing next to her, still and silent, just watching her, his dark eyes observing and noting everything.

She didn't know what he was thinking and, quite frankly, she didn't care. All she knew was that her son—her baby—was just across the room from her and she didn't know how she could get to him, or even if she dared to try.

'Marco...' she said yet again. Then, as Ricardo's stillness and silence got through to her once more, she cleared her throat and forced the words out.

'"Something we have to see", you said,' she croaked in reproach.

'This is what you came for, isn't it? You wanted to see Marco.'

Lucy could only nod silently, the one accusing outburst she'd managed seemed to have drained all her strength so that she couldn't find any words to answer him.

What was happening here? What was in Ricardo's mind? Why had he brought her here like this—to see her baby—and yet once again be so near and yet so far? How had he come from *Not while I live* to actually leading her to the nursery, dismissing the nanny?

He couldn't be so cruel as to let her see Marco, come within touching distance of the baby and...

'Then go and see him,' Ricardo said, stunning her.

He wasn't touching her, wasn't doing anything to push her forward or to hold her back either. The hand that had been on her arm had dropped to his side and he was standing back, waiting—and watching. She could feel the burn of his gaze on her face so fiercely that she didn't dare to turn to meet the darkness of his eyes.

'I can't...'

This couldn't be happening. Not after she had dreamed of

it for so many weeks, ever since the doctors had told her that she was fine now. That they were sure she could handle things, and that she was no longer a danger to her baby or to herself. Without that assurance she would never have dared even to try to make contact. But she had wanted this moment so much that now she could not believe it was actually real.

'Yes, you can.' Ricardo's voice was surprisingly soft, though still without any trace of emotion in it. 'He's real, Lucia. Our baby—our son. You can…'

'No, I can't!' It was a cry of raw pain, dragged from her as if it was tearing her soul out by the roots, leaving her bruised and bleeding deep inside. 'I can't—'

'Have you come all this way to give up now? Whatever else I thought of you, Lucia, I never considered you a coward.'

Coward! If he had meant to sting her into action—and Lucy strongly suspected that he had—then it worked. Before she had time to think, rejection of that accusation had pushed her forward, the impetus driving her to the side of the cot before she had time to think.

And from the moment that she looked into her baby's face there was nowhere else she could look at all. Nothing else that mattered.

'Oh, Marco…'

Sinking down onto the floor beside the cot, she curled her fingers around the white-painted bars and just stared, seeing the way that the baby's chest rose and fell, the curl of his lashes onto the soft cheeks, the faint bubble that formed at his lips as he breathed.

'Darling…sweetheart…'

And looking was just not enough. Slowly one hand uncurled itself from the bars, then slid between them, reaching out towards where Marco lay. With soft fingers she touched his cheek, then curved her palm around the top of his small head, resting gently on the fuzz of jet-black hair. It seemed to fit so perfectly, and yet it was so different from the times that she had held him before that it made a terrible sorrow at all that she had missed clog up her throat.

'He's so big…' she choked out, fighting the tears.

The silence that greeted her words tugged hard on her nerves, making her tense suddenly where she sat. Ricardo still stood in the doorway; he didn't seem to have moved a muscle. And it was the fact that he was so very still, so totally, dangerously still that tightened every muscle in her body, made the tiny hairs at the back of her neck lift in a shivering, fearful moment.

He was as still as some fierce hunting predator might be while watching his prey wander innocently on the plains before him. He was just waiting, poised ready to move— ready to pounce.

'Strange…' he said now, and for all it was so quiet, so apparently calm, his tone did nothing to ease the sensation of being hunted down. If anything, it made it so much worse, twisting her nerves in a sense of intuitive terror, though of what she had no idea. 'He still seems so small to me. But then I see him every day—so I expect that the difference between when you saw him last and now is so much more pronounced.'

Could what he said be any more pointed? Could he do anything more to drive home the point that he had been here with Marco all the time, while she had abandoned their baby when she had walked out?

Slowly she raised her head, lifted her eyes to meet his, and when she saw the dark opaqueness of his gaze she knew what was happening.

He was testing her. She was under total scrutiny, like some

small defenceless creature dissected on a laboratory table and then placed under the microscope. He was testing her, and she had no idea whether what she was doing was the right thing in his eyes or exactly the opposite.

As she fought to control the fearful shudder that took her body by storm, she saw the sudden change in his face and knew that the predator had finally grown tired of watching and waiting.

He had decided to pounce.

CHAPTER EIGHT

'ALL right…'

Ricardo had thought that he would have to force himself to keep his voice calm, his body still. He had anticipated that at this point he would have to struggle with himself not to lose the tight grip he had on his emotions and to control the rising rage that was welling up inside him. But instead it all seemed suddenly so much easier than he had ever anticipated.

It was as if the time he had spent standing unmoving, just waiting and watching, had fixed his limbs in place so that he couldn't move them even if he wanted to. And at the same time a storm of ice had entered his mind, his veins—his heart—freezing them so that there was no feeling, no response in any of them.

He didn't even feel anger any more. Only the icy certainty that there was something he really needed to know here. The suspicion had been planted in his thoughts yesterday and it had taken root there, growing stronger overnight, with each moment of today. On some deep, instinctive gut level he had known that there was something missing in the story Lucy had told him. And what he had just seen had confirmed it.

He had had to see Lucy with Marco. Had to see if the callous indifference she had displayed in her leaving note had been true. And so he had brought her here to see how she reacted.

And she hadn't behaved at all as he had expected.

'I think it's time we got to the truth. The real truth—nothing else. You said you were ill—but there's more to it than that.'

Her behaviour had not been that of the monster mother he had created in his mind. There had been real pain, real fear in that *I can't*… And the way that she had cradled the baby's head had been so needy and yet so desperately gentle, making it plain that she was anxious not to disturb the little boy's sleep.

So what the hell had driven her away, leaving only that appalling note behind?

'What happened to you, Lucia?'

'I—'

She opened her mouth to speak, then closed it again, looking from his face to that of the sleeping baby and then back again. And the way that she had lost all colour from her face until her skin looked bloodless pushed him forward into the room, holding out his hand to her to help her up.

'There is a sitting room just through here—we can talk there. That way we will hear Marco if he stirs.'

'Thank you.'

Did she know what it did to him when she looked up into his face like that, with those soft blue eyes so wide and clear? And the touch of her hand in his had a kick that tightened every nerve in his body, sending stinging electrical sparks running up his arm straight to his heart so that it jerked in instinctive reaction.

Just who was this woman who had been his wife? Still was, on paper. It seemed as if in the single day since she had come back into his life she had been half a dozen diverse characters, none of whom he recognised from the Lucy he had first met. The Lucy he had married. Here and now she was like a completely different person from the hard-faced creature who only yesterday had flung in his face her certainty that she would walk away with a large proportion of everything he possessed.

That, and Marco too.

The nanny's sitting room was a small, comfortable area off the main nursery. There was a settee and armchairs, a tiny kitchenette at the far side of the room. Lucy followed him silently into it, not hesitating or pulling away, though her head turned back towards the cot where the baby lay.

'You will see him again,' Ricardo told her gruffly.

'You promise?'

When she looked at him like that he would promise her anything. But that was the way he had been caught before, when he had let what he had believed was her innocent beauty lure him into her bed.

It would do no harm to promise this much. She would see Marco again; he could guarantee that. Any more would depend on what she told him now.

'I promise,' he said and watched some of the tension seep from her body, the tight mouth loosening, the way she held her shoulders easing.

'Thank you,' she said again and the faint tentative smile that accompanied the words caught on something raw deep inside and twisted hard.

'Save your thanks,' he muttered roughly, 'until I've done something to deserve them. Would you like a drink? Coffee?'

'Some water, perhaps.'

A drink would be a good idea, Lucy acknowledged. Her voice had croaked embarrassingly on her words. If she had to tell him the whole of her story, she was going to need some help.

She did have to tell him, she knew that. There was no going back now. For better or for worse, everything had to come out.

'Your water.'

Ricardo's voice sounded harshly from close by, startling her eyes open so that she looked up and straight into his darkly watchful face, seeing herself reflected, tiny and pale-faced in the polished blackness of his eyes. Blank, unreadable eyes. Eyes that gave nothing away.

And suddenly it was as if she had slipped back through time, back to the moment when she had first arrived at this villa after their wedding. The speedboat had ferried them from the shore across to the island and as they'd stepped ashore she had slipped and almost lost her footing. Immediately Ricardo had moved forward and caught her before she could fall, swinging her up into his arms and carrying her along the wooden jetty that led to the wide stone steps up to the house. As he'd lifted her over the threshold into the villa itself he had suddenly looked down into her eyes, his own deep and dark and totally inscrutable, revealing nothing at all about his thoughts or his feelings.

'Welcome home, wife,' he had said.

Then, as he had let her slip to the floor, he had pressed the palms of his hands, big and warm and strong, to the front of her dress, below which the baby she was carrying—the baby that would eventually become Marco—was as yet just a tiny curve to her belly.

'Welcome, mother of my child.'

It had been in that moment that she had realised that she had fallen desperately, irrevocably in love with this man who was now her husband. But only her husband of convenience, married purely for the sake of that baby.

As the mother of his child, she was welcome in his home. As the mother of his child, his home became her home. But only as the mother of his child. For herself, and in herself she had no place here at all.

'Lucia—your water.'

Cold moisture beaded the sides of the glass Ricardo held out to her and as she took hold her fingers slipped, sliding up against his hand where he held it. The contrast between the coldness of the glass and the warmth of his skin was a shock, startling her and making her nerves fizz as if a bolt of electricity had shot up her arm.

And from the way that those dark eyes burned into hers it was obvious that Ricardo had felt it too. Just for a moment as their gazes locked she felt that he was about to say something—she could almost feel the words in the air. But then he apparently had second thoughts and stepped away again to move to the door and check on Marco. The baby was still sleeping soundly so Ricardo turned back, pushing his hands deep into the pockets of his trousers as he leaned against the wall.

'So,' he said flatly. 'The truth…'

Which was guaranteed to tighten Lucy's throat even more.

Lifting the glass to her mouth, she took a swift, deep gulp of the cooling water as she tried to collect her thoughts. She wished that Ricardo would move somewhere else or that he would come and sit down. Standing there, so tall and lean and dark, he seemed to tower over her oppressively, dominating the room and tightening every one of her muscles just to look at him.

'Why…' Her throat clenched and she had to take another gulp of water. 'Why did you bring me here?'

The look he gave her said that that was a question that didn't need answering but all the same he drew in a long, deep breath and then looked her straight in the eyes.

'I wanted to see you with Marco—how you would react. How you would be when you met him for real.'

So she had been right. He had been testing her. The atmosphere she had sensed in the room earlier had been real and not the product of her overheated imagination.

'And what did you find out?'

'That you lied.'

It was the last thing she had expected but as she opened her mouth to refute the accusation he ignored her attempt at protest.

'You lied in that note you left when you said you wanted your freedom—at least when you said you wanted your freedom from Marco. So something else took you away. You said you were sick—what was wrong?'

'I wasn't exactly sick…' Lucy hedged. 'It was more like a…a breakdown.'

She had his attention now. Those dark eyes couldn't have burned any stronger, or been more fixed on her face.

'A mental breakdown?'

If there had been any hint of shock or horror in his voice then she might not have been able to answer him but the truth was that his tone was completely controlled, totally matter-of-fact. So much so that it was only just a reaction.

'Yes…'

She nodded, keeping her eyes locked with his. That steady black gaze never wavered, never moved. Instead, it stayed fixed on her, probing deeper and further with every breath that she took.

'You were depressed.'

'You could say that.' Lucy's voice was shaky, her weak attempt at laughter even more so. She knew from his quick frown that her laughter seemed out of place but she just couldn't hold it back. *Depressed* seemed such an inadequate word for what she had been through. She had barely known who she was or what she was doing. And the world had seemed like a dark, empty cavern, one that she couldn't find her way out of, no matter how she'd tried. 'Though depressed sounds like the way you'd describe it if you lost a job or your dog died.'

'Not true depression. And if you had a breakdown, then that's what you must have suffered.'

Looking up into Ricardo's face, Lucy blinked hard at the unexpected note in his voice. She hadn't anticipated such sympathy. Was it possible that he might understand after all?

'It was horrible.' She shivered at the memory. 'The whole world seemed black and I didn't know how to make myself get out of bed every day.'

And knowing what she had done to Marco, that by running away she had probably lost him, and the man she'd loved, for ever, had made things so, so much worse. The future had stretched ahead of her, bleak and cold and empty, and she hadn't known how she was going to cope. If it hadn't been for the care of a kind and understanding doctor, the support of therapists, she didn't know how she would have survived.

'There didn't seem to be any point in going on. Any reason to—'

She broke off sharply, startled into awareness of the way that Ricardo had suddenly abandoned his position against the wall and had come close, his fingertips resting lightly on her arm.

'Don't…' he said quietly, pulling her out of the dark fog of her memories.

'Ricardo…' Her voice was all over the place, shaking and quavering in a way that she just couldn't control. And she felt so cold…so horribly cold. She was shivering as if she were in the grip of some horrible fever.

'Give that to me.'

It was only when Ricardo's hand came out and eased the glass from her clenched fingers that she realised how tightly she had been gripping it. She had been holding it so firmly that when her hand had started to shake the water inside the glass had swirled around, slopping over the side and splashing onto the pink linen of her skirt, marring the fine material with ugly dark patches.

She remembered buying this skirt—at least, she thought she did. It had been one of the things she had found on one of the first trips she had made away from the villa a couple of weeks after Marco had been born. She had left him with his nanny and had called Enzo, who took care of and piloted the motorboat, to take her across the lake to the shore. And there she had taken the car into Verona, where she had shopped, hunting for something—anything—that would make her feel more human. Something that would make her feel more alive, more in control of herself and her life.

And something that would make Ricardo look at her like a woman he desired once again.

Without the glass to hold, her hands were shaking even more and when she clasped both of them together on her lap they still kept shaking, shuddering where they lay on the pink skirt. With a terrible effort she twisted them together even more tightly, whimpering faintly when it had no effect.

'Lucia…'

Ricardo's hand, cool from the cold glass, came over both of hers, holding them, stilling them. But he still couldn't calm the waves of despair that were taking her body by storm, making it tremble and shake convulsively.

'Lucia, no,' Ricardo said quietly, calmly. So calm in contrast to the way she was feeling that it stopped her heart for a moment as she tried to take it in. 'There is no need for this.'

'You don't understand…'

Somehow she managed to get the words out, though her voice was as jerky and uneven as her heart.

It was his closeness that was doing that to her. He had slid down now from where he had been sitting on the arm of the settee and onto the cushions beside her. She could feel the warmth of his body, of the long, strong thigh that was pressed close up against hers. And she drew in the scent of his skin with each uneven, ragged breath. The width of his chest in the deep red shirt, the buttons opened at the throat, was level with her eyes, just a hint of dark curling hair revealed in the open neck, and she longed to be able to rest her head against his strength, draw new courage from him. But the distance between them, the yawning emotional chasm that separated her, would always hold her back.

'Oh, but I do.'

To her consternation, she found that Ricardo had somehow seemed to read her mind, to know just exactly what she needed. His strong arms folded round her, drawing her close. At first she tensed, trying to resist. But then the sense of loneliness overwhelmed her and she yielded, soft and yearning, against him.

Her head rested on the hard wall of his ribcage, the steady, thudding beat of his heart pounding under her cheek. She could feel his chest rise and fall with every breath he took and she felt, dangerously, as if she had come home.

Ricardo smoothed one hand over the length of her hair, sliding down her back, raising every tiny nerve in response. The warmth of his palm against the skin of her neck made her heart jolt at the feel of it and a moment when those caressing fingers slid briefly in at the scooped neck of her shirt had her breath catching sharply in her throat. The hard strength of his body was against one breast and as the stroking arm brushed against the other with every slow, gentle movement her nipples tightened in stinging response to the sudden waking need low down between her legs.

'I understand so much better than you could ever believe,' Ricardo murmured, the deep rumble of his voice drowning out the involuntary sigh of longing she had been unable to hold back. 'There's just one thing I want to know.'

Lucy froze against Ricardo's chest. An edge to his voice made her tense in sudden apprehension. The growing sense of warmth and comfort that had been seeping through her body, driving away the chill that had invaded her blood, suddenly seemed to stop and then, shockingly, started to fade again, allowing the shivering cold to start to creep back again.

'I want to know his name.'

She hadn't been wrong about the alteration in his tone, the difference in his mood. It was there too in the sudden change in his position and the way he held her. She was still in his arms, still held close, but it no longer felt like home.

Hard fingers suddenly clamped around her arms, moving her away from him, away from the secure warmth of his lean, hard frame. He held her so that he could look down into her eyes, his dark burning gaze searing her clouded blue one.

'Who the hell is he, Lucia? What's the name of the man who did this to you? The man who drove you to a breakdown when he left you.'

CHAPTER NINE

Who the hell is he, Lucia?... The man who drove you to a breakdown when he left you.

For the first few spinning seconds she hadn't been able to understand what had happened. Ricardo's sharply snapped questions made no sense. She couldn't understand where they came from or why he was even asking them. But then, slowly, reluctantly, she looked back over the conversation and realised the train of thought that Ricardo had been following, the conclusions he had jumped to.

He thought that she had had the breakdown *after* she had left the villa. He really believed—the only way he could possibly see it happening—was that she had run off with another man, leaving him and Marco behind in her determination to start a new life with her lover—his rival.

And then he believed that when that lover had walked out on her, leaving her as she had left him, then and only then had Lucy had the breakdown she had talked about.

'You think that…'

She had stiffened in his arms, pulling away from the warmth and support of his body. And just the tiny movement seemed to take an inordinate amount of effort, bring with it a wrenching pain that was out of all proportion to the distance she put between the two of them.

'You really believe that the only reason I could possibly leave Marco was because there was another man!'

Ricardo didn't need to answer. It was there in his eyes, stamped into the lines of his face. Suddenly, disturbingly, she was seeing her erratic behaviour through his eyes. The excessive spending, the way she had disappeared for most of the day, with no explanation. Had he really thought that she was meeting someone else? That she was having an affair? The thought that she might have put him through that made her shiver inwardly. How could she blame him for thinking so badly of her if that was what he had suspected?

'I can see now that the way I behaved might have made you think that,' she admitted shakily. 'And you don't know how much I regret it if it did. But you have to believe me—there never was anyone else.'

She saw his frown, the way his dark eyes dropped to lock with her own clouded gaze.

'Then why…'

'I wasn't ill—didn't break down after I left here.'

Though leaving Marco had been the last straw. The one that had broken this particular camel's back and driven her in despair and desperation to find a doctor.

'You're saying…'

Ricardo's face changed as realisation dawned. This time his eyes went to the cot where Marco still slept, then came back to her.

'Are you telling me that it was post-natal depression that caused your breakdown? That was why you left?'

Lucy could only nod, her throat too clogged for speech. It was impossible to read the rush of feelings that flashed in

Ricardo's eyes, but she saw the questions there and straightened her spine, waiting for them to come. And now he was the one to move away, putting more distance between them.

'That was like no depression I've ever seen.'

'No,' Lucy admitted.

She couldn't hold it against him that he hadn't recognised what even she hadn't known. She had had the doctor to explain it to her. Ricardo had been looking in from the outside.

When he had been there, which wasn't often.

'You were out all the time. Spending money like water.'

'I know—I was hyper. Manic.'

Post-natal psychosis, the doctor had called it. Not just depression but the more severe form of the illness, which had literally driven her almost out of her mind. So much so that she had been unable to think straight enough to recognise what was happening to her.

It hadn't helped that her relationship with her own mother had been so difficult. The only time that Janet Mottram had shown any real interest in her daughter had been when she had used the child as a pawn in her personal battle with her ex-husband. And, looking back, Lucy knew that what she had feared most was being as distant and unloving a mother to Marco as Janet had been to her.

And, without anyone to confide in, she had been trapped with her own thoughts. Thoughts that had so frightened and appalled her that there was no way she could have admitted them to Ricardo.

So she had put on a front. A cold, distant front that had driven him away from her even more. And she had succeeded so much better than she could have hoped. From the time that Marco had been born, she and Ricardo had barely spoken to each other. It had been what she wanted but at the same time it had added to the aching inside her, creating a spiral of despair from which she had felt that she would never break free.

'You bought clothes, perfume—clothes you never wore when you were with me.'

And he had thought that she had bought them to make herself look good for someone else.

'All that spending—it was just an attempt at distraction. I didn't even want the clothes half the time.'

And the other half she had wanted them to boost her image, to make Ricardo look at her with the desire he had once shown her. But it had seemed that the women she had overheard had been right. She was not the sort of wife who could hold a man like Ricardo. A man who didn't do commitment. Who was used to having his pick of the most glamorous, most sophisticated women of the world.

If only he would speak—say something. Anything, other than subjecting her to the dark, silent stare that seemed to want to probe right into her eyes, burn its way into her head.

'Heaven knows what you must have thought of me!'

'It was only what I expected,' Ricardo stated flatly. 'Normal female behaviour. Every woman I've known has been out for what I could give her. Why should you be any different?'

How could she fight such cynicism? She hadn't been able to do so when they had been together, so why should anything be different now? Besides which the thought that she still hadn't told him absolutely everything, that there were still things she was holding back, things she could hardly bear to think of herself, sat like a leaden weight in her heart, closing off her throat so that there was no way she could make herself speak.

'And you are well now?' he asked, an edge to his voice that she couldn't interpret and she felt too emotionally adrift even to try.

'The doctors say I am,' she managed stiffly. 'They think all should be well and that I'm not likely to relapse. I would never have come back here if I'd thought…'

'I believe you,' Ricardo said when her voice broke too much for her to go on. He was still so very distant, his deep-set eyes hooded and hidden, but his tone gave her a little cause for hope.

'So if you could see your way to letting me spend some time with Marco…'

And, just at that moment, with amazing timing so that it was almost as if he had heard his name spoken, in the other room the baby stirred and started to whimper faintly, still half asleep.

'Marco…'

Instinct drove Lucy to her feet but she was only halfway there when realisation struck and she froze, grabbing at the settee arm for support as she looked back at Ricardo, meeting the deliberately blanked out expression in his narrowed gaze.

'I…I'm sorry…'

She regretted that as soon as she'd said it. She wasn't sorry at all for reacting automatically to the sound of her child's cry. She might not have been the best mother in the world—she knew she hadn't—but that didn't mean that her maternal instincts had died, swamped by the tidal wave of foul stuff that that rushed over her in the depths of those darkest days. After all, she'd only left because of what she was afraid of. Because of the fear that she might do something dreadful to her little boy. That was those mother's instincts working overtime, not losing their way. And now she was doing exactly the same—responding to the way that her baby most needed her.

The memory of that cry had never left her. In her sleep she would hear it and come jerking awake, sitting up in a rush, eyes wide with horror and fear, needing to find Marco…and knowing he wasn't there. That had been the worst, the most terrible moment of all. The thought that somewhere her baby was crying and she couldn't go to him.

Here and now, she could respond to his call. But at the same time she didn't quite dare to. Not with Ricardo watching and not knowing how he would react if she followed her instincts. He had sworn that she would never take the baby from him, so would he let her comfort the little boy—or would he grab at her arm, to hold her back? Or would he, worst of all, wait until she was at the cot's side, about to take her son into her arms and then snatch the little boy away from her—so near and yet so desperately far again.

'I doubt that you'll understand…but…' Her voice trailed off as she met the burning darkness of his eyes, felt herself flinch under their scorching force.

From the other room came a second more wakeful cry, louder this time, drawing Lucy's eyes in a glance of yearning anxiety towards the door.

'I'll call the nanny,' Ricardo said and the words brought back such a rush of memory that it pushed her response from her mouth before she had had a moment to consider if it was wise.

'No!' she said sharply. 'No nanny! Not now.'

'You were happy enough to leave him in her care before.'

'Did you give me any choice?' Lucy flung at him. 'Did you even discuss it with me? No—you made a unilateral declaration that Marco was going to be looked after by a nanny. It may be the way you were brought up—the norm in your wealth driven world to have your children farmed out to the hired help, but it wasn't what I wanted.'

'I had no intention of having him "farmed out",' Ricardo snapped coldly. 'And it certainly wasn't the way that I was brought up. My mother barely had enough money to feed and clothe me, never mind hire a nanny.'

'Then why did you hire one for Marco? Did you think I wasn't good enough to look after your son, the precious Emiliani heir?'

She didn't believe that his eyes could close up any more, or become any more opaque, but it was like looking into the immovable face of a statute. One that was carved from cold, hard marble.

'That was never my aim,' he said at last and if a statue could have spoken then it would have had just that same stiff, icy voice. 'If you want the truth, I was fool enough to think that you might appreciate some help.'

That cold comment twisted a knife in Lucy's already tender conscience. She'd been so caught up in her own misery that she'd never looked at it from this angle. Now she was forced to face the fact that her own lack of self-esteem had turned what had been an attempt to do the right thing into the exact opposite.

'I'm sorry...' she began but as she spoke Marco whimpered again.

'Your son needs you,' Ricardo said.

'What?'

She hadn't quite caught what he had said. Or, if she had, then she wasn't at all sure that she could possibly have heard right.

'Your son needs you,' he repeated, calm, coldly controlled and totally unmistakable this time. 'You had better go to him.'

She knew that look, that assessing scrutiny. He was testing her again. But which was the right way to react? How could she prove herself to him? And just what did he want her to prove?

She could only go with her instincts. There was no way of second-guessing him.

And, as the whimper turned into a wail and then an

outraged cry, she was left with no choice. She no longer gave a damn what Ricardo thought or felt. It was what Marco needed that mattered. She was out of the sitting room in a rush, bending down over the cot before Ricardo could say a word. And she knew that if he had spoken, if he'd tried to stop her, then she would have ignored him completely.

'Hush little one…it's all right. Mu…'

Her throat closed over the words, choking them off. How could she call herself 'Mummy' after all that had happened? Marco would never understand—and would he even let her touch him?

Painfully aware of the way that Ricardo had moved to the doorway, one strong hand resting against the wood of the frame, she could feel the burn of his eyes in her back as she reached in and scooped up the little boy, lifting him gently. He was so much bigger than the last time she had held him that she felt the unexpected weight of him in contrast to then. That dreadful time when she had felt that she had to give him one last hug, in spite of the fears that were whirling in her head, telling her that she wasn't safe with this precious child. That she had no idea just what she might do.

'Careful, darling…'

Was it just the unfamiliar voice, or would she be completely fooling herself to think that the baby recognised her somehow? Lucy's heart clenched sharply as the little boy's big dark eyes opened wide to stare into her face, his wails and his whole body stilling as she lifted him so carefully.

'That's better, isn't it?'

She prayed that he wouldn't feel the way she was trembling all over. That the twisting of her nerves wouldn't communicate itself to him and upset him all over again. She also hoped that Ricardo wouldn't see the fear in her eyes, the determined effort she was making to hide the way she was feeling and misinterpret it as something else.

'Now, let's see…'

Adjusting the baby in her arms, she caught a telltale whiff that left her in no doubt of something that needed dealing with. She didn't have much experience of caring for her child, but this was something practical she'd done for him, even in the short weeks she'd been with him.

'Oh, so that's the problem! Let's see…'

A swift glance around made it clear just where the changing mat and all the things necessary for cleaning and changing a nappy could be found and she moved towards it, taking Marco with her. She was determined not to look in Ricardo's direction, knowing he was still watching her like a hawk. No doubt just waiting for her to make a mistake, show some hesitation. Something he could criticise. Something he could hold against her.

Well, not this time, Signor Emiliani. She almost laughed as she laid Marco on his back on the brightly coloured changing mat. This was something she knew how to do.

'Let's get you cleaned up…'

Unfastening the sleep suit, removing the dirty nappy, cleaning, was the work of moments. And she enjoyed it—doing this simple task for her baby. Even when Marco waved his arms and legs wildly in the air, wriggling so that it was a struggle to get the nappy on and fastened, she couldn't hold back the soft chuckle of appreciation of his life and energy. Forgetting about the dark, watchful man behind her, she bent her head and blew a loud raspberry on his exposed stomach, revelling in its soft roundness, the uncontrollable giggles that burst from him in response.

Perhaps with Marco at least things could come right.

Maybe in time she could make up to him for the way she had left him. If Ricardo gave her that time, she was forced to add as a movement behind her told her that her husband had left his watching position and come closer.

'That's you done,' she said, pretending she hadn't noticed, determined to ignore him as she fastened the baby's clothes, lifted him carefully, cradled him against her shoulder. 'Now, let's see...'

'Give him to me.'

She'd been expecting it but still it was like a blow to her heart. She'd known he wouldn't give her free rein with the baby, that he was just watching and waiting...

Instinctively her arms tightened around the sturdy little body. Every part of her wanted to shout *no*, to refuse to hand him over. But she knew she had to think of Marco. She must not upset him. And yet she couldn't just give in to Ricardo's demand.

'This isn't fair,' she said, keeping her voice as calm and as quiet as she could manage as she swung round on her heel, turning to face the big dark man behind her.

Over Marco's soft dark head she faced the baby's father with rejection sparking in her eyes.

'You let me hold him, come close to him—the next moment you take him from me. It's cruel and...'

'I'm not taking him from you,' Ricardo stunned her by saying. 'It's midday. Marco usually has something to eat around now.'

A wave of his hand indicated the padded high chair close at hand.

'Why don't you put him in there?'

The slight emphasis on that *you* brought a stinging reproach that she had to admit to herself she deserved. The sharp reminder of just how little she knew about Marco's life and routine twisted a cruel knife in her heart.

'I'm sorry.'

Moving rather clumsily as she adjusted to the unfamiliar weight of her son in her arms, she tried to put Marco into the high chair. Luckily, he seemed prepared to help her and, obviously recognising that this meant food was on its way, began banging on the tray with an enthusiastic hand, slapping his palm on to the surface.

'Da!' he said excitedly, waving the other hand wildly in the air. 'Da!'

He was too young to be talking properly yet, Lucy told herself, fighting with the twist of misery that sound brought her. And, besides, having only ever been spoken to in Italian, Marco was unlikely to be trying to form the word 'Daddy'. But it was another way of bringing home to her how much she had lost by being away from him at this important stage of his life. The pain that cut at her had her digging her teeth down hard into the softness of her lower lip as she fought with the tears that burned at the back of her eyes.

Ricardo bent to wipe the high chair's tray, receiving enthusiastic pats on his face from his son as he did so. Careful cleaning of those grasping fingers followed.

'Here—give him this…'

Ricardo passed her a sliced banana on a plate.

'Just put it onto the tray and let him help himself.'

The small domesticated tasks, the time taken to feed the baby, brought a new and unexpected peace between them. Ricardo passed her the food that the nanny had left prepared and Lucy put it before the little boy, some of the tension seeping from her face, a light switching on in her eyes.

Had he been mistaken or had there been the glisten of tears in those eyes just a moment before? Ricardo found himself wondering. And did she know what it did to him to see the way that her sharp white teeth had dug into the pink softness of her lower lip as she had looked down at their little boy?

He had lost any ability to read her expression, thrown off balance by what he had just learned. He had trusted her once and that had had such shocking repercussions that he had vowed never to do so again. But this was very different. Vicious guilt clawed at him at the thought that his already hardened prejudice against her might have blinded him to the truth, driving him to misinterpret her behaviour after Marco's birth.

He should wait and watch, see what happened, he resolved in the same moment that another more primitive response shook his mental balance even harder.

Dio santo, but he had had to fight with himself not to react on the most basic instinctive level. Every male impulse had urged him to reach out for her and pull her to him. To kiss away the imprint of her teeth in her flesh and soothe it with his tongue. He wanted to taste her again, know the soft sweetness of her mouth, explore the moist interior and kiss them both to the verge of oblivion.

He wanted to tangle his hands in the golden fall of her hair and hold her just so—exactly where he could kiss her hardest, strongest, with the deepest passion.

But there was something else he wanted too. Something that combined with the sensual hunger, taking it and twisting it brutally inside him until, looking across at her, he had to push his hands deep into the pockets of his jeans against the temptation to use them in another, very different way.

She was looking down at Marco, laughing softly as the little boy squished his banana in his hand, obviously revelling in the mess he was making and the feel of it between his fingers. And Marco was watching her, his wide smile a beam of delight as he held up the sticky mess for her to see.

A child and his mother. That was what a stranger looking in through the wide open French windows would see in the scene before them. A child and his mother enjoying the moment, sharing the experience of food and fun, while the father, the husband, looked on and laughed with them.

A family.

That was how it should be. It was why he had married her, after all. Because his child, unlike Ricardo himself, his mother before that, should have two caring parents. And, having seen Lucy with Marco, having heard her story, how could he refuse her—and Marco—that in the future? He had to let her back into their son's life.

And back into his?

The cold stab of anger at the thought was like a blade of ice between his ribs, making him clench his teeth tight against it.

He couldn't blame her for the way she had run out on her marriage if she had been as ill as she had described. The evidence of her feelings for Marco were there before him in a natural warmth that no one could mistake. But where did that leave their marriage?

Was Marco truly all she had come back for or was there more to it than that? She needed money, obviously, because she had admitted that she had none now. So was she back, looking for the means of support that he as her wealthy husband was obliged to provide? Did she really just want to be with her son or was the fact that she was Marco's mother still her key to the luxurious lifestyle for which she had married him?

'Oh, Marco! What a mess!'

Lucy's voice, soft and warm with amusement, broke into his thoughts, shattering them and sending them spinning off onto another tangent entirely. As she bent her head, leaning down towards the little boy, laughing again as he reached up and smeared the fall of her hair with banana, he found that he was once more seeing the scene as someone else might see it.

That person would see a happy family. Not knowing the events that had torn the little group apart, they would assume it was still the perfect setting in which to bring up the little boy.

Which it was. Or once had been.

He had wanted a family for his child. Still wanted it more than he could say. And if he played his cards right then there was a way that he could still make it come true for the future. For Marco.

And if there were other reasons—private reasons—for him wanting to keep things the way they had been, could he admit them, even to himself? He had no wish to let anyone know the way that, after just twenty-four hours, he was once more fighting the irresistible, burningly sensual passion that Lucy's slender beauty had always been able to arouse in him. And certainly he was damned if he was ever going to let Lucy begin to suspect that those feelings were there. Sex and money had been the reasons why they had gone into this marriage that was not a marriage in the first place. And sex and money had been the things that had torn it apart too. Those two danger-ous elements had ruined his past. He was not going to let them ruin his future too.

She seemed to have been honest with him. And she truly seemed to want to be back with Marco, for the baby's sake, not for anything she could get out of this, but her concern could easily be faked. Could he really trust her with his beloved son's future? Why should she be so very different from the other women in his past?

The only way to be sure was to test her sincerity one more

time. To make absolutely sure that her reasons for being here were as she claimed. He would offer her the sort of deal that, if she was lying, would surely tempt her into showing her true colours. And the way she responded would tell him all he needed to know.

But if he could get what he wanted out of this situation— if he could keep her here, for Marco's sake, on the terms that suited him—then he would do just that.

CHAPTER TEN

'I THINK he's had enough…'

Lucy bent down to pick up yet another piece of bread that Marco had flung onto the floor, narrowly dodging the plastic mug of milk that landed right beside her as he discarded that too.

'Shall I clean up here and then…'

'Marissa will do that.'

He saw the look she gave him and acknowledged it with a faint inclination of his head.

'She'll take him for a walk too, to get some air. It's better to stick to his routine.'

Ricardo pressed the bell to summon Marco's nanny before wiping the little boy's face and hands with a clean cloth and hoisting him out of the high chair and hitching him on to one hip.

'And we have things we need to discuss.'

'We do?'

But, as she expected, there was no way that Ricardo was going to answer that as he shook his head and concentrated on wiping a stubborn piece of dried banana out of his son's eyebrow, managing Marco's wriggles of protest with an easy skill that wrenched at Lucy's heart.

'Not here.'

Not here. Not now. Not in front of Marco. Lucy added the words he didn't use, acknowledging the cold creeping sense of fear that welled up inside her as she did so.

So was this it? Was this the moment when Ricardo sent her packing? When her all too brief idyll with her little son came to an end and her husband made sure that she left the island?

And if she did, then would she ever see her baby again?

'No...'

Her hands went out to the child in his father's arms, but at that moment the door opened and the nanny she had seen before stepped into the room. After a brief conversation in Italian, too rapid for her to catch, Ricardo passed the little boy to Marissa and turned to Lucy. Something about the look on her face must have hit home to him because, as he took her elbow to turn her away towards the door, he bent his head and spoke swiftly, close to her ear.

'I promised,' he said roughly and just for a moment she stared at him, not quite understanding.

But then her memory cleared and she had a sudden rush of recollection. Ricardo saying, 'You will see him again,' and the conviction in his words that had had her believing him on that when she couldn't trust him on anything else.

And so she didn't fight but let herself be led from the room, with a long lingering glance back at the little boy who had taken over her heart without a chance of ever letting go.

He had always had her love, of course. It was just that her illness had blurred that love and preyed on her fears of not being a good enough mother. The thoughts she had experienced had been the depression, not the reality. She could see that now. But, at the time, lost and lonely, even if never alone, she had not been able to cope.

Now she knew the depth of her love, the way it had always

been there underneath all the horror and the misery. So how would she cope if Ricardo was once more going to deny her access to her child? Could he do that? And, if he did, then how would she ever be able to afford to fight him in the courts if she had to?

'Where are we going?'

'Just here…'

Ricardo pushed open a door to his left, in a position that Lucy recognised. Her heart sank as she walked into the room he had opened, the setting making it plain that her husband had nothing kind or considerate on his mind. His island home's office, with its dark wood furniture, the big L-shaped desk, the array of computer equipment, was a place for business deals, for cold-blooded decisions with nothing of the heart about them.

'Wouldn't you like to sit down?' Ricardo waved a hand in the direction of a chair, one of three gathered around a small coffee table set in the window overlooking the bay.

'Will I need to?'

His beautiful mouth twisted at the sharpness of her response and he met her attacking tone with a half shrug of one of his broad shoulders.

'It depends on how you're going to react to getting everything you wanted.'

'What?'

That nearly did take her legs from under her and she had to reach out for the back of a chair to support herself as the shock hit home.

'You'd do that?' Her voice shook in disbelief.

'Why not?'

This time he shrugged both shoulders, dismissing her stunned question as totally unimportant.

'It's only money. And I can soon make more.'

Only money.

Lucy's fingers had to clench tight over the back of the chair to keep her from letting her trembling give her away. And at the same time she felt her jaw tighten hard against the impulse to let a cry of distress escape. Of course. *Only money.* Did she really think that Ricardo was going to let her walk out of here with Marco? Simply hand the baby over to her and let her go?

Never in a million years.

But she had hoped for *something*. For a hint of recognition that he had recognised how ill she had been to leave her child, that he had seen how she cared for her little boy. A suggestion that he would let her see Marco—have some sort of access to the baby.

'In return for a quick and quiet divorce, I will give you a small fortune,' Ricardo stated bluntly. 'Enough cash to keep you in luxury for many years, without raising a hand to do a thing.'

He moved round to the other side of the desk, pulling out a drawer and snatching up a cheque book from its interior. Tossing it down onto the desk, he flipped it open, grabbed a pen and started to write. Firm bold strokes of the pen wrote numbers, words—and finished it all off with the slashing force of his signature, firmly underlined.

'I don't…' Lucy began but the sound of the cheque being ripped from the stub drowned her attempt to speak. And when he tossed the paper towards her, landing on the edge of the desk where she could see it, all the strength in her vocal cords evaporated in a sense of shock as hard and cruel as if he had actually punched her in her chest, driving all the breath from her body.

It couldn't be true. She had to be seeing things. Either that or Ricardo was playing with her. A small fortune, he had said.

There was nothing small about the amount on the cheque in front of her. It was an enormous amount—an obscenely large amount. More money than she had ever seen in her life. And Ricardo had tossed it at her as if it were a donation of a few pounds or so.

'You don't mean this.' The hand that she used to point at the cheque was trembling in bewilderment. She could barely read the figures clearly because of the disbelief that was blurring her eyes. You can't mean it.'

'Why not? Isn't it enough?' His eyes challenged her to object.

'It's enough for any human being—but it's not what I want.'

'If you want a divorce, then that's all that's on offer.'

It was that word—*divorce*—that felt like a slap in the face. But then he had made no secret of the fact that he wanted her out of his life permanently. The momentary kindness and understanding he had shown her earlier had misled her. She had thought they had come close to at least the beginnings of an understanding. And that had distracted her from the cold-blooded declaration he had made the night before.

How much will you take to leave now, get out of here—and stay out of my life for good?

Taking her silence as agreement, Ricardo jabbed a finger onto a button on the phone, not even looking at her. Speaking in fast Italian, he was obviously issuing instructions. She caught the name Enzo, the word *nave* and could only assume that the order had gone out to prepare the motor launch. He was really determined to get rid of her as quickly as possible. Which put her right in her place. Paid off, dealt with, dismissed from his thoughts. And about to be divorced by the sound of it. So much for his promise that she would see Marco again.

'Your boat is waiting.'

Could his voice get any colder? Could the long body

express hostility any more clearly than the way he stood, rigidly upright, half-turned away from her as if he couldn't wait to move on? Lucy felt a volatile blend of anger and pain well up inside her, pushing her into unguarded speech.

'No—*your* boat is waiting. The boat you've decided I should take. You never even waited for an answer...'

'So tell me, Lucy, what would you have said if I had asked you? Last night you were so determined to get away from here. Now are you telling me that you want to stay?'

She didn't dare to answer that truthfully. In fact her response was so clear and strong in her mind that she lowered her eyes, afraid that the truth would show in her gaze. It seemed that since she had first made her way onto the island—was it really less than twenty-four hours ago?—she had been on a wild roller coaster of emotions, shooting up and down with dizzying force and speed, never quite knowing which was true and which was safe.

Safer. None of the choices before her had been really *safe*. Last night she had been finding her way, groping blindfolded through the pitch-darkness, with only vaguely formed ideas of what she wanted most, and little understanding of how to approach things. Now she knew exactly what she wanted. She wanted to be a mother to her child and...

It was that *and* that made her thought processes stop dead, made her heart jolt in fear and apprehension and had her concealing her eyes and her thoughts from the man in front of her.

She didn't yet know quite what that *and* implied and until she did then she wasn't prepared to reveal the truth to him. Perhaps even then—perhaps even more than ever then—she would need to conceal the facts from him.

'I don't want to stay here but I do want to be with Marco. I want my son.'

It was the perfect summer afternoon, with the sun streaming in through the window, beyond which the lake water sparkled clear and blue in the light, but when Ricardo's face closed up like that it seemed to drain all the warmth from the atmosphere, dim the light, as if a cloud had passed in front of the sun.

'And you know that I would rather die than let you take him from me.'

'I want my rights as his mother… And, before you tell me that I gave those up when I ran out on him, I defy you to take me to court over it! We'll see what a judge has to say when I explain how things happened.'

'So you would fight for him?' He actually sounded pleased that she had challenged him on this. 'I was beginning to wonder.'

It wasn't that she hadn't been prepared to fight for Marco before. More that, until now, she hadn't been sure that she was the right person to do so. Until she had actually spent time with Marco, touched him, held him, felt the heavy warmth of his little body, inhaled the scent of his skin, that she had known this was what she had to do. That she could no longer live without her baby in her life.

'But, be warned, I'll fight right back. I'll see you in court if I have to.'

'You'd use the fact that I was ill against me?'

'What sort of monster do you think I am? But because I understand that you were ill it doesn't mean that I am going to hand my son over to you without a thought. If I have to fight you for custody then I will and I warn you, Lucy—I intend to win.'

Tension was tying Lucy's over stretched nerves into painful knots. Deep inside she quailed at the prospect of a court battle with Ricardo and the legal team that his wealth would bring him. And the truth was that she couldn't fault the way Marco's father had cared for the little boy. The thought of taking the baby from his father tore at her heart.

'Ricardo, neither of us wants this—surely it doesn't have to be this way? I was the subject of a battle between my parents, both of them wanting me, both of them using me just as a pawn in their private battle. I don't want to do that to Marco.'

'And I don't want the Emiliani name dragged through the gossip columns, my private life exposed. But Marco is my son. I didn't go through a marriage I didn't want just to see you take him from me and turn me into an absentee father.'

'And I don't want to be an absentee mother either…'

What had she said to put that sudden gleam of dark satisfaction into those black eyes? It looked almost as if she had done exactly as he had wanted. Lucy had the sudden, deeply uncomfortable feeling that she had been manoeuvred into a corner, checkmated somehow, and she hadn't even seen it happen.

'Then it seems that there is only one way to handle this.'

'There is? And what's that?'

To her astonishment, Ricardo leaned forward and snatched up the cheque from where it still lay on his desk between them.

'Look at that,' he said and, totally bemused, Lucy let him push the slip of paper into her unresisting hand.

'A small fortune,' he said, his voice disturbing in its icy intensity. '"Enough for any human being". And it's yours—if you leave.'

He saw the way that her head came up, the defiant words forming on her lips to fling his offer back at him and the faintest flicker of something that was almost a smile curled the corners of his mouth.

'Or…'

If Ricardo's tone had been glacial, then his eyes seemed to sear right to the core of her soul.

'You can have it the way you want it—if you stay here.'

Unnerved and mentally armed for a fight as she was, Lucy at first didn't catch the apparent concession. But when she did it was with a sense of shocked realisation.

'Stay?' she queried uncertainly. 'For how long?'

Ricardo's stony gaze burned into her, unflinching, unyielding.

'For good.'

One arrogant wave of his hand towards the window indicated where the boat waited, Enzo standing at the wheel, the subdued pulse of the engine seeming unnaturally loud in the silence. Another took in the room they stood in, the whole of the beautiful villa.

'There is your choice. The boat or the island. If you want to talk about this, then you stay here. If you want to leave, then the subject is closed. For ever.'

'But…'

Lucy's thoughts were spinning in a new and different kind of panic. She had the terrible feeling of being trapped. She had been manoeuvred into a very tight corner and it seemed that there was no way out of it.

'You can't keep me here!'

'No, but Marco can.'

'I…don't understand.'

Despairingly, Lucy shook her head, unable to make sense of what he was saying.

'It's quite simple. If you want the money, then you leave—get on the boat and let Enzo take you wherever you want. But if you want contact with Marco—and I think you do—then you stay here.'

'You'd let…'

'But, in that case, then the money is no longer yours. I'll stop the cheque…'

'You won't need to.'

The rush of delight at the thought that he might let her stay was dizzying in its force. How would this work? Perhaps Ricardo had some idea of letting her replace the nanny, or at the very least act as back-up… She didn't know and didn't care. She wanted to stay.

Without thinking, she took the cheque in a firm grip and ripped it into a thousand tiny pieces, tossing them wildly in the air so that they scattered around their heads, floating down softly to the ground like a fall of confetti. Drifting around Ricardo's dark head, several tiny white pieces lodged in the silk of his hair, on the broad straight shoulders, settling softly. He barely spared them a glance, his dark-eyed gaze still locked with hers as he watched her response with cool, distant assessment.

And it was in that moment, as she recalled another day, when the confetti had been real, when the tiny coloured pieces of paper had been thrown around them as they'd emerged from the church after their wedding, that her heart gave a painful lurch of realisation. Then, just as now, the confetti had fluttered around them, landing on Ricardo's hair and shoulders. She remembered how on that occasion he had shaken his head in impatience, sending the delicate pieces of paper flying once again as he'd rid himself of the tiny symbols of luck and love.

This time he was still and unmoving, his eyes seeming blank as they looked into her face. And it was that complete lack of expression that made her stomach clench on a cruel twist of apprehension.

'Are you sure?' he asked, his voice as cold as his expression.

'Totally.' She couldn't afford to let him see any doubt in her face, hear it in her tone.

'You will stay?'

'I'll stay.'

She had no alternative. No other alternative she even wanted to consider.

She had already run from this house once and she knew that she couldn't do it again. Then she had known that her heart was being torn in two at the thought of leaving her child behind but she hadn't been able to feel it. The misery that her life had become had battered her brain so badly that it was numbed by the bruising. Today, with her reunion with Marco so fresh and clear in her mind, the scent of his skin on her clothes, her arms still warm from holding him, she felt every dreadful raw, tearing sensation that threatened to break her heart into pieces, leaving her shattered and destroyed.

'*Buono…*'

Once more the phone was in Ricardo's hand.

'You will not be needed today, after all.' He spoke to Enzo but his eyes were on Lucy.

Beyond the window, Enzo leaned forward and turned a key, switching off the boat's engine. The silence that descended was sudden, still and very, very taut, stretching Lucy's nerves until she winced in distress. And in the silence she suddenly realised that she had agreed to stay and yet she had no real idea just what she was agreeing to.

'Just one thing,' she managed, the dryness of her constricted throat making the words come out as a rough-edged croak. 'There's something I need to clear up. If I'm staying…how am I staying? On what terms? Will I be a replacement for the nanny or…'

Silhouetted against the window, Ricardo was just a dark figure against the brightness of the afternoon sun. The sun that was blinding her so that she couldn't read the look on his face, no matter how much she screwed up her eyes.

'I mean…what…who am I staying as?'

'I would have thought that was obvious.' Ricardo's voice was coldly emphatic, totally clear in a way that his expression was not. 'The only way you'll stay in this house is as my wife.'

CHAPTER ELEVEN

THE big ornate clock out in the hallway was striking midnight, the deep, ominous tones sounding clearly up the curving staircase to where Lucy was sitting in the darkness of the bedroom. Slowly she counted the strokes—anything to distract her mind and give herself something else to think about, no matter how briefly.

'Six…seven…'

It was no good, the distraction didn't work. Her thoughts would keep drifting off to the rest of the day and the time that had passed since Ricardo had decreed that if she stayed at the villa then she did so as his wife.

In the first moments after he'd flung the declaration at her, pure blinding shock had held her frozen, immobile as if someone had aimed a hard blow at her head and left her reeling.

The only way you'll stay in this house is as my wife.

In the silence of the night, the autocratic words sounded so clear that she almost looked around, expecting to see that Ricardo had come into the room to find her and that he was standing right behind her, between her and the door, so that there was no hope of escape.

But the room was as dark and silent as before and the only sound was the faint lapping of the waves of the lake against the shore beyond the partly opened window. She had no idea where Ricardo was or what he was doing.

She hadn't had a chance to speak to him after that one high-handed statement. By the time she had pulled herself together to respond to him, needing to demand exactly what he meant, the phone had rung and Ricardo had swiftly snatched it up.

'Pronto?'

Pausing for a moment, he'd spared Lucy a swift flashing glance before saying sharply, 'I have to take this.'

In case she hadn't got the message, he'd moved to the door and held it open, the pointed dismissal only too clear. There'd been no point in arguing either; his attention was totally focused on the call and she had been completely wiped from his thoughts.

She hadn't seen him since. He had never come back to any part of the house she had been in, but had sent a message to say that he had been called away on business and wouldn't be back until very late that evening.

Well, it was very late now and Ricardo was still not back. She had no idea where he was, or what his plans for her involved.

The only way you'll stay in this house is as my wife.

Why could he possibly want her as his wife, when he had made it plain from the start that he hated her? And… A shiver ran down Lucy's spine that had nothing at all to do with the coolness of the temperature since the sun had gone down…

Just how much of a wife did he expect her to be?

Her whole body felt stiff and cramped and she stretched carefully, easing limbs that had been still for too long. She had fallen fast asleep, lying on the top of the bed as she'd waited for Ricardo's return, and had woken to find the room in darkness and the house silent.

She'd filled the hours between Ricardo's departure and

the onset of evening with enjoying more of Marco's precious company. Upstairs in the nursery flat, still not daring to be on her own with him but, together with the nanny, she had played with him, fed him again. And then, most special of all, she had bathed him and settled him down for sleep in his cosy cot, sitting beside him and singing lullaby after lullaby as she'd watched his eyelids grow heavier and heavier, his breathing slowing until she knew he was deeply asleep.

Even then she had not been able to drag herself away but had stayed, her arms resting on the cot's side, her head on her hands, watching him sleeping for as long as she could. It was only when darkness had finally fallen that she had forced herself from the room and had gone looking for her husband.

Her husband. That, it seemed was what she must now get used to calling him all over again. The man who for his own private reasons wanted her back as his wife—but obviously only on his terms.

And she had yet to find out exactly what those terms were.

So she had come here to the room that Marissa, with carefully disguised curiosity and an obvious struggle not to ask the questions that were burning on her lips, had told her was Ricardo's. Wherever he had been and wherever else he went once he came home, this was where he would have to end up eventually. She had wandered round it, taking in the severe blue and grey, starkly masculine décor that was so unlike the room they had once shared as husband and wife. Here there was little place for comfort, little scope for the softening effects of design or decoration. It was a room that was plain and functional.

It told her nothing new about her husband, nothing about the sort of life he had lived while she had been apart from him. If he had brought other women back to the huge king-sized bed, then it showed no sign of them. If they had been there, then they had been and gone, leaving no scent, no trace behind. To her relief, there was also no sign of any female clothes, no scented toiletries in the bathroom, no make-up scattered in the dressing room. Lucy didn't know what she would have done if she had found them there.

Eventually, the effects of a long stressful day and the build-up of lack of sleep for over a week before that had caught up with her. Telling herself that she would just rest until Ricardo came back, she had lain down on the soft grey and blue covering of the bed, rested her head on the crisp cotton of the pillowcase that still retained some of the most personal scent of Ricardo's skin and hair, inhaled it deeply and letting a single exhausted tear slide down her cheek, she'd fallen fast asleep.

But now she was wide awake again—and Ricardo had not come back. Swinging her legs off the bed, Lucy padded across the thick carpet to the uncurtained window and stared out at the silent, still lake that glistened in the moonlight. From this side of the house she couldn't see the mooring point so she had no idea if Enzo had brought the launch back and Ricardo with him. All the other staff must surely be asleep by now and so...

'What the hell are you doing here?'

The voice came so suddenly and harshly from behind her that she started violently, caught off balance as she spun round in an ungainly movement, gaping at the tall dark figure of the man who stood silhouetted in the doorway.

Her mind had been so preoccupied that she hadn't heard the footsteps on the stairs, or coming rapidly down the corridor. She hadn't known that Ricardo was even in the house until he had appeared without warning and tossed the rough-voiced demand at her, obviously none too pleased to find her there.

'I'm waiting for you,' she managed at last, awkward and un-comfortable. And her unease was aggravated by the way that his dark head went back, his shadowed face tensing suddenly.

'And what the devil gave you the idea that I would want that? This is my room, and what you're doing here at this time of night…'

'But you said that the only way I would stay here would be *as your wife*. Where else should a wife be…but in her husband's room? Isn't that what anyone would expect…would understand from the simple fact that we are married?'

'Anyone would be a fool if they did,' Ricardo growled back. 'This is the last place I expected to see you—the last place I want you to be.'

The effect of the rejection was so powerful that Lucy actually staggered as she stood, reaching out an uncertain hand to grab at the curtains for support. It was only now that she realised how her own feelings had misled her into this situation.

Could see that the hot, hungry need she felt for Ricardo whenever he was near had meant she had put two and two together and come up with an awkward and inaccurate five. She had assumed that he still felt the same about her physi-cally. That at least the burning passion that had brought them together in the first place, rushing them into bed before they had ever had a chance to get to know each other, still blazed unappeased. And it had done—hadn't it? Last night, in her room in the boarding house—and again out on the balcony…

So when Ricardo had declared that he wanted her as his wife then, naturally, she had believed that it was this part of their married relationship that he had wanted to revive.

An assumption that perhaps was not as natural as she had believed.

'But Marissa showed me the way…'

'If Marissa assumed that I wanted you in my bedroom then she overstepped the mark. She…'

'Oh, but that was my fault,' Lucy broke in urgently, terrified that she might get the young nanny into trouble. 'I asked…I thought…'

The words shrivelled on her tongue as Ricardo stepped forward into the room. The light of the moon falling on his handsome face made it look as if it had been carved from marble, tight and cold, his eyes opaque and unreadable.

'You thought that I would want you in my bed?'

His tone made it plain that that had been the furthest thing from his thoughts. Lucy was so grateful for the lack of clear light in the room and the way that it hid the flood of hot colour she could feel rushing up her neck and into her face. Had she got it so terribly wrong?

'You said that if I stayed here then it had to be as your wife.'

'My wife, and Marco's mother.'

Ricardo moved further into the room and flung himself down into a chair at the end of the bed. The change in his position should have made him seem less imposing, less overwhelming in the way that he now no longer towered over her but instead it had the opposite effect. Looking at him as he was now, with his jet-dark eyes gleaming coldly in the wash of moonlight, he seemed even more dangerously distant. If she had ever let herself believe that his decision to allow her to stay had been based on hot-blooded passion then she could no longer think of any such thing.

The man who faced her in this moment looked as if he didn't have a hot-blooded cell in his body. He was all steel and ice, brutal control imposed over any trace of humanity he might have been tempted to show.

'You only want me as Marco's mother?'

What else could there possibly be? the cold burn of his eyes demanded. *What else could I want from you?*

'A child needs two parents—both his mother and his father. That is what I want for Marco. And from the way that I've seen you with him, I can tell that whatever problems you have with our marriage, you don't feel them with him.'

'Yes, you told me about that.'

He'd explained to her in detail, in one of the rare moments of opening up to her about his past. He'd told her then how first his mother, and then Ricardo himself had been turned away from their family's homes because they had been born to the unmarried daughters. The memory of standing on the doorstep as a boy of five with his mother, who had been looking for help, only to have the door slammed in their faces, had burned deep into his soul and made him resolve from then onwards that no one would ever shut him out in that way again. And they would certainly never do it to his child. It was part of what had made him the man he was—ruthless, determined, never taking any help from anyone.

'I understood. It was why I married you.'

'That and the moment that you set eyes on the island, and the villa,' Ricardo returned cynically, lifting one hand in an arrogant flicking gesture that took in their luxurious surroundings, referring to the rest of the beautiful house, the stunning private island.

'Well, yes…' Lucy admitted. 'I saw that this was where your child belonged. That it was our baby's—Marco's inheritance. I didn't want to risk depriving him of this any more than you did.'

What had she said to make him look at her in that way? Why had he suddenly become so still, so focused, with those dark burning eyes fixed on her face as if they wanted to bore

right through her skull and into her mind, read her thoughts—
dig right into the depths of her soul?

'And that is why you married me?'

'Yes, that's exactly why I married you,' she said, fearful
that he might see in her face the evidence of those other very
different reasons why she had agreed to be his wife. The vulnerable, dangerous feelings that she had so longed to see re-
ciprocated. The love that had taken her by storm and left her
unable to bear the thought of life without him. So much so
that she had agreed to a marriage in which she knew that
Ricardo's heart was not involved and never would be.

'So we can work on the same arrangement again.'

'We can?'

Lucy's throat worked convulsively as she swallowed down
the heavy lump that threatened to close it off. From those
moments of half-fearful but—yes, go on, admit it to yourself,
Lucy—half-excited waiting for Ricardo to appear, she now felt
as if she was in a lift that had suddenly plummeted a hundred—
a thousand metres downwards, taking her stomach—and her
heart with it. She had let herself think—let herself imagine—
dream that maybe Ricardo wanted her back as his wife because
in one way at least he couldn't live without her. She'd let
herself think that perhaps he still wanted her in his bed as he
had done before and although the thought had scared her, it had
thrilled in the same moment, sending shivers of reaction along
every nerve that were a form of such nervous exhilaration that
she'd felt as if she had pins and needles all over her skin.

So now the realisation that his plans for her were as cold-
blooded and callous as they had been before made her fight
hard against the bitter tears that burned at the back of her eyes,
clenching her hands in the fall of her pink skirt as she struggled for a control to match his icy composure.

Ricardo was nodding slowly, not seeming to have noticed her tension and the way that she shifted uneasily from one foot to the other.

'Marco needs a mother—you are the natural candidate.'

'Of course,' Lucy confirmed hollowly, unable to drag her voice above a flat murmur.

'But this time things will be different.'

Ricardo placed his hands on the arms of his chair, pushing himself upright with an abrupt movement that took him part way over the floor towards her where she stood at the window. And, as his shadow fell over her, the dark bulk of his body obscuring the light of the moon, she shivered again but this time in pure apprehension, with nothing at all in it of the exhilaration of the time she had spent waiting for him.

'How different?'

To her astonishment Ricardo reached out one hand and touched her cheek, Just once, very softly. It was almost a caress and yet there was something missing. There was such a coldness in it that even when he cupped her cheek there was no sensuality in his touch, no gentleness. It was withdrawn, objective distant. And then he moved again, changing the position of his hand, drawing back all his fingers but one so that there was just one forefinger extended. It barely rested against her cheekbone, a contact and yet not a connection. It was as if he held her prisoner with that one small touch so that she dared not move away in case it tore at her skin to do so.

'If you come back, then this time you will stay. Our child needs you and you will stay with him until he is grown.'

'But of course…'

It was what she wanted so much. Not all that she wanted but a vital, valuable part of it so that she had no hesitation in saying yes.

'This time there will be no running away, no matter what. We will be a couple—at least publicly.'

'Just publicly?' Lucy managed shakily.

Ricardo nodded his dark head so adamantly so that his black hair became tousled, a single lock falling forward onto his broad forehead, making Lucy's fingers itch to reach up and smooth it back, though she knew that he would repulse the gesture violently if she tried.

'All I ask is that you do not bring scandal to my door. That you are discreet. In public we will be seen together—united— the perfect couple. In private it will be different.'

Was he saying that in private he didn't mind if she took a lover? The pain that came from knowing that not only did he not want her any more for himself but that he didn't even seem to give a damn if she slept with someone else, just so long as it didn't get into the papers or create a scandal, was more than she could bear.

'And what about you? Can you manage to be *discreet* as well?' she flung at him, the anguish tearing at her heart making the words cold and harsh in a way that pure anger could never manage.

'I will manage fine,' Ricardo tossed back at her. 'I have already done just that.'

'You have? Really? I don't believe…'

'Why not?' Ricardo challenged. 'Have you heard of anything while you were away? Have you seen my name in the gossip magazines—in the gutter press?'

Which was as good as telling her that he had been clever and careful while they had been apart. That there had been other women—because, of course, being Ricardo, how could there not have been other women?—but that no one would ever find out who they had been.

And no one would in the future. Because it was clear that he planned on keeping his mistresses—*discreetly*—while acting the role of her husband and Marco's father. Because he wanted those other women in his bed when he did not want her at all.

'So…' Ricardo questioned softly. 'What is your answer? Do you agree to this? Are you prepared to act as my wife?'

Did she have any choice? If she gave up on this then she would have to leave and she would be parted from Marco. But if she stayed…

'What do I get out of it?'

'Isn't it obvious?'

What was that look in his eyes, the momentary dulling of their glittering blackness? In anyone else she would have called it disappointment—but in Ricardo?

'You get to be with Marco—to be a mother to your child. And in that time you will live in all the luxury you could want. You will have an allowance that I doubt even you could spend. And when Marco comes of age you will walk away with the full amount—together with all the accruing interest—on that cheque that you so crazily tore to shreds earlier.'

'All of it?' Lucy knew that her eyes had widened in stunned surprise. She couldn't believe the amount that Ricardo was prepared to hand over simply to get his way. 'You'd do all that?'

A shrug of one shoulder dismissed her question as irrelevant.

'My son is worth it,' he said, prowling away to stand staring out of the window at the moonlit lake that surrounded the island. 'The question is, can you say the same?'

'And I suppose you think that this is a very…*civilised* arrangement?' Lucy managed, the words sounding strangled in the tightness of her throat.

'You don't think so?'

'It doesn't seem human to me. I can't imagine why anyone would want to live that way—live a lie.'

Her tone had sharpened on the words and in response she surprised a sudden look in those dark eyes. A flash of something unexpected, as if she had somehow caught him on the raw. It was there and gone again in the space of a heartbeat, leaving her wondering if she had ever really seen it at all.

'Are you saying that it's not what you wanted?' he demanded roughly. 'That you've changed your mind after all?'

'No, that's not what I'm saying.'

'You will stay?'

'I'll stay,' Lucy whispered.

He would never know that the reason why she had so much trouble getting the words out was because of the terms on which he demanded that she stay. Having lived in a loveless marriage with Ricardo once before, she knew how badly it had affected her. Given the choice, there was no way she was willing to endure that again.

But she didn't have a choice. There was Marco to consider and, just as the first time, the only reason Ricardo was considering this marriage was for his son's sake. Once again, she was going to have to accept the little he was prepared to offer.

And this time he was offering even less than before. At least then they had shared a blazing passion that had warmed their nights and put a spark into their days. Even as she'd grown big with her pregnancy, that fire had been there. It was only when she had given birth to Marco, when Ricardo had his precious legitimate heir, that things had started to change.

If it had stayed that way then she might have been able to bear it. She could at least feel he wanted her in some way. Now it seemed that he didn't want her at all except to create the façade of a respectable marriage.

'I'll stay,' she said again, putting more strength into the words this time. 'My son is worth it.'

She couldn't be in any doubt that he had caught her deliberate echoing of his own words. She had no way of knowing if he understood the very different way she had meant them.

'I will make sure you won't regret it.'

The low-voiced response was so unexpected that it rocked her sense of reality.

'Thank you.'

'*Prego...*'

The twist to his mouth was wry and in the now bright light the fine lines around his eyes, the faint shadows underneath them seemed suddenly more pronounced. He actually looked tired. Was it possible that the last twenty-four hours had knocked him off balance, as they had done to her?

'What made you like this, Ricardo?' The words just wouldn't be held back, even though rational thought warned they might not be wise. 'What made you feel that everything—and everyone—has a price and all you have to do is to pay it to get what you want?'

That twist became more pronounced, turning from sarcasm to out-and-out cynicism. For a moment she thought that he had no intention of answering her but then he shrugged off whatever restraint had been holding him back and started to check off his answers on the fingers of his right hand.

'A grandfather who believed that his daughter was unfit to inherit because she had a child out of wedlock. A father who wanted nothing to do with his bastard son because he did not want to divide his wealth between two children but to leave all to one. Lovers who saw relationships as a passport to wealth and luxury, bought with their bodies in my bed.'

'Then they weren't *lovers*, were they?' Lucy put in, taken

aback by the matter-of-fact tone, the coldly indifferent expression. 'Not really?'

'They called themselves that.'

'Then they lied. Love isn't like that.'

'No? Then tell me—what is it like?'

How did she explain love to a man who didn't even believe that it existed? Who saw relationships only in terms of trade and deals. Of one person giving only because of what they could get in return.

'I…' she began but Ricardo clearly wasn't prepared to wait for her response.

'Are you saying that what we had was this elusive "love"?' Ricardo demanded and the raw edge to his voice caught on something jagged and vulnerable in her heart, twisting brutally. 'Are you saying that what we had was something so very special that nothing could come between us? That we would have each other—hold each other till death us do part?'

'No.' Lucy answered him softly, sadly, because she couldn't say that. Not when it wasn't true, on Ricardo's part at least. 'No, I'm not saying that.'

It was only when she saw the flash of something dark and desolate in his eyes that she had to wonder whether that might have been, after all, what he had been looking for. What he had been trying to find all his life and had never succeeded, with rejection and greed twisting his heart, turning him bitterly cynical, as he was now. The ache inside at the thought was almost unbearable. A terrible sense of what might have been and what they had both lost in the mess they had made of their marriage.

On an impulse, as unexpected to her as it obviously was to Ricardo, suddenly something was pushing her forward, lifting her hands to grasp his arms, pressing her lips against the lean hardness of his cheek.

Immediately everything changed. The scent of his skin was in her nostrils, the taste of him on her tongue, and the rough growth of a day's beard scraped against her cheek, scouring the tender flesh. It was all so wonderfully familiar, so shockingly sensually appealing that her heart kicked once, high up in her chest, then lurched into an uneven rhythm that had her breath escaping on a shaken little gasp.

A gasp that met and blended with the heat and moisture of Ricardo's mouth as he turned and reached for her. Reacting blindly, his eyes half closed, his arms enfolded her as a sharp twist of his body brought him to a position where he was hard against her as his mouth came down on hers in a harsh, possessive kiss. In the space of a single heartbeat it was as if they had both gone up in flames, with the heat and the hunger that built between them taking over their senses, melting their bones and driving them into a burning delirium where nothing existed but each other.

'Lucia…'

Her name was rough and raw against her lips, the taste of his breath as she caught it and blended it with her own inside her mouth was as fiercely intoxicating as any potent spirit, sending her senses spinning out of control. She felt as if the earth were shifting beneath her feet, flinging up her arms to fasten them around Ricardo's neck to steady herself. The action drew his head down to hers to deepen and prolong the kiss in the same moment that it brought their yearning bodies even closer together, clamped tight from breast to hip and thigh, so that she felt the heated evidence of his need, hard and hot against her stomach.

'Rico…'

She couldn't hold back on the once familiar name. The only name she had ever used for him in the intimacy of their

bed, in the heat of their lovemaking. She was incapable of
getting the full number of syllables out, too greedy for his
kisses to separate their mouths for long enough to do so. She
didn't even want to snatch a chance to breathe, even though
her consciousness threatened to leave her under the sensual
assault that ravaged through her senses.

Ricardo's hands were hot on her body, smoothing, caressing, sliding over her hips and cupping the curve of her buttocks,
pulling her closer against him. Her breasts were aching and
heavy where they crushed against the wall of his chest and the
burn of his body heat through the cotton of his shirt combined
with the blaze of her own need to make her almost wonder if
the night had somehow passed in a flash and the cool light of
the moon had been replaced by the scorching heat of the day.

'Yes…' she muttered roughly against his demanding
mouth. 'Oh, yes…'

She'd made a terrible mistake and she knew it by the way
he froze, his long body going completely still, his mouth
wrenching away from her.

'*No!*' he declared roughly, breathing as hard as if he had
just run a marathon. '*Maledizione*, no!'

With a violent movement he flung himself away from her,
his hands out as if he felt that he needed to hold her at bay,
keep her distant from him.

'This is not how it's going to be. We got caught this way
once before. It is not going to happen again.'

'Caught?' Lucy questioned, fighting a losing battle with the
quaver in her voice.

The look Ricardo turned on her drained all the lingering
warmth from her body, shocking her from heat to freezing
cold in the space of a single devastated heartbeat.

'Trapped into a marriage that neither of us wanted. That

isn't going to happen again. I will not go there again. Just to look at you, kiss you, might drive me to the edge of madness but I do not have to jump right over the edge. I will not!'

And who was that last declaration directed at? Lucy wondered. At her or at himself? But she didn't have the strength to form the question.

And she didn't have time even to consider an answer because the words had barely died away before Ricardo had raked both hands roughly through his hair, smoothing it back from his face in the same moment that, by some amazingly brutal effort, he brought his breathing and obviously his mind back under total control once more.

'Marissa showed you to the wrong room,' he said, shocking her with the way that he seemed to have taken up the conversation again from the moment that he had first come into the room, as if all the time, all that had happened in between had never existed at all. 'Your suite is down the corridor.'

He clearly expected that she would follow him from the way that he didn't spare a look back but just strode down the corridor to a door that he flung wide open and then stood back to let her in.

With a terrible sense of inevitability, Lucy recognised the room she was in. Ricardo had taken her back to the other bedroom. The one where she had woken—was it really only that morning? The one where he had moved all her clothes, all her belongings, eradicating every trace of her as his wife from his personal space, filing them—and her—away like discarded paperwork.

Finished with. Done.

She had barely stepped inside the room when Ricardo was moving again, turning back towards the room they had just left, dismissing her totally from his thoughts.

'Goodnight, Lucia, *dorme bene*,' he said as the door swung to behind him, cutting him off from her.

Dorme bene. Sleep well.

How could she ever sleep well? How would she manage to sleep at all with all that had happened whirling round and round in her head?

And how was she going to be able to face the first day—and every one after—of this new form of 'marriage' that Ricardo had decreed they would have?

CHAPTER TWELVE

THERE was no way he could sleep. Not now. Not ever, it felt like.

Ricardo's mind was so wired, his whole body burning with the electric aftershock of fierce arousal that he knew there was no way he could lie in a bed and even *think* about sleep. He couldn't even keep still, pacing around his room again and again, wishing to hell that he could get out of here—head for the lake and swim himself into exhaustion. Or work off some of his frustration in the gym, lifting weights and pounding the punchbag until he had managed some form of mental calm.

Calm—hah! That was a joke. A very, very bad joke.

He hadn't had a moment's calm since the day that Lucy Mottram had first walked into his life not quite two years before. He'd been knocked off balance by the wild, heated passion that had rushed them into bed so soon after meeting and he wasn't sure if he'd had a sane thought since then. At least not where she was concerned.

So this time he had decided it would be different. If she came back to the marriage for Marco's sake then he was going to take it so much more slowly. He was going to act with his head and not with the more primitive parts of his anatomy.

It should have made him feel so much more in control, but the truth was that it had had the exact opposite effect. When

Lucy had kissed him he had almost lost it completely. Imposing control for both of them had been a far harder struggle than he had ever imagined. He could fight himself, but fighting Lucy, when she had made it plain how much she wanted him, had been damn near impossible.

He'd even resorted to lying—by implication at least—and letting her think that there had been a stream of women warming his bed in the months they had been apart. Of course there hadn't been. How could there be? He hadn't been able to spare another woman a single glance from the moment that Lucy had walked into his life, and to his total consternation, it had been exactly the same even after she had walked *out* of it again. It seemed that she had taken his libido with her, and memories of how it had been had been all that he'd been left with.

How many times had he scorned, even laughed at the idea when a friend had said that there was only one woman for him? Now he was having to face up to the fact that the damn idea might be true after all. And that Lucy Emiliani, plague of his life, bane of his existence, had turned out to be the one for him. Even when he'd believed that she was only after him for his money, he hadn't cared. Just so long as she stayed in his home, in his bed.

And he still wasn't sure that he'd made the right decision. *Padreterno*—he knew that he hadn't. Not for himself—and not for Lucy, if the look in her eyes when he had walked away from her, leaving her in that other bedroom had been anything to go by.

She hadn't wanted him to leave and he was damn sure that he hadn't wanted to go either. So what the hell was he doing here, fighting with his need for a woman who could affect him like no other female in his life before, when she…?

When she…? What the devil was she doing?

He didn't know—didn't care—because he knew what *he* was doing. There was no going back, no other way out of this. His hand was on the door before he had even realised that he had crossed the room.

In a history of making bad decisions where Lucy Mottram Emiliani was concerned, he was about to make another one. Very possibly the worst he had ever made.

And the truth was that he really didn't give a single damn. He didn't care at all what the consequences might be. He only knew that if he didn't have Lucy in his bed tonight then he would go slowly but surely out of his mind.

He flung the door open, stepped outside.

And stopped dead at the sight of Lucy just emerging from her own room, heading in the direction of his.

Her hair was tumbled about her face and she had made no effort to prepare for bed, still wearing the pink top and skirt that she had worn all day. But her feet were bare, pale and silent on the wooden floor. She froze into stillness in the exact same moment as he did, staring, huge-eyed, straight at him. He only needed one glance at her face, looking deep into her eyes, to know why she was there.

'Rico…' she said and the use of that once intimate, once affectionate form of his name was all he needed to push him right over the edge and into action.

'Lucia…'

He thought that he moved first but they met so fast, so short a way down the silent corridor that she must have come towards him. They collided with a hungry force, each of them with arms coming out to enfold the other, haul them close while their mouths met, clamped, fused in burning need. The strength of the impact slammed them against the wall, Ricardo's body covering Lucy's, his hips cradled in her pelvis, the pressure of her warmth and softness against the hard ache of need he had for her.

His hands were in her hair, twisting in the long golden strands, pulling her face towards him, angling her head just so, so that he could deepen the kiss, plunder her mouth, tangle his tongue with hers. His own breathing was raw in his ears, and hers was every bit as ragged and uneven. Her arms were up around his neck, holding him close, her fingers clenching in the soft short hair at the base of his skull. She was not just being kissed but kissing him back with equal wild enthusiasm.

'Lucia...' he managed in a gasping mutter when the need to snatch in a breath or surrender to unconsciousness forced him to reluctantly release her mouth for a moment. 'I have wanted this—needed this...'

Her soft, uneven little laugh was a sound of acquiescence and agreement, part excitement, part embarrassment. Totally beguiling. But his pulse stilled when she shook her head as it rested against his, her gaze downcast, not looking him in the eyes.

'But you...' The words failed her and she swallowed hard. 'I thought you didn't want a proper marriage.'

Her eyes came up on the last two words, long lashes sweeping the air as blue gaze locked with opaque black. And, with her looking straight into his eyes as she did, what could he say but the truth?

'I lied.'

It was an effort to get the words from a throat that was so raw and thick with need that it seemed it might close up completely but he needed her to hear this. Resting his forehead against hers, looking deep into those clear, beautiful eyes, he tried again.

'*Ho mentito, angelo mio*, I lied.'

I lied...

It was all that Lucy needed to hear. Knowing that Ricardo

had not been able to reject her totally, as she had first believed, sent a rush of heat through her veins, making her pulse throb even more than before. He wanted her as much as she wanted him and, for now, that was enough.

Enough to put an extra urgency into the hungry kiss she pressed on his beautiful mouth. Enough to make her stir against him as the need that throbbed in every nerve became more and more demanding, turning pleasure into something so intense it was close to pain.

Her hands clenched over his strong shoulders, digging into taut muscle in an attempt to get even closer and at the same time keep herself upright as her legs threatened to give way, bones seeming to melt in the blaze of desire that took her by storm. If it wasn't for his powerful support, she felt that she would be sliding down the wall, to land in a molten heap on the floor at his feet.

Ricardo's touch seemed to be everywhere on her body. Hard palms curving over the shape of her buttocks, drawing her even more onto the heat and hardness of his erection, then drifting upwards to tug the pink top free at her waistband, the burn of his fingertips against her bared flesh making her jolt and moan in sharp response.

His lips were on her throat now, making her arch her neck so that his hot mouth could move lower, lingering on the frantic pulse that beat at the base of her neck. And in the same moment he was walking her sideways, along that wall, moving inexorably towards his room where the door had swung open again. He had obviously not stopped to shut it properly in the moment that she had looked up and seen Ricardo in the corridor coming towards her—coming for her.

Her hands were hungry for the feel of him now, needing the warm satin of his skin against them. She pulled his shirt loose, slipped her hands underneath and felt his hot breath catch against her throat as he registered her touch. Whirling away from the support of the wall, he took her with him down the corridor, blundering from one side to another, slamming into each wall with such force that she almost feared they might wake the household, have someone come to find out what was happening.

But then at last they were in the sanctuary of the room, the door kicked to behind them. Ricardo swung her up into his arms, his lips still welded to hers as he carried her across to the bed, dropping her onto the softly quilted surface and coming down hard and fast beside her. Her clothes were no obstacle to his impatient, hungry hands, or his to hers, and soon everything—shirts, skirt, jeans, underwear—lay in a tangled heap on the floor, as intimately entwined as their now naked limbs on the bed.

'I lied,' Ricardo muttered, rough and raw, as first his hands and then his demanding mouth made contact with her shivering skin. '*Madre de Dio*, but I lied… How could I not want this…?'

His kiss on her breast made her convulse with a shaken cry, the pleasure so stunning that it blanked her mind for a moment, surrendering totally to delight.

'Or this…'

Strong hands smoothed their way down her slender frame, over the cluster of curls at the core of her body, caressing fingers sliding knowingly against the tiny focus of her need, stoking the fire with each touch, building it higher and higher.

It had never been like this before. Not even in the beginning when they had first come together, when the mind-blowing passion had taken all thought, all sense away from them, leaving them with only hunger and need. But then everything had been new, a fresh and exciting exploration of each other's bodies, each other's senses. Now they knew what that passion was like, the intensity of pleasure it could bring, but they had been without it for long, long months, time and distance sharpening hunger, increasing sensation, putting an edge on need.

Then Lucy had been innocent, a touch afraid, unsure of where all this was leading. She had wanted Ricardo so much but at the same time she had been unsure whether he would stay, doubting that she could offer him more than a passing fling and soon he would be on his way again, looking for pastures new. But now, with that deep spoken, heartfelt admission that he had lied about not wanting her still sounding over and over inside her head, she felt newly strong, deeply aware of her feminine power over him. A power revealed in the racing thud of his heart, the streak of burning heat across his hard carved cheekbones, the ragged breathing that he clearly could not pull back under control.

And control was not what she wanted from him. What she wanted was...

'Rico...please...bring us together...make us one.'

'Do you have to ask?' was Ricardo's shaken response.

And then it was as if all his English deserted him, burned up in the heat of the inferno they had built between them and, as he separated her legs, pushing them apart with one long powerful thigh, he resorted to his native Italian to mutter roughly, 'Lucia...*sei bella...quanta ti voglio. Madre de Dio... quanto ti voglio.*'

His ardent litany of need was all that registered in Lucy's mind; the rest of her was totally lost in the sensual assault that was swamping every inch of her body. Her head was spinning, every nerve awake and throbbing, and she was lost and adrift on heated waves of pleasure. Waves that grew higher and

higher with each forceful move of Ricardo's powerful possession, taking her with him further and further until at last they
broke on one final wildest, soaring crest of passion, throwing
her out, his name just a cry on her lips, into the tumbling
oblivion of the most devastating orgasm she had ever known.

It was a long long time before she came back to any sort of
consciousness and then it was only to a drifting, half in and half
out form of reality that held her safe and warm, cushioned in a
hazy oblivion. She was curled up, lax and sated, against the hard
heat of Ricardo's powerful form, enclosed in his arms, hearing
his thudding heart slowly ease into calm under her head, his
breathing even out as, like her, he drifted towards sleep.

'You are mine now,' he muttered, his breath hot against her
neck, his lips pressing kisses on her skin with every word.
'Mine. No one else will ever have you…'

There is no one else…never has been since the day I met you.

The words were there inside Lucy's head, needing to be
said. But, before she could summon up the energy to even
form them, the dark clouds of exhaustion from the day had
rolled over her, taking her mind and her consciousness with
her and dragging her down into the mindlessness of sleep.

Down so deep into the darkness that she should have known.
Should have recognised the mindless, almost comatose state
that always took her over just before the dreams began. The
bleak, lonely dreams filled with terrifying images and sounds.

The dreams that had once driven her out of this house and
away from the man she loved. Away from her child.

Disaster was coming. She could feel it, see it on the
horizon. She had to get away…

'No…'

She was going to have to run all over again. It was much
too dangerous to stay…

…But something was holding her back. Something had hold of her arm, restraining her, and no matter how she tugged…

'Lucy…'

'No…no…'

She couldn't stay. It was too dangerous. Much, much too…

'Lucia, *tesoro*… Listen to me…I'm here…*angelo mio*…'

Suddenly there was a faint light in her eyes. And in that faint light a darker shape. A strength and solidity that stood out from the shadows, making her blink in shock and confusion.

'Lucia…' the voice said softly again.

Warm arms came round her, holding her softly, comforting, protecting, not restraining. Where was she? Who was with her?

What the devil was happening here? Ricardo asked himself as he tried to keep his hold on Lucy careful and soft. Never wake a sleepwalker, everyone said. But then everyone had not been confronted by the sight of their wife heading for the stairs, totally naked and with her eyes so blank that it was obvious she wasn't seeing anything in reality.

He'd been woken by her restlessness. The tossing and turning in her sleep that had made it plain that, whatever was happening in her dreams, it was far from pleasant. The dawn had just been breaking when she had first actually sat up, throwing back the bedclothes and swinging her feet to the ground.

'What is it? Where are you going?' he'd asked but she hadn't replied. Instead she'd ignored him completely, standing up and heading for the door. In the end, realising that she was walking in her sleep, he had been left with no choice but to follow her, snatching up the robe that lay across the bed as he went, knowing she was going to need that, whatever happened.

He'd followed her down the corridor, stunned to see she found her way without any hesitation even though her eyes were wide and unfocused, staring straight at nothing.

But when she'd headed for the top of the stairs, that had been a different matter. In spite of everything he'd heard, he couldn't just stand back and watch. He 'd taken her hand very gently, holding her back without a word. But now she had stopped and had turned away from the danger. She was looking at him—looking but not seeing with those wide unfocused eyes.

'Where are you going, *cara*?' he asked again.

'I…I was looking for Marco. My baby.'

'He's fine…' Ricardo began reassuringly but Lucy just talked across him as if he hadn't spoken, her voice rising sharply in evident distress.

'I have to find him. But I mustn't touch him—I mustn't *harm* him!'

Harm? The word sounded shocking, appalling in Ricardo's thoughts. How could she even think that she might harm the baby? Anyone who had ever seen her with him would know that that was an impossibility. That was why he had been so shocked when she had run out on their child. His thoughts went back to the way that Lucy has described her illness earlier that day. She had explained, but it seemed that she hadn't told him everything that had happened. Hadn't told him everything she had been through.

'You won't harm Marco, *tesoro*. He's quite safe.'

He kept his voice quiet, steady, and she seemed to respond to it. The wide-eyed stare was just a little less wild and her slender body perhaps not quite so tense. She was shivering though, whether from nerves or the cool of the pre-dawn, he didn't know, but he slipped the robe around her as gently as he could and knew an almost shocking sense of satisfaction to see her respond and huddle herself into it, drawing it closer round her.

'I have to keep Marco safe,' she said again and he was relieved to hear that some of the frantic note had left her voice too.

'He's safe. I promise you he is. He's completely safe.'

And then she said the words that stunned him completely, hitting him like a punch in the gut so that he almost doubled up from it.

'He will be,' she said. 'He'll be safe when I'm gone.'

Just what could he say to answer that? There was nothing. He could think of nothing and, besides, you couldn't argue or even discuss something with a woman who, for all she was walking and talking, was still actually sound asleep.

'He'll be fine,' he managed, knowing he had to say something. 'And so will you. You'll see him in the morning. But you should get some sleep first—come back to bed.'

To his relief, she didn't resist, letting him lead her carefully away from the danger of the wide, curving staircase, back down the corridor. She followed him, placid as an exhausted child, only slowing, then resisting as they neared his bedroom door.

'Not this way…my husband…Ricardo…mustn't know. He'll hate me.'

Hate?

Lucy was obviously fading now and, needing to make sure she didn't collapse, on he hastily led her past the half-closed door and took her to her own room instead. Once inside she seemed to relax, losing all the tension that gripped her and slumping back against the wall in obvious exhaustion. Swinging her up into his arms, Ricardo carried her to the bed and laid her on it carefully, pulling the covers up around her. Lucy sighed softly, already drifting away back into sleep.

'Stay…' she whispered, tightening the fingers that were still entwined with his. 'Stay.'

'Of course.'

As he slid in beside her she turned, snuggling closer, resting her head against his shoulder, the fine strands of her hair lying like silk against his chest. Ricardo folded his arms around her, holding her so that he felt her slim body relax into sleep, the nightmare or whatever it had been forgotten in the oblivion of unconsciousness.

But he could not forget. And as she slept so deeply beside him he lay wide awake, staring with unseeing eyes up at the ceiling, remembering and thinking.

And later, when he was sure that he would not disturb her, he slipped from the bed, moving as silently as he could, heading out of the room and down the long corridor towards his office.

CHAPTER THIRTEEN

IT WAS the sense of something being wrong that dragged Lucy from her sleep the next morning. A feeling that something had changed forcing her into unwilling wakefulness, making her stir in the comfort of the bed.

And that was when a feeling of loss slid into her mind so that she frowned uncertainly, still keeping her eyes closed.

Something wasn't right here. The bed felt too big, too empty. She had fallen asleep feeling safe, secure for the first time in months, had slept soundly, dreamlessly, but now it felt as if something was missing.

She opened her eyes slowly, slowly, reluctantly. She felt as if she had been dragged from the depths of a dark pit, surfacing unwillingly into the living world. It almost seemed as if she had a hangover, except that she knew she hadn't had a single drink the night before.

And then memory returned. Hazy images of being out of bed, in the corridor outside surfacing in her mind. She knew what this feeling meant. It was one that she had experienced so often before, in the darkest days of her illness. When the staff at the hospital would tell her the next morning what had happened in the night.

She had been sleepwalking again.

But why? In the past such episodes had been linked to stress. To the fears and miseries she'd endured after leaving the villa. She had thought—had hoped that they were over for good. But it seemed that she'd been wrong. The realisation made her turn her face into the pillow, groaning aloud at the thought.

'*Buon giorno*, Lucia.'

The voice came from near the window, bringing her eyes open in a rush to stare straight into Ricardo's watchful face as other memories flooded her thoughts, making them reel.

That final confrontation; the cold-blooded declaration he had made that she should act as his wife and yet not *be* his wife, that was a source enough for the stress that had triggered the attack. And not just that…

Heat ran through every inch of her body as she recalled that the evening had not ended with Ricardo's declaration. She had tried to stay in her room, determined, for now, to work with what she had. At least Ricardo had agreed to let her stay. At least she could be a mother to Marco. Just forty-eight hours before, she would have settled for that and been thankful for it. But here, now, she knew there was no way she could do so.

So she had left her room, going back to talk to Ricardo…

And she had met him in the corridor, coming to find her.

As she struggled to sit up, the realisation that she wore a black towelling robe, gaping at the front, brought other memories flooding back in a rush. Memories that made her skin burn with remembered heat. The molten passion that had brought them together had seared her right to her soul, leaving her stunned and shattered, not knowing what this meant for the future of their relationship, if they had one. It was no wonder that her old fears had resurfaced, driving her out of her bed and into wandering the house while still asleep.

And there had been one other thing, one final straw that

had truly broken her back, emotionally at least. It had been there, in her mind, as she fell asleep and it had obviously filled her thoughts, disturbed her dreams.

There is no one else...never has been since the day I met you.

In the twilight place between waking and sleeping, her mind had broken free of the restraints she had tried to impose on it. In that half-and-half world, she had been unable to pretend to herself any more, as the need, the yearning—the love she still felt had forced its way into her unshielded mind.

She might have told herself that she was staying for Marco. She might declare that fact to Ricardo's face and assure him that the baby was what she wanted. She might try to believe it, need to believe it was the truth for her own emotional safety. But the reality was very far from that.

She wanted to stay *to be with Ricardo*. No matter what conditions he imposed on her living on the island; no matter what role he expected her to play, she would take the little he offered with both hands, grab it and hold it for as long as he let her, so long as it meant that she could be close to the man that she loved.

'G-good morning,' she managed, wondering as she spoke whether the words were really appropriate. The atmosphere in the room felt thick and clouded, as if a fog were filling up her lungs, choking her, making it difficult to breathe. She had the most unnerving feeling that the Ricardo she was facing this morning was a man she had never met before in her life.

He was sitting in a chair near the window, his long body apparently relaxed, long legs stretched out in front of him, crossed at the ankle. But his face denied the appearance of relaxation, with every muscle looking tight and drawn in a way that hardened his jaw, thinned his beautiful mouth and made his eyes into piercing lasers that subjected her face to such scrutiny that she almost felt as if they might scour off a layer or more of skin.

In contrast to her rumpled and still half-awake state, Ricardo must have been up and out of the bed for some time. He had obviously showered and shaved; his black hair was still slick with moisture and just beginning to dry in the warmth of the day. And he was fully dressed in tailored shirt and trousers, the formal style of his clothes, together with their sombre, all black colouring combining to create an impression that was cold and remote as well as ominously dangerous and controlled.

'I made some coffee,' was his surprisingly casual comment, a wave of his hand indicating the tray that stood on a table by his chair. 'Would you like some?'

'OK. Yes, please.'

If her voice shook slightly it was because of the confusion in her mind. However she had seen this 'morning after the night before' working out, it was not like this.

She had hoped—dreamed—that she might wake up in Ricardo's arms. That, safe and warm—and close—they might have a chance to start the new day in a very different way from how they had yesterday. A chance to start again. What she had feared, the fears growing stronger when she had sensed that the bed beside her was empty and Ricardo had got up, was that he had decided that their night together had been a terrible mistake and that he would decree they must go back to the no sex non-marriage he had declared they must have.

Instead, what she had was a near exact repeat of waking up the previous day. As if nothing had changed when in fact everything had.

Deciding she would feel better if she could face him on more equal terms, she scrambled out of bed while Ricardo was pouring coffee and pulled on the robe that lay over the end of the bed, knotting the tie belt and yanking it tight around her waist. The sleeves hung loosely over her hands, the length of it falling almost to her ankles, and she could probably have wrapped the front a couple of times around herself and still have plenty to spare. Only now did she belatedly realise that the reason it was so big and ill fitting was because it was actually Ricardo's robe and so more than several sizes too big for her.

That thought made her distinctly nervous, as it pushed her to recall yet more of the night before. It was the touch and the feel of the towelling robe that brought it back, the evocative scent of Ricardo's skin on the soft material. In the night when she had been sleepwalking, someone had put that robe around her and…

Her throat was so tight that it hurt as she recalled how he had called her *tesoro*, *angelo mio*, the soft voice full of concern. A voice so very different from the one he had used since she had woken this morning.

So what had happened in the night? What had she done? What had she said? The questions sent a sensation like the slither of something nasty and very cold down her spine so that when Ricardo brought the coffee over to her she reached for it with enthusiasm, hoping it would warm her chilled body, ease the tension in her throat.

'Thank you.'

She was relieved to find that this time her voice was actually quite strong and even. At least the way she felt inside was hidden from him for now. But how long that would last when he stood so close, the clean scent of his fresh-from-the-shower skin reaching out to enclose her, the softness of his newly drying hair making her fingers itch to touch, she didn't know. Just to look at his mouth was to recall how it had felt on her skin, the sinful pleasures it had awoken, the hunger she hadn't been able to control.

Edging carefully back, she came up against the bed and perched awkwardly on the side, struggling with the drowning looseness of the robe. A quick sip of the coffee brought some much needed warmth into her veins.

'About last night…' she began, edgy and unsure but knowing that she couldn't leave the topic hanging between them, with both of them avoiding it.

'Last night was last night,' Ricardo answered calmly, his carved features showing no response. 'And what happened then is one thing. Today is a whole new day—and things have changed.'

'Changed how?' Lucy questioned edgily, unease making her shift uncomfortably from one foot to another on the soft cream coloured carpet. 'And where do we go from here?'

'That's what I want to find out.'

Ricardo didn't return to his chair, instead he paced around the room, back and forth.

'And the only way forward is for you to tell me the real truth.'

That made Lucy's heart clench, her throat tightening so that she almost choked on her coffee.

'I have been telling you the truth!'

'Not the whole truth. At least not where your illness was concerned.'

And then Lucy knew where he was going with this. In spite of the weight and warmth of the robe, her skin felt suddenly chilled and clammy, so that she had to fight to control a shiver of real apprehension.

How had she revealed things last night? What had she told him of the darkest days of her illness, the terrible fears and thoughts that had assailed her? And how was that going to affect their relationship from now on? The future that she had thought they would have together?

'Ricardo…' she began stumblingly but he held up a hand to silence her.

'No—let me.'

Prowling over to the window again, he sat down on the wide window seat, staring out for a moment at where the waters of the lake sparkled in the sunlight, before he turned back to her. His expression was totally blanked off, eyes dark and hooded.

'You told me you were ill. You didn't tell how ill. You said you had a breakdown.'

'Post-natal depression.' Lucy's voice was low and unsteady.

'But it wasn't just that, was it? You weren't just depressed—you were…'

With a rough, almost angry movement he raked both his hands through his hair, shaking his head roughly as he did so.

'Last night you went sleepwalking—out of the room, along the corridor. You said you were looking for Marco.'

As Lucy drew in a sharp, uneasy breath his dark eyes flashed to her face and locked with her own worried gaze.

'You were lost. Frightened. You thought you'd lost him. But you were also scared of finding him—scared that you might harm him.'

'That was the way I felt sometimes. I felt…separate from him—I couldn't bond with him.'

And with those words—the words she had struggled with most—finally said, suddenly it was as if the wall in her mind had come down and the words were just tumbling out, faster and faster, falling over each other in the need to have them said.

'There were times when I couldn't even believe that Marco

was mine—ours. I thought that I was going mad—or that the world I lived in was crazy. I dreamed that I'd harmed him—maybe even killed him and so I'd go into his nursery to check if he was all right. But if he woke then he just cried and cried until the nanny came and only then would he stop. The nanny could stop him crying but I couldn't. I felt that he hated me—that I wasn't really his mother and he sensed that.'

'Post-natal psychosis,' Ricardo said when at last she came to a halt. 'Not just post-natal depression but the psychosis I looked it up on the Internet,' he added at her start of surprise. 'I've been reading all damn night. Why the hell didn't you tell someone?'

Carefully Lucy put down her cup on the bedside table so that the way her hands were shaking wouldn't mean that she spilled the rapidly cooling coffee all over the floor. She couldn't drink it anyway. Her stomach was tying itself in knots and she felt sick. Ricardo had accepted the depression but this was something else entirely. This was something that affected his precious son.

'I didn't know what was happening to me and I was afraid to tell anyone. I was scared—terrified.'

'Terrified of what?' Ricardo demanded harshly.

'Of you.'

Her low-voiced response might actually have been a blow aimed at him. She saw his long body jerk just once in response to it.

'Terrified that you would throw me out. That you wouldn't want me when you had what you wanted—Marco. Specially not when you thought that I was a danger to him—and at the time I was convinced that I would harm him. Perhaps I already had.'

'And so you left.'

Ricardo got slowly to his feet once more, resuming that restless pacing up and down as if he felt imprisoned and was hunting for a way out—any way out.

'I couldn't see any other way to go. I thought I'd feel better if I just got away. But I didn't feel any better—the truth was that I felt a whole lot worse. And that was when I knew I needed help.'

'And you turned to a doctor.'

It was impossible to interpret the meaning in Ricardo's comment. She couldn't read anything from the flat, inflexionless words.

'Who else was there for me to turn to? You know my mother and I have never been able to talk—not properly. And there wasn't anyone else. Certainly not you. I could never have gone to you. We didn't have that sort of marriage. Not any sort of real marriage. Not then—not now.'

'You're damn right not now!'

Even as the words were flung in her face, Ricardo was turning on his heel and heading for the door. Lucy could only stare after him in blank bemusement, not knowing what had happened or what was going through his head.

'Ricardo…'

Her shaken use of his name brought him to an abrupt halt. Just for a moment he paused, then he turned back very slowly. For a long drawn-out moment he simply stared at her, eyes narrowed, his mouth clamped into a thin hard line. Then at last he drew in a deep, uneven breath.

'What you're saying,' he said at last and the sound of the ruthless control he was imposing on his voice made a horrible sensation like the march of tiny, icy footprints move slowly up and down Lucy's spine. 'What you're saying is that it wasn't the illness—the post-natal depression—that drove you away from here. It wasn't anything that was wrong with you—it was everything that was wrong with us. We should never have married and that was what was at the root of things all along.'

His words dropped into a silence that Lucy had no idea how to fill. How could she when the only words that she could say were *yes* and *you're right*? That was exactly where the problem lay and hearing it stated in such blunt, unequivocal terms stripped all the strength to respond from her, paralysing her voice so that she could only nod in silent, desperate agreement.

'The only thing I do not understand,' Ricardo went on, still in that terrible flat, emotionless voice, 'is why the devil you ever came back. Once you had got away, why not stay away— as far away as possible?'

And there was only one answer to that.

'You know why,' Lucy managed, her voice just a thin thread of sound. 'Marco.'

'Marco,' Ricardo echoed heavily, nodding slowly in impassive agreement. 'Of course.'

'You do see…'

'Of course I see.' He almost smiled but it was a terrible, bleak smile, one that had no light in it whatsoever. 'What else could you do? For Marco. You were quite right about that— and right about our marriage too. That was the worst possible mistake, right from the start. It was never going to work. It is never going to work.'

He'd turned again, was wrenching the door wide open with a violence that almost tore it from its hinges.

'It ends now,' he tossed over his shoulder, not looking back, striding determinedly away from her as if he couldn't wait to put distance between them. 'I'm ending it now. It's best we forget the whole marriage idea and go our separate ways, I'll get my solicitor onto it right away.'

CHAPTER FOURTEEN

SOMEHOW Lucy managed to force herself to get dressed.

It was a struggle to make herself take off Ricardo's robe and drape it over a chair, when she was longing to hold onto it, to huddle inside it, inhale the lingering traces of his personal scent that clung to the fabric in a way she clearly could no longer do with the man who owned it.

But she needed to feel covered, protected—armoured against whatever might come next. She had no idea when Ricardo might come back and what he had planned if he did, but she had to be ready. She found a pair of jeans and a T-shirt amongst the clothes in the wardrobe and pulled them on, grimacing at the way that the jeans hung off her. Had she really lost that much weight while she'd been ill?

The knock at the door came just as she was fastening a belt around her waist to hold them up. Had Ricardo come back already? And, if he had, then was that good news or bad? Had he changed his mind…?

The thoughts died in her head as she opened the door to find one of the maids standing outside.

Of course. Ricardo would never have knocked. He would have just marched straight in without waiting to be asked.

'Yes?' she asked uncertainly, the apprehension that gripped

her growing as the young woman poured out a string of rapid Italian. Lucy couldn't completely understand, but got the gist of something that sounded like 'Pack now? Are you ready for me to pack all your clothes?' And the way that the maid indicated a suitcase she had brought with her seemed to confirm that that was what she meant.

'I don't understand… Why would you want to pack for me?'

The answer was another tirade of Italian, foremost of which—and totally without needing any translation—was the constantly repeated 'Signor Emiliani'.

Signor Emiliani said this… Signor Emiliani did that… Signor Emiliani had instructed her to pack, ready for the Signora to leave.

Oh, *had* he?

Lucy didn't stop to think, only reacted. She was out of the door in a second, rushing down the corridor before she had time to think. He was throwing her out. After he'd had what he wanted, he was getting rid of her. So much for all his promises to let her stay.

She didn't know if what she was feeling was agonising pain, sheer blind fury or a dangerously volatile and potentially lethal combination of both. She only knew that she was going to find him and have this out with him. She couldn't settle until she did.

He was no longer in his bedroom, but she had a strong suspicion of just where she might find him. If he was busy organising things and issuing orders left, right and centre, then there was one place he was likely to be.

She was right. When she marched straight into his office—not allowing herself to pause at the doorway for fear she might lose all her courage and back down, maybe even run away—it was to find Ricardo sitting at his desk, a litter of papers spread out before him, his dark head bent over something he was writing.

'I said come back in half an hour!' he snapped, not looking up and obviously mistaking her for someone else.

'Oh, really?' Lucy questioned cynically. 'I got the impression that I was to go away and not come back at all—ever—wasn't that what you said?'

Ricardo's head came up fast in astonishment, and the look she caught in his dark eyes shocked and disturbed her. For just a moment he looked like a completely different man.

She couldn't put a name to what she had seen and it didn't stay around long enough for her to take it further. One swift blink and it was gone and in its place was cold, hard rejection.

'Lucia! I sent someone to…'

'I know you sent someone to pack for me—to make sure I got out of your house as quickly as possible—but I have news for you. I'm not going.'

Deliberately she folded her arms across her chest, chin lifting defiantly. She even planted her feet wide apart on the gold and blue rug before the desk, challenging him to come and move her if he dared.

'And don't call me Lucia.'

She wasn't going to let him know how much it hurt to hear his own personal version of her name on his lips, spoken in that seductive accent. It had once meant so much to her. But that had been when she had believed they had a relationship.

'My name is Lucy.'

Ricardo's mouth twisted in a wry smile.

'I know,' he said and there was almost a note of amusement in his tone. 'Lucy is what I just wrote here. Lucy Emiliani, soon to be Lucy Mottram again.'

He tapped his pen down on the topmost piece of paper on

his desk, making Lucy crane forward to read. She gasped as she realised that it was a cheque—obviously a replacement for the one he had written before, which she had torn to shreds and scattered to the winds. A cheque for the same impossibly huge amount of money that he had offered her then.

'I told you I didn't want that. As I recall, I ripped up one cheque already—'

'That was when I thought I wanted you to stay.'

If he'd flung the pen right at her heart he couldn't have made a deadlier hit, and Lucy could only be glad that she already had her arms folded around herself because they went some way towards holding her together when she felt she was falling apart.

'And now?'

The look Ricardo turned on her told its own story. *What do you think?* was stamped onto those hard, unyielding features.

'Is this your answer to everything, Ricardo? Throw money at it until it goes away? So you think you can pay me to leave, do you?'

'It's something I can do for you. The only thing. Pay to support you when you do leave,' Ricardo corrected but Lucy was too far gone to recognise exactly what the difference was in what he said.

'Well, you can think again. I'm not leaving. Not now—not ever—not when you think you can break your promise and get away with it.'

'Promise?' Ricardo pounced on the word as if she had said something exceptional and his dark brows snapped together in a quick hard frown. 'Break what promise?'

That had Lucy unfolding her arms and flinging them in the air in total exasperation.

'What promise? Oh, come on, Ricardo! You know perfectly well! You promised me that I would see my baby—see Marco again—'

'And you will.'

'What—to say goodbye?' Lucy choked on the words, finding them almost impossible to get out through the thickness of tears clogging up her throat. Tears she was determined that Ricardo was not going to see her shed. 'You'll allow me that? Well, thank you so very much! How cruel can you be!'

'Not to say goodbye.' Ricardo pushed back his chair roughly, getting to his feet and raking both hands roughly through his hair in a gesture of frustration. 'You'll see him when you collect him ready for the journey.'

She had to be imagining things, Lucy told herself. The stress had finally got to her and she was hearing things that there was no way that Ricardo could ever have said.

'What journey? I don't understand,' she stammered. 'Where is he going?'

'Wherever you're going.'

Then, when she still gaped at him, too bemused to take anything in, he shook his head with a strange mixture of resignation and impatience.

'Wherever you're going, then Marco is going with you. He's leaving with you. You're both going together.'

'He…you are joking. You have to be.'

'No joke. Why would I joke about this?'

Ricardo's eyes met hers with a burning intensity that left her no room for doubt that he meant exactly what he said.

'When you leave, Marco is going with you. I won't contest your custody. All that I ask is that you allow me access as often as possible.'

'Of course I…' Lucy couldn't complete the sentence but broke off in total confusion. This couldn't be happening. You don't need to do this. You have custody of Marco and you can keep him here. Why are you doing this?'

'If I keep Marco here, then you will never leave,' Ricardo told her starkly. In a series of impossible things that he'd said since she had come into the room, that was the most unbelievable of all.

'You're so determined to get rid of me that you'll give your son away to achieve it?'

'You are his mother. I know you will love him and care for him. I also know it cannot be any other way.' Ricardo's voice seemed to have developed a raw and disturbing edge. He sounded as if his words were coming unravelled at the edges, disintegrating as he spoke them. 'I know that you won't leave without him. So how can I set you free unless I do this?'

Now Lucy knew that she was hearing things. Had he really said *set you free*?

'How can you set me free—and, more importantly, why?'

'Oh, Lucy…'

The deliberate effort he made to use the English form of her name caught on something raw and painful deep in Lucy's heart.

'Isn't it obvious? I'm letting you out of this marriage. That's what you want, isn't it? I trapped you into a marriage you didn't want once before. I'll not do so again.'

A marriage *you* didn't want. Was it possible that Ricardo was saying that *he* had wanted it? No—no way! Hadn't he always emphasised that he had never wanted marriage? That he was only marrying her because of the baby.

But hadn't she been the one to drive that home too? Saying she would marry him for the baby—and only for the baby. Because it was what she'd thought he'd wanted.

'You didn't trap me,' Lucy said carefully. She was manoeuvring blind here, feeling her way inch, by wary inch and if she put a foot wrong then she might fall flat on her face from a very great height. 'If anything, I trapped myself by being so stupid—so naïve about the contraception thing. But when you asked me, I went into our marriage of my own free will. I didn't have to marry you. But it was…I knew it was what you wanted. For Marco.'

'For Marco at the beginning, perhaps, but later…'

'Are you saying…?'

Oh, dear heaven, no! She wasn't brave enough to go so far so fast. Not without something from him that would give her room to hope. Carefully, nervously, she took a couple of steps forward towards where Ricardo now stood by the side of the desk. This close she could see the faintly bruised shadows under his eyes, the fine lines of strain that feathered out from the corners, and had to wonder just what stress had put them there.

'We could have made a better job of it,' she began but Ricardo had launched into speech at the same time.

'If you hadn't felt trapped you would never have left— would never have gone to some doctor hundreds of miles away. Someone you'd never seen before.'

It seemed to Lucy as if the atmosphere in the room had totally changed again, so that she felt as if the earth were shifting under her feet, dangerously rocking her sense of reality.

'But I needed help.'

'You could have had help. You did have help.'

'I did?'

That was too much to take in. Lucy's hand went to her head to try and ease the intolerable pressure there as she fought to absorb what was happening.

Had she got this so terribly wrong?

'You could have come to me—you *should* have come to me. If we had had any sort of a marriage, if I had been any sort of a husband, I would have been there for you. I was there for you. All you had to do was ask.' Fire blazed in Ricardo's eyes, burning away the dazed look that she now realised had been there before. 'Why did you not come to me? Did you not trust me?'

That wasn't anger in his voice. It was pain—a real, deep, soul-destroying pain. She had *hurt* him. Not just by running out on their marriage, on Marco, but, earlier than that, worse than that, by not trusting him, not telling him that she needed help and giving him the chance to offer it.

'We didn't have that sort of a marriage. I knew that what mattered most to you was your child. I knew you'd fight anything, destroy anything that threatened his safety.'

'Did you truly think that I would destroy you?'

The raw hoarseness of his voice gave her the answer to that question and the painful sting of her conscience had her reaching out, catching his hands and holding them tightly. He let his fingers lie in hers, not responding, but at least he didn't pull away.

'I was afraid,' Lucy managed, her own voice not much stronger than his, but it had to work. She had to make him believe what she was saying. 'Afraid that you'd throw me out.'

'And so you pre-empted my actions—the actions you thought I'd take. You didn't wait around for me to throw you out. You went yourself.'

'I thought that was my only way out. I didn't know how to talk to you. You were always so busy. And we hadn't made love for weeks.'

'You were the one who moved into another room. And I let you go because I thought that you were tired—exhausted from having the baby.'

'I was…' Lucy put in but Ricardo continued as if she hadn't spoken.

'You went away for days and would never say where you'd been.'

Lucy felt tears burn at the back of her eyes as she recalled the flippant, careless way she had dismissed his questions, the way she had felt that he was criticising her, trying to control her life.

'The truth was that I didn't know where I'd been—I was living in a haze most of the time. I just went out, went over to the mainland and walked…'

'I should have gone with you—followed you. I should have tried harder. I knew that something was wrong but I was too damn blind to see what it was. When I met you I wanted you so badly—you seemed so fresh and so innocent. So different from any woman I'd known before.'

But then she had turned him down at that first meeting. Only to fall into his arms—into his bed—when she had met the real Ricardo Emiliani a few days later.

'I always regretted saying no to you that first time. You don't know how much I regretted it—wished for a second chance. When I got that second chance I knew I had to grab at it with both hands—not risk letting it escape me again. I didn't even stop to think…'

Something was different, though, she realised. He was actually holding her hands now, having twisted his own round in her grip until his fingers were the ones curled around hers. It was a little thing but it was progress.

'I *wanted* you to be different. I was starting to believe that you could be different. But when the spending started—it was the pattern I'd seen before. I was so disappointed. So angry that it blinded me to any other possible reason for your behaviour.'

'I actually thought that the things I bought would make me feel better,' Lucy admitted. 'That this dress or that top would

be the one that would restore my self-esteem, make me look good again. But then, when I got it home, it wasn't the magic I needed. And…' Her voice caught on the words, a small gasping sob escaping from the rawness of her throat. 'I wanted you to see me again—really see me. I wanted you to think that I was beautiful…'

That got a reaction from him. His head came up sharply, black eyes blazing into blue.

'But you were so beautiful—more beautiful then than at any time since I'd met you.' Ricardo freed one hand, lifting it and smoothing it through her hair before cradling her cheek in his palm. 'Except for now,' he murmured. 'From the moment I saw you on the beach, I knew I was lost. I wasn't prepared to admit it to myself at the time, but I knew that I had to have you back in my life. No matter what it took.'

'Even to the extent of declaring that you didn't want a proper marriage?' Lucy risked, and a tiny bubble of joy danced in her throat when she heard his faint laughter in response.

'And implying that I had had other women since you left— that was another lie too,' Ricardo acknowledged. 'Not one of my better decisions, I admit. But I was determined to take things steady this time, work with my head, not the passion I feel for you. The passion that scrambles my thoughts, makes me act irrationally—crazily. This time I wanted to keep a clear head.' His mouth twisted wryly. 'I didn't manage to last very long.'

'Nor did I,' Lucy reminded him. 'It was what we both wanted.'

'But it was too soon—too fast—just like the first time. That was when we made the mistake. This time I wanted us to have space to get to know each other. Time to…'

Lucy's breath caught in her throat. *Time to…* Had he been about to say *time to learn to love each other*? But Ricardo didn't complete the sentence.

'If you had known me better when Marco was born, then you might have been able to talk to me. You should have been able to talk to me but I failed you. Do you know what it did to me when you said that you had been afraid to talk—afraid of me?'

There was no need for words to describe what he'd felt. It was there in the sheen on his eyes, the tremor of pain in his voice, the way his hands tightened around hers. She could be in no doubt as to what he'd gone through, hearing those words.

'I felt that I'd lost you—that there was no way back from that. That was when I decided I had to let you go.'

'I tried…' Lucy broke off sharply, her breath catching in her throat as she felt Ricardo's strong arms come round her. He drew her close, held her against his side. And it was not a sexual approach, not at heart, but a gesture of comfort and support, warm and gentle.

She would almost dare to say it was a gesture of love.

'I was wrong to make you feel that,' he admitted deeply. 'At the time you didn't seem to need me. I know now that you needed me more than ever before in your life, but I was too blind to see that. I'll never forgive myself…'

He broke off as Lucy's hand came over his mouth to still the words.

'But you must! You must forgive yourself. If I can forgive you—and myself—for what happened then, you can. You must!'

Her heart leapt as she felt the pressure of his kiss, soft and warm against her fingers. Looking up into those deep, dark eyes, she drew on all her courage to ask the most important question. She felt she knew that the answer she wanted was there, but she needed to hear it, to have him say it.

'Ricardo, you said that you wanted to set me free. Why did…?'

'Because I can't keep you here in a marriage you don't

want. It would be like caging a beautiful bird and I can't do that to the woman I love. If you don't want our marriage then I want you to be happy. I want you to be free—free to go out into the world and find someone you can love, as I love you. As I will love you for the rest of my life.'

…someone you can love, as I love you. As I will love you for the rest of my life.

What more could she ask for? What more did she need? Everything she had dreamed of, longed for, was in those two sentences. Words that would sustain her for as long as she lived.

'I don't think I can,' she said slowly and saw his dark head go back, his eyes widening in shock as he looked down into her intent face. 'I don't think I can ever be free—that I can ever *want* to be free. I can't go out into the world and be happy because I can't leave our marriage—it would kill me to do so. And I can't find someone to love—because I've already found him… He's here…'

Slowly, carefully, she lifted her hands and rested them on either side of his handsome face, cupping it between both of her palms, and she met his searching gaze with a whole new confidence.

'You're here. And you're the man—the only man—I want. I love you, Ricardo. Love you with all my heart. I want nothing more than to start again. To have a future with you. To be married to you. A real marriage this time. A marriage of two hearts.'

'A marriage of love,' Ricardo murmured as he bent his head to take her lips in a long, loving caress. 'I couldn't ask for anything more.'

His kiss made her senses swim, set her heart racing. And the way that his strong arms held her close, tight up against the heated power of his hard body, left her in no doubt that

Ricardo too was as forcefully affected as she was. And that left her with one more thing she needed to say.

'Ricardo,' she whispered against his lips, taking tiny gentle kisses from them with each word. 'In this marriage of love that we'll have—at some time in the future I'd love a brother or sister for Marco. But I'm scared—terrified it might happen again.'

Ricardo's arms tightened around her and feeling his strength seeming to pour into her she already felt her fears start to ebb away before its force.

'If it does, then this time I'll be there at your side, night and day, however long it takes,' Ricardo assured her, his voice deep and husky with love. 'I'll be with you—give you whatever support, whatever help you need. I promise.'

His kiss was long and slow, an affirmation of love that would be there for her no matter what happened. And Lucy felt her heart lift in response to it, the certainty that they could handle this if it came.

'And this time I won't be afraid to ask for it,' she murmured, returning his kiss, deepening it. Putting all her heart and her soul into it.

'This time we'll do it together,' Ricardo said and she knew that it was a promise, not just for now but for the whole of their future.

THE COSTANZO
BABY SECRET

BY
CATHERINE SPENCER

Catherine Spencer, once an English teacher, fell into writing through eavesdropping on a conversation about Mills & Boon® romances. Within two months she changed careers, and sold her first book to Mills & Boon in 1984. She moved to Canada from England thirty years ago and lives in Vancouver. She is married to a Canadian and has four grown children—two daughters and two sons (and now eight grandchildren)—plus two dogs. In her spare time she plays the piano, collects antiques, and grows tropical shrubs. You can visit Catherine Spencer's website at www.catherinespencer.com.

CHAPTER ONE

AT TEN o'clock on the morning of September 4, exactly one month to the day since the accident, Dario Costanzo received a phone call he'd begun to fear would never arrive.

"I have news, *signor*," Arturo Peruzzi, chief neurologist in charge of Maeve's case, announced. "This morning, your wife awoke from her coma."

Sensing from the man's neutral tone that there was more to come that didn't bode well, Dario steeled himself to hear the rest. Over the last several weeks, he'd conducted enough research to know that brain damage resulting from a head injury came in many shapes and sizes, none of them good. "But? There is a 'but,' is there not, Doctor?"

"That is correct."

He'd thought himself prepared and found he wasn't prepared at all. Images of her as she'd looked the last time he'd seen her, with her head swathed in bandages and the rest of her hooked up to a bewildering array of tubes to keep her alive, clashed horribly with the way she'd been before everything began to go wrong.

Lovely, graceful, elegant.

Sunlight in motion.

His.

And now? Abruptly, he sat down at his desk, afraid his legs would give way beneath him. "Tell me," he said.

"Physically she shows every sign of making a full recovery. Naturally she's very weak at present, but with appropriate therapy, we anticipate she'll soon be well enough to continue her convalescence at home. The problem, Signor Costanzo, is her mind."

Ah, *Dio,* not that! Better she had died than—

"...not to alarm you unduly. This is quite common following the kind of trauma she sustained, and is by no means as serious as you might suppose."

Realizing that in leaping to the worst possible conclusion, he'd missed what appeared to be a more optimistic prognosis, Dario wrenched his attention back to the neurologist's measured tones. "Exactly what are you suggesting, Doctor?"

"I'm suggesting nothing, *signor.* I'm telling you bluntly that your wife is suffering from retrograde amnesia. In short, she has no memory of her...recent past."

Peruzzi's hesitation was brief, but telling enough to arouse Dario's worst fears all over again. "How recent?"

"That's what makes her case unusual. As a rule, retrograde amnesia applies only to events immediately prior to the injury. In this instance, however, your wife's memory loss extends over a longer period. I am sorry to say that she does not appear to remember you or the life you shared."

Psychogenic amnesia...hysterical amnesia.... Terms that had meant little or nothing to him a month ago, but with which he'd become all too familiar since, floated to the forefront of Dario's mind. "Are you saying her amnesia is psychologically induced, as opposed to physiologically?"

"It would appear so. But the good news is that, regardless of which label we apply, the condition is rarely permanent. In time she will almost certainly regain her memory."

"How much time?"

"That I cannot predict. No one can. It's possible that she could recall everything within minutes of her returning to familiar territory. More likely, it will take days or even weeks, with flashes of memory trickling back in random order. What you must understand is that nothing is to be gained by trying to force her to remember that which, for whatever reason, she cannot recollect. Doing so could be highly detrimental to her well-being. And that, Signor Costanzo, brings me to the crux of this conversation. We have done our part. Now you must do yours."

"How?"

How—the word had hounded him for over a month, begging for answers no one could give. How had he so badly misjudged the depth of her discontent? How, after all they'd promised each other, could she have turned to another man? How had she shown so little faith in *him*, her husband?

"Patience is the key. Bring her home when she's ready to leave the clinic, but don't immediately expose her to a crowd of strangers. Begin by making her feel safe and secure with you."

"How do I do that if she doesn't even remember me?"

"Once she is a little stronger, we'll explain to her who

you are. We have no choice. You're her only next of kin, and she needs to know she is not alone in this world. But she has lost a year of her life, a frightening thing for anyone to face. Let her see that you care about the person she remembers herself to be. Then, as her trust in you grows, slowly reintroduce her to the rest of your family."

"The rest of my family happens to include our seven-month-old son. What do you suggest I do with him in the meantime? Pass him off as belonging to the cook?"

If the good doctor picked up on his sarcasm, he gave no sign. "Hide him," he said bluntly. "You have a sister and parents living close by. Surely one of them will look after him for a while?"

"Deceive her, you mean? How is that helping her?"

"The burden of guilt associated with her learning she has an infant son whom she's wiped from her memory might well shatter her sense of worth and leave her with permanent emotional scars. It goes against the very nature of motherhood for any normal woman to forget she bore a child. Of everything that has made up the fabric of your wife's life over the last year, *this* is the most delicate, and how you handle it, definitely the most critical."

"I see." And he did. Maeve might have woken up from her coma, but she was far from healed. "Is there anything else?"

"Yes. For now, do not expect her to be more than a wife in name only. Intimacy and what it connotes, with a man who might be her husband, but is, in fact, a virtual stranger, is a complication she can do without."

Fantastic! The one thing they'd always been good at was no longer in the cards, and he had to farm out Sebastiano to relatives. "Is there anything I *can* do to help her—besides sleep in another room and send our son to live somewhere else?"

"Certainly there is," Peruzzi informed him. "Your wife has lost her memory, not her intellect. She will have questions. Answer them truthfully, but only as much as she asks for. In other words, don't elaborate, and above all don't try to rush matters. Think of each small fact you reveal as a building block in the empty canvas of her memory. When enough blocks are in place, she'll begin filling in the rest by herself."

"And if she doesn't like everything she learns?"

"It then becomes imperative that you, *signor*, remain calm and supportive. She must know that she can rely on you, regardless of what has happened in the past. Can you do that?"

"Yes," he said dully. What other choice did he have? "May I visit her in the meantime?"

"I cannot forbid it, but I urge against it. Regaining her physical stamina is enough for her to deal with at present, and your inserting yourself into the picture is more likely to compromise her progress than help it. Let it be enough that you'll soon be together again, with the rest of your lives to reestablish your connection to each other."

"I understand," Dario said, even though it was so far from the truth as to be laughable. "And I appreciate your taking time from your busy schedule to speak with me."

"It has been my pleasure. Would that I had such encouraging news to offer the families of all my patients. I will be in touch again when your wife is ready to come home. Meanwhile, I and her other doctors are always available to discuss her progress and address any concerns you might have. *Ciao,* Signor Costanzo, and good luck."

"Grazie e ciao."

Returning the phone to its cradle, Dario paced moodily to the window. In the shelter of the walled garden directly outside his study, Marietta Pavia, the young nanny he'd hired, sat on a blanket, singing to her charge. That a wife could forget the husband she'd grown tired of was understandable, if far from flattering. But how was it possible, he wondered bleakly, that a mother could erase from her mind and heart all memory of her firstborn?

Behind him another voice, cultured, authoritative, interrupted his musings. "I overheard enough to gather there's been a change in her condition."

Swinging around, he confronted his visitor. Black hair smoothed in a perfect classic chignon, and immaculately turned out in a slim-fitting ecru linen dress relieved only by the baroque pearls at her throat and ears, Celeste Costanzo belied her fifty-nine years and could easily have passed for a well-preserved forty-five. "You look ready to take the Milan fashion world by storm, Mother, rather than relaxing on the island," he remarked.

"Just because one is out of the public eye on Pantelleria is no reason to be slovenly, Dario—and don't change the subject. What is the latest news?"

"Maeve has emerged from her coma and is expected to make a full recovery."

"Then she's going to live?"

"Try not to sound so disappointed," he said drily. "She is, after all, the mother of your only grandson."

"She is an unmitigated disaster and I fail to understand why, in light of everything that happened, you continue to defend her."

"But that's the whole point, Mother. We can only guess

at what really happened. Of the two people who know for sure, one is dead and the other has lost her memory."

"So that's her game now, is it? Pretending she can't remember she was leaving you and taking your son with her?" His mother curled her lip scornfully. "How convenient!"

"That's preposterous and you know it. Maeve's in no shape to put on any sort of act, and even if she were, her doctors are too experienced to be taken in by it."

"So you buy their diagnosis?"

"I do, and so must you."

"I'm afraid not, my son."

"I advise you to rethink that decision if you wish to be made welcome in my home," he suggested coldly.

Celeste's smooth olive complexion paled. "I am your mother!"

"And Maeve is still my wife."

"For how long? Until she decides to run away again? Until you find Sebastiano living on the other side of the world and calling some other man *Papa?* Tell me what it will take, Dario, to make you see her for the kind of woman she is."

"She's the woman who bore my son," he ground out, the anger that had festered for weeks threatening to boil over. "For all our sakes, kindly refrain from pointing out what you deem to be her shortcomings as a parent or a wife."

Unmoved, his mother said, "I don't imagine I'll have to, my dear. She'll do so for me."

Everyone at the clinic, from the lowliest aide to the loftiest doctor, who'd been so kind to her and looked after her so well came to say goodbye.

And who, when she'd asked what had happened to her, had said only that she'd been in a car accident and shouldn't worry that she couldn't remember because, eventually, it would all come back.

And who'd steadfastly waved aside her concerns about who was sending her flowers and paying the bills—all except for one young aide who'd carelessly let slip that "he" was, before the charge nurse shushed him with a glare that would have turned the Sahara to solid ice.

He who? Maeve wanted to demand, but sensing that answer wouldn't be forthcoming, instead asked, "Am I at least allowed to know where I'm going when I leave here?"

"Of course," the nurse said, adopting the sort of soothing tone one might apply to a fractious child. "Back to the place where you lived before, with the people who love you."

Wherever that was!

A few days before she was discharged, the doctors told her she was going to convalesce in a place called Pantelleria. She'd never heard of it.

"Who'll be there?" she asked.

"Dario Costanzo…"

She'd never heard of him, either.

"…your husband," they said.

And that left her too speechless to persist with any more questions.

Gathered now around the black limousine waiting to take her away, they all showered her with good wishes. "We'll miss you," they chorused, smiling and waving. "Stop in and see us when you're in the neighborhood, but under your own steam the next time."

And suddenly, after days of wanting nothing more than to be free of their round-the-clock vigilance, she was afraid to leave them. They were "after the accident" and all that anchored her to the present. "Before" was a missing chapter in the book of her life. That she was about to rediscover it and the man she'd apparently married during that time, should have filled her with elation. Instead it left her terrified.

Sensing her panic, the young nurse accompanying her to the airport touched her arm sympathetically. "Don't be alarmed," she said. "I'll see you safely to the plane."

The thought of mingling with the general public appalled her. She'd seen herself in a mirror and knew what a spectacle she presented. Despite the clinic's excellent food and the hours she'd lately spent in the sunlit gardens, she remained gaunt and pale. Her hair, once long and thick, was short now, no more than four or five inches, and barely covered the long curving scar above her left ear. Her clothes hung on her as if she'd lost a ton of weight or was suffering from some unspeakable illness.

When the car she was in arrived at the airport, though, it drew up not outside the departure terminal, but took a side road to a tarmac quite separate from the main runways, where a private jet stood and a uniformed steward waited to usher her aboard.

What kind of man was her husband, that she was entitled to such luxury, she who'd grown up in a working-class neighborhood in east Vancouver, the only child of a plumber and a supermarket cashier?

Remembering her parents and how much they'd loved the daughter born to them years after they'd given up hope of ever having children brought a rush of tears to her eyes.

If they were still alive, she'd be going home to them, to the safe, neat little rancher on the maple-shaded street, half a block from the park where she'd learned to ride a two-wheeler bike when she was seven.

Her mom would fuss over her and bake her a blackberry pie, and her dad would tell her again how proud of her he was that she'd made something of herself and become such a success. But they were both dead, her father within weeks of retiring at sixty-eight, her mother three years later, and the neat little rancher sold to strangers. As a result, Maeve, already exhausted by the emotional upheaval of the day, was strapped in a divinely comfortable leather seat in an obscenely luxurious private aircraft, headed for a life that was nothing but a big, mysterious question mark.

CHAPTER TWO

ALTHOUGH not exactly chatty, when Mauve asked more about the place she was being taken to, the flight attendant wasn't quite as tight-lipped as the medical personnel had been.

"It is called Pantelleria," he said in careful English, as he served her a late lunch of poached chicken breast and asparagus spears so tender and young, they were almost premature.

"So I understand. But I don't think I'm familiar with it."

"It is an island, known also as the black pearl of the Mediterranean."

"And still part of Italy?"

"*Sì, signora.* Close to one hundred kilometers southwest of the extreme tip of Sicily and less than eighty from Tunisia, which is in Africa."

She hadn't lost all her marbles. She knew where Africa was, *and* Tunisia, but Pantelleria? The name still didn't ring a bell. "Tell me about this black pearl."

"It is small, windy and isolated, and the road circling the island is not good, but the grapes are sweet, the sea is a clear, beautiful blue, the snorkeling and the sunsets *magnifico*."

It sounded like a paradise. Or a prison. "Do many people live there?"

"Except for the tourists, not so many."

"Have I lived there very long?"

She'd veered too far from the geographical to the personal. His face closed, and he straightened his posture as if he were on a parade ground and about to undergo military inspection. "May I offer you something to drink, *signora*?" he inquired woodenly.

She smiled, hoping to trick him into another revelation. "What do I usually have?"

The effort was wasted. His guard was up. "We have wine, juice, milk and *acqua minerale frizzante* on board or, if you wish, I can serve you espresso."

"Sparkling mineral water," she said testily, and decided that whoever met her when she arrived had better be prepared to give her some straightforward answers, because this whole secrecy conspiracy was getting old very fast.

But the questions bursting to be asked fled her mind when the aircraft skimmed in for landing and, descending the steps to the tarmac, she saw the man waiting to greet her.

If Pantelleria was the black pearl of the Mediterranean, he was its imperial topaz prince. Well over six feet tall, broad, sun-bronzed and so handsome she had to avert her gaze lest she inadvertently started drooling, he took her hand and said, "*Ciao,* Maeve. I'm your husband. It's good to have you home again and see you looking so well."

His thick black hair was expertly barbered, his jaw clean shaven. He had on tan linen trousers and a light blue shirt she recognized was made of Egyptian cotton, and sported a Bulgari watch on his wrist. By comparison, she looked like something the cat dragged in, and ludicrously out of place juxtaposed next to this well-dressed stranger and presumable owner the sleek private jet.

Privately he must have thought so, too, because, despite his kind words, when she ventured another glance at him, she saw the same pity in his dark gray eyes that had dogged her throughout her teenage years.

Desperate to give her advantages neither of them had enjoyed, her parents had almost bankrupted themselves to send her to one of the best private high schools in the city, never realizing the misery their sacrifice had caused her. They'd hidden their words behind their hands, those snooty fellow students born to old money and pedigrees, but she'd heard them anyway, and they had left scars worse than anything a car accident could inflict.

Poor thing, she could eat corn through a picket fence with those teeth....

No wonder she hides behind all that hair....

I feel bad not inviting her to my party, but she just doesn't fit in....

An orthodontist had eventually given her a perfect smile, and flashing it now to hide the crippling shyness that still struck when she felt at a disadvantage, she said, "You'll have to forgive me. I'm afraid your name's slipped my mind."

They had to be the most absurd words ever to fall out of her mouth, but if he thought so, too, he managed to hide it and said simply, "It's Dario."

"Dario." She tried out the word, splitting it into three distinct syllables as he had and copying his intonation, as if doing so would somehow make it taste familiar on her tongue. It didn't. She paused, hoping he'd enlarge on their relationship with a few pertinent details, and caught something else in his eyes. Disappointment? Reproach?

Whatever it was, he masked it quickly and gestured at the vehicle parked a few yards away. Not a long black limousine this time, but a metallic-gray Porsche Cayenne Turbo, which, although much smaller, she knew came with a hefty price tag attached. "Let's get in the car," he said. "The wind is like a blast furnace this afternoon."

Indeed, yes. Her hair, or what remained of it, stood up like wheat stalks, and perspiration trickled between her breasts. She was glad to slide into the front passenger seat and relax in the cooling draft from the air conditioner; glad that she was on the last leg of the journey to wherever. Though the flight had lasted no more than a couple of hours from takeoff to landing, fearful anticipation of what lay ahead had left her weary to the bone.

Since Dario was so clearly disinclined to talk, she turned her attention to the passing scene as he drove away from the little airport, praying something she saw might trigger a memory, however slight. Soon they were headed south along the coast road the flight attendant had mentioned. It was narrow and winding, but picturesque enough.

To the left, neat patchwork vineyards protected by stone walls rose up the hillsides. Groves of stunted olive trees hugged the earth as if only by doing so could they prevent the winds from sweeping them out to sea.

On the right, turquoise waves shot through with emerald surged over slabs of lava rock rising black along the jagged shoreline. Hence the island's other name, no doubt.

At one point they passed through a charming fishing village. Odd, cube-shaped houses were clustered next to each other with perforated domes or channels on their flat roofs.

"To catch the rainwater," Dario explained, when curiosity got the better of her enough that she dared break his rather forbidding silence and ask what they were for. "Pantelleria is a volcanic island with many underground springs, but the sulphur content makes the water undrinkable."

Disappointingly, this meager tidbit of information struck no more of a chord than anything else she saw. Which left quizzing her laconic husband her only other option if she wanted to arrive at her destination with at least some point of reference in a life dismayingly bereft of landmarks.

"Your flight attendant told me this island's quite small," she said, as the minutes ticked by and he made no further effort to engage her in conversation.

"Sì."

"So your house isn't very far away?"

"Nothing's very far away. Pantelleria is only fourteen and a half kilometers long and less than five kilometers wide."

"So we'll arrive soon?"

"Sì."

"I understand that's where we lived before the accident."

A muscle twitched in his jaw. "Sì."

Talk about a man of few words! "And we've been married how long?"

"A little more than a year."

"Are we happy?"

He tensed visibly, a scowl marring his forehead. "Apparently not."

Distressed, she stared at him. She had exchanged vows with this gorgeous man. Taken his name and presumably once worn his ring, although there was no sign of it now. Had slept in his arms, awakened to his kisses. And somehow let it all slip away.

"Why not?"

He shrugged and gripped the steering wheel more tightly. He had beautiful hands. Long-fingered and elegant. And there was no sign of a wedding ring. "Our living arrangement was not ideal."

She ached to ask him what he meant by that, but the reserve in his voice was hard to miss even for someone in her impaired mental state, so she once again focused her attention on her surroundings.

He'd turned the car off the main road and was navigating a private lane leading to an enclave of secluded villas perched on a headland. By some high-tech method she couldn't begin to fathom, a pair of iron gates set in a high rock wall opened as he approached, then swung smoothly closed again immediately afer the car had passed through.

A drive bordered with dwarf palm trees wound through extensive grounds to a residence which, while remaining true to what appeared to be a traditional island dwelling, was much larger than any they'd passed on the way, and bore an air of unmistakable opulence. Single-storied, it sprawled over the land in a series of terraced cubes, with a domed roof over the larger, central section.

Dario stopped the car outside a massive front door and switched off the ignition. "This is it?" she breathed.

"This is it," he said. "Welcome home, Maeve."

She opened her door and stepped out. The wind had dropped and a stand of pine trees dusted with the mauve shadows of dusk filled the air with their scent. The first stars blinked in the sky. Even from this vantage point, the estate—and *estate* was the only word to describe it—commanded a magnificent view across the Mediterranean.

Closing her eyes, she breathed in the peace and wondered how she could not remember such a place.

For a moment he leaned against the car and watched. The sight of her body, silhouetted sharp and brittle against the deepening twilight, brought back the shock he'd experienced when she first stepped out of the aircraft. The very second he saw her, he'd wanted to establish his husbandly right to enfold her in his arms. Peruzzi's warning not to crowd her had been all that stopped him. That, and his fear that he might inadvertently break her ribs.

She had always been slender, but never to the point that the siroccos of autumn might blow her away if she ventured too close to the edge of the cliffs. Never to the point of such fragility that she was almost transparent. Small wonder the good doctor had urged him to patience. Restoring her physical stamina had to come first. The rest—their history, the accident and the events leading up to it—could wait. Ambushed by her intuitive questions, he'd already revealed more than he intended, but he wouldn't make the same mistake again. He hadn't risen to the top of a world-wide multi-billion-dollar business empire without learning to dissemble if the occasion called for it. And from where he stood, this amounted to one of those occasions.

"Would you like to stay out here for a while?" he asked her. "Perhaps stretch your legs with a stroll through the gardens?"

She ran her fingers through her short, silky hair. "No, thank you. Even though it's still early, I find I'm quite tired."

"Come then, and I'll have my housekeeper show you to your room."

"Do I know her?"

"No. She started working for me just last week. Her predecessor moved to Palermo to be closer to her grandchildren."

He took her one small suitcase from the back of the car and pushed open the front door, then stood back to let her precede him inside the house.

She stepped into the wide foyer and slowly inspected her surroundings, taking in the lazy motion of the fans suspended from the high ceiling, the cool white walls, the black marble floors. "Do you live here all the time?" she asked, her voice hushed.

"Not as a rule. Usually I'm here on the weekends only. It's where I come to unwind."

A shiver passed over her. "So I'll be on my own after today?"

"No, Maeve. Until you feel more at home, I'll stay with you."

"In the same room and the same…bed?"

Is that what you'd like? he wanted to ask, beset by memories he almost wished he could forget. Once upon a time, they had shared such insatiable passion for each other. "You have your own room for as long as you want it, but I'll never be far away if you need me," he said instead, and congratulated himself on providing an answer that neither threatened her, nor shut the door on their resuming a more normal married life at some future point. Peruzzi would be proud of him.

"Oh," she said, and he might almost have thought she sounded disappointed. "Well, that's very nice and considerate of you. Thank you."

"*Prego.*"

She inched a little closer. "Um…are my clothes and personal effects still here?"

"Yes," he assured her. "Everything is exactly as you left it." Except for the blood-soaked outfit she wore the day of the accident. That was one memory he wished he could erase and hoped she'd never recall. "Here's Antonia now," he continued, relieved to be able to change the subject as the housekeeper arrived on the scene. "She'll take you to your suite and make sure you have everything you need."

She exchanged a tentative smile with Antonia, then turned to him one last time. "Thank you again for everything you've done today."

"It was nothing," he said. "Sleep well and I'll see you in the morning."

As soon as the two women, one so sturdy, the other so frail, left the entrance hall and disappeared toward the lower left wing of the house where the guest bedrooms were located, he turned in the opposite direction and along the corridor that led to the library and his home office. Closing himself in the latter, he picked up the phone and called Giuliana, his sister, who lived next door.

"I was hoping I'd hear from you," she said, picking up on the first ring. "Did Maeve arrive home safely?"

"She did."

"And how is she? Is it as bad as we feared?"

"Ah, Giuliana!" Horrified, he heard his voice crack and had to take a moment to collect himself. "She's fragile as spun glass, inside and out. The journey down here exhausted her. We got in just a few minutes ago and she went straight to bed."

"Poor thing! I wish I could see her and tell her how much I love her and how glad I am to have her back among us."

"I wish it, too. I wish you could bring her son home and have her look at him and recognize at once that she's his mother. Sadly, the time's not yet right."

"I know, Dario. Small steps, isn't that what her doctor said?"

"Yes, but not, I fear, as small as he'd like. Already she's wormed too much information out of me and knows our marriage was on shaky ground. Not exactly the best way for us to start trying to put our lives back together, is it?"

"But it can be done if you love each other enough to fight for what you once had. The question is, do you?"

"I can't speak for her, Giuliana."

"Then speak for yourself. I know that the way you started out together wasn't ideal, and that you married her because you believed it was the honorable thing to do and you had no other choice, but it seemed to me that you were making it work."

"Until it all went horribly wrong."

And therein lay the crux of the matter. Could either of them get past what had happened, or had they lost too much ground ever to trust each other again?

Seeming to read his thoughts, his sister said softly, "Maeve loves you, Dario. I am certain of that."

"Are you?" he said wearily. "I wish I was. But I didn't call to burden you with my doubts, I called to find out how you're holding up having an extra child to care for. Is Sebastiano wearing you out?"

"Not in the least. Marietta is an enormous help. You were lucky to find so capable and willing a nanny. As for Cristina, she loves her little cousin and plays with him all the time. And he's such a contented baby. He only ever cries if he's hungry or tired, or needs to be changed."

"He's the one bright spot in this whole unfortunate business."

"And too young to understand what's happened."

"Let's hope he never will." Dario paused. "Has anyone else in the family stopped by to see him?"

"If by that you mean our mother, then, yes. She came by this morning and again this afternoon. She's quite adamant that he should be staying with her, and I'm equally adamant that he should not."

"I'd hoped she'd go back to Milan with our father. The last thing Maeve needs right now is to run afoul of her."

"Unfortunately, she seems set on staying here. But don't worry, Dario. I can hold my own with her, as you very well know, and Lorenzo certainly can. He won't stand for her interfering in our arrangement."

That much he knew to be true. His mother might be a handful at times, but his brother-in-law was no more a man to be pushed around than Dario himself was. "I'm grateful to both of you for your support. Kiss my son good-night for me, will you? I'd come over and do it myself, but—"

"No," his sister cut in. "Tonight, at least, it's more important that you stay home in case Maeve needs you. It wouldn't do for her to find herself alone before she gets her bearings."

And how long before that happened, he wondered moodily, ending the call and pouring himself a stiff drink. It was all very fine for Arturo Peruzzi to counsel patience, but Dario had never been a particularly patient man. Already, after little more than an hour, his tolerance was tested to the limit as far as letting nature take its course in its own sweet time. He'd spent too many days neglecting work because he couldn't concentrate. Too many evenings like this, with a bottle of single-malt Scotch for company. And a damn sight too many nights alone in a bed designed for two.

Irritably, he threw open the glass doors and stepped out onto the terrace. Night had fallen and the dozens of solar lights dotted throughout the garden and around the perimeter of the pool gleamed softly in the dark.

Once upon a time not so very long ago, Maeve had wanted him as much as he wanted her. They'd slipped naked into the warm, limpid depths of the private spa outside their bedroom and made love with an urgency that bordered on desperation. He'd buried his mouth against hers for fear that someone might hear her cries of surrender. He'd withheld his own pleasure in order to prolong hers, and finally come so hard and fast within the confines of her sleek, tight flesh that his heart almost stopped.

So why was he standing here alone now, hard and aching, and she was sleeping in a guest suite? *Dannazione,* she was his wife!

A sound punctured the night, closer than the murmur of the restless sea, fainter than a whisper. A footfall so hesitant he might have dismissed it as a figment of his imagination had it not been accompanied by a fragrance he recognized: bergamot, juniper and Sicilian mandarin softened with a touch of rosemary. *Her* fragrance, and he ought to know. He'd bought it for her.

Turning his head, he found her framed in the open

doorway behind him, her silhouette softened this time by the long, loose garment she'd put on. She had never looked more ethereal or desirable.

"I thought you'd turned in for the night," he said when he was able to speak.

"I couldn't sleep."

"Too much excitement?"

"Perhaps." She took a step toward him and then another. "Or perhaps I've done enough sleeping and it's time for me to wake up."

CHAPTER THREE

HE REMAINED so still and watched her so warily that she almost lost her nerve and scuttled back to the safety of her suite. Decorated in shades of celadon and cream, nice soothing colors designed not to agitate the amnesiac mistress of the house, it was more luxurious than anything she could have imagined. The gorgeous bathroom had a steam shower and a tub deep enough to drown in. Adjacent to the bedroom was a sitting room, and outside in the private garden overlooking the sea, a swimming pool.

An oasis of tranquility, she'd have thought, yet she'd found neither answers nor rest there. From the minute she stepped over the threshold into the house, an air of utter desolation had engulfed her. She felt hollow inside. Bereft beyond anything words could describe.

Something bad had happened here. Something that went beyond a less than perfect marriage, and try though she might to dismiss it, the weight of unspeakable tragedy, of an event or events too horrific to contemplate, continued to haunt her. This spectacular seaside villa held a dark and dreadful secret, one she was determined to unearth.

And whether or not he wanted to, her tight-lipped husband was the man who'd reveal it to her.

"Are you going to offer me a drink?" she asked boldly, even though her pulse ran so fast that she could hardly breathe. Nothing new there, though. She'd lived with subdued panic most of her life, and had long ago learned to disguise it behind a facade of manufactured poise.

"If you're asking for alcohol, I'm not sure that I should," Dario said.

"Why not? Am I a raging dipsomaniac?"

He actually laughed at that, a lovely rich ripple of sound that played over her nerve endings like the bass keys of a finely tuned piano. "Hardly."

"That's a relief. For a moment, I was afraid I might be a good-time girl who danced on the table after one beer."

"I've never known you to drink beer. You prefer good champagne, and never more than a glass or two at that. Nor have I ever seen you dance on a table."

"Then why the reluctance to humor me now?"

"Medication and alcohol aren't a good mix."

"I'm not taking any medication. Haven't for more than two weeks."

"I see," he said and ran a hand over his jaw. "In that case, I'll make you a deal. Join me for dinner and I'll crack open a bottle of your favorite vintage. It was always your favorite."

Not wanting to appear too eager, she pretended to give the matter some thought. "All right. Now that you mention it, I am rather hungry."

"*Eccellente*. If you'll excuse me for a moment, I'll let the cook know there'll be two of us dining tonight."

"Of course." She waited until he'd disappeared then,

weak at the knees from his departing smile, she tottered to a pair of sun lounges upholstered in blue-and-white-striped cotton, and practically fell onto the one nearest.

The view spread out in front of her was breathtaking. A big oval infinity pool, strategically placed for maximum dramatic effect, appeared to cling to the very rim of the cliff. An illusion, of course, brought about by the sort of complicated engineering feat only the very rich and famous could afford. But the profusion of bougainvillea framing the picture was nature's handiwork alone.

Dario returned in a matter of minutes with two slender tulip-shaped flutes and a silver ice bucket containing a bottle of champagne. He poured the wine, sat down beside her and touched the rim of his glass to hers. *"Salute!"*

"Salute! And thank you."

"For what?"

"For everything you've done since I've been ill. They told me at the hospital that you're the one who sent me flowers every day and who took care of all my expenses."

"What else would you have had me do, Maeve? I'm your husband."

"Yes, well…about that…"

"Relax, *cara,*" he advised her gently. "I didn't mention our relationship as a prelude to demanding my conjugal rights."

"Oh," she said, swallowing a wave of disappointment along with a sip of champagne. Not that she was raring to make love to a man she didn't know, but that he presumably knew her very well indeed, yet was so willing to keep his distance, wasn't exactly flattering. On the other hand, what else did she expect? "Under the circumstances, it never occurred to me that you were."

He turned his head sharply and fixed her in a probing stare. "What do you mean by that?"

"I might not remember marrying you, Dario, but I've still got twenty-twenty vision. I know I look more like a scarecrow than a woman."

"You're still recovering from an accident that almost cost you your life. You can't expect to look the same as you did before."

"Even so, my hair…" She tugged self-consciously at the pathetic remains of what had once been her crowning glory, as if doing so might persuade it to sprout another few inches.

Reaching across the space separating them, he stilled her hand and brought it down to rest beneath his. It was the kind of thing a parent might do to stop a child picking at a scab, but however he might have intended it, his touch electrified her in places not referred to in polite society. Involuntarily she clamped her knees together as primly as a virgin defending her innocence.

Fortunately, he couldn't read her mind. Or if he could, he didn't like the direction it had taken, because he let go of her hand as quickly as he'd grasped it. "You have beautiful hair," he said. "It reminds me of sunshine on satin."

"It's too short."

"I like it short. It shows more of your face, which, like the rest of you, is also quite beautiful, regardless of how you might view it."

Even though he delivered it as matter-of-factly as a Kennel Club judge might appraise a freshly trimmed poodle, his compliment was more than she'd hoped for or deserved. After her bath, she'd done her best to find something flattering to wear among the clothes she'd discovered in the small dressing room connecting her bedroom to the bath-room, and heaven knew there was quite a bit to choose from.

Layers of lingerie in glass-fronted drawers filled one side, with a shelf of shoes below, and another holding several big floppy sun hats above. Opposite was a row of loose-fitting day dresses, skirts and tops, with two or three more elegant dinner outfits on padded hangers arranged at one end. Nothing too formal, though. Judging by the plethora of beach and patio wear, and the pairs of straw sandals and flip-flops encrusted with crystals, Pantelleria was not the social center of the world.

The quality of the clothes, however, was unmistakable. She'd fingered the expensive fabrics, admiring the cut and color of the various garments. Fashion was in her blood and whatever else might have slipped her mind, her eye for style had not. That most items appeared at least two sizes too large might have proved something of a chal-lenge to a person of lesser experience, but she was on familiar territory when it came to making a woman look her best. Bypassing silky lace-trimmed bras and panties, she'd chosen cotton knit underwear that forgave her di-minished curves, and topped it with a loose-flowing caftan in vibrant purple that whispered over her body like a breeze and softened the sharp jut of her hip bones.

Regarding her efforts in the full-length mirror, she'd felt a woman a little more in charge of herself again. But although it had given her the courage to seek out Dario and try to worm more information out of him, now that he was inspecting her so thoroughly, she almost cowered.

"You're embarrassing me," she protested.

"Why?" he countered mildly. "You're lovely, and I can't possibly be the first man to tell you so."

"No. My father used to say the same thing, but he was prejudiced. In truth, I was an ugly duckling, especially as a teenager."

"I quite believe it."

Her jaw dropped. "You do?"

"Certainly. How else could you have turned into such an elegant swan?"

He was laughing at her, and suddenly she was laughing, too.

It had been so long since she'd done that, and the result was startling, as if she'd opened an inner door and set free a hard, dark knot of misery. For the first time in weeks, she felt light and could breathe again. "Thank you for saying that. You're very kind."

"And you're your own worst critic." He touched her again, stroking the back of her hand, his fingers warm and strong. "What happened to make you that way, Maeve?"

"I'd have thought I told you that already, seeing that we're married."

"Perhaps you did," he said, "but since we're starting out all over again, tell me a second time."

"Well, I was always shy, but never more than when I entered my teens. I'd become paralyzed with self-consciousness in a crowd, and had a miserable adolescence as a result."

"Didn't most of us at that age, at one time or another?"

"I suppose, but mine was made worse because, when I turned thirteen, my parents sent me to a very prestigious girls-only private academy, light-years removed from the kind of school I was used to and the few friends I had. Not that I came from the wrong side of the tracks or anything, but the day I walked into that elite establishment sitting across town on its high-priced five acres of prime real estate, I entered a different world, one in which I was a definite outsider."

"You made no new friends?"

"Not really. Teenage girls can be very cruel, even if they don't always mean to be. At best I was tolerated. At worst, ignored. I wasn't entirely blameless, either. I compensated by withdrawing and trying to make myself invisible, which isn't easy when you're taller than everyone else, and painfully awkward to boot. I suppose that's when I became fixated on long hair. I used to hide behind it all the time."

She took another sip of champagne and stared at the empty sea, for the second time in one day harking back to that awful, unhappy era. "I wanted to be different. Be braver, more outgoing, more interesting and lively. More like those other girls who were so sure of themselves and so at ease in their environment. But I was me. Ordinary, dull. Academically acceptable, but socially and athletically inept."

"When did all that change?"

"How do you know it did?"

"Because the person you describe isn't the woman I know."

Not on the outside, perhaps, and usually not on the inside either. Until someone poked too cruelly at those hidden insecurities and made them bleed. Then she was exactly that girl all over again. Not good enough. A nobody masquerading as somebody.

"Maeve," he said, watching her closely, "what happened to make you see yourself in a different light?"

She remembered as if it had occurred just last week. "The day in my senior year that the headmistress called me up on stage during morning assembly and ordered the entire student body to look at Maeve Montgomery and take notice. Believing I was about to be castigated for having broken some unwritten rule of decorum, and to hide the fact that I was shaking inside, I stood very erect and stared out at that sea of faces without blinking."

"And?"

"And what she said was, 'When members of the general public meet girls from this academy walking down the street or waiting at the bus stop, this is what I expect them to see. Someone who doesn't feel the need to raise her voice to draw attention to herself, but who behaves with quiet dignity. Someone proud to wear our uniform, with her blouse tucked in at the waist, her shoes polished and her hair neatly arranged.'"

Maeve paused and shot Dario a wry glance. "In case you're wondering, by then I'd progressed to the point that I wore my hair in a French braid, instead of letting it hang in my face."

"I see. So the girl who thought she was an outsider turned out to fit in very well, after all."

"I suppose I did, in a way. I'm not sure if I was really the paragon of virtue the headmistress made me out to be, or if she understood that I needed a morale boost and that was her way of giving it to me, but after that morning the other seniors regarded me with a sort of surprised respect, and those in the lower grades with something approaching awe."

"What matters, *cara,* is how did you see yourself?"

"Differently," she admitted. That night she'd looked in the mirror, something she normally avoided, and discovered not a flat-chested, gangly teenager forever tripping over her own feet, but a long-legged stranger with soft curves, straight teeth and clear blue eyes.

Not that she said as much to Dario, of course. She'd have sounded too conceited. Instead she explained, "I realized it was time to get over myself. I vowed I'd never again be ashamed of who I was, but would face the world with courage, and honor the ideals my parents had instilled in me. In other words, to value honesty and loyalty and decency."

"People don't necessarily abide by their promises though, do they?"

Taken aback by the sudden and inexplicably bitter note underlying his remark, she said, "I can't speak for other people, Dario, but I can tell you that I've always tried hard to stick to mine."

He stared her at her for a second or two, his beautiful face so immobile it might have been carved from granite. When he spoke, his voice was as distant as the cold stars littering the sky. "If you say so, my dear. It's such a fine night that I ordered dinner served out here. I hope you don't mind."

"Not at all," she answered, "but I do mind your changing the subject so abruptly."

He turned away with a shrug, as if to say, *And I should care because?* But she was having none of that. She'd been stonewalled long enough by doctors and nurses and therapists. She'd be damned if she'd put up with the same treatment from a man claiming to be her husband.

Grasping his arm, she stopped him before he could put more distance between them. "Don't ignore me, Dario. You implied that I'm lying, and I want to know why. What have I done to make you not believe me?"

Before he could answer, the housekeeper came to announce that dinner was ready. Obviously relieved at the interruption, he took Maeve by the elbow and steered her the length of the terrace, to a table and chairs set under a section of roof that extended from the house. Long white curtains hung to the floor on the open three sides, no doubt to provide protection from the sun and wind during the day, but they were tied back now and gave an unobstructed view of the moon casting a glittering path across the sea.

It was, she thought, as he seated her and took his place opposite, like a scene out of the *Arabian Nights*. Candles glowed in crystal bowls and sent flickering shadows over a marble-topped table dressed with crisp linen napkins and heavy sterling cutlery. Music with a distinctly Middle-Eastern flavor filtered softly from hidden speakers. Some night-blooming flower filled the air with fragrance. Yet the harmony was tainted by the tension still simmering between her and Dario.

Antonia reappeared from inside the house and proceeded to serve from a sideboard positioned next to the wall. The meal began with a salad of tomatoes, olives, onions and capers dressed in oil flavored with basil, followed by grilled swordfish on a bed of linguine. And since Antonia remained at her post well within earshot as they ate, the opportunity to pursue the cause of Dario's sudden change of mood had to go on hold in favor of inconsequential chitchat.

At length, however, the meal was over, the dishes removed and they were alone again. Pushing aside her water goblet, Maeve interrupted him as he waxed eloquent about the therapeutic benefits of the many hot springs on the island, and said, "Okay, Dario, it's just you and me now, so please forget being a tour guide and answer the question I put to you before your housekeeper interrupted us. And don't even think about telling me to forget it, because I've had about as much as I can stand of people not being straight with me."

"I spoke out of turn," he said carefully, seeming to find the contents of his wineglass more riveting than her face. "I've met more than a few business acquaintances whose idea of a gentleman's agreement turned out to be as meaningless as their handshake. Sad to say, it's left me somewhat jaded as a result."

"That's a shame."

"Yes, it is," he agreed, finally meeting her gaze. "I apologize if I insulted you, Maeve. It was not my intention, and I quite understand if you feel compelled to kick me under the table for being such a brute."

His smile was back, dazzling as ever. Basking in its warmth, she said, "I'll forgive you on one condition. So far tonight I've done most of the talking, when what I'd really like is to learn more about you."

"All right."

"And I wouldn't mind going for a walk while I quiz you."

"Are you sure you're up to it? This is your first day out of hospital, after all."

"But I haven't been bedridden for a few weeks now. As long as I don't have to rappel down a cliff or run a marathon, I'm quite sure I'll be fine."

"Then we'll take a stroll through the grounds."

He led her along a crushed stone path that meandered around to the landward side of the villa and through a series of small gardens.

"Why is each one enclosed like this?" she wanted to know, finding the high stone walls almost claustrophobic.

"To protect them from the winds. These lemon trees here, for instance, would never survive if they were exposed to the sirocco."

She supposed she once knew that, along with the thousand other trivial details that made up daily life on this tiny island, but rediscovering them could wait. For now, sketching in the major figures that shaped her particular situation had to take precedence. "I can see I have a lot to relearn, so let's get started."

"*D'accordo.* Where shall I begin?"

"With your family, since they're also now my family by marriage. Do they live here some of the time, as well?"

"Yes."

"Are they here now?"

"Yes."

"I haven't seen any sign of them."

"They don't actually live in my *dammuso.*"

"You're *what?*"

"*Dammuso,*" he repeated, his grin gleaming in the dark. "Plural, *dammusi.* It's an Arabic word loosely translated as *house* although more accurately meaning *vaulted structure.* The style and method of construction is the same for all residences on Pantelleria."

Not quite, she thought. They might all be shaped like sugar cubes with arched openings and domed roofs, but most were a far cry from the elegant luxury that defined his and the others perched on this remote headland. "Then where *do* they live?"

"Here, we're close neighbors. My sister lives next door, and my parents next door to her."

"And when you're not on the island?"

"Our home base is Milan where our corporate head-quarters are located. But we're not on top of each other there the way we are here. In the city, you and I have a penthouse, my parents also, but not in the same building, and my sister and her husband have a villa in the suburbs."

"You have no brothers? Just the one sister?"

"That's right."

"Does she have children?"

"Yes, but it's probably not a good idea to confuse you with too many names and numbers just yet."

"Okay, then tell me about these corporate headquarters, which sound imposingly grand. Exactly what sort of corporation is it?"

"A family business going back over ninety years. Costanzo Industrie del Ricorso Internazionali. You might have heard of it."

She frowned. "I don't think so."

"My great-grandfather started it in the early 1920s. After hearing about and reading of the misery and destruction during World War I, particularly of children left orphaned and homeless, he vowed he'd dedicate himself to creating a better, more beautiful world for those who'd been born into poverty. He began small here in Italy, buying aban-doned land and creating parks in areas of our cities where before, rat-infested alleys were the only playgrounds."

"Then you do know of at least one man who kept his word."

"*Sì.*" He acknowledged her gentle dig with another smile. "Eventually, he expanded his idea to include holi-day camps in the country for needy children, some of whom had never seen the sea or a lake. To subsidize their operation and make it possible for cash-strapped families to send their sons and daughters away for a few weeks every summer, he turned his entrepreneurial skills in a more lucrative direction, developing ski, golf and beach resorts, at first on his home turf, then in neighboring countries. A portion of the profits went toward setting up endowment funds for his charity work."

"I wish I'd known him. He sounds like a very fine gentleman."

"From all accounts, he was. When he died in the mid-1960s, CIR Internazionali was a household name in Italy. Today, it's recognized worldwide and supports a variety of nonprofit organizations for underprivileged children."

"And where do you fit in the corporate structure?"

"I'm senior vice-president to my father, the chairman and CEO. Specifically, I oversee our European and North American operations."

"So I married an executive giant."

"I suppose you did." By then they'd come to a flight of stone steps that brought them back to the seaward side of the property. "Be careful. These are a little uneven in places," he warned, taking her hand.

This time he didn't release it at the first opportunity, but tucked it more firmly in his. Except for the glow of lamps inside the house and the lights illuminating the infinity pool, the scene was locked in dark blue moon shadows, creating a sense of such isolation that she instinctively tightened her fingers around his. "We might be the only two people left in the world," she murmured.

He caught her other hand and drew her closer. So close that even though their bodies weren't quite touching, such an electrifying awareness sprang up that she wouldn't have been surprised to see blue sparks arcing between them. "Would it trouble you if, in fact, we were?"

"No," she said, lifting her face to his. "I can think of no one else I'd rather be alone with."

He did then what she'd been wanting him to do from the moment she set eyes on him that afternoon. He lowered his head and kissed her. Not on the cheek, as he had before, but on the mouth. Not coolly, as one person greeting another, but like a man possessed of a hunger he could barely keep in check.

She swayed under the impact. Closed her eyes, dazzled by sudden splendor. Felt his arms go around her and pin her hard against him.

His tongue slid between her lips and she tasted desire. His, hers, theirs, more intoxicating than champagne. And for as long as the kiss lasted, the emptiness that had gripped her from the moment of her arrival at the villa eased just a little.

Then it all slipped away. Lifting his head, he put her at arm's length, his breathing as ragged as hers. "I think you've learned enough for one day," he muttered.

"Not quite," she whispered, the desolation he left behind striking through her heart like a darning needle. "I have one more question begging to be answered."

"What is it?"

"If we can kiss like that, Dario, how is it we weren't happily married?"

CHAPTER FOUR

PERUZZI would not be pleased. "Answer truthfully, but only as much as she asks for," the good doctor had counseled. "Above all, don't try to rush matters."

In theory it had all sounded simple enough. In fact, applying the advice was as dicey as picking a path through a minefield. And kissing her, Dario realized, frustrated on more levels than he cared to number, ranked high on the list of rushing things, at least from his perspective. He was hard and aching and half-blind with hunger for a woman who wouldn't have known him from Adam if she'd happened to pass him on the street. All of which most definitely left him in no shape to field another round of her astute questions.

Playing for time, he said, "What makes you think we weren't happy?"

"You told me so, remember?"

Unfortunately he did, and wished he'd had the good sense to think before he spoke or, failing that, to keep his mouth shut altogether. A chunk of recent history might have gone missing from her memory, but the rest of Maeve's brain was firing on all cylinders.

Despite not being able to see her clearly, the intensity of her gaze burned in the gloom. "Were we on the brink of divorce, Dario?" she persisted.

Were they? Only she knew the answer to that one. "No," he said, sticking strictly to the facts. After all, no papers had been filed, no lawyers called in to divide the marital assets or mediate custodial rights.

"Then what was the problem?"

Racking his brains for a misleadingly truthful reply, he said, "All marriages go through rough patches once in a while."

"But we've been married such a short time," she mourned. "We should have been still on our honeymoon."

Dannazione! Next, she'd be asking where they *spent* their honeymoon, and getting into the circumstances surrounding their wedding would certainly not meet with Peruzzi's approval. "Don't assume, because we might have hit a few bumps along the way, that our marriage was a failure," he temporized. "For every disappointment there were a hundred joys, and for me, having you home again rates as one of the latter."

"If you care that much, why did you never visit me in the hospital?"

Dio dare lui forza! Raising his eyes heavenward, he appealed for help. "I did visit you, Maeve. I sat by your bed day and night for weeks after the accident, praying that you'd live."

"But then you stopped coming. Why?"

Because we have a son who was also hospitalized, and he needed me, too. "For a start, I'd had you transferred to a clinic outside Rome, one renowned for its success in treating brain injuries. But you didn't know I was there, and since I was able to do nothing for you, I focused on what I could do."

"Turned to work to distract you, you mean?"

"Yes," he lied, because he knew the truth would be more than she was ready to hear.

"What about when I woke up from the coma?"

"I would have come to you immediately, but your doctors advised against it. You still had a long way to go before being discharged, and they didn't want anything to interfere with your recovery."

"Since when does seeing her husband impede a woman's recovery?"

"When she doesn't remember him?" he suggested drily.

"Oh." She bit her lip. "Yes, I suppose so."

As much by good luck as good judgment, he'd steered the conversation into safer channels. Before she derailed it with another question he couldn't or shouldn't answer, he said, "Difficult though it might be, you have to slow down, Maeve. When last we spoke, Peruzzi warned me against letting you overdo it. If he were here now, I guarantee he'd be appalled that, after the kind of day you've put in, you're not yet in bed."

"But there's still so much I don't know!"

Ushering her inside the house, he said firmly, "And a hundred tomorrows in which to learn it. At this point, what you need above all else is to get some rest. The last thing either of us wants is for you to suffer a relapse."

He'd found the magic word. "Heavens, no!" she exclaimed with a shudder. "That's the one thing I couldn't face."

"Then I'll say good-night." Keeping a safe distance between them, he bent and brushed his mouth across her cheek. But even so chaste a benediction tempted him beyond bearing. The fabric of her dress whispered over her skin in invitation, reminding him of the smooth, creamy flesh it concealed. And the color, a purple as deep as midnight in the tropics, turned her beautiful eyes an iridescent amethyst.

Clinging to him suddenly, she said on a trembling breath, "I am going to remember us eventually, aren't I?"

"Yes."

"Promise?"

"You have my word." He disentangled himself and shooed her away. "Off you go now. Sleep well, and I'll see you in the morning."

With a last doe-eyed look, she went. Expelling a breath of relief, he strode to the liquor cabinet and poured himself a stiff measure of grappa. The brandy seared his throat, but did nothing to ease the turmoil consuming him.

He hadn't climbed to the top of the corporate ladder through indecision, but through sound judgment and an uncanny ability to read other men. He could sense weakness, detect lack of integrity before an opponent so much as opened his mouth. Yet *she* left him riddled with self-doubt.

Had she surrendered to his kiss because the desire that had run riot in him had taken her hostage, too, or because she saw pandering to his sexual appetite as a way to buy forgiveness for past transgressions? When she'd talked of abiding by her promises and he'd hinted at her duplicity, had her dismay been sincere or a disingenuous cover-up?

He had no answers. Not for her or himself.

That night she dreamed of home. Except it wasn't home any longer. Someone else had moved into her apartment and she stood at her parents' graveside, with all her worldly possessions stacked around her in various crates and traveling trunks. "I'm going away and never coming back," she told her mother and father, "but you'll always be with me in my heart."

The leaves on the trees chattered in a gust of wind. "You can't go. You belong here."

"I must," she protested, indicating a shadowy figure in the distance. "He needs me. I hear him…"

"No." The branches swooped low, binding themselves around her. The leaves piled on top of her, smothering her, holding her captive.

She awoke, tangled in fine cotton sheets, her body bathed in sweat, the blood thundering in her ears. Sunlight flooded the room.

Desperately she tried to hold on to the dream, certain she'd been on the brink of a memory breakthrough. Closing her eyes, she fought to recall the image of that elusive background shape, but the clouds that had inhabited her mind for so long now, closed in again, blotting out the picture. Perhaps tonight or tomorrow…

A knock came at the door. Dario? she wondered.

Full of anticipation, she stumbled out of bed and hurried into the sitting room. "Just a sec," she called, pushing her fingers through her hair in a futile attempt to restore it to some sort of order. Once upon a time, the weight of it would have brought it falling around her shoulders in acceptable disarray. Now it sprang up from her scalp in demented whorls, as if she'd accidentally poked a steel knitting needle into an electrical outlet while she happened to be standing in a tub of water.

Opening the door, she came face-to-face not, as she'd

hoped, with her husband, but with Antonia bearing a tray with coffee and a plate of fresh fruit.

Seeming not at all surprised to find Maeve wearing nothing but a short nightgown, the housekeeper nodded amiably and deposited the tray on a table on the terrace. Her English was almost nonexistent, and her Italian laced with a dialect that made it more or less incomprehensible, but, aided by gestures, she managed to convey the fact that the *signor* had eaten breakfast several hours earlier, was not presently at home, but would join the *signora* for lunch at one.

Puzzled, Maeve glanced at the brass clock on a side table, appalled to see that it was after ten already and she'd slept half the morning away. Dismissing the housekeeper, she poured an inch of espresso into a tall narrow latte cup and filled it the rest of the way from a jug of foamy hot milk. She might not remember anything about her previous life in this luxurious hideaway, but she did know she'd never cared for strong black coffee and so, apparently, did the kitchen staff.

The caffeine chased away the lingering remnants of sleep, and left her filled with restless energy. Cradling her latte, she paced the small enclosed garden, stopping occasionally at the table to sample the black grapes, wedges of persimmon and sliced peaches on the fruit plate. Questions dogged her every step. Where had Dario gone? What was the significance of her dream? Why was it haunting her still? What else would she learn today? How long before she remembered everything?

The sun beat down, not the least bit tempered by the steady wind blowing in from the sea. A smudge of land appearing to float on the horizon must be the coast of north Africa, she surmised. Closer at hand a flowering vine sprawled over the stone wall on her right. To the left another wall, similarly clad, had a solid, tight-fitting gate in its center. Almost at her feet, protected from the wind by a shoulder-high glass screen, the pool shimmered and glimmered in cool invitation.

Well, why not go for a swim? At the very least it might deflect the endless circle of questions parading through her mind. And for that matter, why bother with a bikini since, at her present weight, it'd probably end up around her ankles the minute she hit the water? She was, after all, quite alone. Beyond the glass barrier, the land dropped down some eight feet or more to a terraced garden. The walls on either side were high enough that no one could see over them.

In the lee of the building stood a cart containing, among other things, a stack of folded beach towels. She took one, dropped it on the pool deck, then quickly, before she lost her nerve, she shed her nightgown and dived cleanly into the water.

It felt heavenly; cool satin streaming over her limbs. Surfacing, she swam the length of the pool and back, seven or eight times. Then, breathless from the unaccustomed exercise, she flipped over on her back and floated, loving the freedom, the sense of physical well-being that suffused her body.

Quite when she became aware she was no longer alone, she wasn't certain. It might have been the reflected glint of light on the lens of sunglasses that caught her attention, or the door in the wall standing open where, previously, it had been firmly closed. Or perhaps it was the unpleasant prickle of awareness creeping stealthily up her spine, and the sudden chill in the atmosphere, as if a menacing shadow had passed between her and the sun. But the "how" really didn't matter; what did was that she'd been caught stark naked.

Her reaction was instantaneous. She jack-knifed swiftly under water again and swam to the side of the pool closest to the intruder. Once there, she huddled in the corner, next to the steps, with her knees drawn up to her waist and her arms crossed over her bare breasts.

"It is a little late to be overcome by modesty, my dear," her unwanted visitor declared, lowering her glasses far enough down her patrician nose to inspect her thoroughly. "But then, propriety never has been your forte, has it?"

"I…wasn't expecting company," Maeve stammered, so mortified she wished the bottom would drop out of the pool and sweep her straight into the sea.

"Apparently not."

"I gather we've met before?"

The woman sighed. "Unfortunately, yes."

"I see." And she did. Whatever else this stranger might be, she was no friend. "I'm sorry to say I don't remember you."

"So I've been led to believe." Whoever she was expelled another sigh, more long-suffering than its predecessor. "Would that I were blessed with a similar affliction regarding you. Sadly, that is not so. I remember you all too well."

"And for some reason, don't like me. May I ask why not?"

"You are not one of us. You never will be. Why my son ever spared you a second glance is beyond my understanding."

This woman was her mother-in-law?

The ludicrous indignity of the occasion, with her cowering naked under her adversary's withering scrutiny, revived an old, familiar despair in Maeve. It crept over her like a second skin, cold, clammy and soul destroying. Numbly, she said, "Regardless of what you think of me, will you at least pass me my towel?"

The woman spared her another blistering glare then, with the toe of her elegant shoe, inched the towel within reach. Seizing it, Maeve used it to screen herself until she'd climbed out of the pool, then wound it around her body to cover everything from her breasts to her knees. As a fashion statement, it hardly compared to her mother-in-law's sleek outfit, but it was better than the nothing she'd had on before.

"I regret meeting you again under such embarrassing circumstances," she said, scraping together her tattered pride and daring to look her visitor in the eye. "To avoid its happening again, perhaps in future you'd be so kind as not to show up unannounced in my private quarters."

"Or perhaps in future," a steely masculine voice interrupted from the open garden door, "you wait for an invitation before so much as setting foot on my property, Mother."

Oh, perfect! As if she hadn't been humiliated enough for one morning, now Dario had shown up in time to witness Maeve's near-naked body in all its scrawny glory!

Women of character, she'd once read, always stood their ground and never ran away from a challenge.

She didn't care what women of character did. She fled.

Taking his mother ungently by the elbow, Dario marched her through the garden door and far enough away from the villa that they could not be overheard.

"You are angry," she observed, when at last he released her.

"Angry doesn't begin to cover it, Mother," he informed her in a low, furious tone. "What the devil are you doing here?"

"I assure you my intentions were completely innocent, Dario. I merely dropped in to say hello."

"Innocent, my left foot! You've always got an agenda. Exactly how much did you tell her?"

"Not nearly as much as I might have."

"You had no right to say a word. No right to confront her at all. After everything I've told you, what were you thinking?"

"That I might have misjudged her and, because I knew it would please you, I should give her the chance to redeem herself. And that is all I intended when I came here. But she…! *Madre di Dio,* Dario, she was cavorting naked in the pool. Flaunting herself without a milligram of shame. Can you imagine that?"

All too easily! She'd have looked like a sea nymph. And if he'd been the one to discover her, he'd have stripped off his own clothes and leaped into the pool with her.

Turning aside to hide the smile such an image evoked, he said, "Where's the sin in that?"

"Any one of your staff—a gardener or a housemaid—might have seen her. What do you suppose they would have done?"

"What you should have done, Mother. Disappear. As quickly and discreetly as possible."

She smoothed a fastidious hand over her hair. "Well, since I have no interest in witnessing a repeat performance, I won't disturb her again."

"No, you won't," he assured her, propelling her around to the front of the house and hustling her into her car. "Much though I regret having to take such a drastic step, until such time as the situation with my wife is resolved, you will stick to your own property and stay away from mine."

She lowered the window and pinned him with a reproachful gaze. "I see."

"Do you?" he said, his anger boiling over again. "Do you have any idea, or indeed any interest, in learning of the kind of damage you could have done with your interference? If you had told Maeve about Sebastiano, the consequences could have been disastrous."

"I would never tell her about Sebastiano. If I had my way, she'd be sent packing without ever knowing she bore you a son."

He turned away in disgust. "Which is precisely why you will stay away from her until she recovers her memory."

"And what about you, Dario?" his mother called after him. "Can you stay away from her? Or will you once again fall victim to her cheap, superficial charms and let her entrap you a second time?"

His mother drove away then in a burst of speed that sent crushed rock spraying out from under the car's tires. His harshness had hurt her, he knew, and he wished it could be otherwise. But since he had no intention of allowing her to sabotage his marriage, the change in attitude, if ever there was to be one, had to come from her.

There was no sign of Maeve when he returned to the guest wing. The gate to her garden was closed, and she didn't answer when he knocked on her door. In fact, he neither saw nor heard anything from her until he found her waiting on the terrace to join him for lunch, although *hovering* might have more accurately described her. Wearing a full-skirted dress in varying shades of pink, she resembled a delicate butterfly poised to take flight.

"Nice outfit," he remarked, attempting to lighten the atmosphere, "although I quite liked the towel ensemble, too."

She flushed. "I'm so sorry about that, Dario."

"Why? You're not the one who showed up uninvited. My mother is."

"Still, I wish I'd made a better impression. As it is, I'm afraid I've reinforced her already poor opinion of me. What did I do to make her dislike me so much?"

"You married me," he said, pouring them each an aperitif from the decanter on the sideboard. "Italian mammas always have a hard time accepting their sons' wives. She'll change her attitude when she gets to know you better."

"Perhaps when we have children of our own?"

He choked on his wine. "Possibly," he managed, when he was able to draw breath again, "but there'll be time enough to worry about that when you're feeling yourself again."

"I suppose." She frowned and chewed her lip. "I've been thinking a lot since last night."

In his opinion, she was thinking altogether too much, but saying so wasn't likely to stop her. "About what?"

"You mentioned you oversee the North American side of your family's business. Does that include Canada?"

"It does," he admitted, already uncomfortable with the direction the conversation was taking.

"Have you ever been to Vancouver? Is that where we met?"

"I've been to Vancouver, yes," he said guardedly. "But no, we didn't meet there."

"Then where?"

He hesitated. Less than ten minutes in her company and already he was picking his way through that metaphorical minefield again. "You were on holiday in Italy."

"Alone?"

"No. With a woman friend."

"Where in Italy?"

"Portofino."

"Were you on holiday, as well?"

"You could say so. I keep my yacht moored in the harbor and often used to spend summer weekends there." Carousing the night away with friends, but she didn't need to know that.

"Before you married me, you mean?"

Definitely before he married her! "That's right."

"And we met on your yacht? That's hard to picture. What was I doing there?"

"You weren't. You were in the casino." He grinned as her expression changed from skeptical to outright appalled. "At the roulette table."

"That's even harder to believe. I've never been a gambler."

She wasn't that night, either, which was why he'd been able to lure her away and ply her with enough champagne to loosen her inhibitions. Profligate that he'd been back then, he'd thought it would be amusing to give such a lovely young thing a night to remember. What he hadn't bargained on was finding himself tied to her for life.

CHAPTER FIVE

HE'D noticed her at once. Needing nothing more than pearls and a straight, strapless gown in basic black to enhance her blond beauty, she carried herself with the grace and dignity of a duchess. But what captured his interest was less her elegance and style than the indifference in her blue eyes when she caught him looking at her. He wasn't accustomed to being ignored by the opposite sex, especially not on his recreational home turf.

The woman with her, flamboyant in feathers and crimson ruffles, more accurately portrayed the kind of tourist found in the casinos—which was to say, wearing too much jewelry and attracting attention to herself by working too hard at having a good time. "Save my place, Maeve," she squealed, raking in her pile of chips. "I'm off to powder my nose."

"Is that really what women do?" he said, moving into the spot she vacated.

The duchess spared him a lofty glance. "I beg your pardon?"

"Do women really still powder their noses?"

"I have no idea," she replied stiffly. "I don't make a habit of asking them. And by the way, that seat is taken."

"By your friend." He nodded. "Yes, I heard. I'll hold it for her until she returns." Then, as a new game began, went on, "Are you not placing any bets?"

"No. I'm here to keep Pamela company, and don't have any chips."

He slid a pile of his own in front of her. "You do now."

She shied away as if he'd thrust a loaded pistol at her, and wrinkled her dainty nose. "I can't possibly take yours. For heaven's sake, I don't even know you. You could be anyone."

Both amused and piqued by her unsophisticated candor, he said with as much solemnity as he could manage, "I'm Dario Costanzo and perfectly respectable, as *anyone* here will tell you."

Not missing his deliberate emphasis on the word, she blushed disarmingly. "I wasn't trying to be offensive."

"I'm sure you weren't."

"Even so, I can't accept your money."

"It isn't money until you win."

Very firmly, she returned his chips to him. "Which I'm not likely to do since I haven't a clue how the game is played."

"I could teach you."

"No, thank you."

He eyed her thoughtfully. "You're not enjoying yourself much, are you?"

"No," she admitted. "This isn't my kind of place. I wouldn't be here at all if it weren't for my friend."

"What is your kind of place?"

"Somewhere quieter and less crowded."

"Come with me. I know the perfect spot."

She shot down that suggestion with a glance that would

have turned a less determined man to stone. "I don't think so, thank you!"

"Because you're still worried that I might be the local ax murderer?"

She pressed her lips together, but wasn't quite able to hide her smile. "The thought has crossed my mind."

"Then allow me to put your fears to rest." He signaled the manager, a man in his late fifties who epitomized silver-haired respectability and whom he'd known for years. "Federico, would you be so kind as to vouch for me to this young lady? She's not sure I'm to be trusted."

Federico straightened his impeccably clad shoulders. "Signor Costanzo is one of our most valued clients, *signora,*" he told her, subtly conveying shock than anyone might assume otherwise. "I speak from long and personal experience when I say you find yourself in excellent company."

"Well?" Dario eyed her questioningly as the man departed. "Did that change your mind at all?"

She flinched at a sudden burst of raucous laughter behind her. "I admit I'd be tempted to take you up on your offer if it weren't for Pamela. I can't just abandon her."

But Pamela, as he pointed out, had found diversion at the next table with a man old enough to be her father. "Sure," she brayed, flapping her beringed hand as if dismissing an annoying fly when the duchess stopped by to mention she was leaving. "See you whenever, but probably not before tomorrow. I have big plans for tonight."

And so, Dario thought, had he. Increasingly intrigued by the duchess's cool reserve, he ushered her out of the casino. "Shall we stroll for a while?"

"I'd love to," she said, breathing deeply of the balmy night air. "I found it unbearably stuffy inside."

Although his ultimate goal was to lure her aboard the yacht, he took her first to a tiny supper club tucked away in a quiet corner of *la piazetta*. A frequent visitor, he was shown immediately to one of the candlelit tables on the covered patio.

"Better?" he inquired.

"Much," she sighed, slipping out of her evening sandals and wiggling her bare toes.

More charmed by the minute, he undid his black bow tie and the top button of his dress shirt, ordered champagne cocktails, and encouraged her to talk about herself.

The wine loosened her tongue and in short order he learned her name was Maeve Montgomery and she was from Vancouver, Canada. After two years in college, she'd worked as a sales assistant in a bridal salon, been promoted to fashion director at the ripe old age of twenty-two, but found her true calling when she became a personal shopper for clients long on money, but short on taste. She was an unapologetic clothes horse, sewed many of her own outfits and lived in a sixth-floor apartment with a west-facing view of Georgia Strait and the Gulf Islands.

She'd been very close to her parents, both of whom had died within the past five years. Her father, never sick a day in his life, had suffered a ruptured abdominal aneurysm as he sat watching television. He was gone in less time than it took to phone for an ambulance. Thirty-four months later her mother, a severe asthmatic, had succumbed to pneumonia at age seventy. "I miss them dreadfully," she confessed.

That she was in Italy at all had been a last-minute arrangement and a bonus of sorts from Mrs. Samuel Elliott-Rhys, a grateful, longtime client who happened also to be

Pamela's mother. "The friend who was supposed to come with Pamela slipped and broke her leg the week before last," Maeve explained. "Mrs. Elliott-Rhys persuaded me to take the friend's place because she wasn't comfortable having Pamela traveling alone."

I wouldn't be, either, if Pamela were my daughter, Dario thought, but declined to say so. After all, he had her to thank for the way the evening was turning out. "How much longer will you be in Portofino?"

"Five days. We fly home next Wednesday."

Perfect! Enough time for an enjoyable fling, without the entanglement of her expecting a lasting association. "More champagne?" he suggested smoothly.

"I don't think so, thanks. I don't like to drink too much."

She'd had two glasses only. "Can one ever have too much of a good thing?"

"Maybe not, but if it's all the same to you, I'd rather walk some more before I have anything else."

"By all means." He pulled back her chair and knelt to slip her narrow, elegant feet into her shoes.

They set off again, along the cobbled promenade toward the harbor. She didn't object when, as they approached the ramp leading down to the docks, he held her hand firmly and said, "Be careful. Those high heels weren't designed for this kind of walking, and I'd hate to see you trip."

"I'm more concerned about getting arrested," she confided, taking in the flotilla of expensive yachts at anchor in the bay. "Are you sure it's okay for us to be wandering around like this?"

"Perfectly. I keep my own boat here."

"If it's anything like these others, I'm way out of my league."

"Don't let them intimidate you. Most are charters," he said, but didn't bother to add that his was larger than any she'd yet seen and never available for charter. She was antsy enough as it was.

He always anchored as far from the docks as possible, a smart decision in more ways than one. When he felt inclined to go sailing, he was soon clear of the harbor and into open water. When he had seduction in mind, he was assured of privacy. And tonight he definitely had seduction in mind.

As soon as she was seated in the dinghy he kept moored at the end of the last dock, he fired up the outboard engine and sped across the water to the big boat. Once aboard, he wasted no time setting the mood. A little champagne, a little soft music. Just enough lantern glow on the promenade deck to compensate for the absence of moonlight. Precisely the right kind of casual conversation to put her at ease.

No, he didn't live on the yacht, but did spend days at a time cruising the Mediterranean with friends. Yes, being able to get away from it all helped him unwind. He'd take her out tomorrow, if she liked—let her experience the pleasure for herself. Meanwhile, would she like to dance?

"If I can go barefoot," she said.

She could go stark naked if she wanted to, but again he refrained from voicing his opinion aloud. The night was still relatively young. Time enough to think about undressing her later. "Of course," he said, and took her in his arms.

At first, she held herself a little stiffly, but he'd selected the music well. Trendier names might top the charts these days, but as far as he was concerned, if romantic ambience was on the menu, nothing could beat the melodies of the legendary Nat King Cole.

At six-two, Dario was taller than most Italians, but Maeve was tall, too, close to five-nine, he'd guess, and that was without the heels. It made for a stimulating fit of male and female anatomy. As the timeless magic of the music wound around them, she relaxed enough to let him mold her body to his. Her hair smelled of bergamot and thyme. Her skin was as soft and warm as a sun-kissed gardenia petal.

He slid his hand to the small of her back and deliberately urged her closer still. Close enough that she couldn't miss the erection he made no attempt to hide. He felt the accelerated puff of her breath through his shirt front, the wild flutter of her lashes against his cheek.

The music died. Tilting her face up to his, he held her captive in his gaze. Across the water a ship's bell sounded, haunting and soulful. As it, too, faded, he let the silence spin out just long enough to stoke the sexual tension arcing between them so that, when at last he kissed her, she melted in his arms.

Never one to rush his pleasures—and without question she promised pure, unadulterated pleasure—he backed her under the canvas awning, which offered utter seclusion from prying eyes, and kissed her again. At her temple and her ear. Down her throat to the hollow of her shoulder. Then hearing her murmur his name on a sigh of entreaty, he brought his mouth again to hers. Felt it soften beneath his and knew victory lay within his grasp.

Still he lingered. Why hurry to sample the entire feast when the night lay ahead, inviting him to savor each course at leisure?

Her arms stole around his neck. He kissed her again, more deeply this time, and ran his tongue lightly over the seam of her lips. They parted softly, allowing him access to the secrets of her mouth. She tasted of champagne. Intoxicating, irresistible. And he wanted more of her. Lots more.

Stealthily he unzipped her gown. It slithered the length of her to puddle blackly around her ankles. She wore no bra, and panties so brief and flimsy that even he, who thought he understood all the mysteries women's lingerie had to offer, wasn't sure how she held them up. His finger hooked inside the elasticized strip at her hips, and with one slight tug disposed of the scrap of fabric.

Appearing almost dazed, she obediently stepped out of the heap of silk clinging to her ankles and submitted herself to his awed inspection. Fully clothed she had been beautiful. Naked she was breathtaking. Long legged, narrow-waisted, sweetly curved. Pure symmetry of form encased in skin as smooth as cream and lustrous as the pearls at her throat. And suddenly, feasting his eyes on her wasn't enough. He wanted all of her and he wanted her now with an urgency that should have embarrassed him.

Any attempt at leisurely seduction shot to blazes, he stripped off his own clothes with unpolished haste and tossed them in a heap beside hers on the deck. He'd planned to kiss every inch of her until she begged him to lay full claim to her. Instead, he found himself begging her, his voice hoarse with need as he urged her to touch him as intimately as he was touching her.

She did so tentatively, her fingers skimming shyly down his belly and closing around him with such exquisite care that he almost came, when what he'd planned, what he hoped, was first to bring her to orgasm with his tongue.

It wasn't going to happen, not this time. He teetered too close to the edge of destruction to postpone the inevitable, and it was either make a complete ass of himself, or take her now and pray he could last long enough to give her some satisfaction.

He chose the latter. Lowering her to the cushioned seat, he straddled her and pushed her legs apart with his knee. In a moment of madness, he teased her flesh with the tip of his penis, nudging himself against her for the pure pleasure of feeling her silken heat against his unprotected skin. Her scent rose, dark and sweet, a drugging combination so erotic that he barely had time to roll on a condom before driving into her.

Unexpectedly, he met with faint but unmistakable resistance. He heard her tiny whimper and felt the brief, convulsive clutch of her hands at his shoulders. They told him all he needed to know, and if he'd possessed a shred of integrity, he'd have stopped then. But he'd passed the point of no return. Blind hunger obliterated all sense of decency, he thrust harder, and in a matter of seconds was shuddering within her in helpless release.

And she? *Dio perdonare lui,* she lay trembling beneath him, her eyes wide dark pools in the dim light.

"Mi displace," he muttered, when he could speak again, and stroked his hand down her cheek. "Maeve, I'm sorry… I had no idea…!"

She turned her face and pressed a kiss into his palm. "Don't be," she whispered. "I'm glad you were the one."

Cursing himself with every foul expletive at his command, he went below deck and returned a minute later, wearing a terry cloth robe and bringing another for her. Wrapping it around her, he scooped her onto his lap. "How are you feeling? Did I hurt you?"

"Not really, no." She curled up in his arms like a child.

Except she wasn't a child—or was she? How was a man to tell these days, with girls of fourteen dressing and behaving like adults? Gripped by fresh consternation, he asked the question begging to be answered. "How old are you, Maeve?"

"Twenty-eight."

He expelled a sigh of relief laced with astonishment. "And until tonight you were a virgin?"

"Yes. I've never had the time for a serious relationship."

A different kind of alarm swept over him then. Did she think making love equaled a serious relationship? Surely not. At twenty-eight she couldn't be that far out of touch with reality. "A woman's first time should be special," he said. "I must have disappointed you."

"No. I'll remember this night for as long as I live."

So would he, but not for the reasons she supposed. He couldn't recall the last time he'd been so rattled. "And a very long night it's been, too. You must be exhausted." He slid her off his lap and picked up her dress and the ridiculous panties. "I'll show you where you can get dressed, then take you back to your hotel."

"Oh…yes. All right."

Refusing to acknowledge the disappointment he heard in her voice, he showed her to a guest stateroom and stuffed her clothes in after her. "No need to rush. I'll wait for you on deck."

He had the outboard running when she reappeared, and

wasted no time whisking her ashore. He couldn't wait to be rid of her. Not because, having had his way with her, he'd lost all interest, but because he felt lower than dirt and hardly knew how to face her.

She was staying at the Splendido Mare. He walked her as far as the front entrance, but made no move to go inside with her. He wasn't about to risk having her invite him up to her room. He wasn't sure he'd be able to say no. "Thank you for a very special evening, sweet Maeve," he said, kissing her on both cheeks. "Sleep well, and *buona notte*."

He'd already turned away when she called out, "What time shall I see you tomorrow?"

"Tomorrow?" He spun back toward her.

"Yes. You said you'd take me out for a spin on your yacht, remember?"

Unfortunately, he did, and if she'd been any other woman, he'd have come up with an excuse to rescind the invitation, but she was looking at him with such artless anticipation that he hadn't the heart to dash her hopes. "Let's say two o'clock at the marina."

"Wonderful. I'll see you then."

The radiance of her smile shamed him even further. *"Sì,"* he mumbled. *"A domani."*

By the time she showed up the next afternoon, he'd rounded up a small group of friends to join them, and brought his crew onboard to ferry passengers back and forth and serve drinks and meals. Safety in numbers and all that, he'd reasoned.

Once her initial shyness wore off, she seemed to enjoy herself. Certainly none of the others would have guessed she wasn't part of the in crowd. However humble her background, she looked and acted as if she'd been born to high society.

"I like your friends," she said, lacing her fingers in his when, after dinner served on the same deck where he'd deflowered her less than twenty-four hours earlier, he found himself alone with her. Most likely in a misguided effort to give the pair of them some privacy, his other guests had drifted over to stand at the rail. "Thank you for introducing me to them. I feel I know you so much better now."

Oh, *inferno!* That hadn't been the message he'd intended to get across. "You've made quite an impression on them, too, especially Eduardo," he said, knowing he could count on his old friend to back him up in this. They went back a long way and had helped each other out of similar awkward situations more than once in the past. "Don't be surprised if he wants to see you again before you leave."

"As if I'd agree to that!"

"Well, why not? He knows more about the history of the area than anyone you could ask to meet, and can show you places never mentioned in the guide books."

"And you wouldn't object?" she asked, looking woebegone as a lost puppy.

"I'd have no right. I don't own you."

Her face fell. "No, of course not." She patted his hand and reached for her straw beach bag. "Listen, Dario, I think I've had a touch too much sun and feel a headache coming on, so if you don't mind, I'm going to slip away quietly and call it a night."

"Are you sure?"

"Oh, quite," she said, leaving him in no doubt he'd got his message across loud and clear.

"In that case, I'll take you ashore." It was, he figured,

the least he could do, especially as the crew was occupied clearing away the remains of dinner.

She didn't speak again until he tied up at the dock and handed her out of the dinghy. Then, fending him off as he went to accompany her up the ramp, she said, "That's far enough. I can manage on my own now."

He might be a cad, but he wasn't entirely without chivalry. "Nonsense. I insist on seeing you safely back at the hotel."

"No." She shook her head. "There's no need to keep up the pretense. I'm not a child, Dario, and although I probably strike you as pitifully unsophisticated, I'm not completely naive. You've had your fun with me, and now it's over. I get it."

Shame, thick and bitter, coated his tongue. "I'm not sure I know how you expect me to respond to that," he muttered.

"Then let me make it easy for you. We made love or had sex or however you choose to describe it, by mutual consent. It was a one-night stand or a short-lived holiday romance, again depending on your point of view. And since that's all it was, let's chalk it up to its being just one of those things, and say goodbye with no hard feelings."

She might be sexually inexperienced, but she was a pro when it came to making a man feel lower than a worm. "If I've deceived you, Maeve, and clearly you think I have, then I'm sorry. In my own defense, however, I have to say you deceived me also, even if you never intended to."

"Because I didn't warn you ahead of time that I was a virgin, you mean?"

"Yes."

"Would it have made any difference if I had?"

"All the difference in the world," he said gently. "I

would never have laid a hand on you, no matter how desirable I found you."

She blinked back a tear. "I never thought I'd come to regret saving myself until the right man came along."

"That's my whole point, *cara*. Sadly, I'm not the right man for you, at least not long-term."

"And I'm not cut out to be some rich playboy's toy." She wiped her eyes and leaned forward to kiss his cheek. "Goodbye, Dario. Thank you for everything," she said, and quickly walked away.

She was wrong, he thought regretfully, curbing the urge to run after her as she disappeared. He did not see women as toys. He had the utmost respect for them and, for the most part, had remained on good terms with his former lovers.

He did, however, look for a certain level of sophistication in those he took to bed. He was straightforward and did not make promises he had no intention of keeping. When an affair had run its course, he expected his partners to accept the end gracefully. No histrionics, no tearful protestations of undying love, no public scenes.

For that reason the charming ingenue was not for him. At least, she hadn't been until Maeve Montgomery had shown up in his life.

CHAPTER SIX

"DARIO?"

He blinked and shook his head, as though trying to throw off the effects of sleep. "Sorry," he mumbled. "Did you say something?"

"I'm wondering where you went to, just now. One minute you were here, the next, you were gone. Lost in thought."

"I was remembering," he said.

Lucky him! She wished she could. "Remembering what?"

"Nothing special."

"Nothing pleasant, either, if the look on your face is any indication. Are you going to tell me about it?"

"No," he said. "You wouldn't be interested."

"Why don't you let me be the judge of that?"

Draining his glass, he strode to the sideboard and removed the heavy glass stopper from the decanter. "I haven't used the yacht in months," he said, pouring himself another aperitif, "and was thinking I should get someone to check and make sure everything's ship-shape on board."

She no more believed him than she believed the moon

was made of green cheese, but the set of his shoulders and the stubborn cast to his mouth told her she'd get nowhere by saying so. Clearly, as far as he was concerned, the subject was closed.

For now, maybe. But not for long. Not if she had any say in the matter.

The next several days passed uneventfully. Too uneventfully. Although attentive and pleasant when they were together, which wasn't nearly often enough in Maeve's opinion, Dario deftly turned aside any attempt on her part to get him to reveal details of their shared past.

He wasn't quite as reticent about his life and background before he'd known her. His parents set great store by education, he told her, and their children had not disappointed them. He'd earned an MBA from Harvard; his elusive sister had a degree in art history from the Sorbonne. And if that wasn't academic glory enough to satisfy them, his brother-in-law was a graduate of the London School of Economics.

Small wonder his mother was so hostile, Maeve thought when she heard all this. A diploma in sales from the local community college, which was all the foreign wife could bring to the table, didn't stack up too well beside such impressive credentials.

Had he arrived at the same conclusion and decided he'd made a mistake in marrying her? she wondered. Was that what lay behind her nagging sense of impending doom, and why he never kissed her again as he had that first evening?

The most he'd permitted himself since was a chaste peck on both her cheeks when he bade her good-night. The rest of the time, he kept his distance both physically and emotionally. Once in a while, she thought she saw the subdued light of desire smoldering in his gaze as he sat across the candlelit dinner table from her, but he always managed to dampen it when he realized she was observing him.

When she wasn't with him, she could have set her watch by the fixed routine that marked the passing hours. She slept late, ate breakfast by herself in her suite, swam in her private pool, lolled in the endless sun on her private terrace and either played solitaire or thumbed through the magazines on the coffee table in her private sitting room until she met him for lunch.

In the afternoon she napped for an hour or two, swam and lazed some more. At four o'clock she was served Earl Grey tea in china cups so translucent, she could practically read print through them, and *mostazzoli panteschi,* intricate little pastries filled with sweetened semolina, which the cook baked specially for her because she happened to mention once how much she liked them.

In fact, no matter how discontented she might be about other aspects of her "new" life, food was the one thing she couldn't fault. Meals were invariably delicious, an extravaganza of island specialties: fresh seafood, capers in a variety of sauces and salads, pasta, an abundance of exotic fruit and wonderful desserts made with honey and almonds. Enough of those and she'd soon put back the pounds she'd lost—and then some. That Dario managed to remain so fit and trim was simply one more unresolved mystery.

As twilight fell, she went about the business of making herself look presentable for the coming evening with a mixture of anticipation and dread. Would this be the night

her memory returned and she discovered why she sometimes felt a sense of loss so acute that it left her sick to her
stomach?

But it never was, and she was back in bed no later than
ten-thirty or eleven, at the mercy of an exhaustion she
couldn't overcome. Or was it that she sought escape in
sleep so as not to have to acknowledge the demons hound-
ing her when she was awake?

Questions. Always questions. And never any answers.

Apart from joining her at lunch and in the evening,
Dario spent most of his time on the phone or glued to the
computer in his study, keeping abreast of developments
in the company's head office, or consulting on business-
related matters with those members of the family who
were also in residence on the island. At least, she assumed
that's why around the same time every day he'd disappear for an hour or so. But all she really knew for sure
was that, wherever he went, he never invited her to accompany him.

Not that she was ever left alone. The household staff
smothered her with attention. About the only thing they
didn't offer to do was hold her hand while she went to the
toilet.

Finally she'd had enough and confronted him at lunch,
the Wednesday after she arrived on the island.

He gave her the perfect opening. "I have to fly up to the
city tomorrow," he said, fixing them each a campari and
soda.

"You're going to Milan?" Her heart lifted at the prospect of escaping this place and the dark, overwhelming air
of sadness that so often hounded her. To be around other
people who didn't look at her as if she wasn't quite all

there, to get her hair styled, instead of snipping at it herself with a pair of manicure scissors, that would be bliss! "Good. I'll come with you."

"No," he said flatly. "The pace of the city's much too frantic. You're supposed to stay quiet and take it easy."

"But if we have a penthouse there—"

"We have an entire house here, and I'll be gone only a couple of days, or as long as it takes me to attend a few meetings. I don't need the distraction of worrying about what you're up to when I'm in the middle of sensitive business negotiations."

Annoyed by his autocratic refusal, she said, "And what am I supposed to do while you're away, Dario? There's nothing here to keep me occupied."

"You can relax, recuperate—"

"I've done nothing but relax and recuperate for the past several weeks, not to mention being comatose for a whole month before that, and frankly I'm tired of it. I'm marking time when what I want is to pick up my life where I left it off."

He shrugged. "You already are. You're back home with your husband. Can't you let that be enough for now?"

"No, because there's something missing."

"If you're talking about us and our present living arrangement, I can't imagine you want to engage in marital relations with a man you don't remember marrying."

Actually, that wasn't quite true. She might have no memory of *when* she married him, but the more she saw of him, the better she understood *why*. His smile left her weak at the knees. His voice reverberated throughout her body with the deep, exotic resonance of a jungle drum. As for his touch, whether he intended it to be so or not, it turned her insides to a molten lava that rivaled anything the island volcanoes had ever produced.

But there was more to him than pure sex appeal. She'd soon seen beyond the striking good looks to the intelligence, the integrity, the decency. A man half as attractive would have been insulted that his wife didn't remember him. But Dario continued to treat her with the utmost patience and respect, asking nothing more than that she enjoy herself and get well again.

Misreading her introspection, he said, "Don't think it's easy, living in the same house with you, Maeve, and not giving in to my baser instincts. I'm a man, not a saint."

Oh, hallelujah! She wasn't the only one lying alone in bed every night and wishing it were otherwise. But, "There's more to it than that," she confessed. "Something I can't quite put my finger on." Her voice broke and she pressed a clenched fist to her heart. "I feel a deep emptiness here that nothing, not even you, can fill. I have, ever since I set foot in this house."

Quickly setting down his glass, he pulled her into the curve of his arm and stroked her back. "Because you're pushing yourself too hard and letting frustration get the better of you."

"Can you blame me?" She tugged free of his hold, not about to be swayed from her original course by her runaway hormones. "There's a limit to how much mollycoddling I can take, and I've reached it."

"You're not enjoying being taken care of?"

"Did Napoleon enjoy being exiled on Elba?"

"You're not a prisoner, *mio dolce*."

"I might as well be. I can't blink without someone taking note of the fact, and as for wanting to roam freely about the house the way any other wife would, or discuss menus with the cook, forget it! It's not my place to do any such thing. I'm essentially confined to barracks unless I'm with you. It's like living in boot camp!"

He laughed, so relaxed and charming that she knew if she didn't keep her wits about her, she was in danger of finding him even more adorable than she already did. "Oh, not quite that bad, surely?"

Worse, in fact. She was treated like visiting royalty. And therein lay the problem. She wasn't a visitor, she was the mistress of the house. Or at least she was supposed to be. But the one time she'd ventured as far as the kitchen, the cook had descended on her, clucking like an overwrought hen, and shooed her away.

"It sometimes feels that way. Take today, for instance. Because I was dressed and ready for lunch early, instead of doing as I usually do and sticking to my own little garden, I decided to wander farther afield and explore the rest of the grounds to see if something—anything—might jog my memory.

"First, I practically had to wrestle my way past a maid who didn't think I should be allowed through the front door. Then, once I was outside, no matter which way I turned, I kept running into people—gardeners, mainte- nance men, you name it—who made it clear I shouldn't wander off the main paths or go too close to the edge of the cliff. So I went down the drive, thinking I'd take a walk along the road, and got as far as the gates only to find them locked. When I asked one of the workers why, he pre- tended he didn't understand me, even though I spoke to him in Italian."

"Not surprising." Turning away, Dario busied himself

refilling his glass. "He speaks the local dialect, which is quite different from anything you hear on the mainland. Even native Italians have trouble communicating with the islanders. Another campari and soda?"

Refusing to let him distract her, she shook her head. "No, thanks. Look, I can see why you'd want to keep strangers from wandering all over your property, but surely those of us living here should be able to get out if we feel like it? Why, even the door in my garden wall is now kept locked."

"I know. I ordered it to preserve your privacy after my mother's unscheduled visit."

"The point I'm making," she went on, doggedly ignoring the interruption, "is that I've been here almost a week, and to put it bluntly, I'm suffocating. I step out of my suite, and a maid immediately shows up to escort me to wherever I'm supposed to go next. I try to familiarize myself with my surroundings, and I'm stymied at every turn. I feel like a hamster running endlessly on a wheel, but never getting anywhere."

"Then how about this?" he said soothingly. "I'll take the afternoon off and, after lunch, we'll tour the island by boat. If you feel up to it, we can even stop in your favorite cove and go snorkeling. Would you like that?"

She'd like it better if he'd just be straight with her, instead of stalling for time. Before he'd squelched it, she'd seen the brief flash of dismay in his eyes when she'd mentioned the emptiness inside, and guessed he knew exactly what caused it. And if he thought a dip in the sea would be enough to wash it from her thoughts, he was mistaken. Either he gave her the answers she sought, or she'd find someone who would.

On the other hand, after whining about boredom and lack of freedom, she could hardly turn down his invitation to do something different, and visiting a place that had meant something to her in the past might prove to be the key that would unlock her mind.

"Yes, I would," she said, swallowing her frustration and doing her best to sound suitably appeased. "Thank you."

Viewing Pantelleria by boat instead of from the air gave her a whole new perspective on the island. In places, giant cliffs swept down to isolated pockets of pebble beach. In others, great outcroppings of purple-black lava rose up from the cobalt Mediterranean to encircle dreamy lagoons.

Montagna Grande, towering nearly three thousand feet above sea level, stood guard over bright green fertile valleys crisscrossed with ancient stone walls. In other areas, the softer gray-green of low-growing juniper, heather and myrtle that Dario said was called *macchia,* ran wild over the land. "The scent when the wind blows from the west is enough to knock your head off," he told her.

They sailed past isolated farms and a tiny fishing village where water bubbled up from the thermal springs in its harbor. Another village clung to the edge of a sheer cliff, with glorious views across the sea. But awe inspiring though all that was, the spectacle much closer at hand stirred Maeve's blood more.

Dario in tailored black trousers and white shirt was a sight that would kick any woman's heart rate up a notch. But Dario in swimming trunks, with the wind ruffling his hair, was enough to stop a woman's pulse altogether.

Seated beside him in the eighteen-foot Donzi runabout, Maeve had to keep reminding herself that this man really was her husband, and of all the women in the world he might have chosen, he'd picked her to be his wife.

His bronzed torso gleamed in the sun. The only shadows came from the play of muscle in his forearms as he effortlessly navigated Pantelleria's jagged coastline. The hands loosely gripping the steering wheel were strong and capable. Once, they had touched her intimately. She knew it, even though she couldn't remember when, because looking at them sent a spasm of awareness shooting through her body.

And his mouth—had it done the same thing? Or was the sudden damp flood at her core brought on by wishful thinking?

Catching her inspecting him and quite misunderstanding the reason, he grinned and said, "Relax, Maeve, I know what I'm doing. We're not going to run aground."

"I wasn't watching you," she said, rolling truth and fib together into a seamless whole. "I was admiring the view."

"Then you're facing the wrong way." Shifting the throttle so that the boat idled in Neutral, he lifted his arm and pointed off the starboard bow. "Look over there."

She turned and let out a gasp of delight. No more than twenty yards away, a pod of dolphins frolicked in the turquoise water. "I would give the world to be like them," she breathed, entranced. "They're everything I wish I was. Playful, graceful, beautiful."

"You're beautiful, Maeve. I told you so the first night you came home again, and nothing's changed my mind since then."

"No, you don't understand. I'm not fishing for compliments, I'm talking about their spirit. They embody a joie de vivre I seem to have lost. I'm in limbo—a stranger inside my own skin."

"Not to me," he murmured, for once leaning so close that his breath teased the outer rim of her ear. "You're the woman I married."

She leaned against him, loving his closeness, the heat of his body, the scent of his sun-kissed skin. Loving him. "Tell me about that—about our getting married, I mean. Did we have a big wedding?"

He hesitated just long enough for a shiver of apprehension to steal over her. "No. It was a very quiet, intimate affair."

"Why?"

Again that ominous pause before he said, "Because we were married in Vancouver. I could spare only a few days before returning to Italy, which made planning an elaborate affair out of the question."

"So it was a spur-of-the-moment thing?"

"More or less. I took you by surprise, and popped the question, to coin the rather odd English way of putting it. You had just enough time to run out and find a dress to wear."

"What color?"

"Blue," he said. "The same shade as your eyes."

"And flowers?"

"You carried a small bouquet of white lilies and roses."

"My favorites!"

"Yes."

"Who else was there?"

"Two witnesses. A former colleague of yours whose name I don't recall, and a business associate of mine."

"Did we have rings?"

"Yes. White-gold wedding bands, yours studded with diamonds."

"Where are they now?"

"The clinic administrator gave yours to me for safe-keeping."

"What about a honeymoon?"

"Just four short days on the yacht. I couldn't spare more time."

She splayed the fingers of her left hand across her knee. "I think I'd like to wear my ring again. Is it at the house?"

"No. It's with mine, in the penthouse safe, in Milan. I'll get them both the next time I'm in the city." He slid back behind the wheel and put the engine in gear again. "For now, we have more to do and see out here."

Slowly they continued their tour of the island, and finally, with the worst heat of the day past, he guided the Donzi between upthrust spears of basalt rock and dropped anchor in a quiet, secluded cove.

Donning masks, snorkels and fins, they slipped over the side of the boat and drifted facedown over water teeming with marine life. Schools of black-and-orange-striped fish darted among the coral beds. Red starfish, their color made all the more vivid by contrast, clung to dark volcanic rock. Tiny crustaceans scuttled into the protection of miniature forests of algae the likes of which, as far as she knew, she'd never seen before. Close to the mouth of the cove, she came across the remains of an ancient amphora, relic of a shipwreck that had taken place centuries before.

When, after more than an hour in the water, they at last climbed aboard the runabout again, the sun had slipped low on the western horizon. Tired, content and wrapped in a huge beach towel, she snuggled close to Dario as he weighed anchor and set the Donzi on its homeward course.

* * *

As usual, that evening they dined on the terrace, or *ducchena* as Dario had taught her to call it. Maeve dressed with particular care before joining him. Much though she'd enjoyed the afternoon, it hadn't produced the results she'd hoped for. She had no more recollection of visiting the cove previously than she had of marrying Dario, and she was determined that not another night would pass without her making some sort of progress. If that meant having to seduce him into revealing all he knew, then that's what she was prepared to do. It was a case of the ends justifying the means, although why justification should be necessary was a moot point. He was her husband, after all, and had more or less admitted he'd grown as weary of celibacy as she had.

Inspecting the more formal dinner dresses in her closet, none of which she'd yet worn, she rejected the first two, which, though lovely, weren't as eye-catching as the third, a silk charmeuse in deepest jade-green, with a high empire waistline. In contrast to the modesty of the softly flared long sleeves, the low-cut neckline could be described as nothing short of daring. A huge pearl buckle centered below the bust brought together the artfully draped fabric of the bodice, and released it in a free fall of dramatic, shimmering color almost to her ankles. Simple but sophisticated, it required only a pair of teardrop pearl earrings and high-heeled black sandals to complement it.

"Lei è una visione, mia bella," Dario said reverently, when he saw her.

She cast him a deliberately provocative glance from beneath demurely lowered eyelashes. "Thank you."

That she'd achieved the effect she'd been hoping for was immediately apparent. He almost missed the flutes he was filling and came close to splashing vintage champagne all over his shoes.

Recovering himself, he gestured to the sun chaises and said solicitously, "You must have found this afternoon very tiring. Why don't you put your feet up while we wait for dinner to be served?"

The chaises were separated by a low table that allowed for no body contact, but down by the pool was a canopied patio swing built for two. "Why don't we have our drinks on the lower deck, for a change?" she suggested, running a deliberate fingertip from the top of her plunging neckline to her cleavage. "The pool looks so lovely in the moonlight. It reminds me of a huge cabochon sapphire."

Eyeing her suspiciously, he shrugged. "*Certo.* Whatever pleases you. But take my arm going down the steps. You might trip in those heels otherwise."

For a brief, startling second, she forgot her plans to seduce him as another flower-scented night, and a narrow street paved with uneven cobblestones illuminated by streetlamps, flashed before her eyes. And then, as quickly as it appeared, the picture was gone. Imagination? she wondered, her pulse jumping. Or a bone fide memory slipping through the layers clouding her mind?

There was only one way to find out. "I seem to recall your saying that to me before."

He laughed and tucked her hand beneath his elbow. "Only about a hundred times."

"Why? I know I made a practice of falling over my own feet when I was a teenager, but I'd hoped I'm not quite as clumsy anymore."

"You aren't," he assured her. "You're one of the most

graceful women I've ever met. But that doesn't mean I shouldn't go out of my way to keep you safe."

They'd reached the pool deck by then. Not waiting for him to suggest they occupy any of the several chaises lined up around its perimeter, she slipped her hand free of his arm and wandered ever so casually to the swing, leaving him with little choice but to follow and sit down next to her. "Where were you, then, the day of my accident?" she asked.

Even though he wasn't quite touching her, she felt the sudden tension emanating from his body as acutely as if static electricity had leaped between them. "Obviously not doing my job."

"I'm not blaming you, Dario," she amended hurriedly. "No one can be expected to look out for someone else all the time, especially not an adult who should be able to look out for herself."

"But I do blame myself," he said, his voice raw.

She opened her mouth to refute such a notion, then closed it again as another thought occurred. "Oh, dear!" she exclaimed softly. "Are you telling me you were driving the car, and hold yourself responsible for my injuries? Is that why you won't talk to me about it?"

He swung around to face her with such leashed anger that she flinched. "No. If I'd been at the wheel, you never would have been hurt and…"

"And what?"

"And we wouldn't be sitting here like this."

"Like what?"

"Brother and sister," he exploded. "Good friends. Polite strangers. Take your pick."

"You don't like our status quo?"

"What do you take me for?" he ground out. "Of course I don't like our status quo! What red-blooded man would?"

She inched closer until her thigh touched his, and put her hand on his knee. "Then why don't you do something about it, Dario?" she said.

CHAPTER SEVEN

HE'D never thought to see the day or night that he would turn down a beautiful, sexy woman's advances. But when he'd married Maeve, he'd cast aside his role of quintessential playboy and relied on his moral compass to make a success of a union he'd neither anticipated nor wanted. The same inborn sense of decency kicked in now, reining in his response to her.

"Because I'm not convinced you know what you're asking for," he said.

She cupped his jaw and turned his face to hers. "Will this change your mind?" she whispered, her sweetly fragrant breath feathering over his lips to infiltrate his mouth.

At once bold and hungry, her kiss inflamed his soul. This was the Maeve he'd married, he thought, his senses swimming; the girl in a woman's body whom he'd coaxed into shedding the inhibitions that had dogged her most of her life. He had taught her well. She'd blossomed under his expert tutelage; had reveled in her newfound sexuality. And now she was using it to destroy him.

Still he fought, bolstered by doubts he'd never fully acknowledged before. Who was it she really craved: her husband, or Yves Gauthier, the French-Canadian summer visitor with whom she'd struck up such a close alliance, and in whose rented car she'd been traveling when the accident occurred?

"Until you regain your memory, you don't even know me, Maeve," he said, forcing the words past the strangling constriction in his throat.

"I know I want you, and have ever since last week when I walked down the steps from that jet and into your waiting arms."

Did she? Or was she merely responding to the same wild hormonal attraction that had lured her to surrender her innocence to him in the first place? He wished he knew.

As though sensing his uncertainty, she upped the ante by angling her body so that her breast nudged his biceps. "Please, Dario…"

Cursing inwardly, he closed his eyes against the temptation. Undeterred, she murmured his name again and guided his hand inside her low-cut gown to cradle her fullness. Her nipple surged against his palm, eager and responsive. Unbearably aroused already, he clenched his teeth against the increased onslaught to his stamina.

Impatient with his resistance, and with an abandon that left him reeling, she made a sound deep in her throat and, pulling her skirt up around her waist, moved swiftly to sit astride his lap.

Her long bare legs, pale as ivory in the moonlight and his for the taking, leveled his defenses. He couldn't help himself. He touched her, skimming his palms over the slender curve of her thighs, lured by the siren call of their warm, smooth skin. Wove a path to the damp patch of fabric between them and, slipping his finger under the edge of her panties, found the hidden nub of flesh at her core.

She trembled and gave an inarticulate cry at the spasm that seized her. He touched her again, knowing well the exact spot that would give her the most pleasure. A subtle increase in pressure, a more urgent rhythm. Then the hiss of delicate silk giving way as he inserted three fingers between her and her underwear, the middle one sliding inside her dark wet confines at the same time that he relented and let his tongue dance with hers.

The sublime torture of having her tilt her hips backward in fluid compliance, and not take what she so willingly offered, almost killed him. The blood pounded through his veins, his lungs seized up, and how he didn't grind his teeth to dust was nothing short of miraculous. If she touched him, even fleetingly and even with the barrier of clothing depriving him of the intimacy he was affording her, he would explode. But she did not. His contained agony was eclipsed by her soft scream as she climaxed and collapsed against him, sobbing.

He held her until she grew calm again, then lifted her clear of his lap and deposited her back on the seat beside him.

"No," she begged, clinging to him. "Not until we both…together…please, Dario…!"

But he'd played a similar game of Russian roulette with her once before, and look where it had landed them. He wasn't going to make the same mistake again. "I didn't come prepared."

"What does it matter? You're my husband."

Oh, it mattered. It would continue to matter until they

both knew without a shadow of doubt that he was the man she wanted, not just for a night, but forever.

Removing himself from further temptation, he stood up and stepped away from the swing. "This is hardly the time or the place, Maeve," he said. "Our absence has already been noticed. Antonia's serving dinner, and if we don't show up fast, she'll be sending someone to come looking for us."

She let out a horrified little yelp. "I hope you're joking."

"See for yourself."

She peeked around the side of the canopy, which had so effectively camouflaged them from view. The housekeeper, having set out the first course, was casting a searching glance around the empty terrace.

"Well, do something, for heaven's sake," Maeve whimpered, running agitated fingers through her hair. "I'm a mess. I can't have anyone see me looking like this."

No more could he. He might be talking good sense, but his body wasn't listening. He ached so viciously, he'd have plunged fully dressed into the pool, except it would only draw more attention to a situation he never should have allowed to get so far out of hand to begin with. "I'll go ahead and distract her," he said, collecting the champagne flutes and steadfastly willing his rebellious nether regions to behave. "Slip through the library to get back to your room, and join me when you're ready."

Regaining the sanctuary of her suite undetected, Maeve locked herself in the bathroom and, almost as baffled as she was ashamed, regarded herself in the full-length mirror. Her face was flushed, her lip gloss smeared, and her eyes glittered like demented beacons.

What in the world had come over her? Planning to

seduce her husband was one thing, but attempting to do so where they might have been discovered ranked right up there with deciding to swim naked in broad daylight. Both were completely out of character, which gave rise to some disturbing questions.

Had she undergone a major personality change as a result of her head injury, and was that why Dario had so firmly resisted her? Was she proving to be as much of a stranger to him as he was to her? Or was it simply, as he'd tried to tell her before, that she was pushing too hard and too fast to find her way back to him?

One thing she did know. Whether or not he admitted it, he wanted her as ardently as she wanted him. He'd implied that their marriage hadn't been all smooth sailing before the accident, but regardless of what had transpired in the past, the sexual attraction between them had survived intact. Why, then, was he so unwilling to give in to it?

She had no answers but, as she freshened up and made herself presentable again, she determined she wouldn't rest until she found some. Since her husband was so unwilling to provide them and she'd rather eat worms than ask anything of her mother-in-law, she'd rely on her own ingenuity to put together the missing pieces that comprised the jigsaw puzzle of her life. That those answers existed, just a breath out of reach, had been made evident by the brief flash of memory that had assailed her earlier in the evening.

Her opportunity to do some sleuthing came the next day, when Dario left for Milan. Or, more accurately, the next night.

To make sure she didn't trip over the ever-vigilant

Antonia or one of her minions, Maeve waited until after midnight before stealing out of her suite. Her first stop was his study, a room far enough removed from the staff quarters that she was in no danger of alerting anyone to her activities.

Although his desk was littered with the kind of paperwork one would expect of any corporate executive operating out of his home, there was absolutely nothing personal among it that she could see from her cursory investigation. None of the drawers were locked, which suggested they, too, were devoid of anything that might spark a memory, nor did the bookshelves yield any clues. Which left the computer. But even she, desperate though she was to reclaim her past, drew the line at going quite that far. Coming across something that happened to be lying out more or less in full view was one thing; violating his privacy by snooping through his files or e-mail, quite another.

Leaving the study exactly as she'd found it, she crept past the library and the media room, the big formal dining room and the elegant day salon. A few yards farther on, a set of tall double doors blocked her progress, but they opened at her touch and, as she'd suspected, marked the entrance to the master suite.

Like hers, it formed an arm of the villa's E-shaped floor plan. Unlike hers, it didn't share the space with two other suites, but occupied the entire wing.

When she touched the electric switch to her left, four wall sconces shed subdued light on a foyer that was almost as spacious as her living room in Vancouver. Oyster-white walls contrasted sharply with a jewel-toned Turkish area rug covering part of the black marble floor. Equally eye-catching were the vibrant colors of a bird-of-paradise bouquet on a table set against one wall. Two doors took up most of the third wall, with an arched opening leading to a sitting room filling the fourth.

She chose to explore the sitting area first. Tastefully furnished with sofas upholstered in crisp black-and-white-striped linen, the usual complement of occasional tables, strategically placed lamps, a sound system and a small ladies' writing desk, the room's most striking feature was the wall of floor-to-ceiling windows. They offered an unsurpassed view across the moonlit sea and gave access to yet another private pool and terrace furnished with table, chairs and sun lounges.

What struck her most forcibly, though, was the complete lack of personal touches within the room. No objets d'art or magazines littered the surface of the tables. No framed photographs graced the walls. No evidence at all, in fact, that anyone had ever actually used the place. Even the writing desk, which might reasonably be expected to contain some item of interest, revealed nothing but a couple of silver pens, a stack of embossed stationery and a small English-Italian dictionary.

Hoping for better luck elsewhere, she returned to the foyer and opened the first door on her left. A short hall led to the master bedroom, which, decorated chiefly in restful shades of misty blue-gray and white, made her ache for all the nights she'd not shared it with her husband.

Filmy draperies hung at the sliding glass doors that gave access to the pool and terrace. White fur rugs were scattered over the floor. In one corner, a potted tibouchina covered with purple blossoms stood beside a Victorian chaise longue upholstered in a soft gray toile depicting exotic birds. On the other side, a tulip-shaped Art Deco reading lamp fashioned from opaque glass stood on a little carved table, with just enough room next to it for a book and maybe a cup of hot chocolate.

In the opposite corner, a black iron floor candelabra shaped like a tree made a bold fashion statement, even though it lacked candles. The other source of light came from black-shaded lamps with heavy brass bases on the nightstands.

And then there was the most dominant feature of the room, the bed itself. Sumptuously proportioned and extravagantly dressed in the finest linens, it brought to mind images so stirring and erotic, Maeve's stomach turned over in a rolling somersault. Her mind might not remember writhing in ecstasy as she and Dario made love on its thick mattress, but her body certainly did.

Double en suite bath and dressing rooms opened off this room. Body lotions, bath oils and hand-milled soaps, as well as thick velvet towels monogrammed with her initials were meticulously set out in her bathroom. Those clothes not in her temporary quarters were arranged by color in the closets, along with shoes, wide-brimmed hats and other accessories.

But as with the bed and sitting rooms, they struck not a single chord of memory. And to add to the mystery of her past, a second door leading from the bedroom and connecting to who knew what, was locked, as was its counterpart in the foyer.

Disappointed, she retraced her steps throughout the entire suite. Everything was undeniably attractive, but the most important element, the one that made it home, was missing. It was all too eerily immaculate; a residence-in-waiting from which every conceivable flaw had been carefully erased. No trace of human trial and error or interaction remained. Whatever imperfections made up its past had been removed.

And she knew where they were hidden. Behind those locked doors.

Well, at least she'd narrowed down her search. Now all she had to do was find the missing key. But where to look? The most obvious places had turned up nothing. Probably Dario had a safe hidden somewhere, but even if she found it, without knowing the code to open it, she'd be no further ahead.

No, her only recourse lay with her husband. He was the real repository of her history, and one way or another she had to persuade him to share it with her.

As promised, he returned from Milan just in time to shower and change before dinner the following evening. As always, he looked divine in slim-fitting charcoal-gray trousers and a pearl-colored shirt against which his skin glowed like polished copper.

"You seem weary, Maeve," he commented, holding her at arm's length and inspecting her critically when he joined her. "There are dark smudges under your pretty eyes."

Guilt welled up in her. Of course she looked weary! For a start, duplicity didn't sit well with her. Add to that snooping through the house, then mulling over what might be behind those locked doors, and she'd managed only about four hours of sleep last night. "I missed you," she said. That much at least was no lie.

He traced his finger over her mouth. "Did you?"

"Yes," she quavered, finding his touch so wildly exciting that it was all she could do to breathe. "The villa isn't the same when you're not here. I hope you're not planning on going away again anytime soon."

"As a matter of fact, yes, I am. Tomorrow, in fact, to spend the weekend in Tunisia."

All the lovely warm sensations he so easily aroused vanished as if he'd flung cold water in her face. Not bothering to hide her disappointment, she said, "A man in your lofty position having to work on the weekend? Can't you send someone else in your place?"

"I wouldn't dream of it," he replied, filling their champagne flutes from the bottle of Cristal chilling in the wine bucket. "This trip will be strictly for pleasure."

"I see. Well, I hope you have a very lovely time." She tilted her chin, praying for pride to conceal her hurt, and took an inelegant but fortifying swig of champagne.

"And *I* hope," he continued, amusement silvering his voice at her conspicuously acidic response, "that you'll come with me."

She choked as her next mouthful went down the wrong way. Had she heard him correctly? "Go with you?" she spluttered.

"Provided you feel up to it, of course. If not, we'll forget the whole idea."

She swallowed an unseemly hiccup. "Surely a more pertinent question is, are you quite sure *you're* up to it?"

"Well, who else would I take? You are my wife, after all."

"I know. It's one of the few things I *am* aware of."

"Then why the hesitation? I thought you'd welcome a change of scene."

"I would," she agreed. "It's your about-face that's giving me pause. Or is your memory as faulty as mine and you've forgotten that, as recently as two days ago, you insisted I'm not yet well enough to face the outside world?"

"I've forgotten nothing, but you've made so little progress since you came home that I'm no longer sure keeping you secluded is helping your recovery. Perhaps, instead of trying to revive old memories, we should concentrate on forging new ones, and where better to begin than in a place you've never been before?" He looked at her expectantly. "Well? What do you think?"

She lifted her shoulders, bemused. "I hardly know what to say."

"Say yes. Let's start over and see where it leads us."

"A second honeymoon, you mean?"

"*Sì.*"

"As in you and I…um…you know…?"

"Precisely. Starting tonight. It's either that, or I enter a monastery, because keeping my distance from you is having a most deleterious effect on my health, not to mention my sanity."

"Is it really?" For the life of her, she couldn't quite contain her delight. "My goodness, I'd never have guessed."

Laughing, he reached across the table and grasped her hands. "You certainly would, you little minx. You know exactly the effect you have on me."

"But I never thought you'd give in to it."

"Don't underestimate your power, Maeve. I have missed holding you close while you sleep, missed waking up next to you each morning, and deeply missed making love with you. But not furtively or hastily, as almost happened the other night, which is why, before I left for Milan, I instructed Antonia to prepare our private rooms for your return."

Resuming her married life was what she'd wanted almost from day one, but now that it lay within her grasp, some of its luster faded. She'd been right in thinking the master wing looked naked under all its chic finery. It had indeed been swept clean. The secrets of the past were not about to be revealed, after all, merely shoved out of sight. And she'd bet her last dollar they were securely under lock and key in that other room.

That a deafening hush had descended over the terrace became apparent when Dario said, "I hoped for a more enthusiastic response, *mio dolce*."

"This is all so unexpected, I'm still trying to take it in," she said, to cover up the suspicions racing around in her head. "I suppose, if I'm really honest, I half expect you to change your mind again."

Coming to where she sat, he pulled her to her feet, extracted a small leather pouch from his shirt pocket and tipped the contents onto the table. A pair of white-gold wedding bands rolled over the polished surface and came to rest at the base of her wineglass. Taking her left hand, he slipped the smaller of the two on the third finger. "Once again, Maeve Montgomery, I take you for my lawful wife. Is that enough to reassure you?"

The ring, though a little loose fitting, gleamed in the candlelight and felt so deliciously right that for the moment only one thing mattered. She picked up the other ring, slid it on his finger. "And I once again take you, Dario Costanzo, to be my husband."

He handed her her wineglass and raised his in a toast. "Then here's to us, *mia bella*."

"To us."

The intensity of his gaze as they sipped made her blush.

"I do believe," he murmured hoarsely, setting both flutes back on the table and reaching for her, "that it's customary at this point for the groom to kiss his bride."

Struggling to breathe normally, she nodded. "I do believe you're right."

He cupped her face between his palms and lowered his head.

Brushed his lips over hers lightly, fleetingly, then with crushing urgency, as one hand stroked past her shoulders to settle intimately at her waist. "After which," he said, lifting his head to gaze deep into her eyes, "comes the first dance."

Slowly he clasped his other hand with hers and guided her across the terrace. They moved together effortlessly, his longer legs accommodating her shorter steps, his lips skimming her temples.

A clock inside the villa rang out the hour, nine musical chimes that briefly drowned out a silken-voiced tenor crooning softly from stereo speakers mounted on the outside wall, then drifted out into the night.

Caught in a sudden powerful tide of déjà vu, Maeve yearned toward her husband. Once before he had held her in his arms, and a chime had echoed across the quiet sea. As the bell-like tone died away, he'd kissed her just so, under the same stars that sprinkled the heavens now. And it had been wonderful. Magical. She knew it as surely as she knew her own name.

"I remember," she breathed. "Dario, it's all coming back to me."

CHAPTER EIGHT

"ALL what?"

"Kissing you like this. Dancing with you under the stars."

"Nothing unusual in that." In marked contrast to her excitement, Dario kept his response determinedly casual. "It's the sort of thing married couples do all the time."

Except that, in their case, it had happened only once before, the night he'd seduced her. Considering the aftermath, he'd as soon it didn't all come rushing back in vivid Technicolor now. They wouldn't stand much chance of starting over if she recalled the embarrassment and hurt she'd suffered at his hands, the day after she'd surrendered her virginity to him. And in his opinion, a fresh start was long overdue.

He was tired of fighting his feelings for her, and of living like a monk despite being tempted beyond human endurance. Among other considerations, walking around with a permanent erection was humiliating, as he'd discovered during his meetings in Milan when his thoughts had repeatedly strayed from the serious business of international finance, to the much more pleasurable contemplation of soon making love to his wife.

Maeve wasn't helping matters, either, in looking more desirable by the day. Plenty of homemade pasta, good, fresh seafood washed down with excellent local wine, and the *mostazzoli panteschi* and other pastries she enjoyed so much had eliminated her gaunt angles and restored her delicious curves. Add to that her impeccable sense of style, and he'd have had to be both neutered and brain dead not to desire her.

Plainly put, he missed the wife he'd grown to love, and not just because of the sex or lack thereof. He missed her companionship, her sharp intelligence and her quick wit. He missed how they would lock glances across a roomful of people at a dreary corporate party, and smile in complicit understanding that they'd enjoy their own private celebration at the first opportunity. Yet he'd been forced to keep his distance from her because he didn't trust himself to be close.

Even worse, Maeve hadn't seen their son in nearly nine weeks. The longer the separation continued, the harder it would be on everyone. Already she'd missed so much of their child's development; milestones that would never be repeated. Sebastiano had three teeth now, which was three more than he'd had the last time she'd seen him. He pretty much sat up unaided, and already was trying to crawl by pulling himself over the floor like a baby seal. He gurgled with pleasure every time he saw his little cousin, Cristina, and had bonded with his aunt to the point that he'd cried and reached out for her the last time Dario had tried to pick him up. Tearing him away from the people who'd become his primary family was going to be painful for everyone involved.

That Dario was hugely indebted to Giuliana and her

husband, Lorenzo, for helping out by taking the baby into their household and into their hearts, went without saying. But the boy should be riding around on his own father's shoulders and sleeping in his own crib, with his own mother singing him to sleep at night.

Dario had had enough of feeling more like a visitor than a parent, and more than enough of paying discreet visits to his sister's, in order to spend a stolen hour or two with his son. It irked him to be put in such a position. No man should have to sneak around to see his own child.

But Peruzzi's warnings had left their mark. Dario had no way of knowing how Maeve would react when her memory returned, but he did know he wouldn't be responsible for causing her more grief than she'd already have to face. Whether Yves Gauthier had been friend or lover scarcely counted for much, compared to her having wiped all knowledge of her son from her mind.

Nor was that all. As her husband, Dario was beyond weary of the half-truths and evasions he was feeding his wife. He didn't handle well not being in control, and if it were up to him, he'd tell her everything, sort out the mess they'd found themselves in and go forward from there. In light of Peruzzi's warnings, however, it was a risk he dared not take.

Unaware of the direction his thoughts had gone, Maeve sagged against him now. "You believe I'm grasping at straws, don't you?"

"Not necessarily," he said, "but if you're determined to immortalize a particular night, why not let this be the one?"

"You're right." Drifting back to the table, she sat down and toyed with the cook's very excellent *linguine allo scoglia*, mounds of clams, prawns, shrimp and mussels bathed in a rich tomato sauce. "Tell me more about our trip tomorrow. Exactly where are we going in Tunisia?"

"The capital itself, Tunis. It's an interesting city that I think you'll enjoy."

She nibbled a fat prawn thoughtfully. "What should I pack in the way of clothes?"

"For the evening, one of your pretty dinner dresses. During the day, something in cool cotton, a couple of wide-brimmed hats, comfortable flat-heeled sandals and sunscreen," he said, tackling his own meal. "Walking's the only way to appreciate everything the city has to offer, and it's going to be hot. Oh, and fairly modest clothes—I won't stand for strange men burping at you."

"Burping?" She choked back a laugh. "No wonder you call them strange!"

"That's not why. Burping's the Tunisian way of showing appreciation for a pretty woman, and since most local women cover themselves from head to toe in public, tourists are fair game for any man with a roving eye."

"If I didn't know better, I'd think you were jealous."

"Perhaps I have reason to be," he said, an unexpectedly bitter note coating his reply.

"What?" She stared at him, shocked.

Cursing himself—the festering accusation was out before he could contain it, and hardly an auspicious way to effect the kind of reconciliation he was hoping for—he added swiftly, "It's the price every husband pays for having a beautiful wife, Maeve."

"Well, let me put this particular husband's mind at rest," she said flatly. "I don't care how many men burp at me, I only have eyes for you."

There it was again, the erection that never slept! "How hungry are you?" he inquired huskily.

"For this?" She poked her fork around in the unquestionably delicious food remaining on her plate. "Not very."

No more was he. "Then what do you say to our continuing this conversation someplace more private?"

"I think it's the best idea you've had in ages."

Earlier, Antonia or one of the maids had added a few more romantic touches to the master suite. A bouquet of lilies filled the sitting area with fragrance. In the bedroom, a single rose in a bud vase stood on the little table next to the Victorian chaise longue. More than a dozen squat candles in glass cups suspended from the tree-shaped floor candelabra cast a glimmering light over the bed, but left the corners of the room swathed in moon-shot darkness.

All this Maeve took in with what she hoped showed just the right degree of curiosity. But despite her best efforts, her gaze repeatedly wandered to the locked doors, first the one in the foyer, and then the other, there in the bedroom.

That Dario noticed quickly became apparent. "It doesn't matter that you don't recognize anything," he said, rather firmly steering her away from the room at large, and through the open glass doors to the terrace. "Tonight's about us and the future, *tesoro*."

Outside, more candles burned in faceted glass hurricane lamps set around the pool, and waiting on the table was an ice bucket containing another bottle of champagne and two long-stemmed frosted glasses. As the perfect introduction to a night of seduction, she could hardly have asked for better. Yet her delight was tainted by something far less pleasant. "It's not that, exactly," she muttered, treading a fine line between truth and lie.

"Nor is it about rushing to make love before you're ready," he assured her. "We take this at your pace, Maeve. I wouldn't have it any other way."

It wasn't that, either. The simple fact was, she was riddled with guilt. If only she'd known this was how the evening would end, she'd never have come sneaking through the suite, the night before.

A good marriage should be based on trust and respect, so what did it say about theirs, that she'd behaved so shabbily? Yet to admit to her transgression now was more than she could bring herself to do. After all, it wasn't as if she'd discovered anything significant, or tried to pick the locks on the doors to that other room.

But that line of reasoning offered cold comfort and prompted her to say, "That's not what's bothering me, Dario. It's my conscience. You've been so patient with me ever since I came home, but I've been a pretty poor wife, and I'm sorry for that."

"You're here now, and that's all I ask for," Dario almost purred, drawing her down to sit on his lap. "Do you have any idea, *innamorata,* how empty these rooms have been without you, or how long the nights that you have not shared our bed?"

If he never did anything more than speak to her like that, with his voice resonating over her nerve endings until her entire being hummed with awareness, she could die a happy woman.

He mesmerized her. Rescued her from the mundane and, with a fleeting kiss here, a featherlight touch there, transported her to a world far removed from the ordinary.

He shaped her mouth with his thumb, a tactile benediction so exquisite that she quivered uncontrollably. Stroked his fingertip the length of her arm, from her wrist to her shoulder, imbuing the caress with a tenderness that made her want to weep. He traced the line of her collarbone, the contour of her throat, and left her gasping for more. Did all with such consummate finesse that she was hardly aware of when they returned to the intimacy of the bedroom, or how it was that they were standing naked before each other.

As though seeing her for the first time, he held her at arm's length and let his eyes roam from her breasts to the indentation of her waist, then past the curve of her hips to the shadowed juncture of her thighs. And every place his gaze touched caught fire until she was burning all over.

"I thought I remembered how lovely you are," he finally murmured in hushed tones, "but would you believe I did not do you justice?"

"Yes," she said on a breathless sigh, raging desire giving her the courage to scrutinize him with the same minute attention to every detail of his physique that he had afforded to hers. "Memory so often plays us false."

The candle flames bathed his olive skin in tongues of shimmering light. They played over his torso, illuminating the muscled slope of his shoulders, the breadth of his chest, the hard, flat plane of his midriff, and the long, strong length of his legs. They showcased the urgent thrust of his erection that told her more plainly than anything words could convey how much he desired her.

The day over a week ago that she'd stepped out of his private jet and seen him for what, as far as she was concerned, was the first time, she'd thought him the most handsome man she'd ever met. But only now did she appreciate the extent of his masculine beauty. He stood before her like a god hammered from bronze and dusted with gold. Proud, powerful, invincible.

He left her weak with longing; dazed with wonder. "Dario?" she whispered.

"I'm here, and I'm yours," he said, the timbre of his voice chasing new thrills over her skin. "Show me what you want, *amore mio,* and I will give it to you."

Hypnotized by his unwavering stare, she put her hand to his chest. Felt the strong, steady beat of his heart. Circled his flat nipple with her forefinger. "I want you all of you," she told him and, with new daring, slid her hand past his waist and flexed her fingers possessively around his erection. How smooth and heavy it was. Soft as silk, strong as steel.

"I want to feel you hard against me and hear your breath catch in your throat," she whispered, her words vibrating with suppressed passion. "I want you to take me to bed and fill me so that there are no empty corners left where I can hide."

With a muffled groan, he swung her into his arms. The mattress sighed as he lowered her to it and lay down beside her.

Stirred by the night wind, the filmy drapes at the open glass doors whispered applause. The candlelight winked.

As though he'd been waiting permission from all three, he finally kissed her. Deeply, hungrily. And when that wasn't enough to satisfy either of them, he put his mouth in other places, scorching a path from her breasts to her navel, and lower still to her thighs. Boldly, he flicked his tongue between them, searing their tender skin and inching them apart.

Momentarily shocked, she stiffened. But he'd done more than inch her legs apart. He'd forced open a chink in her memory of other such times. Times her body recalled with aching intensity, even if clouds continued to swirl in her mind.

He had done this before. *They* had done this before, with her clawing at his shoulders as she writhed before the onrushing waves of ecstasy threatening to drown her. And with him holding her hips captive so that she could not escape the pleasure he was so determined to give to her.

Tension caught her in an unforgiving spiral. Wound tighter and tighter. So tight that perspiration dimmed her vision. A silent scream rose in her throat, but before it could find voice, she soared, exploding into a hundred thousand prisms of light, each more blinding than its predecessor.

Desperate to anchor herself to earth, to him, she cried his name. He heard her unspoken plea and, bracing himself on his forearms, he lowered himself until his flesh was touching hers, there where she craved him the most.

Smoothly he filled her. Carried her in a rhythm at first slow and easy and so deeply intimate that her eyes flooded with tears. Then, as the momentum built, a different kind of emotion swept over her, one laced with greed because a little wasn't enough. She wanted everything he had to give her. She wanted his soul in exchange for the one he'd taken from her.

But she should have known that nothing worth having ever came without a price. As she took from him, so he robbed her a second time. Even as he groaned and shuddered in release, her world splintered again with such unrestrained abandon, she thought her heart would burst.

He collapsed on top of her, his chest heaving. The thudding silence that followed roared through her mind like a tornado. If this was how it had been between them before, drenched in glorious passion, how could she not have remembered, and why had he hinted that all was not well in their marriage?

Yesterday she thought finding the answers would dispel the sense of doom haunting her. Now she wasn't sure she wanted to tamper with perfection. Better to do as he suggested: leave the past behind and carve a new path into the future.

Stirring, he lifted his head and stared down at her, his eyes smoldering in the subdued light. "Did I please you, *tesoro?*"

"Oh, you pleased me," she said. "You pleased me very much. I have not felt so complete in a very long time."

The dark shadow forever looming over her had lifted somewhat, and for the first time in weeks she slept deeply, dreamlessly, safe in her husband's arms.

They left early the next morning, shortly after sunrise, which put paid to any idea she'd harbored of a more intimate start to the day. Dario was all business as he'd shooed her out of bed and into the bathroom.

"Ordinarily I'd have taken you by boat," he explained, during the short drive to the airport at the north end of the island, "but Tunis is a fascinating city and with only two days in which to show it to you, I've saved us some time by chartering a private aircraft. We'll be there in time for breakfast."

A perfectly logical explanation, at least on the surface, but she was convinced there was another reason he was so anxious to vacate the villa.

"Storage," he'd informed her tersely when, in the course of getting ready to leave, she'd inquired ever so casually what lay behind the locked doors in their suite.

"Storage for what?"

"Just stuff," he replied, and practically strong-armed her out of the house and into the Porsche.

He was lying. She knew it as surely as she knew her own name. But she could hardly call him on it since she wasn't entirely without guile herself.

By nine o'clock they were seated at a sidewalk café on the Avenue Habib Bouguiba, breakfasting on peaches, figs, oven-warm brioches spread with quince jam, and rich, flavorful coffee. The slight tension that had marked their departure from Pantelleria melted in the North African sun, and Dario was again the ideal husband from last night, trapping her knee between both of his under the table, hypnotizing her with his smile and devouring her in his sultry gaze.

Afterward, they strolled hand in hand past old bookstores, galleries and flower stands to the Cathedral of St. Vincent-de-Paul, and stood in awe before its impressive neo-Romanesque facade. An excellent tour guide, Dario explained that in addition to containing the tomb of the Unknown Soldier, the cathedral was also the largest surviving building from the French Colonial era.

From there they entered the Medina, the medieval Muslim town situated only a stone's throw away from the Christian church, yet a world removed from the bustling modern city beyond its gateway. Graceful minarets rose up white and dazzling against the deep-blue sky. Ancient palaces and mosques vied for space with crowded souks selling everything from spices to clothing, perfume to jewelry. Pottery, brass and carpets spilled out of tiny shops into the street.

Men wearing flowers in their hair infused the morning with the fragrance of jasmine that vied with cloves and incense to permeate the air. Merchants bargained in Arabic and a smattering of French, English, Italian and German with tourists looking to take home souvenirs. Barbers plied their trade on every corner.

Maeve was enchanted by it all: the scents, the sounds, the atmosphere, the exotic foreignness. Nothing here hinted at a troubled past. No disapproving mother-in-law lurked nearby. No secrets were hidden behind locked doors. She was happy and in love, and for as long as it lasted, she intended to savor every second.

"I'm so glad to be here with you," she told Dario, when they stopped midmorning to refresh themselves with tiny cups of sweetened mint tea.

"And I with you." He touched her hand, tracing his finger over her wedding ring. "I must have been mad to wait so long to claim you as my wife again."

His words filled her heart to overflowing.

They resumed their explorations, wending their way through the maze of street to Ez Zitouna, the Mosque of the Olive Tree. Here the gold souks and other so-called "clean" professions stood closest to the walls, while the "unclean" professions such as dyeing and crude metal work were farther away.

It was a shopper's paradise and Maeve was fascinated by the delicate silver jewelry, sequined and embroidered accessories, and finely woven wool which only the very wealthy could afford.

"Some of my former clients would kill to own this,"

she remarked, examining a beautiful fringed shawl in vibrant shades of blue and crimson.

"But it was designed with you in mind," Dario said, and over her objections promptly started bargaining with the merchant to acquire it for her.

When they finally left the Medina around three o'clock, he'd also bought her an exquisite antique perfume bottle and a bird cage intricately carved from white wood, "because," he insisted, "no wife of mine is leaving here without something to remind her of her second honeymoon."

"But I don't own a bird," she protested, laughing as he juggled the cage through the crowds.

Unfazed, he said, "I'm sure they sell those, as well. We'll come back tomorrow and look for one."

The driver he'd hired to pick them up at the airport had dropped off their luggage at the place they were staying. A French Colonial mansion converted to a small boutique hotel, it was exclusive, elegant and charming. Their suite, overlooking the rear gardens and the Mediterranean, was shielded from the city noise and cooled by ceiling fans. The floors were marble; the furniture, antique provincial; the wall hangings, silk.

By then, worn-out from the early start to the day and the heat, Maeve was glad to kick off her sandals, shed her dress for a cotton robe and stretch out on the bed for a late-afternoon nap. But that plan went awry when Dario, who'd gone out to the terrace to make a phone call, came back into the room.

She felt the mattress give under his weight, then his lips were on hers, his kisses sliding from soft and persuasive to hard and commanding.

Love in the afternoon, she discovered, had much to

recommend it. Leisurely, splashed with sunshine, it invited a different kind of intimacy from that of the night before; a more acute visual scrutiny than candle flame and moonlight allowed.

She saw his mouth curve with pleasure when her nipples peaked under his grazing caress, and the slow, sultry sweep of his lashes as he buried himself deep inside her. She watched the passion flare in his eyes, the sweat beading his brow and the hard line of his clenched jaw as he fought the tide threatening to overpower him.

Clutching his shoulders and rising to meet him as her own body answered the demands of his, she glimpsed the reflection of their tangled limbs in the gilt-framed mirror hanging above the dresser on the opposite wall, his burnished by the Mediterranean sun to the color of brown sugar against her paler skin tones. Even as her eyes closed in surrender, his taut buttocks, the sensual rhythm of his hips, the flexing and contracting of his back muscles, imprinted themselves forever in her mind.

Drowsy and sated, with the damp heat of utter gratification still binding her to him, she kissed his throat and whispered, "Nothing that happened in the past matters to me any longer, Dario. From now on, this day, this moment are all I care about, and all I need on which to build our future."

Somehow she'd said the wrong thing. Although he didn't move a muscle, sudden distance sprang up between them, induced by a tension so potent that it filled the entire room. "I wish it were that simple, my darling wife," he said. "Unfortunately, it isn't."

CHAPTER NINE

"I THOUGHT," she said in a small, crushed voice, "that's what you wanted."

More fool him, he'd thought so, too. But that, Dario realized grimly, was what happened when a man let his carnal appetite get the better of his judgment. He rationalized every decision he arrived at, even when none made sense. The truth was, there was no escaping the past and there never would be.

"What I want," he said carefully, "is to put the past behind us. That's not quite the same thing as pretending it never happened. Our history—what we've done, where we've been, who we've known—makes us who we are today, Maeve."

"What if we find we don't like who we are?"

"Then we make changes and try to put right the things that went wrong. We don't lop off an arm or leg because it hurts, and we can't just cut out a chunk of our past if we happen not to like it."

"Then why did you bring me here?"

He propped himself on one elbow and looked down at her. Her face remained flushed from lovemaking, but the light in her beautiful blue eyes was bruised with pain. "Because I see you struggling to regain your focus, and I hoped a new scene, new faces, might help. And because I'm a selfish bastard who wanted you all to myself for a couple of days."

"I wanted that, as well." She sighed tremulously. "I wish we could stay here. I wish we never had to go back to Pantelleria."

"Can you tell me what it is about the place that disturbs you so?"

"I feel too…confined. My entire life has narrowed to what lies within the walls of the villa, and it's suffocating me."

It hadn't always been like that, but for her own sake, it had to be that way now. There wasn't a soul on the island who hadn't heard about the accident and the circumstances surrounding it. It had been all anyone had talked about for weeks. Left to roam about at will as she once had, she'd be recognized and, if there was a greater risk than his telling her all that had come to pass, it was having her hear it from someone else.

"There's something about the place that haunts me," she went on, with a tiny, helpless shudder. "It's as if something dark and fearful is lurking in the corner, waiting to jump out and destroy me. I wish, if you know what it is, that you'd just tell me."

"It might be that we argued and said some hurtful things to each other, the last time we were together before the accident."

"What kind of things?"

"Outside commitments. My obligations as a businessman and a husband, yours as my wife. Loyalties, priorities, casting blame, and misunderstandings in general." He shrugged. "It's not something I'm very proud to look back on."

She regarded him in sudden hope. "Is that how the car crash came about—we argued, I got upset and drove off, and you're afraid I'll blame you for letting me go when I was in no fit state to drive?"

He wished he'd kept his mouth shut because, at this rate, she'd stumble on the truth before much longer, and he wasn't sure he'd know how to handle the fallout. "No. I wasn't on the island the day that happened. I was in Milan."

"Oh," she said thoughtfully. "Then who was driving?"

Dio, the one question he'd hoped to avoid! "A summer visitor who'd rented a nearby villa for a few weeks. I can't tell you much more than that."

"But—"

Loath to continue a subject painfully fraught with conjecture, he took her hand and urged it down his belly to cradle him, knowing her touch was all it would take to make him hard again. "But nothing, *amore mio!*" he muttered against her mouth, tormenting her in deliberate seduction exactly as she was tormenting him, because it was the only way he could think of to silence her questions. "Why are we talking about other people, when a second honeymoon should be only about a man and his bride?"

She responded as he'd hoped she would. "I don't know," she gasped, her eyes glazing with pleasure as he found the erogenous spot between her legs.

He stroked her until she came, and when at last he took her completely, burying himself deep in her soft, welcoming depths, it was with something approaching desperation, as if by doing so he might bury his own doubts, as well as hers.

Because she wasn't the only one afraid that the truth might smash their newfound happiness into oblivion.

She must have drifted to sleep in his arms because when next she opened her eyes, darkness had fallen and Dario was gone, but a patch of light from the open bathroom door and the sound of running water told her where she might find him.

With a boldness that would have shocked her a week ago, she went to join him. A towel slung around his hips, he stood before one of the two hand-painted wash bowls, scraping a razor over his soap-lathered jaw. Drops of water glinted in his thick hair and sparkled on his shoulders.

"*Ciao,* sleepyhead," he crooned, inspecting her naked body with such unabashed appreciation that she blushed from head to toe. "*Venire qui e darmi un bacio.* Come and give me a kiss."

"Not a chance," she squealed, ducking away as he advanced on her with the clear intention of smearing shaving soap all over as much of her as he could reach.

He was quicker though, and cornered her in the big double shower stall. In the ensuing scuffle, his towel slipped its anchor and fell off. Feigning dismay at the sight of his virile proportions, she shielded her eyes. "Oh, dear! I didn't mean to have *that* kind of effect on you."

Laughing, he pinned her against the tiled wall and turned on the cold water, full force. "Sure you did, *la mia principessa nuda,* and now you'll have to pay the price."

"Stop!" she shrieked, goose bumps the size of raisins puckering her skin under the chilly blast. "There has to be a more humane way to resolve the issue that's…um, arisen between us."

"In fact there is, and believe me I'd resort to it in a flash if I hadn't made a dinner reservation that leaves us only half an hour to dress and get to the restaurant." He slapped her playfully on the bottom. "So hop to it, honey, as they say in your country, and we'll resume this discussion later."

The dinner dress she'd brought with her was one she'd come across by accident, stashed at the back of her closet behind all the others, many of them still too large for her. Long and black, with a narrow skirt and silver embroidery along the neckline and at the hem, it was chic and elegant without being overly formal. A gauzy wrap spattered with tiny silver stars, silver sandals and matching clutch purse, and white-gold hoop earrings completed the ensemble, and from Dario's low, drawn-out whistle when he saw her, she'd chosen well.

He took her to a wonderful restaurant in the very heart of the Medina. Hundreds of years old, it oozed pure exotic atmosphere with its flowing draperies, brass oil lamps, and pointed arches fronted by gilt lattices reminiscent of the kind seen in old Hollywood spy movies.

Taking off their shoes, they sat on rush matting on a raised platform and dined on fresh Mediterranean lobster and succulent lamb flavored with coriander and saffron, accompanied by traditional couscous and a fine local wine. This last surprised Maeve, not just because of its quality, but that it was available at all.

"Alcohol's allowed because Islamic law isn't adhered to quite as rigidly in Tunisia as in other Muslim countries,"

Dario explained, when she commented. "Most restaurants serve wine, at least in the city, probably a leftover custom from French colonial times. How's your lamb, by the way?"

"Can't you tell?" She closed her eyes in pure enjoyment. She'd been too hot to eat much during the day and was starving. "It's delectable, and so is the lobster."

"Make sure you leave room for dessert. They have first-rate honey cakes stuffed with dates on the menu, as well as honey and almonds in layers of pastry like Greek baklava, except they call it baklawa here. With your sweet tooth, you'll probably want to try some of both."

"You seem to know the place pretty well. Do I take it this isn't your first visit?"

"I've been here a time or two, yes," he admitted. "Back in my wild bachelor days, before I met you."

"Hmm." She pursed her lips and looked teasingly at him from the corner of her eye. "I don't think I want to know about that."

"There's nothing much to tell. Being here now with you is far more memorable."

"For me, too. I'm enjoying myself so much, Dario."

He lifted her hand to his lips and kissed her fingertips. "Then we'll come back another time, stay longer and ride camels in the Sahara."

"I'm not sure I'm ready for that. I've never even been on a horse."

"You've probably never tried belly dancing, either, but there's a first time for everything," he said, pointing to where a team of young women appeared from behind a curtain.

They began to weave their sinuous way across the floor,

watched by men lounging against the walls and smoking hookah pipes. The music, provided by a quartet clad in bedouin robes, consisted of a sort of zither, a simple recorder, a small hand drum and a tambourine. Even to Maeve's untutored ear, the repetitive melody and persistent rhythm bore an unmistakably Arabic flavor.

The dancers wore wide, filmy pajama bottoms and bralike tops draped with gold-beaded fringes that shimmied with every undulation. In view of the amount of skin exposed between the two, how the bottoms stayed up and tops stayed on was nothing short of amazing.

Noting her absorbed interest in the spectacle, Dario said with an evil grin, "Would you like me to ask if they'll give you a lesson, my dear? I'm sure they'd be happy to oblige."

"Okay—if you'll try a hookah pipe."

"Sorry, I don't smoke."

"Then I don't shimmy," she said, and settled in the curve of his arm, content to watch the show, nibble baklawa, and sip Tunisian brandy made from figs and Turkish-style coffee served in tiny cups.

They left the restaurant slightly before eleven o'clock. Tunis after sundown was something of a surprise, she discovered. Instead of rushing around as they had during the day, people sat peacefully wherever they happened to find themselves, whether it be a park bench or their own doorstep, talking quietly as they recovered from the intense heat of the day.

Once back at the hotel, Maeve leaned against the wall of their suite's little terrace and gazed out at the nighttime view. Directly ahead, the dark mass of the sea rolled somnolently ashore. To her right, floodlit domes and minarets made up the city skyline. "This has been the experience of a lifetime, Dario," she told him, her senses alive with all she'd seen and heard and tasted. "I feel as if I'm living a scene from *One Thousand and One Nights*."

Standing behind her, he lowered the zipper on her dress slightly and pressed a hot, openmouthed kiss on her exposed shoulder. The tactile impact reverberated all the way to the soles of her feet.

"And this particular night isn't yet over. As I recall, we have unfinished business to attend to," he murmured. "Slip into something more comfortable, *mio dolce,* while I order us a bottle of champagne."

But she didn't need champagne to set the mood, any more than she needed the peignoir she'd so carefully included in her suitcase. The wine grew warm, the negligee spent the night on the floor in a heap of white lace, and Dario loved her with an inventiveness and passion that stole her breath away.

He explored every inch of her, cherishing her toes, her instep, the soft, sensitive skin at the back of her knees. He kissed her breasts, swirled his tongue at her navel, buried his mouth between her legs.

He made her tremble and shudder. And when she thought she'd slide into madness from the sheer exquisite ache of wanting, he'd sidle against her, then retreat before she could imprison him within the folds of her eager flesh.

When finally he took possession of her, she contracted around him in endless spasms of ecstasy that racked her body and left it glistening with sweat. But when at last he climaxed and took her with him yet again, it was glorious: a wild, delirious ride to the ends of the earth and back again.

Limp and spent, she collapsed in his arms, knowing that no matter what the future held, this was a night she would never forget.

She slept like a child, utterly relaxed, her body warm and soft, her breathing smooth and even. Her hair curled damply on her forehead. Her lashes lay thick against her cheek. Her hand curled trustingly on his chest.

Had he somehow effected a miracle? Dario wondered. Could a weekend of hot sex and romance mend a marriage that had grown progressively shakier with each passing month and culminated in a row that had almost cost her her life?

Unwilling to get down to specifics, he'd been deliberately vague when she'd asked what their last argument had been about, before the accident. But far from fading over time, the details remained sharp in his mind, stained with guilt and ugly suspicion.

It had started the first weekend in August when he came home from an unusually long business trip to Australia. The previous summer, after he'd brought Maeve to Italy as his bride, he'd explained that his work involved a lot of travel and they'd agreed it made sense for her to remain in the penthouse in Milan during his absences. His family was close by, and so was her obstetrician. After Sebastiano was born at the end of January, however, she began spending increasing time on Pantelleria, whether or not Dario was out of town.

"It's more relaxed here," she explained, when he asked her about it. "I'm under less social pressure and have more time to enjoy my baby. You're so busy during the week that we hardly see each other, anyway, but if you fly down on

Friday evening and stay until Monday morning, we can at least be together then."

What she didn't say, but which he knew to be true, was that she wanted to escape his mother, who doted on her new grandson, but made no secret of her aversion to Maeve. "She's a spineless nobody who entrapped our son, and not the daughter-in-law I hoped for," he'd overheard Celeste remark to his father, during one of her periodic visits to corporate headquarters.

"You weren't the daughter-in-law my mother envisaged, either," his father had replied, "but she finally accepted you, and I suggest you learn from her example. Dario's his own man, just as I was. He's made his choice, and from everything I see, done not too badly for himself."

But in May and the onset of hotter weather, the entire Costanzo clan moved to their summer homes on Pantelleria. Like him, his father and brother-in-law spent the week in Milan and joined their families on the weekend, leaving the women to keep each other company the rest of the time. And that's when the rot really set in. Giuliana and Maeve had connected from the first and grown close as sisters. But his mother and Maeve were a whole other story, as Dario learned on his return from Australia.

Celeste wasted no time airing her grievances and cornered him in the garden his first day back. "She's inexperienced and should be grateful for my help," she complained, referring to a confrontation that had taken place a few days earlier to do with what she perceived to be Maeve's inept mothering skills. "I know what's best for my grandson."

"You need to take a step back and stop interfering,"

Dario informed her flatly. "And stop trying to undermine Maeve's self-confidence, as well, while you're at it."

"I'd have thought you'd appreciate my keeping an eye on her when you're not here," she retaliated. "All things considered."

He wasn't about to give her satisfaction by asking what *all things considered* amounted to. "She doesn't need anyone keeping an eye on her in my absence. I trust her judgment implicitly."

"A little too much, if you ask me," his mother said ambiguously, and when he responded by starting to walk away, stopped him short by bringing up the subject of Yves Gauthier, a man new to the island of whom Dario had previously been only vaguely aware.

"He's Canadian, just like her," Celeste continued scornfully, "and calls himself an artist, although not one any of us has ever heard of. He's leased the Belvisi place for the summer, but it's no secret that while you were away, he was seen more often at your home than his own. From all appearances, he and your wife have become, shall we say for want of a better description, very close *friends*."

Still refusing to rise to the intended bait, Dario said, "Not surprising. They share a common background."

His mother sniffed disparagingly. "'Common' being the operative word."

"I'd have thought that by now you'd learned your lesson and knew better than to go around stirring up trouble where none exists," he told her sharply. "It didn't work when you tried it with Giuliana and Lorenzo, and it won't work now. Maeve is my wife and the mother of my son, and that's never going to change."

She lifted her shoulders in her signature elegant shrug.

"If that's really what you want, then at least let me say this. It's just as well you're planning to take a break from the office and spend a week or two here because, whether or not you believe me, Yves Gauthier needs to be reminded of his proper place, and it is not making himself at home on your territory."

Dario had laughed, and accused her of letting her imagination run away with her, but the seed of doubt had been planted. He began to notice how frequently Maeve brought up Gauthier's name in conversation, and how the Canadian had insinuated himself into their tight social circle.

Dario had never been jealous of another man in his life. The women he'd dated in the past had never given him cause to be. That, as a husband, he found himself at the mercy of such demeaning weakness now both shamed and infuriated him.

Determined not to let it gain the upper hand, he did his best to stamp it out, but it got the better of him just three days into his supposed vacation time, when he and his parents were recalled to the head office for an emergency meeting of the board of directors. Giuliana and Lorenzo, the other two involved, were visiting friends in Paris and flew directly from there to Milan.

"But you only just got home," Maeve complained, when she heard. "Can't they manage without you, for once?"

"Not this time," he said. "We've run into a major snag with an overseas operation that could cost us millions."

"But we never get any alone time anymore."

He forbore to point out that was as much by her choice as his, and said reasonably, "Come with me for a change. Show Sebastiano the city of his birth. Go shopping and visit the museums. It'd do you good."

"Tag along like an extra piece of luggage?" she scoffed. "No, thanks! I've had enough of being made to feel small and insignificant. I'd rather stay here."

He knew her run-in with his mother lay behind her response, and if he was half the man he liked to think he was, he'd have shown more understanding. But he had bigger issues to resolve. The company his great-grandfather had created was hemorrhaging money and it had to be stopped. So instead of giving her the reassurance he knew she needed, to his horror and later regret, he heard himself roar, "Well, at least you can always call on the obliging Monsieur Gauthier to keep you company if the nights prove too long and lonely."

She blanched. *"What?"* she gasped.

"You heard me."

"Yes," she said after a pause, her eyes welling with tears. "I imagine half the island probably did."

Doing his best to moderate his tone, he said, "You're not the only one who's tired of our being apart more than we're together, Maeve. If I wanted to live like a bachelor, I wouldn't have married you in the first place."

"Perhaps that was your big mistake," she said, struggling to keep her voice steady. "But since you did, and since you have so little trust in me, perhaps the best thing you can do is put an end to what was never a love match in the first place."

And leave the door open for some half-assed wannabe artist to move onto his turf? Like hell! "Regardless of the reason for our marriage, the fact remains that it happened, and I have done my best to make it work. You have unlimited freedom and the wherewithal to enjoy it pretty much however you please. So forget any ideas you have of walking out on it. That is not, nor will it ever be an option."

"Watch me!" she spat. "I don't care how rich and famous you are, I will not sink back into that pathetic, brow-beaten creature I once was, just for the privilege of being the great Dario Gabriele Costanzo's charity bride."

"I didn't marry you because I felt sorry for you, Maeve."

She swiped at the tears running down her face. "Oh, we all know very well why you married me," she said bitterly. "You had to do the right thing."

"Yes. Doing the right thing has always been important to me."

"Then how do you explain this?" Seizing a tabloid magazine lying on the coffee table, she thrust it at him. It fell open at a photograph showing him leaving a restaurant apparently in the company of blond, tanned beauty wearing a white dress so minuscule, it was barely decent.

"I can't," he said, tossing the magazine aside. "I won't lie to you. When I'm away, I'm frequently entertained by business men and their wives, many of whom are extremely attractive, but this woman is not one of them. I have no idea who she is nor, to my certain knowledge, have I ever so much as spoken a word to her."

"You didn't spend much time speaking to me, either, the night we met," she sobbed, "but that didn't stop you from—"

"I'm well aware how that night ended, Maeve. I made a mistake and I'm doing my best to live with it. But if you're determined to point fingers, let me remind you that at least some of the blame lay with you. All you ever had to say was stop."

Livid with himself and with her, he left her then, stopped just long enough to grab his briefcase from his desk, and strode out to the car. Within the hour he was onboard the company jet, headed for Milan.

The next afternoon the police contacted him. There'd been an accident. A car had spun out of control and gone over the edge of a cliff, some five or six kilometers from the villa on Pantelleria. Sebastiano had suffered minor injuries, Maeve was clinging to life, and the driver, Yves Gauthier, was dead.

CHAPTER TEN

GLOOMILY, Maeve watched as the aircraft gained height and headed due east over the Mediterranean. Too soon the Tunisian coastline sank into the hazy sunset distance and the black dot that was Pantelleria assumed more distinctive shape and color.

The day had flown by. She'd woken first and spent a minute or two inspecting the man she'd married. His face was more vulnerable in sleep, making him appear less the powerful business magnate. She loved the lean, firm line of his jaw, even dusted as it was with new-beard growth, and the way his black hair, normally so well behaved, spilled riotously over his forehead. She loved his strong neck, his dark, dense lashes that were enough to make a woman weep with envy, the sweeping arc of his eyebrows. She loved his mouth, its shape, its texture and its amazing talent as an instrument of seduction.

More than all that, she loved the inherent strength of him, the kind that had to do with something other than muscle and sinew. She might not remember their past relationship, but she knew instinctively that she could count on him. He was not a man to shirk his duty, renege on a promise or betray a friend. Although undoubtedly hand-some as a god and sexier than was good for him or her, his real beauty came from within, and that was what she loved most about him.

Love…a word so often spoken without thought for what it should mean, yet sometimes the *only* word that would do, even if she couldn't recall it ever having crossed Dario's lips since their reunion. Yet perhaps that wasn't so strange, given that although they'd been married for over a year, because of her illness she'd really only known him for the last few weeks. Was it possible to fall in love with him all over again in so short a time, or was the up-swell of emotion he aroused in her something her heart remembered, even if her brain did not?

He stirred, stretched and raised his eyelids to half-mast, as if the weight of their lashes was more than they could be expected to cope with so early in the day. *"Buon giorno,"* he muttered, his voice so raspy and sensual that she tingled all over. "You have the look of a woman with much on her mind."

"I was just thinking."

"About?"

"What I'd like for breakfast."

"Come up with any ideas?"

"Yes," she said, drawing the sheet down past his waist and very precisely placing the tip of her forefinger exactly where she wanted it to go on his very male anatomy. "I'd like you."

His gray eyes darkened. "Help yourself, *amore mio*. I'm all yours."

After such a start to the morning, the famed mosaics in the Bardo Museum, which they visited later, weren't nearly as impressive as they might otherwise have been.

"I don't want to go back there," she said now, the words falling into a silence broken only by the hum of the airplane's engines.

Dario looked up from the newspaper he was reading. "That's not what you told me yesterday. Yesterday you were captivated by Tunis."

"You don't understand," she said. "What I mean is, I don't want to go back to Pantelleria. Please, Dario, can't we go straight to Milan instead? I want to see my other home, and I can't believe you'd rather be trying to run your end of the business from the villa when it would be so much more efficient and convenient to be at the heart of things at corporate headquarters."

"Are you sure you're ready for such a radical step?" he asked her doubtfully. "Milan's a big city, and there was a time that you preferred the slower pace of life on Pantelleria."

"Not anymore," she said, with an inward shudder. "Antonia and the rest of the household staff have been most kind, and I don't mean to sound ungrateful, but I want to be around people who don't look at me as if I'm some sort of walking freak, or treat me as if I might break if I don't follow the exact same routine every day. Plus, we're almost into the second week of October now, and you said yourself there's not much to do on the island once summer's over."

"True. And with the fall fashion season getting underway in Milan, you'd enjoy seeing what's on the runway, I'm sure."

The chance to witness creative design at its most innovative transfused her with a well-remembered excitement. "Oh, I would!"

He rolled up the paper and regarded her thoughtfully.

"What?" she said, wishing she could read his mind.

"I'm wondering if there's something else you might be interested in, as well. Next Saturday is our company's annual benefit to raise awareness of *Parchi Per Bambini,* my great-grandfather's children's charity, which is as important today as it was when he first introduced it. There are now more than a hundred playgrounds in the poorer areas of various cities around the country, but not as many as we'd like to see, especially in the south. It'll be quite the gala occasion. How do you feel about attending it with me?"

"I'd love to."

"Think twice it before you say that. The whole family will be there, which you might find overwhelming since it'll be like meeting them all for the first time."

She grimaced. "Except for your mother. She and I, if you recall, already renewed our acquaintance with a singular lack of success, I might add."

"*Sì.* Except for my mother."

"Well, I have to face her again sooner or later, and the same goes for the others."

"You didn't feel that way a couple of weeks ago."

"A couple of weeks ago I hadn't rediscovered my marriage." Or fallen in love with her husband all over again. But perhaps it was too soon to tell him that, so she said instead, "I'm not the same woman I was back then."

"No, I don't believe you are. You're emerging from a chrysalis into a butterfly more than ready to spread her wings." He slapped the newspaper against his knee. "*D'accordo!* It's a date. I'll send for the company jet and we'll fly to Milan in the morning."

At last, no more marking time! Elation and relief fizzed through her blood like champagne. She was a step away from rediscovering the other half of her lost life; hopefully one free of covert glances from anxious domestics, and secrets hidden behind locked doors.

"Well, this is it." Stepping out of the elevator, which they'd entered from a sunny private courtyard, Dario flung open the double doors to the penthouse.

Maeve stepped into a small marble foyer and paused, more than a little dazzled by what lay beyond. If the island villa was luxurious, this residence was palatial. Gleaming hardwood floors and paneled white walls graced an entrance hall grand enough to host a sixteenth-century masked ball. At one end, a spiral staircase rose to a gallery, above which a beveled glass dome flooded the entire area with natural light.

Apparently unnerved by her silence, Dario touched her arm tentatively. "If you're concerned at being left alone, I'll cancel my meeting," he offered, referring to the in-flight phone call he'd received after they'd left Pantelleria.

"Don't be silly," she said. "What do I have to be nervous about? The place isn't haunted, is it?"

"Not that I'm aware of."

"Then go with an easy mind."

"The meeting shouldn't last more than an hour or two, but call if you need anything. My assistant will put you through right away. Meanwhile, pour yourself a glass of wine and make yourself at home while I'm gone. I called ahead and had the maid service stock up the refrigerator. Better yet, take a nap. We left Pantelleria pretty early and you're probably tired."

Tired? She'd never felt more energized in her life, at least that she could recall. "Really, Dario, stop worrying. I'll be perfectly fine."

"All right, then." He hugged her and dropped a kiss on her mouth. "We'll go somewhere nice for lunch when I get back," he promised, the look in his eyes suggesting lunch wasn't the only thing he had in mind.

"I look forward to it." She shooed him away, eager to reacquaint herself with her sort-of-new home. "Now go!"

She waited until the elevator doors whispered closed behind him before passing through the entrance hall and an arched opening flanked by marble pillars to the living room—except so mundane a term scarcely did justice to the gracious expanse confronting her.

Elaborate white moldings stood in stark contrast to walls covered with burgundy-colored silk damask. Oil paintings, some portraits, some landscapes, hung in heavy carved frames. Thick ivory carpets cushioned the floors. An ebony grand piano stood in one corner, its highly polished lid reflecting the graceful fronds of a tall areca palm in a Chinese jardiniere. The remaining furniture was antique, Italian provincial mostly, with the sofas and arm-chairs upholstered in cream silk brocade. In the center of one wall was an elegant marble fireplace. The remaining walls boasted French doors that opened onto a wrap-around terrace with breathtaking views of the Duomo.

Pillared archways on either side of the fireplace gave access to a formal dining room large enough to seat a dinner party of twelve. A magnificent chandelier hung above the long table, its crystal prisms shooting fiery sparks in the bright sunlight. A butler's pantry connected this room to a superbly outfitted kitchen with a small but charming breakfast room set off to one side. There, another door opened directly into the big entrance hall.

Upstairs were three bedrooms each with its own marble bathroom. A four-poster occupied pride of place in the master suite, which also had a recessed sitting area set up with two armchairs. More ornate white molding show-cased deep-ocher walls, with matching watered-silk drapes at the tall casement windows.

All comfort and luxury aside, though, the most inter-esting item, at least to Maeve, was a silver-framed photo-graph she found on a bureau. It showed her and Dario at some social function that required them both to wear evening dress. Although the camera had captured only their heads and shoulders, his black bow tie, starched white dress shirt with its pointy collar and the silk lapels of his dinner jacket were visible, as was the opal and silver or platinum filigree pendant nestled in the vee-shaped neck of her off-the-shoulder dark blue gown. Dario was suave sophistication personified, his smile dazzling and assured. Maeve wore the look of a deer caught in the head-lights.

"I had a lot more cleavage in those days," she mused, taking a closer look at the picture, "and a lot more hair."

A quick survey of her dressing room told another story. Numerous famous designers were represented in all their expensive glory, filling the mirrored closets with outfits to suit every occasion. Stiletto-heeled shoes, jeweled evening sandals and limited-edition ankle boots lined the shoe racks, with handbags to match on a shelf above. All were designer labels she'd long admired and even coveted, but never expected to own. That she did so now was, she rec-ognized, entirely thanks to Dario.

Overwhelmed by his unstinting generosity, she retraced her steps through the various rooms. His largesse went much farther than the contents of her wardrobe. The opulence surrounding her exceeded anything she could have imagined and quite how she'd managed to wipe all memory of it from her mind defied explanation. The girl who'd grown up in a tidy little rancher in east Vancouver had come a long way, and once upon a time such splendor would have intimidated her. Now the rich, warm colors and sumptuous textures seemed to fold themselves around her and welcome her in a manner that the cool blues and grays of the villa on Pantelleria never had. She felt at home. Safe and secure. Mistress of her own house, with no dark shadows peering over her shoulder.

Grateful beyond words for Dario having agreed to let her come here and for giving their marriage another boost, she racked her brains, trying to come up with a way to show her appreciation. She wanted to present him with something that didn't depend on wealth or position, both of which he had in abundance, but with a simple gift that came straight from her heart.

Finding herself back in the kitchen again, inspiration struck. As a teenager her other great interest, apart from designing and sewing her own clothes, had been cooking. Many a time she'd helped her mother make the big Sunday dinner, learning the importance of a light hand with pastry, the art of folding ingredients to create the perfect cake, and the secret of using herbs and spices to turn an otherwise bland sauce into a treat for the tastebuds. But as the wife of Dario Costanzo, multimillionaire and international business magnate, she'd never so much as made toast. At least, not in recent weeks. But as of today that was about to change.

Dario had mentioned having the maid service stock up on supplies, but a quick inspection of the refrigerator revealed only wine, cheese, grapes and coffee beans. Granted, there were oranges and bananas in a bowl on the granite counter, and a selection of crackers and biscotti in the cupboards, but that didn't exactly amount to what she'd call a well-stocked pantry, so she grabbed her purse and went shopping.

She found what she was looking for tucked into a narrow street behind the Plaza Duomo. A delicatessen with a few iron tables and chairs under an awning outside lured her over the threshold with the astonishing selection of gourmet foods she glimpsed through its open door. Braids of garlic hung from the ceiling. Olive oils, aromatic vinegars, foie gras, truffles and preserves lined one shelf; chocolates, another. Baskets of fresh bread stood on the counter. Trays of cooked poultry, smoked meats, cheeses and other dairy products were arranged in refrigerated display cases.

She made her choices and within the hour was home again, which, by her reckoning, left her exactly one hour more in which to whip together a meal and set the scene. She managed it all with minutes to spare before Dario showed up at half past one.

"What's all this?" he asked, stepping out to the terrace and surveying the table she'd set with dark green linens, white china and a small arrangement of white roses she'd bought from a street flower seller.

She handed him a glass of chilled white wine. "I made us lunch," she said, so proud of herself she was fit to burst. "I thought, seeing that it's such a lovely day, it would be nice to eat here."

"But I said I'd take you out."

"I decided to save you the trouble."

Mystified, he shook his head. "Costanzo wives don't cook for their husbands."

"This one does." She ushered him to the table. "Sit and enjoy your wine while I serve."

"We hire maids to do that."

"Not today," she said, and hurried back to the kitchen to put the finishing touches to the main dish.

Following her, he leaned against the center island and watched, bemused as she drizzled toasted almond slivers over chicken breasts coated with tarragon-flavored cream sauce. "I didn't know you could cook."

"Unlike you, I didn't grow up surrounded by servants, Dario. I can cook and clean house if I have to."

"Not our house, you can't. I draw the line at that."

"Really?" She angled a smile his way. "Were you always this bossy, or is it because I'm showing some independence that you're suddenly oozing testosterone from every pore?"

"Is that what I'm doing?"

"Well, let's just say you're being very much the macho Italian. It wouldn't surprise if, any minute how, you started beating your chest."

He lowered his lashes and favored her with an outrageously lascivious leer. "I'd rather beat yours."

"Behave yourself," she said severely. "And if you insist on getting in my way, make yourself useful and slice the bread."

"You'll be making me wear an apron next," he grumbled, brandishing the bread knife with an expertise that told her he wasn't quite as averse to the domestic arts as he'd like her to believe.

"An excellent idea." Not missing a beat, she took off her apron, a pretty flowered affair with a ruffle along the hem, which she'd picked up in an open-air market near the delicatessen, and tied it around his waist.

Abandoning the bread, he pinned her between him and the center island. "Now you've gone too far, *principessa*. It's time I taught you a lesson."

She tried to wriggle free, at which his pupils flared and a splash of color stained the skin along his cheekbones. "Know what it's like to make love on a kitchen counter, Maeve?" he inquired, his voice raw and dangerous with desire.

Breathless herself, she whispered. "I don't imagine it'd be very comfortable."

He kissed her so hard she went weak at the knees. "Then stop tempting fate and serve me my lunch. Your punishment can wait until later."

The uninhibited banter and passion of that day left its mark on those that followed. With no household staff to monitor their comings and goings, they lived like ordinary people.

She wore her bathrobe to make him breakfast, and if he sometimes pulled her onto his lap when she went to serve him his espresso, and the coffee grew cold as a result, she didn't complain. He came home for lunch and often didn't return to his office until late in the afternoon, again because, somehow or other, he became distracted.

Occasionally they went out for dinner, once to a restaurant at the top of a building so tall that it brought them face-to-face with the gargoyles on the Duomo. Another time he took her to an elegant place in the Piazza Republica where they enjoyed an exquisite five-course meal.

On the Thursday she went shopping for something to wear to the benefit. Despite the selection in her dressing room, the evening dresses were more suited for winter or spring wear, and the October weather was still mild. "Use it to buy whatever you want," Dario instructed, pressing a credit card into her hand before he left for the office that morning.

"You're spoiling me."

"It pleases me to do so, *amore mio,*" he returned.

She found the perfect gown in an atelier showroom on the Via Montenapoleone. Made from yard upon yard of ivory chiffon lined in silk, it fell from a strapless bodice nipped in at the waist to a cloud of airy swirls at her feet. Given her fair skin, she'd normally have chosen a deeper shade of fabric, but the delicate color complemented the golden tan she'd acquired on Pantelleria.

She didn't need accessories. She had the bejewelled sandals in her closet and enough evening purses to stock her own boutique. But her hair needed attention, and upon Dario's insistence, she made a Saturday-morning appointment at a very exclusive salon spa. Massage, facial, manicure, pedicure and hairdo, she had them all, with champagne served on the side, along with a tray of little appetizers to keep up her strength.

Such pampering! she thought, amused. In the old days she'd have fixed her own hair and painted her own nails, and done a creditable enough job of both. But tonight was too important for amateur efforts. She wanted so badly to be beautiful for Dario, and was desperate to win favor with his family.

When she emerged from her dressing room a few minutes before they were to leave for the benefit, she knew all the effort had been worthwhile. For once he was speechless and simply stared at her as if he'd never seen her before.

"Look at you," he finally said, his gaze roaming from the top of her head where the stylist had coaxed her hair into a smooth, upswept golden coil, to the jeweled sandals on her feet. "*Una signora cosi bella* and all mine."

"Does that mean you won't be embarrassed to introduce me to your family again?"

"Embarrassed?" He took her chin between his thumb and forefinger and dropped a reverent kiss on her mouth. "Maeve, *innamorata,* I could not be more proud."

His approval buoyed her up during the drive to the hotel where the benefit was being held. It sustained her when he offered his elbow and escorted her into the room adjacent to the ballroom, where a well-dressed crowd was enjoying predinner cocktails. It gave her the courage to meet the discreet stares of strangers, and fortified her enough that she was able to smile when he led her to a group gathered off to one side.

At their approach, an older man with thick silver hair and dark gray eyes like Dario's stepped forward.

"My father, Edmondo," Dario murmured.

"Buona sera, signor," she said, horribly aware of being the center of attention of just about everyone in the room, most particularly Dario's mother, whose expression suggested she'd been assaulted by an unpleasant odor.

"What is this *signor* all about?" his father exclaimed, embracing Maeve warmly. "You might have forgotten that you once called me *Papa,* but I have not."

His kindness, especially in the face of his wife's overt hostility, made Maeve's eyes sting with incipient tears. "Oh," she said, and cringed at her inane response.

"And my sister, Giuliana," Dario continued, bracing her with an arm at her waist.

"Maeve, *cara!*" His sister swept her into a hug that pretty much squeezed the breath from her lungs, but went a long way toward restoring her equilibrium. "I am so happy to see you again. You look wonderful, doesn't she, Lorenzo?"

"Sì," the tall man who was with her agreed, and brushed a kiss over both Maeve's cheeks. *"Ciao,* Maeve. We have all missed you."

Throughout the introductions, Dario's mother continued to observe her disdainfully. "This is an unexpected turn of events, Dario," she finally announced, in a stage whisper that probably carried as far as Pantelleria. "Are you sure it was wise to bring her here?"

"And you've met my mother, of course," he said smoothly, the chilly glare he bestowed on Celeste enough to turn her to stone.

"Yes." Rallying her pride, Maeve extended her hand. "How very nice to see you again, Signora Costanzo."

No affectionate hug from that quarter, or offer to call her *Madre.* Not that Maeve wanted to. Celeste Costanzo was about as far removed from the mother she'd loved so dearly as chalk was from cheese.

"Indeed," Celeste replied. "And may I say how very nice it is to see you more appropriately attired than when we last crossed paths."

The rest of Dario's family might have been happy to see her again, but any hope Maeve had nursed that she and her mother-in-law might make a fresh start died at that. Before the evening so much as got underway, the battle lines had been drawn.

CHAPTER ELEVEN

KEEPING an eye on Maeve, who went into dinner on his father's arm, Dario pulled Giuliana aside and, under cover of the general buzz of conversation surrounding them, asked, "How's Sebastiano? It's been over a week since I last saw him, but it feels more like months."

"He's fine, Dario. As I told you when we spoke this morning, we left him and Cristina with Marietta because we saw no point in dragging them all the way from the island just for one night. But earlier this evening, Lorenzo phoned her to find out how they were doing, and both children were already in bed and asleep. They'll hardly have time to miss us before we're home again."

"While his mother continues to live in ignorance of his very existence." Dario ground his teeth in frustration. "I don't know how much longer I can go on like this, Giuliana. I miss my son."

"But you have your wife back, and that's progress, surely?"

"I tell myself it is and certainly she's seemed much happier this last week. If it weren't for the fact that we have a child, I could let the past go and build on what we've got now. As it is, we're in a holding pattern, waiting for something to jog her memory, and who's to say what that might mean? She could decide she wants no part of me or our marriage."

"I seriously doubt that'll ever happen. She wears the look of a woman in love with her husband."

"Even assuming you're right, love based on misconceptions doesn't stand much chance of surviving, once the truth comes out. I'm deliberately keeping her from her baby. If the situation were reversed, I would find that impossible to forgive."

"You're following her doctor's advice, Dario."

"Barely. Sometimes I come so close to ignoring everything Peruzzi believes is the right way to go about things that it's all I can do not to simply tell her exactly how the accident came about, and let the chips fall where they may."

"Then why don't you?"

"Because it could destroy her. You and I both know self-esteem isn't her strong suit. Unfortunately, patience isn't one of mine."

His sister touched his arm sympathetically. "You must be doing something right, Dario. She's positively glowing."

"For now," he said. "But who knows how long that will last, once her memory returns?"

Weaving his way deftly through the crowd, Edmondo led Maeve to a table at the far end of the ballroom and handed her into her chair with courtly, old-world charm. "Here we are, *cara mia*. I'm putting you next to me in order for us to get to know each other again."

"And I," Lorenzo announced, taking the seat on her other side, "intend to do the same."

"I'm flattered," she said, and scanned the room, trying not to betray how jittery she felt. She was out of her element in this smart, sophisticated crowd. "Where's Dario?"

"Mingling with his guests for a change," Celeste informed her loftily. "In his position, he can scarcely remain so frequently absent from the social scene and not expect to perform double duty when he does choose to appear."

"I'm afraid it's my fault he's spent so much time away, Signora Costanzo."

"We are well aware of the reason, my dear," Edmondo said, patting her hand kindly. "His first duty was, and is, to you, his wife, something we all understand."

All except for Celeste, Maeve thought, silently berating Dario for suggesting she attend this blasted affair, then leaving her to his mother's untender mercies.

Some of her dismay must have been apparent to Lorenzo because he leaned close and murmured, "Don't take Celeste's words to heart, Maeve. Her bark, as they say in English, is much worse than her bite."

"I'm not inclined to put the theory to the test."

Giuliana arrived at the table in time to overhear their exchange and laughed. "Smart lady," she said. "It takes most people years to arrive at that conclusion."

Following close behind, Dario stopped long enough to trace a discreetly intimate finger over the exposed skin of Maeve's back. "Sorry I left you to fend for yourself, *amore*. How are you doing?"

"Better now that you're here," she told him, her annoyance evaporating in the warmth of his touch.

"I'm yours for the rest of the night," he promised, giving

her shoulder a squeeze before taking his place between his mother and sister as a hovering waiter began to pour the wine.

When all the glasses were filled, Edmondo stood up, cleared his throat and turned a benign glance Maeve's way. "This date has long held special meaning for me because it was my grandfather's birthday. I have always been proud of him for his efforts to improve the lot of those less fortunate than himself, and prouder still that my children continue to support the work he began. But I don't know that I've ever been prouder than I am tonight, when I look around this table and see my grown-up family complete again." He raised his glass. "I therefore ask you to join me in a toast to a very special young woman. To you, Maeve, and a full recovery very soon, *cara mia*. We have missed you."

Her father-in-law meant well, she knew, but the last thing Maeve wanted was to be the focus of everyone's attention. She hadn't liked it when she'd been singled out in high school, and she didn't like it now. In an agony of embarrassment she looked across the table to Dario, silently begging him to deflect the spotlight elsewhere.

He met her gaze and held it steady, his calm gray eyes telling her she was not alone, and that whatever surprises the evening might bring, he'd be beside her and together they'd cope. He made it possible for her to breathe air into her beleaguered lungs and unclench her fingers, which lay knotted in her lap. Because of him she was able to return Edmondo's smile, murmur her thanks and not mind too terribly much that Celeste barely managed to acknowledge the toast without gagging.

At length Edmondo sat down again, and general conversation resumed as a melon-and-prosciutto appetizer, the first of several courses, was presented. A delicate chicken consommé came next, followed by artichoke salad with capers brought all the way from Pantelleria, then scampi on a bed of braised endive. Before the entree, palate-cleansing basil and lime sorbet appeared in thimble-size stemmed glasses.

Somehow, Maeve was able to manage it all without dribbling, drooling, using the wrong fork or otherwise embarrassing herself—this, despite having Celeste watch her the entire time like a hawk waiting to pounce on a rabbit. Of course, it helped that throughout the feast, Dario also captured Maeve's glance and smiled a private little smile, one so loaded with sensual promise that she was almost able to ignore Celeste's hooded scrutiny.

Between courses, with a lift of one eyebrow and a meaningful nod at other couples gliding around the floor to the strains of the orchestra, he invited her to dance. She melted dreamily in his arms, her pretty dress floating around her ankles like morning mist, and lost herself in the spicy scent of his aftershave and the firm reassurance of his body pressed close to hers. She wished the evening would never end, at the same time that she wanted it to be over so that they'd be alone again.

He scattered tiny kisses against her brow. Held her ever closer and told her how proud she made him, how beautiful she was. And when the chandeliers dimmed and the music slowed to a sultry beat, he drew her closer still and whispered other things in her ear. Shocking, sexy, outrageously thrilling things not meant for anyone else to hear.

With his every wicked word, desire built, streaming

through her blood and leaving her body and spirits soaring. Suspended in breathless anticipation.

Perhaps she soared too high. How else to account for her clumsiness when she returned to the table after a particularly stirring slow waltz, and somehow managed to knock over Lorenzo's wine? One second she was easing into her chair, preparing to enjoy the medallion of filet mignon on her plate; the next, the glass was tilting in precarious slow motion and the contents spilling out to leave the front of her gown stained a dark purplish-red.

"Oh, my goodness!" she cried, mopping ineffectually at the river of wine still trickling into her lap. "Lorenzo, I'm so sorry."

"Not at all," he insisted with impeccable courtesy. "My fault entirely."

But it wasn't. She knew it, and so did everyone else at the table, except for Giuliana, whose seat was empty. A well-bred commotion arose: Dario summoning a waiter to rectify a situation beyond repair; Edmondo gently insisting such things happened and no one was to blame; Lorenzo apologizing needlessly, again and again. And a sudden hush from nearby tables as attention shifted to the drama unfolding at the Costanzos'.

Maeve shriveled inside and wished she could die. Aware of all eyes on her, the anonymity she craved again denied her, she muttered her excuses, stumbled awkwardly to her feet and fled, her brief Cinderella reign at an end.

The ladies' room, smothered in the scented silence of gardenias, was as elegantly appointed as the ballroom. Low white leather benches on spindly legs fronted a long marble vanity topped by a beveled mirror. Crystal wall sconces shed a flattering light.

Too much light! One glance at her reflection revealed with glaring accuracy in its unwinking surface, the extent of Maeve's fall from grace. Her dress was ruined. The wine had seeped right through the chiffon to the silk lining, putting paid to any far-fetched notion she'd entertained that sponging it with cold water might be able to effect a miracle. She could have wept.

Behind her, the door whispered open and to her added horror, Celeste appeared. *Ah, no,* Maeve thought in despair. *Not this, not now!*

Her mother-in-law glided across the thick carpet, subjected Maeve to a pitying stare and, without so much as a word, took a wand of lip gloss from her beaded purse and applied fresh color to her mouth.

Her silence condemned more thoroughly than any verbal attack she might have launched. Unable to bear it, Maeve said haltingly, "It *was* an accident, Signora Costanzo."

Celeste snapped her lipstick closed and leaned forward to inspect herself in the mirror. "You're rather fond of accidents, it would seem," she drawled.

Maeve sucked in a shocked breath. "Are you saying you think I did this on purpose?"

"I think you're a magnet for disaster, which follows you wherever you go. The pity of it is, it touches the people around you, as my son has discovered to his cost."

Chagrined, Maeve said, "Have I never managed to do anything right in your eyes?"

"You used to dress well enough at least to *look* the part of a Costanzo wife." Celeste's gaze skimmed over her, coldly, pitilessly. "Now you can't even do that."

Although Maeve stood at least three inches taller than

her mother-in-law, at that moment she felt herself shrink into an old, all too familiar insignificance. "I have tried to fit in," she said.

Celeste let out a snort of contempt. "You will never fit in. You're a nobody."

"You're quite right," Maeve said, stung into retaliating. "I was not born with a silver spoon in my mouth. I come from very humble origins. But my parents had their priorities straight. They understood what common decency was all about, and instilled in me a sense of humanity you completely lack. What kind of woman rejects another for something beyond her control? More to the point, what kind of *mother are you,* that you refuse to accept your son's wife?"

Celeste turned white around the mouth. "You have the effrontery to lecture me about how a mother should behave? You, who has turned over responsibility for her—"

"That's enough, *Madre!*" Suddenly Giuliana was there, inserting herself between them. "Not another word, do you hear? Maeve, *mia sorella la più cara,* Dario sent me to find you. Come with me now."

"No," Maeve said, standing her ground. "Not until she finishes what she started to say."

"It is not my mother's place to say anything," Giuliana insisted, grasping her by the elbow and marching her to the door. "This is between you and Dario. Let him be the one to answer your questions."

Shaking from the aftermath of her confrontation with Celeste, Maeve whispered, "How can I face him? This evening is such an important occasion for your family, and I spoiled it."

"You did no such thing." Opening the door, Giuliana

almost shoved her out to where Dario waited. "Get her away from here," she told him urgently. "In fact, get her out of town quickly, before our mother finds a way to finish what she just started. Enough damage has been done for one night."

He nodded, wrapped Maeve's velvet evening cape around her shoulders and ushered her from the hotel to his chauffeured car parked in the forecourt. Bundling her into the backseat, he climbed in after her, slammed closed the door and told his driver, *"A Linate."*

Linate was the airport where the corporate jet had landed on its arrival from Pantelleria, her island prison. "Are we going back to the villa?" she asked in numb resignation.

"No," he said. "We're going back to Portofino, where we began."

"Why bother? It won't change who I am."

"You're my wife."

"Take a good look at me, Dario," she said, throwing open her cape, while the tears she'd so far managed to suppress flooded her eyes. The city streetlights flashed intermittently over her ruined evening gown, turning the stain dark as blood. "I'm a pathetic misfit."

He folded her hands between his and chafed them. "It's only a dress, Maeve," he said gently. "Not worth getting upset about."

"Oh, it's about so much more than that, and we both know it. It's my life, disguised under a veneer of high-society money and sophistication to hide who I really am underneath. Your mother's right. I don't belong with a man like you. You should let me go and find someone from your own strata of society to be your wife."

"It's much too late for that."

"Why?"

He hesitated, and she realized how often he'd done that in response to her questions over the last weeks, as though he had to launder his answer before daring to utter it.

Beside herself, she struck out at his arm with her fist. "Tell me!" she cried. "If it concerns me, I have the right to know."

"Okay!" He threw up his hands in surrender. "But not until we get to Portofino. You've waited this long to hear the whole story. Another hour or two isn't going to make any difference to the outcome."

He'd called ahead for a helicopter to transport them to Rappallo, and for one of his sailing crew to open up the yacht and have a car waiting to drive them the short distance from the heliport to Portofino.

Maeve was shivering by the time they'd taken the dinghy out to the big boat and climbed aboard, though whether from the cool night air or sheer misery was hard to determine. Not that it made any difference to Dario. He'd held out long enough and it was time to come clean. Peruzzi could say what he liked about waiting for nature to take its course, but Peruzzi wasn't the one watching Maeve come unraveled.

Taking her to the aft salon on the promenade deck, he filled two mugs with the hot chocolate he'd ordered prepared, then carried them to where she huddled on the couch and sat down next to her. "Here," he said. "This will warm you up."

She brought her hands out from under her cape and wrapped them around the mug. "Thanks," she said dully. It was the first word she'd uttered since her impassioned plea for the truth, during the drive to Linate.

Her gaze flickered around the salon, and after a while she spoke again. "Is this room where we began?"

"Not quite. We spent that night on deck."

"Tell me about it."

So he did, leaving out nothing. No point trying to whitewash the facts at this stage. He'd behaved badly and she might as well know that from the start.

She sipped her hot chocolate and listened without interrupting until he finished, then said, "So we had sex the first night we met?"

"I prefer to say we made love."

Her face registered her disbelief. "How could I have done that? I'd never been with a man before."

"I know," he said.

"Being saddled with a novice couldn't have been much fun for you."

"*Fun* isn't the word that comes to mind, Maeve." Taking her mug, he set it with his on the low table in front of them and clasped her hands. "Even in your innocence, you were passionate and generous, and I couldn't resist you. But I admit I was taken aback when I realized I was your first lover. You were twenty-eight at the time and beautiful. How is it you were still a virgin?"

"I didn't have much time for romance. I was too busy building a career." She looked at him almost shyly. "I'm glad there's only ever been you."

Had there? Or would she remember another lover, before the night ended?

"So what happened next?" she went on. "Did we know right from the start that we were meant to be together?"

Hearing the sudden lilt in her voice, he averted his gaze. "It didn't happen quite like that. You left for home a few days later and I didn't expect to see you again. But I found you weren't easy to forget."

"Forgetting's always easy. It's the remembering that's hard."

Thinking back to the day he'd proposed, he had to admit that in a way she was right. He'd give his right arm not to remember what happened next....

Late on a stinking hot afternoon at the end of August, he stopped in Vancouver on his way from Seattle to Whistler. Tracking her down was simple enough. There was only one Maeve Montgomery, Personal Shopper, listed in the Vancouver business pages.

She lived in the city's west end, on the sixth floor of a west-facing apartment building in English Bay. The beach was littered with sunbathers soaking up the rays when he arrived. Mothers unpacked picnic hampers and spread towels over huge logs washed up by winter tides. Children held their fathers' hands and splashed in the shallow waves rolling ashore, their shrieks of glee occasionally rising above the muted roar of commuter traffic headed for the suburbs.

A pleasant enough spectacle of domesticity, but not something that held much appeal for him, he decided, searching for Maeve's name in the list of residents posted next to the intercom outside her front door. There were too many beautiful women in the world for him to tie himself down to just one; women who understood how the game of love was played.

Is that why you're here, because Maeve Montgomery's one of those women? The question came at him out of nowhere just as he was about to buzz her number.

He stopped with his finger poised. What the devil was he thinking? They had nothing in common, beyond a night they both wanted to forget. Why would she want to see him again? More to the point, why did he want to see her? For a romp between the sheets, when he knew that's all it would ever amount to for him? To boost his ego at the expense of hers, *again?*

Disgusted with himself, he turned away. At the bottom of the steps, a leggy blond in shorts and a sleeveless T-shirt had stopped to balance a brown paper sack of groceries on one hip while she fumbled in a leather bag hanging from her other shoulder. The setting sun silhouetted the elegant jut of her hip, the curve of her bosom, the rounded swell of her belly.

Preoccupied with finding whatever she was looking for in the purse, she didn't notice him. But he had ample time to study her and what he saw filled him with black despair. The woman was Maeve, and she was unmistakably pregnant. About four and a half months along, he reckoned, recalling how his sister had looked at that stage when she was expecting Cristina. And the last time he'd seen Maeve had been in April….

He'd reached a critical point in his revelations. Either he plunged ahead with a truth that the experts had warned could crush her, or he stopped now and continued to pray for a miracle that he knew in his heart was not going to happen. Neither the island, Milan nor seeing his family again had triggered her memory. Portofino had been his last hope that he'd be spared having to tell her bluntly how they'd come to be husband and wife. And it, too, had drawn a blank.

Cool night air notwithstanding, he was sweating. Ripping off his bow tie, he undid the top two buttons of his shirt, strode out to the promenade deck and leaned on the rail, his chest heaving. The moon slid out from the shadow of the *castello* atop the steep hillside rising behind the town, and shed a pearly glow over the bell tower of the Church of San Giorgio. Closer at hand the sea lapped gently against the yacht's hull. But overriding them all was the scene unfolding in his memory....

Unaware that she was being watched, Maeve had hitched her purse strap more securely over her shoulder, shifted the sack of groceries to the crook of her arm and climbed the steps, a set of keys dangling from her free hand.

He waited until she reached the top before blocking her passage and, removing his sunglasses, said, "*Ciao,* Maeve."

She stopped dead, shock leaching the color from her face. Her mouth fell open, but no sound came forth. Her eyes grew huge and wary. At last, making a visible effort to collect herself, she asked faintly, "Why are you here?"

"I'd have thought that was self-evident. I've come to see you."

As if "come to see you" conveyed a message vastly different from the usual, she tried unsuccessfully to hide her thickened waist behind the sack of groceries. "I'm afraid this isn't a good time. I have other plans for tonight."

"Cancel them," he said flatly. "We obviously have matters to discuss."

"I thought I made it clear the last time we were together that I have nothing to say to you, Dario."

"That was nearly five months ago. Much has changed since then. For a start, you're pregnant."

"What's that got to do with anything?"

"Plenty, if, as I have reason to suspect, it's my baby you're carrying."

She tilted her chin proudly. "Just because you happened to be the first man I slept with doesn't mean you were the last."

"Quite possibly not," he agreed, "but nor does it address the question of the child's paternity."

A crimson flush chased away her pallor. "Are you suggesting I'm the kind of woman who doesn't know who her baby's father is?"

"No," he said pleasantly. "You came up with that improbable scenario all by yourself. And we both know you're lying because that same kind of woman doesn't wait until she's twenty-eight to part with her virginity."

"I'm twenty-nine now. Old enough to live my life without your help, so please go back to wherever you came from."

"I don't care if you're a hundred," he snarled, infuriated by her attitude. "I'm going nowhere until we've established if I'm the one who got you pregnant, so hand over your groceries, lead the way to your apartment, and let's continue this conversation someplace a little less public."

"Don't order me around. I'm not your servant."

"No," he said wearily. "But we both know you're the mother of my child, and whether or not you like it, that gives me the right to a lot more than you appear willing to recognize, so quit stalling and open the damned door."

She complied with a singular lack of grace and rode the elevator to the sixth floor in mutinous silence. Once in her apartment, she flung open the doors to the balcony to let in what little breeze came off the water, then spun around to face him. "All right, now what?"

"Now we talk like reasonable adults, beginning with your admitting the baby's mine."

"I was under the impression you'd already made up your mind you knew the answer to that."

"Nevertheless, I want to hear *you* acknowledge it."

"Fine." She slumped wearily onto a padded ottoman and eased off her sandals. "Congratulations. You're about to become a daddy, though quite how you managed it is something I'm still trying to figure out."

"The same way most men do," he said, her sulky indignation all at once leaving him hard-pressed not to smile. Which would have been inappropriate in more ways than one. She was in no mood to be teased, and there was nothing remotely amusing about the predicament they were facing.

"I didn't think a woman was likely to get pregnant her first time. In any case, you used a condom."

"Not quite soon enough, I'm afraid, and for that I have only myself to blame. I knew better than to run such a risk. My only excuse, and a poor one at that, is that I found you irresistible."

"Oh, please! Once it was over, you couldn't wait to be rid of me. The fact that you didn't once bother to contact me afterward is proof enough of that. Which brings me back to my original question. Why are you here?"

"You weren't as forgettable as you seem to assume. I was passing through the city and decided to look you up. Now that I am here, however, the question uppermost in my mind is, when were you planning to tell me about the pregnancy?"

"I wasn't. All you were interested in was a one-night stand, not a lifetime of responsibility."

"I might be every kind of cad you care to name, Maeve,

but I'm not completely without conscience. You could have contacted me at any time through the Milan office, and I would have come to you."

"What makes you think I wanted you? I already have everything necessary to give my baby a nice, normal life."

"Not quite," he said. "You don't have a husband."

"I won't be the first single mother in town. Thousands of women take on the job every day and do it very well."

"Some mothers have no other choice, but you can't seriously believe a child isn't better off with two parents to love and care for him."

"No," she admitted, after a moment's deliberation. "If you want to be part of this baby's life, I won't try to stop you."

"How very generous of you," he said drily. "But explain to me if you will how that's going to work, with your living here and my being in Italy? A child is not a parcel to be shipped back and forth between us."

"You have a better solution?"

"Of course. We form a merger."

"Merger? As in, another company to add to your corporate assets?"

"Marry, then, if you prefer."

"What I'd prefer," she said tightly, bright spots of color dotting her cheeks, "is for you to take your *merger* and leave—preferably by way of a flying leap off the balcony!"

"I'm making you an honorable offer, Maeve."

"And I'm declining. I'm no more interested in acquiring a reluctant husband than I'm quite sure you are in being saddled with a wife."

He looked at her. At her long, elegant legs, her shining blond hair, the fine texture of her skin and the brilliant blue of her eyes. She was beautiful, desirable, but so were any number of other women, none of whom had spurred him to relinquish his bachelor state in favor of married life. What made her forever different was the bulge beneath her T-shirt for which he was responsible. And in his book, that left him with only one choice.

"It's no longer just about us and what we want," he said. "Like it or not, we are to be a family, and to us Italians, family is everything."

"Well, I'm not Italian. I'm a liberated North American woman who well understands that even under ideal circumstances, marriage is hard work. And you can hardly expect me to believe you think these are ideal circumstances."

"They are unexpected," he conceded, "but not impossible."

And so it had gone back and forth between them for the next hour or more until, eventually, he had worn her down and she had accepted his proposal.

He took her out for dinner to celebrate. She hadn't eaten much because a late meal gave her heartburn. He hadn't eaten much because the enormity of what he now faced sat in his stomach like a lead weight....

The rustle of her gown and faint drift of her perfume brought him back to the present. "Dario?" she said, coming to where he stood at the rail and placing her hand on his arm. "What's wrong?"

He blew out a tormented breath. How did he begin to tell her?

CHAPTER TWELVE

HE DIDN'T answer, but stood as if carved from stone and refused to look at her. Already at the end of her rope, Maeve shook his arm in a burst of near-uncontrollable fury. "Don't ignore me!" she raged. "I asked you a straightforward question. *What's wrong?*"

A shudder ran through him. He inhaled sharply, opened his mouth to answer, then snapped it closed again.

Never in her life had she physically assaulted anyone. The very idea sickened her. But at that moment Maeve's frustration was such that it was all she could do not to kick and bite and scratch and do whatever else it took to jolt him into responding. But no, she thought, her anger subsiding into despair. Not just responding. Telling the whole truth for a change.

"Listen to me," she said, struggling to keep her voice from cracking. "This has to stop now. The searching gazes, the pregnant pauses…I'm tired of them all."

To her astonishment, he let out a bark of ironic laughter.

"You think this is funny?" she gasped.

"No," he said, sobering. "Just an unfortunate choice of words on your part, that's all."

"How so?"

Pushing himself away from the rail, he squared his shoulders and faced her with the dull resignation of a man confronting a firing squad. "Wait here. I'll be right back with the answer."

She watched him go, her insides churning. She wanted to know everything. Wanted it so passionately that it was eating her alive. Yet at the same time, she was afraid, as if, in the deepest recesses of her mind and heart, she knew she wouldn't be able to live with what she learned.

He was back within minutes. Beckoning her into the salon, he switched on a table lamp and gave her a rather large white envelope. "Here," he said. "If it's true that a picture's worth a thousand words, this should tell you plenty."

Inside was a photograph, the second she'd come across in the last week, this latest of her and Dario on their wedding day. It was almost as he'd described it. Almost. She recognized the Vancouver courthouse in the background, her blue dress, the little posy of white lilies and roses. But he'd neglected to mention one not-so-tiny detail that leaped out at her and left her light-headed with shock.

Surely, she thought, groping blindly for the couch, it was a mistake? A trick of light, an optical illusion?

She blinked to clear her vision, and looked again. The picture trembled in her hand like a storm-tossed leaf, but the incriminating evidence remained intact. "Dario," she whimpered in a voice she barely recognized, "are my eyes deceiving me, or was I pregnant?"

"They're not deceiving you," he said.

Then that had to mean...

Her entire body froze, trapped in the path of a conclusion so gravely dark and terrible that to acknowledge it would crush the life out of her. So she attempted to deflect it by seeking escape in the trivial. *No wonder she'd sported such an impressive cleavage in the photograph taken last December. No wonder some of the clothes she'd found in her dressing room at the penthouse appeared so roomy. No wonder…no wonder…*

"And that's why you married me?" she continued, desperate to avoid uttering the word screaming to be heard. "Because you felt you had to?"

"Yes."

For weeks she'd begged him to answer her questions directly, and for weeks he'd edited the facts to spare her feelings. But now that she needed him to cushion the blow, he blasted her with a truth so painful that she cringed.

Scrutinizing the photo again, she said, "I guess that explains why you look so stony-faced."

"You weren't exactly radiant yourself. We had not planned to have a baby."

Baby, baby, baby…

There it was, out in the open, the word she'd so strenuously tried to ignore. And once spoken, it hovered in the atmosphere, a devastating, debilitating accusation that shot her from limbo straight into hell.

"What happened to it?" she whispered, caught in a web of indescribable horror. "Is that why I feel so empty inside—because I miscarried?"

"You didn't miscarry."

This time his stark reply pierced the heavy bank of fog that had been her constant companion for so long and shredded it to ribbons. They began to shift and part, letting in terrifying fragments of memory.

The salon grew dark and fearful, inhabited by ghosts that threatened to devour her. Moaning, she threaded her fingers through her hair and dug them into her scalp. Touched the scar now so well concealed. But the images and sounds leaked through its healed incision.

She relived the sudden jarring impact of a car leaving the road and careening out of control toward the edge of a cliff. Heard again the hideous shriek of tearing metal, the splintering of glass.

She saw the man beside her slumped over the wheel, and herself scrabbling wildly to release her seat belt so that she could climb into the back of the car, because her baby was there, imprisoned in his infant safety seat. Except it wasn't safe at all because the car was rocking and spinning, and she had to free him, had to get him out of there and save him, because he was her darling, her precious son, and she would give her life for him.

She saw the thin line of blood oozing down his pale, still face. Felt herself drowning in his terrifying, soul-screaming silence. And then the world was turning upside down, and the sea was rushing up to meet her, and there was nothing but darkness.

Until now, when the light of her failure shone too brightly before her and so many fragmented pieces came together to make a horrifying whole.

The locked room on the island had been his nursery, filled with magical things to entertain him and keep him safe. Mobiles and music boxes; soft blankets and tiny sleeper sets. A quilt she'd made before he was born. Lullabies she'd sung. Books she'd read to him, even though he was too young to understand the meaning: *Counting Kisses* and *Goodnight Moon*.

Oh, sweet heaven! Oh, dear God, please, *please*…!

The floor came up to meet her as she crumpled over, hugging herself to keep the pain from splitting her in half.

"Maeve?"

She was dimly aware of Dario sinking down beside her, his arms trying to draw her upright on the sofa, his voice layered with concern. In a fit of unprecedented agony, she sagged against him. "How can you bear to be near me?" she sobbed. "How can you bear to touch me? Because of me, our beautiful little boy is dead."

"Not so," he crooned, stroking her hair.

"He is," she wept, driven to near madness by her grief. "I remember it all." Her breath caught at the endless horror movie rolling through her mind. "Dario, I saw him."

Grasping her by the shoulders, he shook her gently but firmly. "Whatever you think you saw, Sebastiano is not dead, *amore mio*. Do you hear me? *He is not dead*."

"You're lying," she cried, flailing wildly to break free from his hold. "You've been lying to me all along."

"Yes, I have lied," he admitted. "By omission. To protect you until you were ready to face the truth. But I would never lie about this. I give you my word that our son is alive and well."

Her adorable baby, with his gummy smiles and big blue eyes, whose skin was softer and sweeter smelling than a rose petal, was *not* alive. He couldn't be.

"His car seat saved him, Maeve."

"No," she said brokenly. "I saw the blood. I saw it, Dario."

"It was nothing. A minor cut caused by something flying loose in the car from the impact."

His certainty, the ring of truth in his words, let a crack

of light into the darkness inhabiting her soul. "A minor cut? That was all?"

"Not quite. He suffered a bruised spleen, as well, and was hospitalized for a few days, but he's fine now. More than fine. He's thriving."

"Then, where is he?" she cried, her arms aching to hold him. "Why haven't I seen him since I left the hospital?"

"I sent him to live with my family until you were better."

"Your family?" She recoiled as if he'd slapped her. "If he's with your mother—"

"He's not with my mother. Giuliana has been looking after him on Pantelleria. He's there now, with her daughter and their nanny."

She hadn't thought Dario could shock her more than he already had, but the sheer audacity of his last disclosure took her breath away. "All this time he was practically living next door and you didn't tell me?" And to think she'd felt guilty about sneaking around behind *his* back! "How dare you!"

"Maeve…" He went to pull her into his arms.

She shook him off. "You kept him from me."

"From me, too, and if you think it was easy, you're wrong." He threw up his hands in surrender. "Stop looking so wounded. I did what I thought was best."

"Best for whom?"

"For you, Maeve. I thought—"

"I don't care what you thought. I want my son." The wretched tears started again, weakening her when she most needed all her strength. "Damn you, I want my baby!"

"Tomorrow," he promised. "We'll go back to the island first thing tomorrow."

"No. I want to go to him now."

"Be reasonable, Maeve. It's after midnight. There's no way we can get there tonight."

"Sure there is. You're Dario Almighty Costanzo. You can charter a jet as easily as other men hail taxis. You can make a child disappear so that no trace of him remains to remind his mother he ever existed. How do I know you haven't sent him away where I'll never find him?"

"Don't be ridiculous," Dario said sharply. "I've done nothing of the sort. On the recommendation of your doctors, I hid all reminders of him until such time as you, of your own accord, were well enough to cope with the events that brought about the accident."

"You had no right. You're not God."

"No," he said. "I'm merely your husband, as subject to making mistakes as any other mortal. In hindsight, perhaps I did the wrong thing, but at the risk of repeating myself ad nauseam, at the time, I thought I was acting in your best interests."

"When is keeping a mother from her child ever in anyone's best interests, Dario?" she asked bitterly.

"When the mother has been traumatized to the point that she has no recollection of giving birth," he suggested, then, regarding her steadily, went on, "Or perhaps if there is reason to believe that said mother intends to desert her husband and abscond with their child."

She stared at him, dumbfounded. *"Abscond?"*

"Run away," he amended helpfully.

"I understand what the word means," she snapped. "What I don't understand and certainly don't like is that you'd think me capable of such a thing."

"I don't like it, either, but the facts appeared to speak for themselves."

"What facts?" she said scornfully.

He subjected her to another steely gaze. "You had most of Sebastiano's things with you in that car, Maeve—his clothes, his favorite toys, even his baby swing—as well as a suitcase of your own stuff. You were with Yves Gauthier, a man who'd shown up out of nowhere in June and who'd insinuated himself into your life so thoroughly that everyone on the island was buzzing about it."

"We were fellow ex-pats. It was natural we should become friends."

"Was it natural for him to lease a villa for three months, then suddenly be headed for the airport within a few weeks, with a return ticket to Canada, via Rome, tucked inside his passport?"

"Did I have a ticket to Rome tucked in my passport? Come to that, did I even have my or Sebastiano's passport with me?"

"No. But in view of the fact that, the day before, you and I had had a flaming row at the end of which you told me in no uncertain terms to leave you the hell alone, you can scarcely blame me for entertaining doubts about what you had in mind."

"I remember our arguing," she said, the sequence of events falling into place with disturbing accuracy. "We fought because you wanted me to come back to Milan with you, and I said I wouldn't because that meant putting up with your mother forever interfering and trying to take over with Sebastiano. You said you hadn't given up your bachelorhood to live like a monk, and if that's what I thought marriage was all about, I was mistaken. You told me to grow up and learn to stand on my own two feet. And then you left—went stamping off without so much as a goodbye."

"That's more or less it, yes."

"I walked the floor all night after you'd gone, knowing you were right. If your mother bullied me, it was my fault for letting her get away with it, and up to me to put an end to it. But by running away from you?" She shook her head incredulously. "I was running *to* you. *To you,* Dario Costanzo, because I decided to be the wife you deserved, instead of sniveling in the corner like a whipped puppy."

"Then where did Gauthier fit into the picture?"

"He didn't. His only sin was coming by the next day to tell me he had to return home for health reasons. He had a heart condition that flared up again unexpectedly. I recall thinking he didn't look well and that it was a good thing he was going back to get treatment, but that's about the extent of it because my concern was mainly with you and our marriage. He had to drop off his rental car at the airport, and offered to give me a lift. He might have been en route to Canada via Rome, but I was headed straight to you in Milan."

"And that's all there was to it?"

"In a nutshell. But since you seem to have so little trust in me or my judgment, why don't you ask Yves yourself?"

"I can't. He died in the accident. In fact," Dario said bluntly, "he caused it, though not through any fault of his own. Apparently, he had a heart attack while he was at the wheel."

She pressed her fingers to her mouth, assailed by one shock too many. "Oh, no! I'm sorry to hear that. I had no idea he was so seriously ill. He was such a gentle person, so kind, and much too young to die."

"I'm sorry to be the bearer of more bad news. And I'm sorry that I doubted your loyalty. I'm your husband. I should have trusted you."

"But you didn't, and maybe the reason is that you were looking for an excuse to be rid of me."

"What the devil are you talking about? I married you, didn't I?"

"Oh, yes," she said, the memory of their early days together rising sharp and clear in her mind. "You put on a very good front, were every bit the dutiful husband, both in public and in the privacy of our bedroom, but a front is all it ever was. You proposed only because, when you found out I was expecting your baby, you felt you had no other choice."

"There's a strong element of truth in that, I admit."

She winced, and wondered why this admission, coming as it had on top of others much worse, should leave her feeling so miserably hollow inside. Hadn't she told herself, their last morning in Tunis, that he was a man of honor who would never shirk his responsibilities? Well, that she could still call herself his wife was living proof she'd been right.

"But let me point out that I didn't know you were pregnant when I went to the trouble of looking you up in Vancouver," he continued. "That I did because I cared about you."

She nodded sadly. "'Cared about' is certainly a nice, inoffensive way of putting it."

"What else do you want me to say?"

"That you were at least a little bit in love with me when you married me, as I was with you."

"I can't," he said, the candor she'd once found so disarming striking a fatal blow. "Love came later."

"Did it? You never once told me so. How do you think it made me feel that all the time I was falling more deeply in love with you, you never once said, 'I love you, Maeve'?"

"I'd have thought it was self-evident. If you remember as much as you say you do, you can't have forgotten the nights we spent making love."

"Sex was never a problem for us, Dario. The last few weeks are proof enough of that."

"It was more than sex."

"Not the night I conceived, it wasn't. You made that abundantly clear the next day."

"I know. And nothing I say now can excuse my actions then. The best I can do is tell you I will regret them for the rest of my life. I treated you appallingly for something that was entirely my fault."

"By seducing me, you mean?"

"Yes."

He looked so haunted, so miserable, that she felt constrained to say, "In all fairness, you didn't exactly drag me off kicking and screaming."

"That doesn't absolve me of what followed. All the signs of your innocence were there, if only I hadn't been too self-absorbed to recognize them. Your timidity, your almost catatonic submission…only much later, after we were married, did I realize that you always react that way when you feel under fire or inadequate."

"Was I very inadequate, that first night?"

"No," he said, his gaze soft and warm. "Your honesty and generosity were beautiful. They were what made you so hard to forget. You were like no other woman I'd ever known. I might not have planned to marry you, *amore mio*, but I can tell you in all truth, that I now consider it to be the best decision I've ever made."

"I want to believe you, Dario, I really do," she sighed. "But I keep coming back to the fact that you couldn't be honest with me. You let me think we were on a second honeymoon, when all the time you harbored suspicions that I was going to leave you and take Sebastiano with me. Although," she added, conscience again prodding her to acknowledge that she'd brought some of that on herself, "I suppose I did give you reason to doubt me."

"Does any of it really matter now?" he said, catching her hand and drawing her to him. "This is no longer about what happened in the past, Maeve. It's about you and me, and where we go from here. Mistakes have been made on both sides. Can we not learn from them, forgive ourselves and each other and start over?"

She felt torn clean down the middle, half of her wanting to hate him for deceiving her so well. And half of her simply wanting him. "I'd like to think so, but the way you cut me out of Sebastiano's life, and hid all evidence that he'd ever been born, and kept everyone else away from me…you treated me as if I'd died!"

"In a way you had, Maeve. You weren't the wife I thought you were. At least, that's how it appeared at first. But I know better now. I *have* known better, more or less from the day you came home again. And this last week…*mio dolce,* it truly has been a perfect second honeymoon."

"Really? Is that why you made sure there was no trace of our son at the penthouse, either?"

"There never was much to start with, and the few things you'd left behind I had put in storage weeks ago."

"What do you mean, *left behind?* Are you suggesting you still believe I was running away with him?"

"No, of course I don't. But he spent only the first few weeks of his life there. When you decided you'd rather stay on the island, you took all his things with you, making it very clear to me that you didn't consider the penthouse was your home. The few items you didn't take—some of his clothes and the bassinet—he outgrew ages ago. But if you'll give us another chance to be a family, I'll make a brand-new nursery for him so that he has his own room no matter which place he calls home."

He tucked a stray wisp of hair behind her ear. "What do you say, my love? Can we pick up the pieces and put them together to make it work for all the right reasons this time?"

"I want to," she admitted. "I think so. But…"

"But what?" he said. "Tell me, *tesoro,* and I'll make it happen."

"What I want most is to be with my baby again. Can you make it morning already?"

"Unfortunately not." He stroked his knuckles along her jaw. "But I can think of a way to make the time pass more quickly."

His touch, his voice, tugged at her heartstrings, disarming her. *Be careful,* the voice of caution warned. *You've been through this many times before, where all he had to do was touch you, and you were putty in his hands. But you're not an innocent anymore. You've learned the hard way that it takes more than great sex to build a marriage.*

But her heart knew better than her head. *It takes forgiveness, too. Love, real love, outweighs anger and disappointment. And you love this man, you know you do. You have found your son again. Happiness is at your fingertips, yours for keeps. All you have to do is reach out and*

*take it. Let yesterday go and celebrate a tomorrow that
promises true contentment.*

Sighing, she melted against him. Joy permeated her
soul. She felt alive, truly alive, at last. She wanted to feel
his lips on hers, his hands on her body.

"Show me how," she said.

CHAPTER THIRTEEN

MAEVE didn't complain about the slow passage of time again. From the outset, there'd been a powerful chemistry between her and Dario, a pulsing awareness that might not have been love on his part, but it had held them together during the rough first weeks of their marriage and it was what held them together now.

Not that she could have resisted him, even if she'd tried. He was too skilled a lover, too utterly, gorgeously seductive. Too everything. Any lingering resentment shriveled to dust in the heat of his kisses. His smile, the slumbrous appreciation in his eyes when he looked at her naked body, made her insides flutter as if a thousand tiny wings were beating to get free.

With no more secrets between them, and all the doubts and fears laid to rest, they had no reason to hold back all that lay in their hearts. Every touch, every glance, every whispered word spoke of a newfound trust, one able to withstand whatever fate might hold in store for them.

They had walked through fire and lived to tell about it. Through it all, sex had been their ally, stoking the furnace of their desire when all else failed to bring them together.

This time it took them further. Past raw physical need to a deep, quiet intimacy that welded them together seamlessly, in body and in soul.

"I love you, my beautiful wife," he muttered on a fractured breath, seconds before he lost himself in her clinging heat.

They were the sweetest words on earth, and she'd waited what seemed like a lifetime to hear him utter them. They were worth every tortured second, healing her as nothing offered by men of medicine ever could.

Dawn had traced a silver line across the eastern horizon when exhaustion finally caught up with them. Maeve curled up in Dario's arms and fell into a sleep no longer haunted by shadows. She didn't stir until the aroma of coffee brought her awake again.

Squinting in the shaft of sunlight piercing the room, she found Dario standing by the bed, dressed in casual trousers and a polo shirt, and bearing a tall, steaming latte cup. *"Buon giorno, innamorata,"* he murmured, his voice a caress. "Time to get moving."

She stretched drowsily and yawned. "Already?"

"If you want the early start you spoke of last night, then yes. We're leaving in half an hour. If, on the other hand," he added teasingly, "you want to spend the morning in bed with me, that also can be arranged."

"Don't tempt me," she scolded on another yawn, and reached for the coffee mug. "Give me a few minutes to make myself presentable, although how I'll manage to do so might be difficult since, unlike you, all I have at my disposal is an evening gown much the worse for wear. Thank goodness I have my cape to cover up the mess."

"Don't worry about it. No one will see you. I've ordered

a helicopter to pick us up here at the yacht and take us to Linate where the company jet's waiting to fly us straight to Pantelleria."

She took a sip of coffee. "I've changed my mind. I want to go to the penthouse to clean myself up and choose something more appropriate to wear for what I have to do before we leave Milan."

"What happened to the mother so anxious to reunite with her son? Last night all you wanted was to be back with Sebastiano as soon as possible."

"I still do. But I have unfinished business to take care of in the city first." She drew in a deep breath and looked him in the eye. "I've made a decision, Dario. I'm going to see your mother. This warfare between us does nobody any good and has to come to an end."

"But Maeve, *angelo mio…!*" He flung out his hands in a manner so quintessentially Italian that she almost laughed. "Are you sure you're up to such an undertaking?"

"I have to be," she said. "I'm a wife and a mother, not a child. It's past time I faced my insecurities for what they really are—weaknesses that only I can conquer. And the place to start is with your mother."

"If that's what you feel you must do, then I'll come with you."

"No. You've protected me long enough. I need to do this alone."

Talk was cheap when more than eighty miles lay between her and her adversary. Bearding the lioness in her den? Not quite as much.

"Thank you for seeing me, Signora Costanzo," Maeve said, so vibrantly aware of the other woman's scrutiny that it took a great deal of effort not to squirm. "I realize my visit has come as a surprise."

"Indeed." Celeste Costanzo nodded permission for her to perch on the edge of one of two white velvet sofas in a drawing room so tastefully furnished that it defied description.

How does she do it? Maeve wondered. How does she manage to look so perfect in cashmere and pearls, with no sign of last night's fracas leaving bags under her eyes, as Maeve was sure she had under hers? Does she never have a bad hair day? Never smudge her mascara or get a run in her stocking or break a heel?

Taking a seat opposite, Celeste crossed her elegant ankles, folded her manicured hands in her lap and waited, her finely plucked eyebrows raised in silent question.

She wasn't going to make this easy. But then, why should she? Maeve asked herself. When have I ever made things easy for her?

Shoring up her courage, she plunged in. "First, I should tell you that I've recovered my memory. I remember all the events of the past year, up to and including the accident."

"Then I suppose congratulations are in order."

Ah, me! Could she not sometimes give a little, for a change?

Burying a sigh, Maeve plowed on. "I understand your reservations about me, *signora*. I am, as you've so astutely observed on more than one occasion, a nobody, and Dario is a very rich man."

"What is your point, Maeve?" Celeste inquired, her icy demeanor remaining unmoved. "Are you asking my forgiveness for your shortcomings?"

"No," she said staunchly. "I've done nothing to require your forgiveness. You have a beautiful grandson because of me, and he, by any measure, makes up for whatever disapproval you might hold for his mother."

"Then exactly why are you here?"

"To set the record straight, once and for all, not about who I am not, but about who I am. I don't pretend to have come from the kind of privileged background Dario enjoyed, nor did I achieve the same level of education. However, I am not unintelligent, and most certainly not ashamed of my upbringing. I know the difference between right and wrong, and I have a deeply ingrained sense of fair play."

"And you're baring your soul to me now because?"

"Because whether or not you choose to believe me, there was no affair between me and Yves Gauthier. We happened both to be Canadian, and that was our only connection. I love Dario. I have from the day I met him, and I always will. We've not had an easy time of it, these last few months, but we *are* a team and I will allow nothing to come between us ever again. Not another man, not a near-death experience…and not you, Signora Costanzo."

"I see. Is that all?"

Was that grudging respect Maeve saw in her eyes? Bolstered by the possibility, she said, "No. If my son one day were to present me with the fait accompli of a pregnant stranger as a daughter-in-law, my initial reaction would be one of deep concern. Words such as *entrapment* and *fortune hunter* and *social climber* might occur to me, as I'm sure they have to you."

"Then we share something in common, after all."

"What we have in common, Signora Costanzo, is that

we both love Dario and we both love Sebastiano. I am not asking you to love me as well, but can we not overlook our differences and, for the sake of our families, forge a closer relationship, one based on mutual respect, if not affection?"

"I don't see that happening," Celeste said.

Her reply, spoken with such uncompromising certainty, reduced Maeve's hard-won courage to a deflated heap.

"At least," Celeste added, a hint of something approaching warmth in her tone, and her mouth almost turning up in a smile, "not if you persist in calling me Signora Costanzo."

She wanted to be called Mother? One day, perhaps, Maeve thought, balking at the idea. But now was too much, too soon.

"*'Madre'* would be a little premature, of course," Celeste continued with unnerving prescience, "but do you suppose you could bring yourself to call me Celeste?"

Maeve had been gone more than two hours, during which time Dario paced the floor like the anxious expectant father of triplets. He never should have allowed her to confront Celeste alone. He loved his mother, but he was under no illusions about her ability to reduce the most assured individual to babbling idiocy, if she so chose. And although Maeve was certainly no idiot, underneath her smart navy blue jacket and skirt, she was a fragile, vulnerable woman.

When she did finally show up at the penthouse, all she'd say was that she'd bring him up to speed later, but that her most immediate concern now was to get to the airport and head home to Sebastiano. Since he was equally anxious to reunite with their son, he called for the car to be brought round.

She settled in the backseat, a Mona Lisa smile on her face, and smoothed her skirt over her long legs. Grinding his teeth, he did his best to curb his trademark impatience. But when, some ten minutes later, they'd left the toll zone and were traveling along the Via Marco Bruto, no more than a couple of kilometers from the airport, he could contain himself no longer.

"You're going to keep me hanging until the last possible minute, aren't you?"

"Yes," she replied saucily. "It's my turn to be the one with all the answers."

"At least tell me it wasn't horrible."

She patted his hand reassuringly. "Do you see blood?"

"No, but nor did I expect to. My mother doesn't need a knife to inflict wounds. She can slice a person open with one look."

"Oh, I learned many years ago to withstand that kind of attack, Dario. You ought to know that by now."

"I'm beginning to think I don't know the half of it. When did my shy, defenseless wife turn into such a warrior?"

She leaned closer and kissed his cheek. "When her husband told her he loved her."

"How could I not?" he muttered, embarrassed to find his throat thick with sudden emotion. "You overwhelm me, my lovely Maeve. I know of no one with a bigger heart, and I thank God that you gave it to me, even if I was at first too blind to recognize how lucky I am."

"It isn't how you start out, it's where you end up," she said sagely. "We're together, and will soon have our son again. For me that means everything. Tell me about him, Dario. What's he like now? Have his eyes changed color? Does he still have lots of hair?"

"He's grown, as you'd expect, has two bottom teeth, one top, and is almost crawling. But his eyes are as blue as yours, and his hair as dark and curly as ever."

"I can't wait to see him," she said wistfully. "Do you think he'll recognize me?"

The car swung into the airport and drew up near the tarmac where the jet waited. "You'll soon find out, *amore,*" he said. "We'll be back on the island in a little more than three hours—just enough time to enjoy a leisurely in-flight lunch with Giuliana and Lorenzo, who are also headed home today."

When he stepped into the main cabin, however, he discovered his parents were onboard, as well. "This is unexpected," he remarked, noting the open bottle of champagne and general air of festivity. "I was under the impression you were staying in Milan for the next few days."

His mother nodded. "We were, but plans changed at the last minute."

He swung his gaze to Maeve, who appeared not the least taken aback by their presence. "You don't seem surprised," he said.

"I'm not," she informed him airily. "I invited your parents to join us when I visited Celeste this morning."

Celeste? Invited?

"Uh-huh," he grunted. "Anything else I should know about?"

Giuliana snickered into her champagne. No great surprise there. She'd always been a giggler. It used to drive him crazy when they were young.

"A little dinner party for six tonight," Maeve warbled. "I phoned Antonia from your mom's this morning to arrange it. It seemed only right that the whole family should be there to celebrate the grand reunion."

"A glass of champagne, son?" his father asked.

"I need something stronger, *Babbo*," he said. "Make it a Scotch, instead."

Almost midnight, with a light breeze lifting the filmy drapes at the open bedroom doors behind her, and the slate tiles beneath her bare feet still warm from the afternoon sun. Across the sea, lights twinkled on the Tunisian coast. The end of a glorious, momentous day, Maeve thought, breathing deeply of the sweetly scented air.

So many memories. Celeste smiling conspiratorially at her across the aircraft cabin. Dario's face, priceless in its astonishment. "People don't effect a coup like this and get away with it," he'd threatened her in an undertone, when they sat down for lunch. "You're safe enough now, but you'll pay for this later, once we're alone."

Arriving at the villa, to find the entire household staff waiting on the front steps to welcome her home. Flowers in every room. Her little niece, Cristina, adorable in white embroidered cotton and lace, planting a shy kiss on her cheek and calling her Zia Maeve. Enrica, the cook, taking her aside to consult on the dinner menu. "Does it meet with your approval, Signora Costanzo?"

Dario disappearing briefly, then returning with their son and placing him in her arms. To hold him again, to smell his sweet, clean baby smell, feel his breath against her neck, his chubby fingers clutching her hair, the warmth of his little body against hers, his wide smile not quite as gummy anymore…that was a heaven on earth made all the more unforgettable by the emotional response of those who witnessed it. Lorenzo and Edmondo blinking furiously. Giuliana sobbing openly. Celeste dabbing fastidiously at her eyes with a scrap of lace that passed for a handkerchief. And Dario whispering, "Look, *angelo mio,* he remembers you. Sebastiano knows his mother."

With a last glance at the star-studded night, Maeve turned and went on silent feet through the bedroom to the nursery. A lamp on the dresser sent out a soft glow, enough to show a yellow plush teddy bear sitting in the rocking chair near the window. She crossed to the crib and looked at her sleeping son. He lay on his back with his arms outflung.

"Perfect, isn't he?" Dario whispered, coming up behind her and slipping his arm around her waist.

"Perfect," she echoed, and pressing a kiss to her fingertip, she placed it gently on her baby's rosy cheek. "I love him so much."

Dario turned her away. "And I love you. Come to bed now, my darling, and let me show you how much."

She went with him, his words alone enough to unfurl the passion always lurking in her soul. She was home at last. The two people who meant the most to her were under this one roof.

They loved her.

She loved them.

It was enough. It was everything.

Joy spilled over her, rich and warm and forever.

HER SECRET,
HIS LOVE-CHILD

BY
TINA DUNCAN

Tina Duncan lives in trendy inner-city Sydney with her partner, Edy. With a background in marketing and event management, she now spends her days running a business with Edy. She's a multi-tasking expert. When she's not busy typing up quotes and processing invoices, she's writing. She loves being physically active, and enjoys tennis (both watching and playing), bushwalking and dancing. Spending quality time with her family and friends also rates high on her priority list. She has a weakness for good food and fine wine, and has a sweet tooth she has to keep under control.

CHAPTER ONE

"'HELLO, Alex." Is that all you have to say to me after disappearing to God knows where for months on end?' Alex Webber demanded.

He regretted the words instantly, not only because he had an audience but because they also demonstrated a rare loss of control on his part.

But that was hardly surprising, was it? He'd been caught way off-guard by Katrina's sudden appearance. Bursting in on him uninvited was not her style at all but, more importantly, she'd been missing for months.

Katrina Ashby shrugged her shoulders, sending her caramel-blonde hair rippling around her leather-clad shoulders. 'I suppose I should have added, *how are you*?'

Alex clenched his hands into fists. Although he wasn't a violent man, and had never lifted a finger against a woman in his life, he wanted nothing more than to stride across the room and shake Katrina until her teeth rattled.

After all of this time, how dared she turn up like this, out of the blue, and say, 'Hello, Alex,' as if nothing had happened?

His insides contracted on a burst of anger as week

upon week of frustration imploded inside him. At the same time, other parts of him were swelling as another far more primitive form of frustration made itself known.

Forget shaking her until her teeth rattled, Alex conceded. What he really wanted to do—even though he shouldn't—was to pull her into his arms and kiss her until she wrapped her arms around his neck and sighed her surrender into his mouth.

Aware they had an interested audience—several board members were openly gawping, others surreptitiously looking backwards and forwards between them behind the cover of hands and folders—Alex did neither.

'Out!' he commanded.

Body rigid and teeth clenched, Alex remained where he was as the board, five men and two women, rose hastily to their feet and competed for who could reach the door first. They knew their boss well. He rarely lost his temper, but, when he did, it was usually a major eruption. Able to read the danger signs, each and every one of them was eager to get out of the firing line.

When the door closed behind them, Alex moved purposefully towards Katrina. She didn't back away from him. She stood her ground and gave him look for look, with a glint of challenge in her eyes he hadn't seen before.

'I asked you a question,' he asked silkily when he stopped in front of her.

She angled her chin into the air. 'And I answered you. Hello, Alex. How are you?'

'I'll tell you how I am.' He stepped closer until they were almost touching. He could smell the scent of her perfume—a gift he'd had his PA send her for her birthday shortly before she'd vanished—and could see the little specks of golden-brown in her cat-like green eyes. 'I'm furious!'

She cocked her head. 'Why?'

'*Why?*' Alex thought the top of his head might explode; he could actually feel the blood pumping at his temples. He grasped her shoulders and put his face close to hers. 'Because you disappeared without a trace, that's why!'

She smiled. 'Without a trace? Isn't that the name of an American TV show?'

'Katrina!'

Her smile faded. 'I didn't disappear, Alex. I just decided to go away for a while, that's all.'

Katrina had always been the cool, collected type—except when they'd been in bed together. Then she'd been wonderfully abandoned, returning kiss for kiss, touch for touch and pleasure for pleasure with a passionate intensity that blew his mind and everything else.

Normally, he liked the fact that she was so self-contained, but today her calm demeanour annoyed the hell out of him.

'Without telling me where you were going or how long you'd be gone for?' Alex prompted through gritted teeth.

'I told the people who mattered,' she said softly.

Alex exhaled sharply, his teeth snapping together. 'And you didn't consider including me in that group?'

Her gaze remained steady on his. 'No. I didn't.'

Alex struggled to keep his anger contained. He knew he was overreacting badly but he couldn't seem to help himself.

'Why not?' he bit out.

'Why should I tell you?' she shot back at him, that

new challenging light in her eyes making them appear greener than usual.

His fingers flexed, digging into the soft leather of her jacket. 'Because you owed it to me,' he grated, the answer dragged from somewhere deep inside him.

Alex wasn't sure what angered him more: the fact that she had run out on him, or that she was the one to have betrayed him.

Of all the women he'd been with over the years, Katrina was the last one he would have picked to put him in this position.

'*Owed it* to you?' Her eyes flashed like quick-silver and the tip of her index finger dug into the centre of his chest, as if she was trying to bore a hole through to the other side. 'I don't owe you a thing, Alex. Not a single thing. And don't you forget it!'

Alex was stunned by her reaction. The Katrina he'd known would never have spoken to him the way this Katrina just had.

Pressure built inside his head until once again Alex thought the top of his head might explode.

Dragging in a breath, he fought for control.

He hated losing his temper. It reminded him of his father's monstrous behaviour, and the last thing he ever planned on doing was following in James Webber's footsteps!

He pulled her closer. Their bodies brushed and a surge of electricity powered through him. 'You're wrong about that. You owe me, all right. We were lovers, damn it!'

'*Lovers?*' She barked out a laugh, but there was no amusement in it. 'Don't you mean I was your mistress?'

Although she'd never said so, Alex had sensed on

more than one occasion that Katrina hadn't been entirely happy with the role she'd played in his life. Like most women, she'd wanted a wedding ring and children, despite the fact he'd warned her up front that neither of those things was on offer.

They weren't on offer to any woman. And never would be.

'I'm not going to argue semantics with you. The point is we were together for almost a year. If that doesn't earn me the right to be told you were leaving Sydney, then what does?'

Katrina tried to shrug out from under his touch. When he refused to let her go she glared up at him. 'The operative word is *were*, Alex: we *were* lovers. We're not any more. The last time I saw you, you told me our relationship was over. Or have you forgotten that?'

'No, I haven't forgotten.'

He hadn't forgotten a thing.

Not what she tasted like.

Or smelled like.

Or how she looked when she fell apart in his arms.

And certainly not what she'd told him on that last fateful day they'd been together. Each and every word was indelibly carved into his brain as if someone had put them there with a hammer and chisel.

Releasing Katrina, Alex stalked to the window where he stood staring out at the Sydney skyline, fists shoved deep in his trouser pockets, tension drawing his shoulders up towards his ears.

'You had to know that wasn't the end of it,' he said quietly. 'You were pregnant, for goodness' sake!'

'What's that got to do with anything?' she asked,

still sounding as cool as a cucumber, her eyes boring a pair of twin holes between his shoulder blades.

'What has that got to do with anything…?' Alex spun around to face her, blue eyes wide and incredulous. His fists clenched and unclenched against the silk lining of his pockets. 'Did you really think you could drop that kind of bombshell and not expect me to contact you again?'

She cleared her throat, and for the first time since bursting unannounced into the boardroom she didn't look quite so sure of herself; the challenge in her eyes was replaced by uncertainty. 'I'm not sure what to say. You were so cold that day. I honestly thought I'd never see you again.'

'Of course I was cold. I was in shock, damn it!'

'And do you think I wasn't?' Katrina demanded, voice rising.

Her words hung in the air like the residue of rifle fire, bouncing off one wall and then another.

Her mouth twisted. 'Oh, that's right!' She slapped an open palm against the centre of her forehead. 'How could I forget? You claimed you weren't the father.'

She looked at him as if she half-expected him to contradict her.

Alex stared stonily back, his silence answering for him.

'How can you believe that? We made love all the time. I could have become pregnant on any of those occasions, and you know it.'

'Aren't you forgetting one little thing?' he asked, dangerously quiet.

'And that is?'

'Protection,' he issued in a hard voice. 'I took care

of our precautions. Too many women have tried to catch themselves a rich husband by getting pregnant deliberately.'

That was obviously what Katrina was trying to do. But what made it worse, so, so much worse, was that she was trying to do it with another man's child.

She had to be.

Because Alex had an even better reason than the precautions he'd just referred to for believing the child wasn't his—a reason that was so strong it put that belief almost beyond question.

Her treachery bit deep, gouging at him with hungry teeth.

It had been there like a thorn in his side, slowly leeching its poison into his system and raising all sorts of questions in his mind.

When she'd taken him to the heights of passion had it merely been a means to an end? Had she been there with him on the journey, feeling what he was feeling, or had she been putting on an act while her brain had clinically thought about her forthcoming plan?

The realisation that what he had thought was real and beautiful might just have been a sham left him feeling empty inside—and angry outside.

She gasped. 'Are you accusing me of being a gold-digger?'

He shrugged. 'If the shoe fits.'

'Well, the shoe doesn't fit. I wouldn't have you even if…even if…' She waved her hands through the air. 'Even if you were served up to me on a platter with a million-dollar cheque in your mouth!'

Alex laughed; he couldn't help it. The suggestion

was so ludicrous he couldn't believe she'd actually had the gall to make it.

She lunged at him, hand arcing through the air. 'You cold-hearted…!'

Alex caught her hand and forced it back to her side before pulling her close. He'd never seen her lose her temper before. Her eyes were glittering with emerald fire, streaks of colour striping razor-sharp cheek bones. An incredible energy was emanating from her, so powerful he felt he could reach out and touch it with his hands.

A surge of lust—a lust he knew he should not be feeling—sent his blood roaring through his veins. He put his face close to hers. 'Don't push me, Katrina. I'm *this* close—' he held up thumb and forefinger with barely a hair's breadth separating them '—to doing something we'll both regret.'

'Don't push you?' she shouted, eyes so wide they dominated her face. 'Are you out of your mind? It's the other way around—don't *you* push—'

Alex silenced her with his mouth.

He hadn't planned on doing it; it just happened.

He kissed her savagely, his mouth hard and uncompromising.

Katrina stiffened until it felt as if he was holding an ironing board in his arms; her hands were like steel braces pressing forcefully against his chest. Alex fed a hand into her hair and cupped the back of her head, the other clamping around her waist at the base of her spine.

She tasted sweet, like the nectar from sun-warmed peaches, and as intoxicating as the finest wine. Something stirred inside him, something he hadn't felt since he'd last been with her. Something that not one of the women he'd slept with in the last seven months had evoked in him.

His mouth softened on hers and he began kissing her as if those months had never existed. As if she'd never told him she was pregnant and he'd never told her it was over.

His head spun.

His body stirred.

He was rock hard in under three seconds flat.

Katrina was the only woman who'd ever been able to do that to him. After all this time, and everything that had happened between them, Alex hadn't expected her appeal to still be so strong. But her effect on him was as powerful as it had ever been, if not more so.

Heart pounding, he ran the tip of his tongue over her lower lip then nibbled on it with his teeth, his hands relaxing until he was cradling her against him.

And slowly, oh, so slowly, the resistance melted out of her body. She sighed, her hands clutching at his shirt front, her lips softly parting.

Then she began kissing him back.

His kisses grew hotter and more demanding, his lips devouring hers, his tongue thrusting into her mouth to savour her inner sweetness. Heat seeped into his bloodstream until he felt saturated with raw desire. The world spun out of control, taking his sanity with it.

He was vaguely thinking about locking the door and carrying her to the long boardroom-table when Katrina began pushing against his chest again.

'Stop it, Alex!' she gasped, dragging her mouth out from under his. She was breathing so fast she could barely get the words out. 'Stop it! I don't want this.'

Alex lifted his head and stared down at her.

Her eyes were wide, the golden-brown specks gleaming, her mouth moist and kiss-swollen. A hectic flush had coloured her cheekbones, and scented heat was radiating off her skin.

She looked the way she'd always looked when they made love, and the familiarity of it sent a wave of satisfaction through him.

'Yes, you do.' He smudged his thumb across her lower lip. 'Do you think I didn't notice the way your eyes ate me up when you burst in here? And just now you were with me kiss for kiss. You're hungry for me—go on, admit it.'

Alex wasn't quite sure why it was so important that she admit she still wanted him, but it was. Important enough that a clamouring sense of urgency to hear her say the words was rising up inside of him.

Katrina tore herself out of his arms and stalked across the room, putting the length of the boardroom table between them. 'That…that kiss was a mistake,' Katrina said, wringing her hands together in front of her as if wringing a tea towel she was trying to extract water from. 'It shouldn't have happened.'

Alex opened his mouth to challenge the truth of that statement but just as quickly closed it again.

Katrina was right.

It *was* over between them.

It had to be.

Why was he thinking any differently?

Because he wasn't thinking with the head, he admitted grudgingly.

He dragged in a breath. 'I couldn't agree more,' he replied coolly.

She blinked at him. 'You…you agree?'

He nodded. 'Of course. I kissed you merely because I was trying to prove a point.'

Her mouth compressed into a straight line. 'And what point is that?'

'You claimed you wouldn't take me even if I was served up to you on a platter,' he drawled softly, refusing to admit the comment had dented his ego. 'That kiss just proved you'd take me any way you can get me. Only I'm not buying.'

'Why you arrogant, egotistical playboy!' she spluttered, green eyes flashing fire at him. 'Might I remind you that I was the one who stopped just now, not you?'

Alex was once again surprised by her outburst. Katrina had lost her temper twice since she'd arrived, something he couldn't recollect her doing even once in the almost-twelve months he'd known her.

'I'm not going to debate that with you. Now, you obviously came here for a reason. Maybe it's time we stopped talking about the past and got to the point of this meeting. Because, frankly, I don't understand what you're doing here.'

A mixture of emotions flashed across her face so fast he couldn't register what each one was. Her breath hissed out of her mouth. Without another word, she spun on her heel and stalked towards the door.

Alex frowned. 'Come back here, Katrina. This meeting isn't over. It's not over until I say it's over.'

She threw him a scathing look over her shoulder and wrenched open the door, disappearing through it before he had a chance to stop her.

Alex lunged after her, then slowed when he heard the murmur of voices. He frowned. It sounded as if Katrina was talking to his PA, Justine.

He was at the door when he almost collided with Katrina, who was coming back into the room.

She was carrying something.

Alex looked down automatically.

He stiffened. The air locked tight in his lungs, his heart knocking against his breast bone as if it was trying to shatter it. His body moved from stiff to rigid in the blink of an eye, as if he'd just been spray-painted with quick-drying cement.

Staring up out of what he now realised was a carry cot was a tiny, gurgling baby.

He looked up. 'What the—?' Alex dragged in a ragged breath, his eyes narrowed on her face. 'I— You—' He snapped his mouth closed, dragged in another breath and then accused harshly, 'You had the baby!'

Katrina frowned. 'Of course I had the baby.' She looked down and her mouth softened. 'Meet your daughter. Her name is Samantha.'

Katrina had never seen Alex speechless before, but that was certainly what he was now. His sensual mouth was working but so far no sound had emerged. At least, nothing intelligible. His blue eyes were fixed with piercing intensity on their tiny daughter, as if he'd never seen a baby before.

'Well, aren't you going to say something?' she asked anxiously, her hands shaking so much she thought she might drop the cot and its precious contents.

Alex lifted his head slowly, his gaze refocussing on her. 'I didn't know you'd had the baby,' he said, sounding dazed.

Katrina frowned. She put the cot down on the end of the table before turning back to Alex. 'That's the second time you've said that. Of course I had the baby. Why are you so surprised?'

He blinked and the dazed look slowly cleared. 'When you disappeared the way you did, I presumed you'd decided to abort the child.'

'What…what did you say?' she asked in a voice that was little more than a whisper.

Alex shrugged. 'It was the only reason I could think of to explain why you packed up and left the way you did.'

'You have to be kidding?' Katrina burst out incredulously. She'd never lost her temper as many times as she had during this meeting. But she'd spent months stewing over the way Alex had treated her, and he was doing the same thing again now: pushing all of the right buttons to send her anger into overdrive. 'I can think of a dozen reasons, and not one of them would be *that*.'

'Then why?'

'You didn't think I might have needed a friend right about then?' When he stared at her blankly, she gritted her teeth. 'I was twenty-two, Alex. Pregnant and alone. The man I loved had just accused me of trying to foist another man's child on to him. What did you think I was going to do—carry on as if everything was normal?'

His mouth curled. 'You're not going to try that old chestnut, are you?'

She blinked at him. 'What old chestnut?'

He waved a hand. 'Love. You just said that you love me. This is the first I've heard of it.'

Her heart resounded in her chest with the same boom as rolling thunder. 'I said *loved*, Alex. Past tense. And I didn't tell you how I felt because it was clear you didn't love me. Or want my love.' She laughed harshly, mocking her feelings and the dream that one day he would love her in return. 'Don't worry. I realise now that it was all an illusion. The man I thought I loved didn't really exist. He was obviously just a figment of my imagination, because he would never have treated me the way you have.'

'And how have I treated you?' Alex demanded in a cool voice.

She wrung her hands together again. She'd been determined to keep calm during this meeting but her anxiety and distress were getting the better of her. 'For one, he would never have accused me of aborting our child without telling him!'

'I'm sorry,' Alex said stiffly. 'It sounded like the most logical explanation.'

'Well, it wasn't. I needed to be with someone who genuinely cared about me. Someone who would give me emotional support instead of blaming me for the situation, like you did.'

He frowned. 'So you went to stay with a friend?'

She nodded. 'Just for a couple of weeks. Until I found somewhere else to live.' She gave him the kind of look that could curdle milk. 'I had no intention of staying in an apartment being paid for by you. So much for your claim that I'm a gold-digger!'

His remark had been totally uncalled for. She hadn't been happy about him renting an apartment for her in the first place. It was only when Alex had explained that its location meant they could see more of each other that she'd given in.

Alex stared at her through narrowed eyes. 'What friend?'

She angled her chin upwards. 'I don't think that's any of your business, do you?'

His mouth hardened. 'Just tell me one thing.'

'And what's that?'

'Was it a man?'

'No, it wasn't a man. What makes you ask that?'

He shrugged. 'It makes sense.'

Katrina frowned. 'It might make sense to you, but it doesn't to me.'

His piercing blue eyes bored into hers. 'I would have thought it made perfect sense for you to stay with the father of your child for the duration of your pregnancy.'

She gasped and pressed a hand to her chest, where her heart was frantically beating. 'What did you say?'

Alex threw a cold glance at the cot. 'Whoever fathered that child, it wasn't me,' he said in a voice that rasped like sandpaper down her spine.

Katrina's stomach churned, her heart kicked, and it was all she could do to remain standing upright.

She was so angry and hurt that she wanted nothing more than to spin on her heel, stalk out the door and never see Alex again.

If it wasn't for Samantha, she would have done exactly that. But her daughter's needs had to come first—and she needed both of her parents.

'She *is* yours,' she finally gritted out.

'No. She's not. I always made sure we were protected.'

'Not always.'

'OK. So I forgot—once,' Alex dismissed.

She sucked in a lungful of much-needed air and glared at him. 'That's all it takes. Besides, all forms of contraception have a failure rate, including condoms. And, since I didn't sleep with anybody else, it's physically impossible for anyone else to be the father.'

Alex frowned. Katrina could tell by the way he was looking at her that the cogs of his mind were grinding as he assessed what she'd just said. Finally, face hardening, he said, 'I don't believe you. The child is not mine. And I will expect you to sign something attesting to that fact.'

Katrina folded her arms defiantly. 'I'm not signing anything.'

'Oh yes, you are. The document will list a number of conditions: one, you will never approach me regarding the child again. Two, you will never ask me for money. And three, you will never publicly try to claim I am the father of your child.'

Katrina was so stunned all she could do was stare and keep on staring.

'When the document is ready, you will sign it,' Alex continued in the same harsh voice.

Katrina surged to her feet, limbs shaking, hands clenched into fists. She'd never felt so insulted in her life—unless she counted his earlier accusation about secretly aborting their child!

Angry—furious, more like it—Katrina stared him in the eye and resisted the urge to smack him across his handsome face.

'*That* is not going to happen.'

Without saying another word, she scooped up the carry cot and stormed out of the boardroom.

CHAPTER TWO

ALEX frowned as he watched Katrina march out of the room. 'Katrina! Come back in here.'

Alex narrowed his eyes as he waited, in no doubt that she'd reappear at any moment. He'd always found her... Well, the truth was he'd always found her rather biddable. She'd always fallen in with his plans, even when he'd known she wasn't entirely happy with them. She'd always said yes, even if it had meant changing her schedule to fit in with his.

Put simply, like every other woman who'd shared his bed, she had never once said no to him.

Any minute now, she would reappear. He would reiterate his intentions. She would leave...and it would all be over.

The thought should have pleased him. But somehow it didn't.

The thought of never seeing Katrina again, never tasting her again, left him feeling oddly unsettled, although he couldn't imagine why.

Forcing the thought aside, Alex scowled.

Realising that Katrina should have reappeared by now, he sprang towards the door.

A quick scan of Justine's private office showed no sign of either Katrina or the carry cot. He strode to Justine's desk. She was on the phone and acknowledged him with a slight smile and a raised eyebrow.

Too impatient to wait, Alex snatched the receiver out of her hand and dropped it unceremoniously into the cradle.

Justine gaped up at him. 'What did you do that for?'

Alex could understand her surprise. In the three years she'd worked for him, he'd never done such a thing. 'Where's Katrina?'

'She left.'

'What do you mean she left?' Alex roared, his insides contracting on a wave of frustration.

Justine blinked up at him. 'Well, she came out and said goodbye, and then she left.'

The words hit Alex in the centre of his back as he left the room and began sprinting down the corridor towards the lift. By the time it offloaded him in the vast foyer on the ground floor, there was no sign of her.

He raced to the exit and lost precious seconds waiting for the glass doors to slide open. Like the lift, they appeared to be moving in slow motion.

Out on the pavement, Alex looked left and right, then scanned the other side of the road.

There was no sign of Katrina.

Alex swore, astounded Katrina had run out on him for a second time. People just didn't do that to him.

Alex returned inside, stopping beside the security guard standing inside the doorway. His name tag read David Greenway.

'David, did you see an attractive woman come

through here a few minutes ago? She has caramel-blonde hair and green eyes. She was wearing a black leather jacket. You couldn't miss her.'

David Greenway's Adam's apple bobbed up and down as he swallowed. 'I'm sorry, sir. We get a lot of people through here.'

Alex clamped his teeth so tightly together he thought they might shatter. He was about to turn away when he thought of something. 'She was carrying a baby in a cot.'

'Ah.' The security guard nodded eagerly. 'Yes, I remember her now.'

'Did you see which way she went?'

David nodded. 'She flagged down a taxi virtually right outside the door.'

'Damn.' Alex stared down at the tips of his shiny black shoes and then up again. 'Did you see what company?'

'As it happens, I did. It was Lime Taxis.'

'Well done, David. Well done,' Alex said, patting him on the shoulder and hurrying away.

Back in his office Alex pressed the speed-dial button for the Royce Agency, the private-detective firm he'd engaged on numerous occasions to do background checks on prospective employees and upgrade the security in his homes and offices.

He'd also engaged the agency to find Katrina. It was the first time the outfit had failed him, which was why they had continued to search for her free of charge.

He was put through to Royce, the owner, straight away.

Briefly and concisely, Alex outlined what had happened.

'Lime Taxis, you said?' Royce confirmed. 'The information is going to cost you.'

'I don't care how much it costs,' Alex grated. 'Find her.'

He'd spent seven months kicking his heels, wondering where Katrina was and what she was doing.

His interest hadn't been in the least personal, of course. The minute he'd discovered she was trying to foist another man's child on him, he'd known their relationship was over. But he had felt it wise to keep an eye on her so that the situation didn't explode in his face.

But Katrina had hidden herself well. He had no intention of letting the same thing happen again; he wanted the experts on the job while her trail was still hot.

'OK,' Royce said. 'I'll call you back as soon as I have the information.'

'Make it fast.'

Alex paced his office like an animal trapped in a much-too-small cage. When his mobile phone rang, Alex almost broke the thing in his eagerness to answer. 'Royce?'

Royce got straight to the point. 'The taxi dropped her off at an apartment in Waverton. Here's the address.'

Alex scribbled the information down on his notepad. Before ending the call, he said, 'I want you to send someone over to the apartment to watch Katrina. They are not to let her out of their sight. I want to know where she goes and who she sees. And I want a report on who she's staying with. Got it?'

Alex didn't wait for a reply. Despite the fact Royce and his people had failed to find Katrina, they were still good operatives. The best, in fact. He had no doubt his request was already spinning into action.

Ripping the page from his notepad, Alex shoved it in his pocket and left the office.

'I'm going to be out for the rest of the day,' he said, striding past Justine's desk without pause.

'But you have appointments all afternoon,' Justine called after him.

'Cancel them,' Alex flung over his shoulder. 'I have more important things to attend to!'

Katrina was scrubbing the stove top when the doorbell rang. There was something therapeutic about making the white enamel gleam. She always cleaned when she was upset or had some serious thinking to do. And right at this moment she could tick the box against both of those things.

The doorbell pealed again.

'Coming,' she called, dropping her cloth then pulling off her green rubber-gloves and flinging them down on the edge of the kitchen sink.

Hurrying to the door, she pulled it open.

She was quite unprepared to find Alex standing on the doorstep.

For one stunned second all she could do was gape up at him like a stranded fish. Then she dragged in a breath, regathered her wits and tried to slam the door in his face.

She was too late.

An expensive black leather shoe wedged itself between the door and the jamb. Then a strong, long-fingered hand curled around the edge of the door and began pushing it open.

Katrina leant against it with all her weight, but it was useless. She was no match for Alex's size and strength. It was like an ant trying to push over an elephant.

Recognising that she was wasting her time, Katrina

stepped away from the door so fast that Alex practically fell into the apartment.

After staring at her long and hard, he looked around.

'You live *here*?'

The slight emphasis he'd given the last word managed to convey exactly what he thought of the apartment. Her hackles, which were already sticking up like the needles on a porcupine after their earlier meeting, bristled some more.

Katrina followed his gaze. She had to admit the carpet needed replacing. It was threadbare in places and stained in others. The walls were also long overdue for a coat of paint.

Peter had apologized for the condition of the unit, but he'd over-extended himself when he'd bought it and was struggling to meet the mortgage repayments.

Katrina had jokingly said it was OK because it didn't show up her furniture. It would be generous to call her stuff 'second hand'. She was probably its third or fourth owner, each piece displaying a series of dents and scratches from each of its previous lives.

But so what?

If he looked hard enough, Alex would notice what was really important. And that was that she kept the place immaculately clean and tidy.

She tossed her head, angled her chin into the air and said coolly, 'Yes, this is where I live. Sorry if it's not up to your high standards, but we can't all be as rich as you. What are you doing here, Alex? How did you find me?'

'I'm here because you ran out on me before we finished our conversation,' he said through clenched teeth. 'As to finding you, that was easy. You were seen getting into a Lime Taxi. Discovering where it had dropped you didn't take long.'

'That's an invasion of privacy. They had no right to tell you where I'd gone.'

'Tell that to someone who cares.' Alex slammed the door behind him and moved determinedly towards her.

Katrina, who had managed to stand her ground at the bank earlier in the day, backed away from him.

His eyes were a glittering, angry blue, his jaw squared with the same emotion. He also looked impossibly, wickedly handsome, and the closer he moved into her personal space the more she was aware of him.

Her heart and her pulse rate both picked up rhythm.

Her back came up against the wall that divided the small living area from the even tinier kitchen. She pressed against it, as if she could somehow go through the painted brick to the other side.

Alex planted a hand against the wall on either side of her head, effectively trapping her.

His heat and his smell were all around her.

Anxiety and awareness coursed through her, making her tremble.

'That's the second time you've run out on me. And the last. Understand?' Alex said in a dangerously soft voice, his breath wafting across her face.

'I didn't run out on you,' she said, angling her chin into the air. 'I walked.'

He growled something completely incomprehensible under his breath. 'Don't split hairs. Why did you leave?'

She snatched in a breath. 'I left because I didn't like what you were saying.'

'So why didn't you just tell me that?'

'I did. I said I wasn't going to sign your stupid document. And I'm not,' she added for good measure. 'I
haven't changed my mind.'

He bared his teeth in the parody of a smile. 'You will
if you know what's good for you.'

The threat stirred her anger to life. She welcomed the
emotion because it banished her awareness of him.

'No, I won't.' She dug the point of her index finger into
the centre of his chest. 'Because Sam *is* your daughter.'

He froze, face twisting. 'Stop saying that. It's not true!'

Her anger evaporated as if it had never existed.
Her heart stilled then took off at a gallop. A shiver
made its way down and then up her spine, setting her
teeth on edge.

For the first time, she appreciated just how much
Alex didn't want it to be true.

She frowned. Surely this was more than just the
normal reaction of a playboy who didn't want to be tied
down? She could practically feel the anxiety seeping out
of his pores into the air surrounding them.

Something else was going on here, although she
didn't have a clue what it was.

'Yes, Alex. It is.'

'It's not. It can't be.' Alex couldn't hide the desperation in his voice. It was clear he was in some form of
denial, which meant he was in for a rude awakening.

'I'm afraid it is.' She paused for a moment before
playing the ace she'd hoped wouldn't be required. 'And
I can prove it.'

He raised a dark eyebrow. 'And just how do you plan
on doing that?'

'A DNA test will prove Sam's paternity.'

Alex was such a logical, facts-and-figures kind of guy. He would have no choice but to believe scientific evidence.

The suggestion had clearly shocked Alex. He was staring at her as if she'd just grown three heads.

While she waited for him to say something, Katrina couldn't stop her eyes from running over him.

There wasn't a man alive who looked as good in a suit as Alex did. All of his clothes were handmade and fitted him like a glove. He was tall and lean, with broad shoulders, a muscled chest and long, powerful legs. The dark fabric accentuated his black hair and piercing blue eyes.

He looked elegant and sophisticated and very, very male.

Heat stirred low in her pelvis. She was nowhere near as immune to him as she liked to think she was. He'd been right when he said her eyes had eaten him up as soon as she'd burst into the boardroom. They were eating him up again now. She couldn't seem to help herself.

And she didn't understand why.

The way he'd treated her should have killed all of the feelings she had for him. And it had—at least on an emotional level. She hadn't been lying when she'd told Alex she didn't love him any more.

Because she didn't. If anything, the reverse was true.

But, on a physical level, it was a different matter entirely.

Physically, she was as attracted to him as the day they'd first met.

She'd pushed open the boardroom door, taken one look at Alex and now the burn was back.

Just like that.

'Are you serious about this?' Alex asked, interrupting her thoughts.

Katrina dragged her eyes back to his face, hoping he hadn't noticed the way she'd been staring at him. 'Frankly, I'd rather not have to go through the humiliation of everyone knowing that you think I sleep around. But if it's the only way you'll accept the truth then I'm more than willing to go through with it.'

'In that case, I'll arrange the test.' His expression gave nothing away. If he had doubts, he wasn't showing them. He glanced at his watch. 'There's no time like the present. The sooner we get this farce over with, the better.'

Alex didn't say a word as the doctor swabbed the inside of the baby's cheek then put the spatula in a thin glass testtube and marked the outside with a bar-coded sticker.

'How soon can we have the results?' he demanded as Dr Kershew extracted a fresh applicator.

'It will take forty-eight hours,' Doctor Kershew replied. 'Open up.'

Alex opened his mouth. The doctor repeated the process on the inside of his mouth.

'Can't you get it done any faster?' Alex asked with a frown as soon as the doctor was finished.

Doctor Kershew placed the two samples side by side on his cluttered desk then looked back and forth between them. He was obviously aware of the tension that had been simmering between them since they'd entered the surgery ten minutes ago. 'I'll see what I can do.'

'You'll call me as soon as you know?' Alex pressed.

Doctor Kershew shook his head. 'They don't call

with the results. They send a written report. Would you like it sent to your home or office?'

'My home. The less people who know about this, the better,' he stated grimly, with a sharp glance in Katrina's direction.

Katrina's response was to jut her chin into the air, and her cat-like green eyes glinted with challenge again.

'And you, Ms Ashby? Where would you like your copy sent?'

She turned to the doctor. 'I don't need it.' She flung Alex a look that he was sure could strip paint. 'I already know what the results will be. I don't need some silly test to tell me something I already know.'

Alex stared at her, his scalp contracting. He'd been discomfited when she'd suggested the DNA testing. Hell, he'd been more than uncomfortable. He'd felt as though she'd smacked him around the head with a plank of wood.

If she'd had any doubts about the child's parentage, then surely she'd have avoided the suggestion like the plague?

Now she was acting supremely confident of the results, so much so that the back of his neck began to prickle and a restless sensation attacked the base of his spine.

What if she was right?

What if the child was his?

Alex let his eyes stray to the baby's cot, which so far he'd avoided looking at.

The baby had fallen into a peaceful sleep, her tiny fist pressed against her flushed cheek, her bow-like mouth softly parted, her little chest rising and falling with each breath.

He'd decided many years ago never to get married

or have children. With his family history, he'd considered it his only option.

It was a decision he'd never regretted.

He'd never even thought about what it would be like to have a child. What was the point when he'd already decided not to?

Now he had to consider it.

He stared at the sleeping infant. She was cute, he had to admit that. But then so was a newborn kitten. But if she was his...

The breath caught in the back of his throat.

If she was his then it was a different matter entirely.

Alex sucked in a deep breath and dragged his gaze away from the cot. His eyes locked with Katrina's. She'd noticed him watching the child. She had a very assessing look on her face, as if she was trying to figure out what he was thinking.

She'd be surprised if she could look inside his head, Alex acknowledged wryly, because his thoughts had just jumped to another aspect of their situation.

If the child was his, then it meant Katrina hadn't betrayed him.

There had been no other man.

No other lover.

And no intention to scam him.

It also meant that what they'd shared was real.

He wasn't quite sure why that was so important to him but it was.

'It's standard procedure,' the doctor said gently. 'Both parents receive a copy.'

Katrina looked back at the doctor and shrugged. 'I don't care where you send it.'

'Oh, for goodness' sake!' Alex rattled off the address.

The doctor made a note on the file before shutting it closed. 'There, all done. Now, if that's all, I'd better see to my next patient. I'm behind schedule.'

'Thank you for squeezing us in,' Alex said, rising to his feet. 'I appreciate it.'

'You said it was important. I always have time for you and your family.' He leaned confidingly towards Katrina. 'I delivered Alex and his brother, you know. I have a soft spot for them.'

'I can imagine,' she said faintly.

The doctor looked back at Alex. 'How is Michael doing?'

Tension gripped him. 'The same,' he bit out. He didn't want to talk about his brother in front of Katrina.

The doctor shook his head sadly. 'Well, if there's anything I can do, all you have to do is call.'

'I know. But the first step is up to Michael.'

Katrina was paying close attention to the conversation. Alex had made a point of keeping his family and Katrina apart, as he did with all of his lovers. He'd wanted to avoid building any expectation of a permanent relationship.

But more and more that looked like it had been a waste of time where Katrina was concerned.

Because, if the baby did turn out to be his, then the future he'd envisaged would be well and truly blown to smithereens.

Alex was trying and failing to process an inbox full of emails when Royce called at eight that night. Once again, the other man got straight to the point. 'I don't have a lot to report. One of my people has been watching the apartment since just before you arrived at two-oh-three.'

Alex was impressed they'd moved so quickly. 'And…?'

'And nothing. Katrina came out with a pram around three-thirty and walked to the local park and back. Other than that she hasn't been out. A number of people have come and gone from the apartment building, but it's been difficult to ascertain whether any of them have visited her. There's been no sign of the guy who owns the apartment.'

Alex stiffened. 'What guy?'

'Let me see.' Alex heard the tapping of computer keys. 'The apartment is owned by a guy called Peter Strauss.'

Something shifted in his chest. 'She's living with a man?'

'That's not clear. We're still looking into it. Katrina's name doesn't appear on any official lease or documentation. At least none that we've found so far. She's either living with the guy or she has a private arrangement with him.'

'I see,' Alex said, not seeing at all, and wishing to hell that he did. 'What else do you know about the guy?'

'Nothing. We're doing a background check now. I should have an answer for you tomorrow or the day after.'

'Make it tomorrow. I want to know everything. When they met. What their relationship is. Everything.'

Alex wasn't sure why he was so interested.

He tried to tell himself it was because the Strauss chap could be the baby's father, but he knew he was just fooling himself.

He was a great believer in the saying 'actions speak

louder than words' and Katrina's behaviour suggested she was telling the truth.

The scales were now firmly tipped in favour of him being the child's father.

So why should he care who this guy was?

Frankly he shouldn't give a flying fig, but he did.

Alex sat stiffly in his chair, body so tense he expected his joints to creak when he moved. A restless sensation attacked the bottom of his spine.

He wanted to storm over to the apartment and demand some answers.

Instead, he cursed under his breath and headed for his bedroom. He pulled on a pair of black running shorts, a white singlet top and a pair of trainers. Leaving the apartment by his private elevator, he headed for the nearby park.

He jogged for an hour most days.

Tonight, he didn't jog.

Tonight, he pounded the pavement as if his very life depended on it.

Sweat dripped from his body.

His lungs burned and his heart raced.

On his twelfth lap, Alex decided to call it quits. He could run until he cut a groove in the cement and it still wouldn't ease his frustration.

He ground to a sudden halt, gasped in a breath and swore viciously.

Jogging at a less frantic pace, he headed back to his apartment.

Then, sweaty, tired and so wired he expected to emit sparks at any moment, he snatched up his car keys.

CHAPTER THREE

KATRINA was cleaning the kitchen sink—gleaming stainless-steel was almost as satisfying as glowing white ceramic—when someone pounded on the door as if they were trying to smash it down.

Worried the racket might wake Samantha, she removed her rubber gloves and hurried to the door.

'Who is it?' she called softly, trying to keep her voice down.

'It's Alex. Open up!'

'Alex?' she asked in surprise, blonde eyebrows shooting towards her hairline.

What was Alex doing here?

'Yes. Alex. Open the door!'

Startled by his forceful order, Katrina slid the door chain along its protective channel and then turned her attention to the lock. In her nervous haste, and hindered by the oversized rubber gloves, her fingers fumbled with the latch and it took her two attempts to get the door open.

'What do you want, Alex?' she asked.

Although she hadn't invited him in, Alex swept past her into the apartment.

As he did, she noticed what he was wearing.

Or, rather, what he *wasn't* wearing.

All he had on was running gear. Skimpy running-gear that left very little to the imagination.

A white singlet top bared the steely strength of his broad, bronzed shoulders, and short shorts left the hair-roughened length of his powerful legs free for her hungry gaze to feast upon.

In an instant, her mouth was parchment dry and her heart was beating ninety-to-the-dozen. 'Alex?' she prompted when he failed to answer her.

Suddenly she realised that while she'd been staring at Alex he'd been staring just as hard at her.

In her eagerness to open the door before Samantha was disturbed, Katrina had forgotten she was wearing her oldest tracksuit. It was tatty and worn, and the black was no longer sharp but faded. She'd taken the jacket off a while ago; scrubbing was hot work. Beneath it she was wearing a black stretchy top with spaghetti-thin straps.

If her outfit wasn't bad enough, her hair had fallen out of the clip she'd used to fasten it to the top of her head. It was now half up and half down, with several strands sticking to her cheeks. To top everything else off, she wasn't wearing a touch of make-up—not even mascara.

Katrina cringed inside at her dowdy appearance and then immediately reprimanded herself.

Who cared what Alex thought?

It wasn't as though he meant anything to her any more.

'What are you doing here, Alex?'

Alex stared at her with hooded eyes, then said abruptly, 'I thought you lived alone.'

Katrina blinked at the comment, which had come out of left field. 'I do. Apart from Sam, of course,' she said, trying to ignore how primal and potently make Alex looked.

'Really?' He raised a brow. 'What about Peter Strauss?'

Katrina blinked again. How did he know about Peter? And why was he asked about him?

'Peter is my landlord,' she said automatically.

'You don't have a lease.'

It was a statement not a question, and it was fired at her as fast as a bullet from a gun.

An uneasy feeling settled at the base of her spine. 'How do you know that?'

He waved a hand. 'Just answer the question.'

'Have you had me investigated?' she asked, still pre-occupied with how he'd come across the information.

'Of course.'

Shock ratcheted up her spine, vertebra by vertebra. 'How dare you?'

'Oh, I dare a lot of things. Why should you care, anyway?' His eyes narrowed. 'Unless you've got something to hide?'

'I've got nothing to hide.'

'Then why won't you answer the question?'

Katrina folded her arms. 'Because it's none of your business, that's why! As far as I'm concerned, you have no right to question me—unless it relates to Sam.'

His eyes flashed with an emotion she couldn't quite define. Suddenly, he was right there in front of her, hand cupping her throat. 'Answer the question!'

The smell of heated male flesh mixed with sweat folded around her like an invisible cloak. As she inhaled, it was as if she were absorbing little particles of Alex that circulated in her bloodstream like a potent drug.

Swallowing against the warmth of his palm, she managed to say huskily, 'What's this all about, Alex?'

What's this all about?

That was a good question, Alex decided.

It was just a shame he didn't have an answer.

At least not one he wanted to share.

He didn't want to admit—even to himself—that jealousy had sent him rushing over here like a man possessed. But there was no other explanation.

And the little green monster was having a field day, eating away at him like acid burning through metal.

Katrina looked unbelievably sexy in an entirely natural way. She might not be wearing any make-up, and her outfit was one that most of his previous lovers would have consigned to the rubbish bin, but all Alex could see was the shapely contours of her body, skin that was glowing with good health and hair that was shining with vitality.

Had Strauss seen Katrina dressed like this? Had he peeled the figure-hugging black top and faded tracksuit-bottoms off the sleek lines of her body before making love to her?

'Who is Peter Strauss to you?' He knew he shouldn't ask the question but was unable to hold it back.

She stiffened beneath the loose hold he had on her throat and her cat-like green eyes flashed quick-silver. '*That* is none of your business. Our relationship is over, remember?' she said, tossing her head.

Her fragrance filtered into the air. Alex inhaled without meaning to, filling his lungs with the smell of her.

His head spun.

His heart pounded.

His body hardened.

Let her go, a little voice in his head instructed with warning. *Let her go before you do something stupid.*

Alex prided himself on his logic. The little voice in his head made a lot of sense.

Still, Alex couldn't bring himself to release her.

Frustration imploded inside of him.

She was right.

He knew she was right.

'I don't care who you sleep with,' Alex said harshly, wondering whether she knew he was lying through his teeth. 'You can sleep with ten men for all I care.' If she did, he would commit murder. 'I'm thinking of the child. She needs to be brought up in a moral environment.'

'The *child* has a name,' Katrina said pointedly. 'And I think that's a little bit rich coming from you!'

'Meaning?'

'Meaning you've had more women than you can probably count, so I don't think you should be pointing fingers.'

His fingers curled more closely around her throat. 'Don't push me, Katrina.'

'Or what? What will you do? Kiss me again like you did this morning?' she goaded.

His eyes dropped to her mouth. She had the most beautiful mouth, just made for kissing.

'Yes,' he said huskily, and did what he'd wanted to do since he'd walked into the room.

Acting on gut instinct, he bent his head and claimed her mouth with his.

Unlike this morning, Katrina didn't put up even a show of resistance.

This time, she kissed him right back with a depth of hunger that struck deep inside him.

Groaning in the back of his throat, Alex hooked an arm around the small of her back and pulled her closer until nothing, not even air, came between them.

He ignored the fact that their relationship was over and he shouldn't be kissing her at all.

He ignored the fact that a young child, in all likelihood his daughter, lay sleeping innocently in the bedroom behind them.

He ignored everything except touching her and tasting her and relishing the familiar feel of her in his arms.

He deepened the kiss. Her arms made their way up and around his neck, where she dug her fingers into his hair.

The flash-fire of primitive desire laid claim to every ounce of tissue in his body. Muscles strained to get closer to her. His skin shrank around his bones. His heart and his pulse didn't feel as if they belonged to him as they beat out a frantic tattoo.

He urged her backwards, instinctively seeking and finding the lounge. The backs of her knees hit the edge of a seat and he tumbled her on to the cushions.

He looked down. One spaghetti-thin strap had slipped off a creamy shoulder, baring the swell of her breast to his gaze.

His body throbbed—hard.

And, then again, even harder.

Then his eyes landed on a stuffed toy sitting in the corner of the lounge.

It was a brown gorilla. And it appeared to be staring at him.

Alex froze.

This was madness. Absolute and utter madness.

Until this situation was sorted, he shouldn't be touching her.

He took a step backwards.

And then another.

Then he said, 'We can't do this.'

Katrina flopped back against the sofa.

She was weak, breathing heavily, body pulsing.

He was right; they shouldn't be doing this.

She closed her eyes.

Why, oh why, had she let Alex kiss her? And why, oh why, had she kissed him back? He thought she was a liar and a cheat. He thought she was low enough to try and foist another man's child on him. She needed her head read for letting him anywhere near her.

She breathed in deeply and willed her heart to stop its frantic beating.

'I think you'd better leave,' she murmured without looking at him.

Katrina could feel him looking at her bent head.

'Are you OK?' he asked finally.

Her eyes snapped open before flashing to his. 'I'm fine. Why wouldn't I be?'

'Why indeed?'

Alex walked to the door and pulled it open. 'I'll call you when I get the results.'

'You do that,' she said, just before the door closed with a quiet click.

* * *

Katrina was cleaning the fridge two days later, trying to take her mind off the fact that today was the day the DNA test results were due, when the doorbell rang.

Immediately, she tensed.

What if it was Alex?

She hadn't received her set of results yet, but that didn't mean Alex hadn't received his.

How was he going to react to the news that Samantha was indeed his daughter?

Stripping off her green rubber-gloves, she tossed them on to the sideboard before hurrying to the door. She paused and took a deep breath before pulling it open.

It was Alex.

But it was an Alex she'd never seen before.

He looked ill. Grey. Strained. Older.

She gripped his arm, which was rock-hard with tension.

'Alex, what's wrong? Are you sick? Do you want me to call a doctor?'

He shook his head but didn't answer her.

She all but pulled him into the apartment.

It was then she noticed the piece of paper gripped in his clenched fist.

Her heart plummeted to her toes with sickening speed, then jolted into the back of her throat.

'Is that…is that the test results?' she choked out.

Alex looked at his hand as if surprised to see he was still clutching the document.

He nodded, his fist unclenching as if it was spring loaded.

The paper bearing the logo of the laboratory dropped to the carpet.

Katrina didn't bother picking it up. Didn't bother because she knew the results.

Alex lifted his head and stared at her. His face was empty of expression and Katrina registered that he was in some kind of shock.

'Samantha is my daughter,' he said simply, his voice so low she could barely hear him.

Katrina nodded.

'I'm a father,' he croaked.

Again, she nodded. 'Yes. Yes, you are.'

He ran a hand through his hair and around the back of his neck. 'I thought I was prepared for this. When you suggested the DNA test, I knew you had to be pretty sure I was the father. But seeing it in black and white…' He shook his head. 'It's knocked me for six.'

Katrina could see that. She'd never seen Alex like this.

But she found it hard to be sympathetic. She'd told him the truth so many times, she'd practically turned blue in the face. But he hadn't listened to her.

Not once.

Even when she'd suggested the DNA test he hadn't given her an inch.

'Do you have something to drink?' Alex asked.

'I presume you're not referring to tea or coffee?'

'Whiskey, if you have it?'

'I think Peter has some,' she said.

She went to the kitchen cabinet where Peter kept his alcohol. Finding a bottle of whiskey towards the back, she poured a decent measure into a tumbler she pulled from the adjoining cupboard.

'Here,' she said, holding the glass out towards him.

Alex walked towards her as stiffly as a store mannequin come to life, took the glass and threw the whiskey down his throat in one fell swoop. The liquid must have burned on the way down, but he looked like he relished the sensation, and when he turned towards her a moment later the spark of life was back in his eyes.

'I want to see her.' His voice was stronger now, his face determined. This was the Alex she knew so well. The successful businessman who knew exactly where he was going and what he wanted.

'Of course.' Katrina didn't hesitate. She'd approached Alex because she wanted him to be a part of Samantha's life. It looked like that started now. She pointed to the corner of the room near the window. 'She's in her pram.'

He nodded. His eyes were fixed with unwavering concentration on the pram as he crossed the room and looked down.

Alex bent over the pram, his heart kicking like a bucking bronco in his chest.

As soon as he did so, the baby smiled up at him.

She had his eyes, Alex realised, his heart squeezing tight in his chest, an emotion he hadn't felt before blossoming inside him.

Or had she?

Didn't all babies have blue eyes when they were born?

He wasn't sure, but he preferred to think she took after him.

'Hello, Samantha,' he said, his voice little more than a croak, his throat so tight he could barely speak.

The baby gurgled and thrashed her little arms and legs. She was wearing some pink all-in-one thing with a bright-pink bunny motif on her chest. She looked so cute, his heart wrenched again.

'She's beautiful.'

Katrina appeared in his peripheral vision. 'Yes. Yes, she is.'

'She's so tiny.'

Katrina laughed. 'She may be small, but she has a good set of lungs on her.'

He turned, a smile tilting the corners of his mouth. 'Does she?'

Katrina nodded. 'Yes. She's a determined little miss. I'd say she takes after you in that regard. When she's hungry, or needs changing, she makes sure everyone in a ten-mile radius know about it.'

'How old is she?' he asked, staring back into the pram.

'She was born on the nineteenth of April, so she's a little over seven weeks old. She weighed two-point-eight kilograms and was fifty-point-seven centimetres long.'

Alex felt his heart turn over. 'I wish I'd been there to see her born.' For the first time, he thought about what Katrina must have gone through. 'Was it a difficult birth?'

She shrugged. 'Difficult enough, I suppose. I was in labour for twenty-one hours.'

'But you're all right?'

She nodded. 'I'm fine.'

'And Samantha?'

'She's fine too.' She smiled. 'She has all her fingers and toes.'

'I should have been there,' he ground out, hands clenched into fists at his side.

Guilt ate into him.

He'd spent years trying not to follow in his father's footsteps.

And on a business front he'd succeeded.

More than succeeded.

He'd worked two jobs to pay for his university fees. He'd studied when other students had been out partying. And when he'd got his first real job he'd worked his tail off, clawing his way to the top with sheer grit and determination.

On a personal front, it was a different story.

Although he was popular with the ladies, Alex didn't want to have the kind of relationship his parents had had. Marriage had trapped them in a cauldron of constant fighting and unhappiness.

He preferred to keep his relationships short, sweet and simple.

The minute things started to go south, he just walked away.

And as to having children? Well, they'd been off the agenda too.

Since his father's blood pumped through his veins, there was a chance—even if it was only a slim one—that he would follow in his father's footsteps.

After all, he'd inherited lots of other things from him: the physical resemblance was almost uncanny. Alex had seen photos of his father when he was younger, and it was like looking at a photo of himself as he was today.

But it was the other traits—little things that didn't mean a lot on their own but when put together meant something else entirely—that sent a chill down his spine.

They were both left-handed.

They were both allergic to peanuts and strawberries.

They both had a habit of running their hands through their hair and around the back of their necks. Every now and then, Alex would catch himself doing it and would shiver at the likeness.

The list was endless.

If he'd inherited all of those things, what was to say his father's abusive nature hadn't been inbred in him and was just waiting for the right time to show itself?

James Webber had abused his children without a second thought.

Alex had considered it far better not to have children in the first place than to risk hurting them later on.

But against all the odds he *had* become a father.

And what had he done?

The first thing he'd done was let his daughter down.

He'd abandoned Samantha—and Katrina—when they'd needed him.

Katrina moved away from him. 'Yes. You should have been.'

Alex stiffened at the recrimination in her voice. Although he had a lot to answer for, he was not alone in that. Anger crackled up his spine. 'I'm willing to take partial responsibility for what happened,' he said harshly. 'But so should you. If you hadn't disappeared the way you did, then we wouldn't be in this situation.'

She jutted her chin defiantly into the air, her eyes spitting emerald fire at him. 'Don't try to blame this on me, Alex. I told you I was pregnant with your child and all you did was insult me. You preferred to think I'd been sleeping around.'

'I told you I was in shock. You should have tried again.'

'Uh-uh. No way!' She shook her head vigorously

from side to side. 'Do you have any idea how offensive you were? Even if I'd been feeling one-hundred percent, I still wouldn't have wanted to face that again. And, since my morning sickness had well and truly kicked in by then the thought of confronting you made me want to throw up.'

Even though Alex had actively avoided having anything to do with children, and the families having them, he had heard enough to know how debilitating morning sickness could be. The fact that Katrina had suffered from it without his support merely deepened his guilt.

'OK. You've made your point. But do you realise it was less than forty-eight hours before I went to your apartment to talk to you?'

Her eyes spat that emerald fire at him again, until Alex half-expected his hair to catch fire. 'If you expect me to applaud you for that, then you're wrong. You should have followed me home straight away and apologised.'

Alex ran a hand through his hair and around the back of his neck, noticed what he was doing and ruthlessly dragged his hand back down to his side. 'You're right. I should have.'

'But you didn't. As a result, I went through my pregnancy and the birth alone without anyone there to support me.'

Alex clamped his hands into fists at his side, an invisible hand clawing at his insides. 'You had no one with you?'

'No.'

Alex turned back to the pram, not so much to look at his daughter as not to look at Katrina. He should have been there to provide her with the support she needed.

It was all well and good kicking himself now, but it couldn't undo the damage he'd done.

As if deciding that she preferred him smiling to scowling, Samantha suddenly started to cry. Despite the gravity of their conversation, Alex found himself smiling as the sound ripped into his eardrums. 'I see what you mean. That's some sound.'

'She's only just started. Give her a few minutes to get to full throttle, and you'll know what she's really capable of.'

Alex grimaced. 'God forbid!' He turned expectantly to Katrina. 'Aren't you supposed to pick her up when she cries?'

She gestured with one hand. 'You're the closest.'

Alex took a step back from the pram. And then another. His heart knocked on his breast bone. 'I couldn't. I might drop her.'

'I'm sure you won't. Just make sure you support her head and neck.'

Alex looked back into the pram. Samantha's face was rapidly changing from pale red to beetroot, and the volume of her cries had grown several decibels.

Dragging in a breath, he gingerly reached in and picked her up.

She weighed practically nothing and almost fit into the palms of his hands. 'You're just perfect, aren't you?' he whispered, feeling the truth of that statement reverberate deep inside him.

Samantha stopped crying and stared up at him. Carefully, he shifted her into the crook of his arm.

She smelled sweet—powdery. Babyish. Completely and utterly unique.

An invisible hand reached into his chest and clamped around his heart. He could hardly breathe, as if a steel band had been slipped around him and tightened until it hurt.

Samantha was his.

Flesh of his flesh.

Blood of his blood.

Something primitive surged inside.

He wanted to hug Samantha to his chest and never let go.

It was a deep-rooted feeling of possession he'd never felt before.

He looked at his daughter and felt tears sting the back of his eyes.

He stroked a gentle hand over her hair, several shades lighter than his own. 'My hair was that colour when I was born. It got darker as I got older.'

'No doubt Sam's will do the same,' Katrina acknowledged.

He swallowed, once. Twice. Three times.

He dragged in a breath. Then another.

And made a silent promise to his daughter—a promise to do all the things his father should have done but hadn't.

And a promise not to do the things his father should not have done but had.

Carefully, he held the baby out to Katrina. 'Here. You'd better take her.' He sniffed. 'I think she needs changing.'

Katrina took Samantha from him and walked to the small dining table, one end of which had been set up as a baby-change table.

Alex thrust his now-empty hands deep into his

trouser pockets as he watched Katrina expertly unsnap the fastenings of the jump suit and begin changing his daughter's nappy.

He'd wondered how he would feel if it turned out Samantha was his.

He now had his answer.

He felt lucky, privileged and terrified all at the same time.

CHAPTER FOUR

KATRINA put Samantha back in the pram and looked up. She found Alex staring at their daughter with an odd expression. 'What?'

He shook his head. 'I still can't believe she's mine.'

'I don't know why you're so surprised. As I told you before, one time using no protection is all it takes.'

'I know.' He gazed back steadily with eyes almost the exact same shade as his daughter's. 'But what you don't realise is that I had a vasectomy in my early twenties.'

Her mouth dropped open.

She blinked.

'What the—?' She snapped her mouth closed, dragged in a breath, and then another. 'You have to be joking?'

He shook his head. 'No. I'm perfectly serious.'

'But the condoms…?' She rubbed her temple, hoping the action would clear the fuzziness in her head—because she was very confused. 'Why would you insist on using condoms if you'd already had a vasectomy?'

'Condoms protect against disease as well as pregnancy, so I've made a habit of wearing them. Since you weren't on the Pill it made sense to keep on using them. If I hadn't, you'd have wondered why. And, frankly, I didn't want to discuss a personal decision which is nobody's business but my own.'

Katrina had heard every single word he'd said, but on one level they just didn't make sense. It was as if he had suddenly started speaking in another language.

'But why on earth would you have a vasectomy?' Katrina said, asking the very question he'd originally set out to avoid answering.

'I would have thought the reason was obvious.' He looked her straight in the eye and made no attempt to soften the blow he was about to deliver. 'Because I didn't want children.'

His answer sucked the air from her lungs. Her chest felt so tight she could hardly breathe. Her heart stopped, stammered and restarted with a wallop.

While she was still reeling, Alex continued. 'The doctor who performed the surgery explained that there was a certain failure rate with the procedure, but I had all the necessary tests and believed it was a success. Since Samantha is my daughter, then obviously it failed somehow.'

Katrina didn't comment. The whys and wherefores were of no interest to her. It was the bottom line that concerned her.

And the bottom line was that Alex didn't want children.

What did that mean for their little girl? she wondered, anxiety tearing her insides to shreds.

'Aren't you going to say "I told you so"?' Alex asked, raising an eyebrow.

She shrugged. 'What's the point? This isn't about who's right and who's wrong. This is about Sam. I only want what's best for her. That's all I've ever wanted.'

Alex grimaced. 'I'm sorry for doubting you.'

She barked out a harsh laugh that had no amusement in it. 'Considering what you've just told me, I suppose you had your reasons. But you still had no right to turn on me the way you did. You said some pretty horrible things to me. I never cheated on you, and I don't believe I ever behaved in a way to suggest that I would. The least you could have done was give me the benefit of the doubt.'

'You're right. I'm sorry.'

Katrina inclined her head. 'Apology accepted.'

He looked surprised but pleased by her response. 'Good. Then we can move forward with a clean slate.'

'And what exactly does moving forward mean? If you don't want children, does that mean you don't want Sam? Because I'll tell you here and now that I want her to have both of her parents in her life. It's important to me.' To emphasise just how important, she added, 'Sam has no other blood relatives on my side of the family. If something happens to me, she's going to need you. I don't want her to be put into an orphanage or the foster-care system. She deserves more than that.'

'You're young and healthy. There's no reason to expect anything will happen to you for many years to come.'

'I'm not willing to take the chance. Accidents happen all the time. And the risk of me not being in her life when she's older is higher than I'd like.' At his enquiring look, she added huskily, 'Breast cancer runs in my family. I lost my grandmother, my aunt and my mother to the disease. I don't like my odds of not getting it.'

His frown deepened. 'Aren't there tests for that kind of thing?'

She nodded. 'Yes, although all it can do is identify whether I have the gene or not, not if I'll get the disease.'

'And you've had the test?'

She nodded.

'And…?'

'And I have the gene,' she replied simply.

Alex paled beneath his skin. 'And there's nothing they can do?'

'I could have a double mastectomy, but I'm not ready to do that. I want more children, and I'd rather breast feed them if I can.' She shrugged. 'Regular mammograms and self-examination is about all I can do—apart from taking care of my overall health, of course.'

Alex just stared at her. It was clear he was stunned by what she'd told him.

'But can you see why it's so important to me that she has both of us?' Katrina said softly.

He nodded. 'Well, you can set your mind at ease. I have every intention of being a part of Samantha's life.'

Relief swept through her, unknotting muscles she hadn't even known she'd had. 'That's great.'

Alex stared at her, face expressionless. She couldn't tell what he was thinking but for some reason she began to feel uneasy, a restless sensation attacking the base of her spine.

'So we're in agreement, then?' he asked. 'We have to do what's best for Samantha?'

Although the question appeared straight forward, there was an odd note in Alex's voice that she couldn't quite decipher. It made her unease expand quickly into out-and-out wariness. 'Of course. That's why I came back.'

But was it the only reason? a little voice whispered in her head.

A couple of days ago her answer would have been a clear and resounding yes.

But now Katrina wasn't so sure.

The way she'd kissed Alex two nights ago had thrown her thought processes into chaos.

She had a sneaky suspicion that a part of her had wanted to come back because she'd wanted to see Alex again.

'Good,' Alex said, breaking into her thoughts. 'Then the only logical course of action is for the two of you to move in with me.'

Katrina blinked. Dragged in a breath. Blinked again.

Surely she hadn't heard him right?

Because she thought he'd just said...

Well, she thought he'd just said...

She shook her head.

No. Whatever she thought she'd heard was wrong. It had to be.

'Say that again,' she said.

He didn't hesitate. 'You heard me. I want you and Samantha to move in with me as soon as it can possibly be arranged.'

The strength and conviction in his voice convinced her.

She'd heard him right the first time. And the second.

Katrina looked away from him.

His suggestion had caught her way off-guard. Whatever she'd expected him to say, it wasn't that.

Bitter irony pinched at her insides with razor-sharp claws. There was a time when she'd wanted nothing more than to live with Alex. If he'd asked her a year ago she'd have been over the moon.

But he hadn't asked, so there was no point wishing he had.

And now...

Well, as far as she was concerned, it was much too late.

'I thought you didn't do permanent live-in relation-ships?' she said, referring to the warning he'd given her when they'd first started sleeping together.

'I don't. Or, at least, I didn't. But circumstances have changed somewhat, wouldn't you say?' he said, with a pointed glance at the pram.

Katrina followed his gaze. 'I suppose they have.' She looked back at him. 'So you're prepared to sacrifice your freedom for Sam—is that what you're saying?'

'I wouldn't put it exactly like that but, essentially, yes.'

His answer shouldn't have hurt but it did.

Those pincers went to work on her insides again, this time getting their razor-sharp edges into the centre of her heart.

Katrina didn't understand her reaction. She didn't love Alex any more. Why should she care that he was prepared to give up his freedom for his daughter when he hadn't cared enough for her to do the same?

'Well…?' Alex prompted when she just stared at him.

'I hardly think living together is necessary,' she said in a cool voice.

'Well, I do.'

She'd heard that tone before. It was the 'I always get what I want, so you might as well give in now' tone.

Well, he wasn't getting what he wanted this time.

Angling her chin, she said, 'Well, that's too bad. I don't want to live with you.'

Alex frowned, clearly surprised by her response. No doubt he'd expected her just to blindly do what she was told.

She could understand why he thought that; once upon a time, that was exactly what she would have done.

But not now.

Becoming a mother had changed her. She had more than just herself to think about now.

She could no longer avoid conversations or situations she wasn't comfortable with. Not when they affected Samantha. Her daughter had to come first.

'I insist.' His tone was smooth but underlined by steel.

'You can insist all you like, but it won't change my mind.' She splayed her hands out wide and adopted a conciliatory tone; arguing wasn't going to get them anywhere. 'If you're worried about access, then don't be. I won't fight you regarding visitation. You can see as much of Sam as you like. I don't want there to be a tug-of-war between us, nor do I ever want her to feel as if she has to choose between us.'

'She won't have to. Because we'll be living together.'

The phrase 'immovable object' immediately sprang into her mind.

Alex could be both stubborn and determined. Those qualities had certainly helped him to become the success he was today. But they could also be extremely annoying.

Because if he thought she was going to move in with him after the way he'd treated her, then he was out of his mind.

'It's the only practical solution. I want to see Samantha every day, not when some schedule tells me I can.' Alex held up a hand as she opened her mouth to speak. 'And don't tell me there wouldn't be some kind of timetable, because we both know there would have to be.'

She sighed. 'OK. I suppose you have a point. But you need to look at the big picture.'

He raised an eyebrow. 'I thought that was exactly what I was doing. Isn't raising Samantha in a family environment the best thing for her?'

'In a real family the mother and father usually love each other,' Katrina shot back. 'That hardly applies in our case.'

'Love is a highly overrated emotion. It doesn't pay the bills and it doesn't keep you warm at night.' Tension drew his shoulders up towards his ears. 'I've seen some pretty horrible things done in the name of love. Frankly, I don't want anything to do with it.'

'If that's the case, then I feel sorry for you. You're going to miss out on so much. But we're straying from the point. What effect do you think living with the two of us will have on Sam? We do nothing but argue. That's hardly a healthy atmosphere for a child to grow up in.'

He gave her a meaningful look. 'I think what happened in this very room two nights ago proves we do more than argue.'

Colour swept up her neck and into her face. 'Hang on a minute. Let me get this straight—when you suggested we move in with you, I thought you were talking about a platonic arrangement. Kind of like one of those marriages of convenience but without the marriage. Are you now suggesting we live together for real? That you and I…?' She stopped and licked her lips. 'Resume intimate relations?'

'Intimate relations? If by that you mean having sex then, yes, that's exactly what I'm suggesting. The aim is to provide Samantha with a *real* family with all that that entails.'

Alex had briefly considered asking Katrina to marry him but had quickly dismissed it as an option.

The DNA test had provided his legal claim to his daughter and living together offered more flexibility. He also liked the idea of being able to walk away if things started to go wrong.

'Sex is hardly a sound basis to build a relationship on,' Katrina said scathingly.

'It's better than having nothing,' Alex shot back with the speed of light. He was determined to get what he wanted, and he was prepared to hammer each and every one of Katrina's arguments into the ground if that was what it was going to take. 'There have been plenty of relationships that have survived with far less. I always thought our physical relationship was rather special. I consider that a real bonus. Besides, aren't you ignoring the fact that we used to get on pretty well?'

'*Used to*, Alex. Past tense. I haven't noticed us getting along too well since I came back.' She shook her head. 'It would never work.'

'How do you know? How can either of us know?' He paused before saying softly, 'But don't you think we owe it to Samantha to try?'

Katrina bit down on her lower lip.

She was obviously thinking about it.

Their daughter was her weak point—a fact that he would use to his advantage.

He would do anything and everything within his power to make Katrina agree to move in with him.

After what seemed like for ever, Katrina slowly shook her head. 'I can't. To put it bluntly, I don't want to get involved with you again. After the way you've treated me, I don't think I can trust you again.'

Alex moved closer to her, his face determined. 'Just

fifteen minutes ago I apologised for those things and you accepted. We agreed we would move forward with a clean slate.'

Katrina frowned. 'You're right, I did. But that only extends so far.'

'A conditional acceptance?' Alex asked with a raised eyebrows.

She nodded. 'If you want to put it that way, then, yes. When I accepted your apology it meant that I'm willing to be civil to you whenever we meet. It also means I'm prepared to work together with you to decide what's best for Sam. It *doesn't* mean I either want to move in with you or start sleeping with you again.'

Alex wagged a finger at her. 'Ah, but now you're contradicting yourself.'

She frowned more deeply, clearly confused. 'And how am I doing that?'

'Aren't you the one who said this was about Samantha?'

She nodded. 'That's what I said. So…?'

'So you're making this all about you and what you want, not what's best for her.'

He heard her sharp inhalation of breath. Saw her eyes widen.

The room fell silent.

Alex waited for a moment and then went for the jugular. 'I'm willing to sacrifice my freedom to give Sam the family she deserves. What are you prepared to sacrifice?'

He'd used the shortened version of their daughter's name quite deliberately. He was playing on Katrina's emotions, but he didn't care.

He had to convince her that moving in with him was the right thing to do.

He intended to be a good father to Samantha, and he couldn't do that if she was living somewhere else.

Honesty also forced him to admit that this wasn't just about Samantha.

This was also about the fact that he wanted Katrina. What had happened here two nights ago proved that beyond a shadow of a doubt.

As he'd just told her, he'd always thought that what they'd shared was special.

So special, in fact, that he wasn't ready to let it go.

Finally, Katrina cleared her throat. 'You're suggesting I sacrifice myself for my daughter?'

'That's a rather melodramatic way of putting it but, yes, that's exactly what I'm suggesting. Besides we both know there wouldn't be any sacrifice involved,' Alex continued confidently. 'You want me.'

Katrina stared at him but didn't answer.

Alex smiled. 'I've kissed you twice in as many days and you've kissed me back both times.'

Her chin made its way into the air. Still, she didn't say anything.

His smile widened. 'Don't worry. You don't need to say anything. I know.'

She tossed her head, sending her caramel-coloured hair swirling around her shoulders. 'You're not omniscient, Alex. You don't know everything.'

His eyes dropped to her mouth. 'I know that it would only take one kiss to prove me right. Shall we try it?'

He crossed the room at the speed of light, grasped her hands and pulled her against him.

She tore herself out of his arms and took a stumbling step backwards. 'No.'

Alex followed her retreat and slid an arm around the small of her back. 'No? You don't sound very sure.'

Again, she wrenched herself out of his arms. This time she put the length of the sofa between them. 'I'm sure.'

Alex eyed the sofa separating them. If Katrina thought that would stop him if he really wanted to get to her, then she had another thing coming.

He shook his head, his mouth quirking at the corners. 'Really? I don't think you are.'

She blinked.

'Remember how you used to cry out my name when I sucked on your nipples?' She licked her lips as if they were dry; colour swept into her cheeks. 'And how you used to dig your nails into my back as you came? You drew blood on more than one occasion.'

The colour in her cheeks deepened until they were burning a bright pink. Her pupils dilated, the golden-brown flecks standing out prominently. Her chest was rising and falling, her nipples pressing against the tan cotton of her top.

'Remember?' he prompted again, his voice thickening.

She licked her lips again. 'I don't remember a thing.'

He crossed the room in a flash, practically vaulting the corner of the sofa. While she was still staring at him, open-mouthed, he pulled her into his arms and said huskily, 'Then let me remind you.'

Katrina shuddered as his mouth claimed hers.

No matter what she'd told Alex, she wanted him.

She might not love him any more, but the chemistry

between them was like an addiction that she had no control over.

Because, instead of pushing him away, she was winding her arms around his neck and pushing her aching breasts against the hard wall of his chest.

And, instead of telling him to get away from her, she was sighing her surrender into his mouth as if this was the first and last place she wanted to be.

Alex prised her lips apart and deepened the kiss. Their mouths danced a duel as erotic and as ageless as time. Light bloomed behind her closed eyelids. Heat blossomed under her skin until she felt as if she were glowing.

Alex lifted his head.

Her lashes fluttered open.

Their eyes met.

'Tell me,' he ordered, feeding a hand into her hair and pulling her head back to expose the fragile length of her neck.

Katrina let her eyes flutter closed again as she felt his mouth nip at the sensitive skin just below her ear. 'Yes,' she breathed.

'Yes what?' he asked, nipping at her again.

She opened her mouth to say the fateful words, 'yes, I want you', but at that exact moment Samantha began to cry.

My God, what was she doing? Katrina asked herself frantically.

She tore herself out of Alex's arms and stumbled towards the pram.

She dragged in a breath and released it slowly, then repeated the process. Gradually, her heartbeat began to slow towards the semblance of a normal rhythm.

When she was calm, she reached into the pram and picked Samantha up. 'Hush, little one. Hush.'

She gently rocked the baby until she quieted then looked at Alex. 'I am *not* going to sleep with you.'

Alex folded his arms across his impressive chest. 'Who are you trying to convince—me? Or yourself? You want me.'

It wasn't a question. It was a statement.

Katrina knew she would be wasting her breath trying to deny it. After the way she'd just kissed him, there was no doubt in either of their minds that he'd spoken the truth.

She tossed her head. 'So what if I do? Didn't your mother ever tell you that you can't always have what you want?'

His mouth twisted. 'Oh, she taught me that, all right.'

The bitterness in his voice immediately roused her curiosity, but satisfying it was hardly a priority.

Sorting out Samantha's future was the only thing that concerned her. And there was one thing she knew for sure.

She looked Alex squarely in the eye. 'I'm sorry, Alex, but I'm not prepared to live with you.'

Alex shook his head, his eyes showing a mixture of surprise and admiration. 'You really have changed, haven't you? You've turned into Little Miss Confrontation.'

She nodded. 'You'd better believe it. I used to be a pushover where you were concerned, but not any more. I can't forgive you for the way you treated me. At least, not enough to get involved with you again. It would make me unhappy, and that wouldn't be good for Sam.'

'And where does that leave me?' Alex challenged. 'Out in the cold?'

'Now who's the one being melodramatic?'

'I hardly think it's melodramatic when you're trying to stop me from being the father I want to be to Sam.' His eyes were as hard as nails, his voice threaded with the same steel. 'If that's your final decision, then you leave me no choice.'

The tone of his voice sent a chill unlike anything she'd known down her spine. A knot of tension formed in the base of her throat. 'What…what do you mean?'

'It means I intend to sue for sole custody.'

His answer sucked the air from her lungs.

'What—?' She stopped, swallowed and tried again. '*What* did you say?'

'You heard me.'

His voice was strong and determined; the look in his eyes was equally resolute.

Katrina staggered backwards.

Alex frowned and held out his hands. 'Give Sam to me before you drop her.'

Katrina backed out of reach, hugged her daughter close to her chest and wrapped her arms protectively around her. She glared at Alex. 'You stay away from her! And you can stay away from me too. In fact, I want you to leave. *Right now!*'

His hands dropped to his sides but he didn't move. A muscle along the line of his jaw bunched as if he were gritting his teeth. 'I'm not going anywhere.'

'I'll call the police,' she threatened.

'No, you won't.'

There it was again, that tone. Forceful. Attacking.

Like a compression wave travelling through the air. When it hit you, it threatened to strike you flat to the floor.

She trembled but she tried to put on a confident front. 'Are you sure about that?'

'Yes, I'm sure. The last thing you want is to make an enemy out of me.'

She barked out a harsh laugh. 'I think it's too late for that, don't you? What you just suggested is, well, it's barbaric. Sam is just a baby. She needs me.'

'Yes, she does.'

'She's too little to—' She stopped, gasped, then said slowly, 'Say that again.'

Alex stared back at her. 'I agreed with you. You are her mother. Of course she needs you. I never said that she didn't.'

She blinked, and breathed deeply. 'But you just said you'd sue me for custody.'

'And I meant it.' For the first time since he'd arrived at the apartment, Alex looked angry, his face hardening and nostrils flaring. 'Did you listen to yourself just now? Talk about being selfish. Have you thought for one moment that Sam needs me as much as she needs you? Have you?'

Katrina flinched. 'I've already said that—'

Alex didn't let her finish. He put his face close to hers and bared his teeth. His eyes were emitting blue sparks, his hands clenching and unclenching at his sides. 'My daughter is going to have a better start in life than I had; I can promise you that. She is *not* going to be raised in some dingy two-bit apartment barely big enough to swing a cat in. She is *not* going to go to bed hungry two out of three nights because there's not enough money to put a proper meal on the table. She is *not* going to be bullied, and she is *not* going to be scared.'

Alex stopped.

Katrina thought he'd finished but he'd only paused long enough to draw breath.

'She is going to have ballet and music and tennis lessons if that's what she wants. She is going to have friends and go to parties and not be embarrassed because she wears clothes that come from the cheapest chain-stores or other kids' hand-me-downs. She is going to feel safe and secure and happy. And I, as her father, am going to see that it happens. And to hell with anyone who gets in my way!'

CHAPTER FIVE

His words hung in the air like a crack of rifle fire, bouncing off one wall and then another before slowly echoing into nothing. The silence that invaded the room prickled at the back of Katrina's neck and made her skin contract over her bones.

As if sensing the tension in the room, Samantha started crying again. Katrina eased her grip, which had unconsciously tightened with each and every word that had exploded from Alex's mouth.

Laying the baby in the crook of her arm, she swayed from side to side.

The rocking motion soothed Samantha, who grew quiet.

It failed, however, to calm Katrina's own shattered nerves.

She was stunned by Alex's outburst. Not only was the sudden flare-up out of character, but the content had knocked her for six.

She knew next to nothing about Alex's family. When they'd been together he'd never talked about them. She knew his mother was still alive, because she'd called him several times, leaving messages he'd always ig-

nored. She also knew he had a brother and, courtesy of
the conversation she'd overheard between Alex and Dr
Kershew that day in his surgery, she knew that his name
was Michael.

Alex had never mentioned his father. Or his background.

She'd always assumed he came from a wealthy
family. She didn't have a particular reason for thinking
that; she'd just never associated a man who owned and
ran his own investment bank with anything but success
and wealth.

But his tirade just now had been full of such passionate intensity there was no doubt he was speaking from
personal experience.

Tears stung the back of her eyes when she realised
he was the little boy who had gone to sleep hungry. *He*
was the little boy who had been bullied and scared.

'I'm sorry,' she said, looking up.

His jaw squared. 'What for? For the fact that I had a
lousy childhood? Or the fact that you want to deny Sam
everything I can offer her?'

Katrina bit back a gasp.

Alex was not holding back. The gloves were well
and truly off.

Every word was like a sword he was thrusting
through her—and each and every one found its mark.

'That isn't fair,' she protested, even though she knew
there was a lot of truth in what he'd just said.

She'd contacted Alex for many reasons—included
amongst them was the fact that she knew he could offer
their daughter more financially than she could.

She had to face it, she was struggling. All she had to

do was look at the pile of unpaid bills pinned to the fridge door with magnets to see that she was just scraping by. She didn't want to see her daughter suffer that way.

'And is it fair that I get only the scraps from the table and not the full feast, which is exactly what I'd be getting if Sam lives with you?'

Katrina winced as that shot also found its target. 'I suppose not.'

'I have as much right to custody as you have.' His eyes met hers squarely. 'The difference is, I have the money to win.'

He was right.

Alex could afford the best legal counsel in Australia. In fact, he could hire a whole team of lawyers if he wanted to, whereas she would have to make do with legal aid.

It wouldn't be a fair contest. It would be over before it had even begun.

Her shoulders slumped, the energy draining out of her. 'OK. You win; I'll move in with you. But I won't sleep with you.'

His eyes seared into hers. 'I am *not* signing on for a lifetime of celibacy!'

She clenched her hands into fists. 'Well, don't think I'm just going to stand by while you sleep with other women!' she burst out before she could stop herself. 'I refuse to be humiliated that way,' she added hastily just in case he thought she was jealous.

Because she wasn't. Was she…?

Katrina was very much afraid that she was—and she didn't like it one little bit.

The look Alex threw her chilled her to the bone. 'What kind of a man do you take me for?' he demanded.

'Do you really think I'd risk doing anything that would hurt or embarrass my daughter if she found out?'

Katrina was ashamed to realise that she hadn't given a thought to how such behaviour would affect Samantha. She'd been too busy worrying about how *she* felt about it.

'I hadn't thought of that,' she admitted grudgingly.

'Well, I have. You either move in with me with the aim of building a proper family with all that that entails, or you don't move in at all.'

Her heart started to thump again. She now knew exactly what the saying 'between a rock and a hard place' meant. She was sandwiched between the two right now.

'You can't just expect me to jump straight into bed with you,' she huffed.

Alex shrugged. 'I don't see why not. It's not as if you haven't slept with me before.'

His insensitivity made her grit her teeth. 'It's not the same, and you know it. I didn't dislike you then the way I do now. I need time. Time to establish a relationship first.'

'We already have a relationship, or are you forgetting the fact that we spent almost a year together?'

Katrina's heart sank to her toes. 'I've forgotten nothing. That's the problem.'

In the end they agreed to a compromise.

Her move to the penthouse was completed with the minimum of fuss the following day. Alex arranged everything; the transfer happened with a speed that made her head spin.

After giving her a quick tour of the apartment, which

was as spacious as it was luxurious, Alex departed for the office. 'I'll be back around eight to see how you're settling in.'

Katrina was surprised he'd left so quickly. But then, she reasoned, he was a busy man who'd obviously taken time out of his schedule to be here to welcome them.

Alex had arranged to give her furniture away to charity, so it didn't take her long to unpack her meagre possessions. Even with her belongings scattered around her room, and a few favourite ornaments and photographs carefully positioned in the lounge, the apartment still didn't feel like home.

She'd never lived in anything so lavish, not even for a night. She felt like a fish out of water and, as a result, found it difficult to relax. So much so that she could hardly wait to put Samantha in her pram and go outside.

After a long walk down to Circular Quay, Katrina returned to the apartment and proceeded to put the baby to bed. The familiar routine of feeding and bathing her daughter was soothing.

Alex arrived home just before eight. Katrina was watching TV and pretending not to watch the clock at the same time.

'Have you eaten?' he asked, pulling off his tie and unbuttoning the collar of his shirt.

Katrina shook her head. 'No. Not yet.'

He undid another button. And another. Katrina tried not to stare, but found her eyes straying to the triangle of golden skin he'd revealed.

'Do you still like Chinese?' Alex asked, his fingers working the next button free.

By this stage half of his muscled chest was bare.

Alex looked good naked; his body was taut and toned. Katrina took full advantage of it before she realised he was waiting for her reply.

Dragging her eyes back to his face, she nodded.

'There's a list of restaurants in the third drawer down in the kitchen. Why don't you call the Chinese and order while I have a quick shower?' he suggested, pulling the open shirt out of the waistband on his trousers.

Katrina forced herself not to look down, even though the temptation to do so was strong. Was he doing this little striptease deliberately? she wondered, dragging in a breath before releasing it slowly. 'Fine. I'll do that.'

Alex shrugged off the shirt and let it dangle off one finger. 'Good. I shouldn't be long.'

'Do you have any preferences?' she choked out.

He flashed her a smile that made her go weak at the knees.

'You choose. You know what I like.'

He turned and walked out of the room.

Katrina stared at the strong planes of his back. She did know what he liked—and she wasn't just thinking about food!

She remembered several memorable occasions when they'd showered together, taking it in turns to wash each other. There was something very sensual about the combination of soap, water and skin that brought her out in goose bumps just thinking about it.

The Chinese food arrived not long after Alex had opened a bottle of crisp white wine. Katrina cautiously dished the food up on to the expensive china plates she'd found in the kitchen.

'One of these days you're going to have to master the art of using chopsticks,' Alex mocked as she picked up her fork.

Her mouth twisted. 'I've tried, but more food ends up in my lap than in my mouth.'

'I know. Do you remember the night I tried to teach you to use them?'

Katrina's eyes met his, the memory of that evening washing over her.

Alex had decided that a penalty-and-reward system would help her to learn more quickly.

Her reward had been a kiss. Her penalty had been the loss of an item of clothing.

She hadn't learned how to use chopsticks that night; she didn't think they'd even finished their meal. But she'd learned a lot about herself and about the depth of her desire for Alex.

Heat flooded her insides until she found it difficult to sit still. 'Don't, Alex. You promised you'd give me time.'

Alex shook his head. 'No, I didn't. I said I was willing to let our relationship progress naturally. There's a big difference.'

Katrina was beginning to realise that. 'I should have known better than to trust you. I thought you meant I could set the pace.'

'I'm not waiting until hell freezes over, if that's what you're thinking. I expect there to be progress.' He gave her a wicked smile. 'And I never said that I wouldn't give the pace a nudge along every now and again, did I?'

'Alex…'

He held up his hands, his electric-blue eyes wide and innocent. 'All we're doing is talking.'

'Is that what you'd call it? I'd call it a trip down memory lane.'

That nudge he'd just mentioned was also a blatant attempt to seduce her with memories.

Alex took a sip of wine before answering. 'And what's wrong with that? I see nothing wrong with re-connecting with our past. We used to have some pretty good times, if you remember.'

That was the problem.

She *did* remember. And she'd rather she didn't.

She remembered their first meeting in her boss's office, where one look from the tall, dark-haired, blue-eyed stranger had left her both breathless and speechless.

She remembered their first kiss that very same evening, when she'd trembled in his arms as if she'd never been kissed before.

But she also remembered each and every time he'd returned to his apartment, leaving her with the smell of him on her skin, the taste of him in her mouth and only the lingering heat of his body to keep her warm.

She looked him in the eye. 'Yes, we had some good times. But it wasn't all a bed of roses. At least, not for me.'

Alex frowned. 'Are you saying I made you unhappy?'

Katrina swallowed. 'Not entirely. I'm just saying I wasn't particularly good mistress material.'

His eyes narrowed to slits of blue. 'You wanted more than I could give you.'

It was a statement, not a question. Her fork clattered down on to her plate. 'You knew?'

He nodded. 'Although you didn't say anything,

you weren't very good at hiding your feelings. I warned you in the beginning that I didn't plan on getting married or having children. You should have listened to me.'

She inclined her head, an empty feeling attacking her insides, draining her of warmth. 'You're right. I should have. The point I'm trying to make is that I don't want to keep revisiting the past. If we're going to make this work we should start afresh.'

'Considering we have a daughter together, don't you think it's a little too late for that?'

She gestured with one hand. 'You know what I mean. Can't we just be friends for now? Until…you know… we get used to each other again?'

Alex looked as though the idea was totally alien to him, and Katrina guessed he'd never had a platonic relationship with a woman in his life. 'We're meant to be building a lasting relationship.'

'Then friendship is an excellent place to start, don't you think?'

'I don't know if that will work.' He picked up his wine and took a sip before saying slowly, 'You can't just pretend we don't want each other, Katrina. It won't make it go away.'

Picking up her fork, Katrina skewered a honey king-prawn and doggedly began eating without giving him a reply.

Alex obviously got the message, because he sighed and picked up his chopsticks.

'Are your rooms OK?' he asked a couple of minutes later.

He'd put her and Samantha in adjoining rooms with

their own bathroom. Her bedroom was large, spacious and luxuriously appointed.

Their daughter's bedroom had already been furnished as a nursery, complete with animal motifs on the walls and a pile of toys that must have cost a bomb.

'They're fabulous. How did you manage to decorate the nursery so fast?'

His mouth twisted. 'Money talks. I'm glad you like it.'

She smiled with genuine warmth. 'How could I not like it? It's fantastic. And whoever chose the toys did a wonderful job. Sam already loves the pink teddy-bear.'

Alex looked away, seemingly fascinated by the rice he'd picked up with his chopsticks.

Instinct prompted her to ask, 'Who bought the toys, Alex?'

He looked up somewhat sheepishly. 'I did.'

'I see.'

Katrina was stunned. Although why she should be she didn't know. Alex was nothing if not thorough; when he did things he went all out, crossing every t and dotting every i.

'I wanted to get Sam something from me,' he said in that same sheepish tone. 'I guess I got a little carried away, didn't I?'

She gave him a warm smile. 'Maybe just a little bit. You bought enough toys to last her until she's five. I don't want her spoilt.'

Alex smiled back. 'I don't want her spoilt either. I'll try not to get so carried away in future.'

Katrina's heart turned over, then wrenched hard.

This was so difficult.

Alex had virtually blackmailed her into moving in

with him. Now that she was here, she had two choices: she could either be as uncooperative as possible—in which case Alex would sue for custody and she would lose her baby—or she could try and make their relationship work, knowing it was the best thing for Samantha.

Obviously, she'd chosen the latter.

But—and it was a big but—she didn't want her emotions to become involved. That was easier said than done; Alex was pretty hard to resist when he turned on the charm.

After dinner they cleared the table. Katrina stacked the dishwasher and was about to retire to her room when Alex suggested she join him in the lounge for another glass of wine.

'There are a couple of things I want to discuss with you,' Alex added persuasively.

'Fine. I'll just check on Sam.' She hesitated and then asked, 'Do you want to come with me?'

He nodded.

Their daughter was sleeping peacefully in her cot, her fan-like lashes soft against her cheek.

'Is there anything more innocent or more wonderful than a sleeping baby?' Alex whispered.

Katrina shook her head. 'No.'

She reached in and straightened the covers then moved aside to allow Alex some space.

He brushed a gentle hand over the top of Samantha's head before stroking a finger down her cheek.

Returning to the lounge, Katrina sat down and folded her hands in her lap. 'What did you want to talk to me about?'

'A couple of things. First, transport.' Alex dug into his pocket and came out with a set of keys. 'Here, take these.'

'What are they?' she asked, automatically reaching out to take them.

'They belong to the silver BMW I had delivered for you this afternoon.'

Katrina put the keys down on the glass-topped coffee table as if they were a hot potato burning a hole in the centre of her palm. 'I don't need a car.'

'Of course you do. I don't want you relying on taxis. You need your own transport to get to and from appointments.'

A car was a luxury she hadn't been able to afford. The little second-hand sedan she'd owned before falling pregnant had been sold to help pay for all the additional expenses that went along with having a baby.

Since Samantha had been born, Katrina had used public transport to get around, just like thousands of other mothers did every day. It was no mean feat, considering all the gear she had to take everywhere with her, but it was adequate.

'I really don't think it's necessary. I'm quite happy to make do with public transport.'

Alex frowned. 'I had to *make do* when I was growing up. My daughter doesn't. I don't want you relying on public transport. End of story.'

Katrina wasn't happy with the way Alex had just laid down the law. She opened her mouth to argue and then quickly shut it again.

Alex had as much right as she did to have a say where their daughter was concerned. And she had to admit that a car would certainly make life easier. At the same time, she was conscious of the expense.

'OK, if you feel that strongly about it. But a BMW

isn't necessary. Any old second-hand car would be just fine for our needs. Is it too late to return it?'

'Yes, it is too late. I've already paid for it. Besides, I don't want to return it. I bought a BMW in the first place because it has an excellent safety record; that still stands. I want something that will protect you both in case of an accident.'

Katrina was warmed by his concern, even though she knew she was going to be terrified driving such an expensive car. 'Fine. If that's what you want.'

'It is. Now, to funds.' He handed her a yellow envelope. 'I've opened two credit cards in your name. Both have a five-thousand-dollar limit, so don't go berserk.'

Katrina shook her head. 'No. No way.' Even before she'd finished speaking, she'd placed the envelope down on the coffee table and pushed it towards him.

'Yes way. You're going to have to buy things for Sam,' Alex said smoothly. 'Prams. Car seats. Clothes. It will all add up. You'll also have your own expenses. I'd prefer it if you didn't return to work, so it's only fair that I support you.'

Katrina straightened her spine. She might have given in over the car, but this was another thing entirely. 'First, I have no plan to give up work. The company I worked for while I was pregnant agreed to take me back part-time after my three months' maternity leave is up. And—'

Alex frowned. 'You worked while you were pregnant?'

Katrina nodded. 'Of course.'

'There's no "of course" about it. You should have been taking it easy.'

'I was pregnant, Alex, not sick. I've always worked; I wouldn't know what to do with myself if I didn't. And

I didn't really have much choice. Having a baby is an expensive business; I had to work to pay the bills. Besides, I wanted to keep busy.'

In those first few months, she'd been agonizingly miserable.

One minute she'd been so angry with Alex she'd half-expected steam to pour from her ears. The next minute she'd been so hurt she'd burst into floods of tears.

No doubt pregnancy hormones had made her feel worse than she might otherwise have felt, but she'd been pretty low to start with.

Working had helped take her mind off Alex. It had also helped her to stop feeling so sorry for herself.

'I'm sorry I wasn't there to help,' he said grimly.

Katrina opted not to respond to that comment. They'd already had this discussion. Going over it *ad nauseum* wasn't going to help anybody.

'Second, I'm not a huge fan of credit cards,' she said, returning to the original conversation. 'My mother always said that if you can't afford to pay for it now you can't afford it at all.'

An odd look crossed his face that she couldn't quite decipher. 'I can assure you we can afford to use credit cards. But if you give me the details of your bank account I'll also transfer some cash to you each month.' He raised a hand. 'Don't say it. I have the right to share the expense of raising my daughter.'

Katrina snapped her mouth closed. She wanted to argue with him, but knew that he was right.

'Lastly, I wanted to discuss the household arrangements. I have a housekeeper who comes in three times a week. Her name is Leslie. She takes care of everything. Washing, cleaning and shopping. If you want to change those arrangements, feel free. I'll leave it up to you to sort out with her. I've told her about you and Sam. She's due here tomorrow around ten. I take it you can introduce yourself?'

Katrina wasn't quite sure what to say. She wasn't used to having household staff, nor did she think she wanted to get used to it. Given the choice, she would rather look after their home herself. But it was obviously an arrangement that suited Alex, and she didn't feel it was right to make waves so soon after arriving.

Suppressing a sigh, she inclined her head. 'Yes. No problem.'

'Now there are just a few logistical matters to take care of.'

Katrina couldn't think of another thing. Alex had taken care of everything with his usual thoroughness and efficiency. 'Such as?'

'Contact numbers.' He extracted a business card from his pocket. 'This has all of my numbers on it. Give me your mobile number so I can contact you when you're out. I think it's really important we keep each other posted about any plans we make. For example, I sometimes have business commitments in the evenings. If I'm going to be out, I'll let you know,' Alex said. 'Otherwise, I suggest we eat together.'

Katrina didn't know whether to welcome the suggestion or not.

She had enjoyed this evening.

If the truth be known, she'd enjoyed it rather more than she should have. This was only her first night here, and already she was fantasising about what it would be like if this was for real. Imagining what it would be like if they were a real family.

A family where she loved Alex and he loved her.

But there was no point building sandcastles in the air.

Alex thought love was an overrated emotion.

And she…

Well, she had lost her heart to Alex once. She had no intention of making the same mistake twice.

CHAPTER SIX

DURING the next few days they fell into a routine. But it was a routine Katrina wasn't the least bit happy with.

She wasn't quite sure what she'd been expecting when she'd agreed to move in with Alex, but it hadn't been this.

She hardly saw Alex. He left the apartment before she got up in the morning and often returned after she'd gone to bed.

The few times she had seen him, he'd been polite but distant. The easy camaraderie they'd shared on her first evening felt like a distant memory.

By the time the fourth night arrived, Katrina had had enough. Her distress wasn't personal, of course; she was upset on her daughter's behalf. Frankly, the less she saw of Alex the better.

But the situation couldn't go on. The only way to resolve it was to stay up and talk to Alex.

Her plan went skew-whiff, however, when she fell asleep.

She woke when strong arms lifted her.

'What the—?' she gasped, jerking awake.

Blue eyes stared down at her. 'You fell asleep.'

'Did I?' She yawned and pushed the hair back off her face. 'What time is it?'

'Eleven-thirty.'

'My goodness! I've been asleep for hours.'

'Have you?' His voice was husky.

Katrina nodded and blinked sleep drenched eyes. She was all too conscious of being cradled against the hard wall of his chest with his heat and all-male smell wrapped seductively around her. Desire flared low in her belly, her heart picking up rhythm.

'You can put me down now,' she suggested softly.

Alex let her legs swing gently to the ground, but he didn't immediately release her. He smoothed a strand of hair back behind her ear, and her stomach clenched at the fierce intensity burning in his eyes. 'I have to kiss you,' he said hoarsely.

He bent his head towards her. She had plenty of time to stop him, but she didn't.

She tried to tell herself that she didn't turn her head away because she was still only half-awake but she wasn't sure she was telling the entire truth.

It wasn't just the fuzziness of half sleep holding her captive. It was anticipation.

Alex claimed her with his mouth, softly at first and then with more intensity, prising her lips apart.

Even though she knew she shouldn't, Katrina closed her eyes and kissed him back.

When he raised his head they were both breathing heavily.

For a moment neither of them spoke.

Desire pulsed softly in the airwaves between them. It was a soundless beat that connected them in a way it was impossible to explain. And the power of it was impossible to ignore.

Katrina knew that if she didn't break the link soon she'd be all but inviting Alex to make love to her.

She had to admit she was tempted. But then she remembered why she'd been waiting up for him in the first place and the spell was broken.

Clearing her throat, she stepped backwards. The arm wrapped around her waist tightened.

Katrina pushed her hands against his chest. 'Let me go, Alex. We need to talk.'

His spare hand cupped her jaw, his thumb tracing the outline of her mouth. 'I'd much rather kiss you again.'

'And I'd rather you let me go,' she said quietly.

Alex searched her face. What he saw must have convinced him she meant what she said, because he sighed and released her. He wiped a hand over his face. 'OK. But before we talk I need something to eat.'

Katrina suddenly noticed how tired he looked. 'Haven't you had dinner?'

He shook his head. 'I didn't get a chance to. One of the big deals we've been working on went right off the rails today. Someone didn't do their job properly.' The hard edge sharpening his voice suggested the culprit had been severely dealt with. 'We spent the evening thrashing out a solution which we'll present to the client tomorrow.'

'I see.' She hesitated before tentatively suggesting, 'Would you like me to make you something?'

He nodded. 'If you don't mind. My usual effort is a sandwich.'

'I think we can do better than that,' she said, leading

the way into the modern kitchen. 'How does an ome-
lette sound?'

'Sounds great.'

Katrina opened the fridge door and pulled out eggs,
bacon, cherry tomatoes, capsicum, baby spinach and
cheese.

'Is there an open bottle of white in there?' Alex asked
from behind her.

She looked in the fridge door. 'Yes.'

She put it on the central bench and pushed it across
to him.

He raised a brow. 'Care to join me in a glass?'

Katrina shook her head. 'It's a little late for me.'

Alex poured a glass of wine and sat on a stool on the
other side of the work bench. 'You said you wanted to
talk to me. What about?'

Katrina broke three eggs into a glass jug and began
whisking them. 'It sounds kind of silly now.'

'It was obviously important enough to keep you up.'

She nodded and took a deep breath. 'It's just that I've
hardly seen anything of you since we moved in.' She
gave him a sheepish look before picking up the pepper
grinder. 'I was beginning to think you were avoiding us.
I realise now you've obviously just been very busy.'

Alex was silent for such a long time that Katrina
looked up.

Their eyes met.

Alex grimaced. 'Not entirely.'

Katrina raised an eyebrow.

'I'm always busy but the deal I was telling you about
earlier only exploded today. Before that…' He grimaced
again. 'Well, let's just say you weren't completely wrong.'

Surprise made her heart leap in her chest. She laid the knife she'd been using to chop the vegetables down on the cutting board. 'You mean you were avoiding us? But why? I don't understand.'

His eyes dropped to her mouth, where they lingered like a physical caress. 'Can't you guess?'

Her colour rose. His implication was clear. 'I...' She trailed off, scrambling for an appropriate response.

'I'm not used to going without something I want.' Alex picked up his glass of wine and took a sip. 'I thought it was prudent to stay out of your way for the time being. I thought it would be less frustrating.' His mouth twisted. 'Not that it's entirely worked.'

Katrina pressed her hands against the granite benchtop, welcoming the coolness against her heated skin. 'I...I don't know what to say.'

'Then don't say anything.' He raised an eyebrow. 'Unless you're ready to change your mind and come to bed with me.'

When Katrina shook her head and looked away, Alex sighed. 'I didn't think so.'

He was resigned to the fact that Katrina was going to make him kick his heels for several weeks before letting him into her bed. Her reasoning was a whole lot of gobbledegook that didn't make a lot of sense to him.

OK, he'd treated her badly. He was the first to admit that his behaviour had been appalling.

But she still wanted him—whether she wanted to admit it or not.

What was the point in making them wait? Frankly, he couldn't see any.

And while he was prepared to give her a bit of leeway he didn't plan on waiting for for ever. Maybe it was time to remind her of that.

'Just be aware that I won't let the current state of affairs continue for too much longer,' he warned softly.

Katrina, who now had her back to him as she busied herself at the stove, swung around. 'And what, pray tell, do you mean by that?'

Alex wasn't the least fazed by her snippy attitude. 'The situation will come to a head at some point. When it does, I won't take no for an answer.'

Her chin angled. 'Yes, you will. Otherwise it will be rape.'

Alex scowled at her. 'I've never had to force a woman to share my bed and I'm not about to start now. When the time comes, you'll be more than willing…you'll be begging me to take you.'

'I don't think so. You'll be lucky to even get to first base if you keep on avoiding me. The whole idea of waiting is so that we can establish a relationship before we sleep together. I need to learn to trust you again. I can't do that if I never see you.' She waved her spatula through the air. 'And have you even given a thought to the fact that by avoiding me you're also avoiding Sam?'

Alex frowned at her. 'I always pop into the nursery before I leave in the morning and again before I go to bed. I see Sam every day.'

'I didn't know that.' She turned to the stove, stirred the eggs for a moment and then swung back to him. 'But it's still not good enough. Not by a long shot. Sam's asleep then. I thought you said you were going to accept your responsibilities. But if you're not willing to make an effort to spend time with your daughter when she's awake then you're honouring diddley-squat!'

Alex immediately took offence. His glass landed on the granite bench-top with enough force to almost shatter it.

His father had neglected many of his responsibilities and had out-and-out abused others. The accusation Katrina had just thrown at him was totally unjustified. Couldn't she see how much effort he'd gone to to make sure his daughter was well provided for?

'How can you say that?' he demanded, his back ramrod straight. 'Sam has wanted for nothing since you moved in here. The second hand pram and capsule you had her in have been replaced by new ones. She has a wonderful nursery and heaps of toys. Everything that money can buy.'

She glared at him. 'This isn't about money. Or things. This is about love.'

'You know my opinion of that emotion,' he bit out coldly.

Her eyes grew so wide they dominated her face. 'I thought you were talking about your feelings regarding women—not your own flesh and blood.'

'Love is just a word that in and of itself means nothing. It's usually used as a substitute for something else. Between men and women, that something is usually lust. With familial relationships, it as often as not represents a combination of liking and respect.' He gave her a hard look. 'Sam will, without a doubt, have those things from me.'

'Well, you can't hope to bond with her on any level

if she's not even awake when you see her,' Katrina shot back at him, each word like a weapon she was using against him.

She really was Little Miss Confrontational these days, particularly where Samantha was concerned. 'That will happen in time. It's only been a couple of days.'

'Well, just remember that they are a couple of days you can never get back.' Katrina stared him in the eye, her face serious. 'Babies grow and develop so quickly; Sam has already changed so much since she was born. You'll both be missing out if you don't start spending time with her.'

Alex topped up his wine. In truth, he had been avoiding Samantha as much as he'd been avoiding Katrina—not that he intended to tell Katrina that. Nor did he intend to explain why he had been avoiding their daughter.

For the first time in years, the nightmares were back. Dreams of incidents from his past.

Some were of real beatings he'd been on the receiving end of. Beatings that had damaged his body but never his spirit.

Others were of his younger brother being similarly abused—despite Alex's attempts to stop it from happening.

Each image was so real it felt as if it had only just happened. Each vision was so authentic that he broke out in a cold sweat and woke trembling.

He knew why the dreams were back, of course—because he'd just learned that he was a father.

Now he had to face his greatest fear: that lurking somewhere inside him was the same monster that had lived inside his father.

Rationally, Alex knew he would never deliberately

hurt any child, least of all his own, in the way his father had taken pleasure in doing.

But what if he hurt Samantha through thoughtlessness or ignorance? What if he lost his temper and lashed out without thinking?

He'd done that once before, many years ago.

The thought of it happening again terrified the life out of him.

He would rather cut off an arm or a leg than hurt a single hair on Samantha's head.

But Katrina was right. There had to be a middle ground. Somewhere where he could build a relationship with his daughter at the same time as keeping her safe.

'OK. You've made your point, Little Miss Confrontation. I'll make sure I spend more time with her. Satisfied?'

She nodded. 'Tomorrow is Friday. I presume you don't work at weekends?'

Alex shook his head. 'I usually spend a couple of hours reading reports and doing emails, but, no, I don't work all weekend.'

'Then you have no objection if I arrange a couple of family outings for us, then, do you?'

If the quickest way into Katrina's bed was to spend time with her, then Alex would willingly spend every spare minute there he possessed.

And this conversation with Katrina forced him to acknowledge that spending quality time with his daughter was something he *must* do.

He'd spent so much time focussing on the practicalities of Samantha's care that he hadn't given a thought to the relationship itself.

Mind you, that was hardly surprising. It was easy to forget what a real father-child relationship should be like when you'd never had it.

Not that that was excuse. He'd watched his friends with their fathers. He'd been envious of the way other fathers had played ball with their sons, and how they'd told stupid jokes and teased each other.

There and then, Alex made a vow to himself: he was going to be a better father than his dad had been.

He would do things with Samantha. Lots of things.

And what better way of doing them than with Katrina at his side?

She was as fiercely protective of their daughter as a lioness with her cub. Nothing would happen while she was around to prevent it.

Alex shook his head and smiled, anticipation making his heart beat strongly in his chest. 'No. I have no objection whatsoever. In fact, I'm looking forward to it!'

The following day Katrina had just started to undress Samantha in preparation for bathing her when a sound made her turn.

She found Alex standing in the doorway, watching them.

He was wearing one of his to-die-for suits and a dark tie dotted with tiny diamonds.

He looked way too handsome for his own good, and Katrina had to swallow before speaking. 'Alex. I didn't hear you come in. You're home early.' Glad of an excuse to take her eyes away from him, she turned back to her daughter. 'Look who's here, Sam. It's Daddy.'

'I took what you said last night seriously. And, since

I managed to put out the fire on that deal earlier than I'd expected, I thought I'd surprise you.' He splayed his hands wide. 'So here I am, reporting for duty.'

'Well, you're just in time for Sam's bath. Why don't you join us?' she suggested softly.

He nodded. 'OK. What do I have to do?'

Katrina smothered a smile at the way Alex had asked the question. He sounded so serious and industrious, as if he had an important job to complete and he was waiting for a list of instructions.

'Well, since you've never bathed a baby before, I'll take care of the actual washing.' Katrina kept her face serious and her voice sober. 'But you have two very important tasks.'

He raised an eyebrow. 'And they are…?'

'First, you need to quack.'

Alex stared at her as if her skin had just broken out in a series of multicoloured spots. 'Quack?'

Katrina nodded and pointed to the yellow rubber-duck already bobbing on the water. 'Yes, quack. Sam likes the rubber duck but she likes it even more when you make quacking noises.'

'Really?' He looked and sounded sceptical.

'Yes, really.'

'And the second task?'

She placed a hand on his arm and leaned closer. 'Relax. Don't forget, you're meant to be having fun.'

Alex stared at her for a moment before his mouth turned up at the corners. 'Am I taking this too seriously?'

'Uh-huh.' She nodded. 'You certainly are. But then, you're an over-achiever. I wouldn't have expected anything less from you.'

His eyes glinted metallic blue. 'You're mocking me.'

'Maybe just a smidge,' she said, holding up thumb and forefinger with barely a hair's breadth between them. 'I used to love bath time. I want Sam to enjoy it too. So we try to have fun, don't we, poppet?'

Samantha cooed her total agreement.

'I see,' Alex said, still not sounding totally convinced.

'My mother was usually in charge of bath times, so it was a special treat when my dad came home early and supervised. I had a whole heap of toys, and Dad had sounds for each and every one of them.' She wrinkled her nose at him. 'He set the bar pretty high so you have a lot to live up to.'

'That's just great,' Alex muttered, as if the pressure of expectation was riding on his shoulders. 'You've never mentioned your father. Where does he live?'

'Nowhere. He died in a work accident when I was little.'

Alex frowned. 'How old were you when your mother died?'

'Thirteen.'

'What happened to you then? You said you had no other blood relatives.'

Tension slithered inside her. 'I went into foster care.'

'I never knew that.'

Katrina shrugged. 'I don't talk about it much. They weren't the happiest years of my life.'

He touched her arm. 'I'm sorry.' He glanced at Samantha then back to her. 'That's another reason you pushed so hard to make me accept Sam as my daughter, isn't it?'

Katrina nodded. 'I'd had quite an idyllic childhood

up until then. But afterwards…' She shivered. 'I don't want Sam to have to go through that—ever!'

'She won't have to.'

'I know. Thanks to you.'

'There's no need to thank me. She's my daughter.' He cleared his throat. 'Now, enough of this serious talk.' He shrugged off his suit jacket and hooked it over the door knob. Pulling his tie free, he neatly folded it before slipping it into his trouser pocket. Finally, he rolled up the sleeves of his business shirt to the elbows. 'I'm ready. Let's do it.'

Katrina finished undressing Samantha and slid her into the water.

The baby cooed and smiled. Quickly, Katrina used the soft sponge to give Samantha a quick all-over wash and then said to Alex, 'OK. It's over to you.'

Alex moved closer. His body brushed up against the side of hers, and the smell of male skin mixed with soap invaded her nostrils.

Katrina wanted to move away but it wasn't feasible. Instead, she tensed her stomach muscles and tried to pretend that it wasn't Alex standing beside her.

Alex hesitated and picked up the duck. He gave her a sideways glance. 'I feel ridiculous doing this.'

Katrina conceded that he did look uncomfortable. 'You don't have to do it if you don't want to.'

He dragged in a breath. 'No, I'll do it.'

Again, Katrina smothered a smile. He sounded as thought she'd just asked him to swallow a tablespoon of particularly obnoxious medicine and was screwing up his courage to do so.

A few half-hearted and less than enthusiastic quacks

followed. Samantha appeared fascinated by the fact that it was her father wielding the duck, but a little unsure about the sound he was making.

Katrina touched his arm for a moment before quickly retreating. 'Relax, Alex. Just remember what you liked when you were a kid and do the same thing.'

'I didn't have those kinds of bath times.'

Katrina looked at him. 'What sort of bath times did you have?'

His eyes met hers for an instant, the expression in them sending a shiver running down and then up her spine. 'Not the fun kind.'

Her heart wrenched. Not only had he gone to bed hungry but he hadn't had fun bath-times. What else had he been deprived of? she wondered, her heart going out to him.

'Well, just imagine what you would have liked and do that instead,' she suggested lightly.

Alex looked back at the duck, studied it for a moment and then let out a quack that immediately made both Katrina and Samantha smile.

Later, Katrina would wonder whether that was the moment she started falling in love with him all over again.

He raised a brow. 'Better?'

She smiled with genuine warmth. 'Much better.'

Katrina was thrilled with the effort Alex was making. Coming home early had earned him a brownie point. Helping with Samantha's bath had earned him another.

There was just one down side to all this. She was seeing another side of Alex. A softer side that she hadn't seen before.

The problem with that was that it made Alex more attractive.

And that was the last thing she needed, because she was already finding him attractive enough.

'I never knew bath time could be so much fun. Or so wet,' Alex said ten minutes later as he looked down at his drenched shirt-front.

Katrina giggled. 'I hope you're not planning on blaming our daughter for that.'

'I certainly am,' he replied indignantly. 'If she didn't laugh every time I whizzed the duck through the water and made those waves, then I wouldn't have kept on doing it.'

'Well, I hope you don't intend being that enthusiastic all the time. I'm saturated.' She plucked at her buttercup yellow blouse which was plastered against her like a second skin.

'I don't know,' Alex said huskily. 'I rather like the wet look.'

In fact, he more than liked it. Katrina's shirt was not only sticking to her like glue, but the water had also made the material semi-transparent. Alex could see the outline of her low-cut cream bra and the texture of the lace running along the edge. He could also see the outline of her erect nipples at the centre.

Unable to resist, Alex tunnelled a hand beneath the fall of her hair, bent his head and kissed her.

He'd barely had a chance to do more than taste the sweetness of her lips before Katrina dragged her mouth from under his. 'Don't, Alex.'

'Why not?' he demanded.

Her eyes didn't meet his. 'Sam is getting cold.'

Because there was a grain of truth in Katrina's statement, Alex didn't argue. But before he let her go he looked her in the eye and said, 'The day is coming when you're going to run out of excuses.'

Her eyes flashed quick-silver and she tossed her head.

Without saying a single word she'd managed to convey—graphically—exactly what she thought of that suggestion.

How had he ever thought that Katrina was biddable? Alex asked himself.

She was about as docile as an atomic bomb.

For some reason he found that fact as arousing as he found it irritating.

He wanted to reach out and haul her into his arms. But he resisted the urge. 'I think you'd better take Sam and get out of here before my baser instincts get the better of me.'

He heard her breath catch, but she didn't move. She just stood there staring at him.

'You have until the count of three,' Alex warned softly. 'And then you'd better not tell me that I didn't warn you. One. Two…'

She scuttled from the room with Samantha, swaddled in a fluffy towel, still in her arms.

Alex dragged in a deep breath. And then another. Slowly his heartbeat returned to normal.

When he felt that he was under control he went through the door to the adjoining nursery. Katrina had just finished dressing Samantha in a pair of pyjamas dotted with pink, blue and yellow teddy-bears.

'What happens now?' he asked lightly.

'It's bed time. I fed her before she had her bath. She seems to prefer it that way.'

'Well, I'd better kiss her goodnight, then.' He stepped forward. Before Katrina had time to object, Alex closed his arms around both of them. 'Goodnight, Princess,' he whispered, brushing his lips across Samantha's forehead and then her cheek.

Sam cooed with pleasure.

The simple sound was as powerful as a sword being thrust through his heart.

Warm pleasure flooded his insides until he felt as if he was glowing.

Holding Katrina and Samantha in his arms felt so right. As if it was meant to be.

Although he wasn't a believer in fate—he preferred to think that a man controlled his own destiny—Alex embraced the feeling.

'Alex, let me go. I need to put Sam down.'

Alex looked down. Already Samantha's lashes were fluttering closed. Reluctantly, he let his arms drop to his sides and then stood watching as Katrina tucked their daughter into her cot.

Samantha was asleep the minute her head hit the pillow.

Katrina picked up what he presumed was a baby monitor and flicked the dial. 'Does she still wake through the night?' he asked, guiltily aware that this was yet another aspect of parenting he hadn't given a thought to.

'Yes. I've been feeding her twice during the night, but it's gradually dropping down to one.'

Alex frowned. 'That must be pretty tiring.'

She nodded. 'It is. But it won't last for for ever. You have to be philosophical about these things.'

'I suppose you do. Now, why don't we get changed

into some dry clothes and then you can tell me what you have planned for the weekend.'

'OK. It will take me a few minutes. I need to clean up the bathroom.' She wrinkled her nose at him but there was a twinkle in her eyes as she said, 'Someone I know got water all over the cabinet and the floor.'

'Oops. I think that's my cue to leave.'

As he left the room Alex felt satisfied by what had transpired in the last few hours.

He'd enjoyed the evening. He'd enjoyed it a lot more than he'd expected.

He had a good feeling about this. About Samantha—and Katrina. His two girls.

He smiled.

That had rather a nice ring to it. Now more than ever he knew he'd done the right thing. His two girls belonged with him.

CHAPTER SEVEN

WHEN Katrina entered the lounge, Alex was there before her. He was seated on one of several brown-leather couches, his long legs stretched out in front of him.

Gone was the business suit. In its place was a pair of worn denims that clung to his lean hips and powerful thighs, and a figure-hugging cotton sports-shirt in a shade of blue paler than his eyes. His hair was damp, as if he'd just had a shower, and his jaw had lost the end-of-day stubble he'd been sporting, suggesting he'd also shaved.

He looked gorgeous and sexy and way too attractive.

Alex saw her and smiled. It was a smile that pierced straight through her. 'I took the liberty of pouring you a glass of white wine. I hope that's all right?'

'That's fine. Thanks.'

Alex scooped up the glass from the coffee table and held it out to her. Katrina crossed the room and took it from his outstretched hand. Their fingers brushed and a tingle of electricity zapped up her arm.

She jerked, almost spilling the wine.

Alex frowned. 'Why are you so jumpy?'

She shrugged. 'I don't know. I'm probably just tired.'

Even as she said the words she knew they weren't true.

She was nervous. She knew it was stupid but she couldn't help it. Sharing Samantha's bath time with Alex made her feel as if she'd been suddenly stripped of all her defences.

It had started with their close physical proximity; it had been impossible to ignore the heat radiating off his body straight into hers. Impossible, too, to ignore the smell of his skin or the scent of his shampoo.

But what had really undone her was seeing the other side of Alex. She was used to Alex as he usually was. Confident. Controlled. Arrogant.

This evening, he'd totally disarmed her with his willingness to be teased and his eagerness to please Samantha and the hint of vulnerability he'd shown.

Alex patted the sofa beside him. 'Well, sit down for a while and relax.'

Katrina hesitated a moment before taking the seat opposite.

Alex frowned and put his wine glass down on the table with a clatter. 'This has to stop.'

Katrina clasped her hands around her glass. 'What does?'

He stared at her through narrowed eyes. 'Last night you accused me of avoiding you. Well, now it's my turn. I'm going to accuse you of doing the exact same thing.'

She folded her arms. 'You can hardly accuse me of avoiding you when we've spent the last hour together.'

'Actually, I can. You might be in the same room, but you're doing your best to prevent me getting close to you. Every time I touch you, you jump. Every time I kiss you, you come up with an excuse to stop me.'

'You said you'd let me set the pace,' Katrina protested.

'And I also said that I'd give the pace a nudge along every now and then. There is a halfway point, you know. Would it really have hurt you to sit beside me for a while? Maybe hold hands, share a couple of kisses?'

Katrina didn't want to answer him.

She didn't want to admit that she had stop him from doing those things because she was scared of what would happen if she didn't.

'You're meant to be trying but you're not,' Alex continued. 'You accused me of honouring diddley-squat but what about you?'

Katrina clenched her hands into fists at her side. 'I'm not the one who started this, Alex. You are. I can't just wave a magic wand and forget all the horrible things you said to me. It's not that easy.'

Alex sat forward and splayed his hands wide, forearms resting on his knees. 'What do you want me to say, Katrina? I *should* have believed you. I know that. I made the biggest mistake of my life when I said those things to you. And we've all paid for it.' His eyes seared into hers. 'I missed seeing you grow big with our child. I missed watching my daughter being born. As you pointed out yesterday, I can never get those things back.'

He paused but only to draw breath. 'And you. You were alone during your pregnancy and the birth. But it's not the same as having the father of your child with you during that special time. And Sam…? She went without a father for the first weeks of her life.'

'Alex—'

He held up a hand, his face gravely serious. 'No, let me finish. I want you to know that I haven't taken any of those things lightly. When I apologised to you, I wasn't just paying lip service. I wasn't going through the motions just for the sake of it. I apologised because I meant it.'

Katrina stared at him.

She didn't say a word. She couldn't. She was stunned by what Alex had just said, and how he'd said it.

His voice was so full of passion that each word had exploded inside her like a bomb detonating.

She had no doubt he meant every word.

'I can't undo the past,' Alex continued. 'But what I *can* do is work on the future. I'm willing to do everything within my power to make us a family. The question is, are you? Or are you so bitter that you can't ever forgive me? Because if that's the case then you should tell me—right here and right now—and we'll call it quits before we go any further.'

Katrina felt as though the bottom had just dropped out of her stomach and her world. A vacuum formed inside her; anxiety clutched at the back of her throat.

Much as she didn't want to admit it, there was a lot of truth in what Alex was saying.

She remembered the moment he'd apologised.

I'm sorry, he'd said.

And she, without a second's hesitation, had said, *apology accepted.*

Why? Because it had been the right thing to do—for Samantha.

But that had been the mother in her talking, the part of her that would do anything for her daughter—including swallowing her pride.

But she wasn't just a mother.

She was a woman too.

And the woman in her had been thinking that Alex's apology was way too little and way too late. The woman in her had clung to every little barb and every little jab of pain as if it were her lover.

Alex said he hadn't just been going through the motions when he'd apologised. Katrina was ashamed to admit that her acceptance of his apology had been exactly that: it had been expedient. A means to an end.

But, deep down, she hadn't forgiven Alex.

There was a ball of bitter resentment inside her that hadn't unravelled in the least. It was as tightly wound as the day it had formed.

She dragged in a breath then met his eyes squarely. 'There's some truth in what you said. I must admit, I didn't think your apology was genuine.'

'And now that you realise it was?'

She couldn't lie. She couldn't take something as pure as his honesty and as deeply felt as his regret and rip them to shreds. It would be like plucking the stars from the sky and trying to squash them under her heel.

'It…it makes a difference,' she said, unable to look away from him.

Already she could feel the ball of resentment and bitterness unravelling, as if it was made out of string and Alex had taken one end and was slowly pulling on it.

'Good.' The fact that he didn't hide his relief underlined the importance he was placing on their conversation. 'But is it enough? Is it enough to allow you to *really* put the past behind you and move forward?'

'I'm not sure,' she said honestly.

She hadn't had a chance to think that far.

She was confused, and scared. As if the world had spun into action and she was no longer sure of her place in it.

There had been a certain security in clinging to those bad memories. Hanging on to them had had the same effect as placing a protective barrier around her heart. They'd made her feel safe.

Realising Alex had meant every word of his apology had just torn that protective barrier to shreds. And spending the evening with him and Samantha had stripped her of her defences.

It was a double whammy that left her feeling exposed and vulnerable.

Alex leaned back against the sofa. Although his movement added only an extra foot to the distance between them, it suddenly felt like miles of wide, open space.

Suddenly, Alex felt as out of reach as a man on the moon.

And she…

Well, she felt very alone and isolated.

'Then I suggest you think about it,' he said in a cool, clipped voice. 'If you can't let go of the past, then we don't stand a chance. If you're not prepared to try, we're wasting our time.'

Her heart thumped. 'And Sam?' she asked, knowing what the answer would be but needing to hear it anyway.

'I told you before—I don't intend to give up my right to being a full-time father.' He sounded as determined as a bulldozer ploughing through a brick wall. 'Think about it: if you decide to call it quits now, everybody loses. You. Me. But most of all Sam.'

Katrina stared at him. Thoughts were spinning with fevered intensity through her brain.

Fear was beating on the inside of her skull.

If she pulled the plug, she would lose Samantha.

She'd rather cut out her heart than let that happen.

Alex sighed, heavily. 'Tell me something, Katrina. When you confronted me in the boardroom what did you hope to achieve?'

It was a good question. It was just a shame that she didn't have a good answer.

'I'm not sure.' She clasped her hands tightly together in her lap. 'I tried not to have too many expectations because I was afraid of being disappointed. Obviously, I wanted you to accept Sam and be a part of her life, but I hadn't thought as far as the practicalities of how we'd go about doing that.'

Alex stared at her for a long moment.

It felt as though he was looking right inside her. Into her mind. Her heart. Her soul.

'You keep on telling me this is about Sam. But do you know what I think? I think you're fooling yourself. If you were really putting Sam first you'd be going out of your way to make this relationship work instead of putting up obstacles at every opportunity. I don't think this is about Sam any more. This is about you. This is about your hurt feelings, your wounded pride.'

His words lingered in the room like the residue of gunfire, bouncing off one wall and then another. They rebounded inside her head with the same ferocity.

Because he was right.

It *was* about her and her hurt feelings.

It was about the things he'd said to her when she'd told him she was pregnant, and it was also about the fact that she'd loved Alex with all her heart and he hadn't loved her.

But more than anything it was about trying to avoid getting on the slippery slide of emotions that would lead to her falling in love with him all over again.

Alex could barely breathe as he waited for Katrina's reply.

He had handled this conversation like a rank amateur. For a man who negotiated multi-million-dollar contracts, and managed billions of dollars worth of investments, he had bungled one of the most important conversations of his life.

He'd pushed too soon.

It was a strategic mistake he never made when he was trying to land a big deal, but he'd made it now.

With every second that passed his stomach muscles grew more and more rigid and his throat felt as if invisible hands were squeezing around it.

All the while his eyes never left her face.

Finally, after what felt like for ever, her chin came up. She looked beautiful, proud, grave and serious. 'You're right. This is meant to be about Sam, but I've let my feelings get in the way. For that I apologise.'

The air rushed from his lungs so quickly he felt light headed.

He'd been half-convinced she was going to tell him their relationship would never work. That she would never be able to forgive him for the things he'd said to her.

What he'd have done then, he didn't have a clue.

He would not have wanted to take Samantha away from her mother, but nor would he have been prepared to abandon her.

It would have been an impossible choice—and one he was glad he didn't have to make.

And Katrina? Well, he wasn't prepared to let her go either.

She was the mother of his child. She was also the woman he wanted more than he thought it was possible to want a woman.

Relief and pleasure burst to life inside him.

'Apology accepted,' he said smoothly.

She raised a delicately plucked eyebrow. 'Just like that?'

He inclined his head. 'Just like that. As we keep on saying, this is about Sam. We've both forgotten that on occasion. We've let our feelings get in the way of what's best for her.' He stared at her, coiled tension strangling his insides. 'Can I take it you're prepared to give it a shot? To try to make *us* work?'

Anticipation held him still.

'I do want to make this work,' she started carefully.

'This…?' he prompted.

Her cheeks flushed with colour. '*Us*. My reasons for wanting both of us in Sam's life still stand. And I have to admit that providing Sam with a real family is by far the best thing for her.'

Alex sat as still as a statue for an entire minute, letting her words filter though his system.

Then he moved.

Rising to his feet, he rounded the coffee table until he was standing right in front of her. Reaching down, he grasped her hands and pulled her upright, straight into his waiting arms.

Her hands went to his chest. 'But that doesn't mean—'

Alex refused to let her go. His eyes drilled into hers. 'Yes. That's exactly what it means.'

'Alex—'

He kissed the words right out of her mouth. His mouth glided over hers, and one hand tangled in the silken length of her hair. Finally, heart pounding, he lifted his head. 'Doesn't it?'

Katrina stared at him. A mixture of emotions flitted across the surface of her eyes like scudding clouds. 'I don't think…'

'Don't think,' Alex whispered. His hand tightened in her hair, pulling her head back on the slender length of her neck. *'Feel!'*

And then he kissed her again. And again.

When he lifted his head Katrina was clutching his shirt front and her body was trembling against him.

He ran a hand over the soft silkiness of her hair. 'I'm going to make love to you,' he warned softly.

He gave her plenty of time to stop him.

But she didn't.

Alex didn't need a second invitation. He smoothed a strand of hair back behind her ear, his fingertips feathering against her cheek. He pulled her closer, so close the smell of female flesh wrapped seductively around him.

He bent his head and claimed her with his mouth, softly at first and then with more intensity, prising her lips apart.

This time when he lifted his head he rested his forehead against hers. 'I want you to be sure,' he whispered. 'If you're not, you'd better tell me now because in another minute or two it will be too late.'

For a heartbeat she didn't say anything.

Alex could hardly breathe. He didn't even think his heart was beating.

And then she smiled. 'I'm sure.'

Not saying a word—he didn't think he could utter a single syllable when she was looking up at him with desire-drenched eyes—he swung her up in his arms and carried her down the corridor.

He was almost at his bedroom door when he hesitated.

He'd always made it a practice to keep the women in his life out of his bed. It was a demarcation line that he had never crossed, a warning to his lovers that their position in his life was limited.

But Katrina was the mother of his child. She was the woman he wanted above all others.

She had just agreed to try and make their relationship work.

Surely those old boundaries had no place in his life any more?

'What is it?' Katrina asked when Alex hesitated in the hallway.

'Nothing.'

Instinctively, Katrina knew that it was far from nothing. In fact, her heart soared when he pulled open the door, the significance of the action not lost on her.

Alex had always found little—and sometimes big— ways of maintaining an emotional distance from her.

Keeping her out of his apartment, and thus out of his own bed, had been one of them. If she'd wanted a sign that he was committed to making their relationship work, he'd just given it to her.

They were both taking steps towards being a real family.

Some were baby steps. Others as significant as man landing on the moon.

Alex put her carefully down in the centre of the king-sized bed. Straightening, he began unbuttoning his shirt before shrugging it off and dropping it on the floor.

Katrina's mouth ran dry. Alex had a fantastic body, the result of daily jogging and strenuous gym sessions. She watched as his fingers went to his belt buckle.

She could hardly draw breath as Alex kicked his trousers aside, divested himself of his underpants and strode to the bed. Although his movements were economical rather than designed to arouse, Katrina couldn't take her eyes off him.

A pulse beat between her legs, and a dragging sensation pulled at her insides. Then she wasn't thinking at all as Alex came down on the bed beside her.

'Sit up,' he instructed, his voice rippling down her spine.

Katrina did as she was told, albeit shakily.

Alex stripped her of her clothes with a speed that left her reeling. When his eyes focussed on her naked breasts, they grew heavy, desire tightening their tips into prominent peaks.

'Back.' His voice was hoarse.

She did as she was told, this time collapsing back against the pillows, her breath coming in little gasps.

Alex looked at her. Just looked at her.

'I'd forgotten how beautiful you are,' he murmured, his voice feathering down her spine. 'You are truly magnificent.'

'So are you.'

He didn't answer her.

At least, not with words.

But his touch told her a lot.

He caressed her almost reverently, as if he were afraid she would disappear in a puff of smoke the minute he touched her.

His hand flattened over her abdomen and his eyes flashed to hers. 'What did you look like when you were pregnant?' he asked huskily.

Her breath hitched in the back of her throat. It was the last question she'd expected. 'Like most women, I suppose—big and fat.'

He shook his head. 'I bet you were stunning. I would have liked to have seen you swollen with my child.'

It was a beautiful thing to say.

Her heart swelled until it was fit to burst. She wasn't sure how to respond so she said nothing.

And then she wasn't capable of thinking at all as Alex bent his head and kissed her.

His hands and mouth were everywhere, fire and silk. He knew exactly what drove her to distraction. Knew what made her cry out loud with ecstasy—and what made her thrash against the pillow.

Unable to contain the sensations coursing through her, she dug her nails into his skin.

Alex lifted his head. 'Drawing blood again, are you, Kat?' he asked huskily, using the pet name he only ever used when they were in bed together.

Katrina smiled and dug them a little bit harder. 'Yes, I am. You'd better be careful you don't bleed to death.'

Surprised appreciation burst from his throat in laughter that soon turned to a groan as she took him in her hand and boldly stroked him. He left her side only long enough to ensure they were protected, then spread her trembling thighs and plunged inside her.

Katrina cried out. The feel of him filling and stretching her sent pleasure rolling through her in waves. She wanted to hang on to this moment for ever.

Alex froze as if she'd shot him. 'Did I hurt you? I didn't think. After the baby…'

'I'm OK.' She moved her hips in an upward motion that drew him in even deeper. 'More than OK.'

His frown turned into a sexy smile as he withdrew and thrust again. 'I can see that.'

They didn't talk any more after that. It was as if a spell had been woven around them, transporting them to a magical place where there was just the two of them, dominated by senses spinning out of control and hearts beating as one.

Alex threaded a strand of Katrina's hair through his fingers and let it drop on to the pillow. It felt like silk and looked like multi-coloured satin, moonbeams picking out strands of cinnamon, gold and honey.

The clock showed it was just gone one in the morning. He should be asleep. Why he wasn't, he had no idea.

He usually slept through the night without stirring—particularly after making love.

Maybe it was because this was the first time he'd shared his bed with a woman. He'd always thought he wouldn't like it. He enjoyed his own space, and was partial to sprawling across the sheets without having to worry about someone else getting in the way.

But waking and finding Katrina's soft, warm body wrapped around his had sent a shaft of pleasure through him.

He picked up another handful of hair and let it play through his fingers. This time some fell against her cheek. Softly, he stroked it back off her face.

Then, giving in to temptation, he reached down and pressed a kiss against the corner of her mouth. She murmured in her sleep and rolled towards him.

Alex wrapped his arms around her and kissed her again.

She blinked and opened her eyes. 'Alex.' His name was a sigh on her lips, a sigh that echoed inside him.

'No regrets?' he whispered.

She shook her head, and then she smiled at him. Not just with her mouth, but with her eyes. A hand reached inside his chest and squeezed tight. It was the way she used to smile at him. Alex didn't realise until that moment just how much he'd missed it.

'No regrets,' she whispered.

Satisfaction, and an emotion he couldn't quite define, swept through him. He rolled over so that she was half-lying beneath him. 'Good...because I want to make love to you again.'

She dug her fingers into his hair. 'I'm not stopping you.'

CHAPTER EIGHT

'Do YOU realise that's the first time Sam has slept right through the night?' Katrina said the next morning.

Alex brushed her hair aside then angled his mouth against the side of her throat. 'Obviously she realised that her parents had more important things to do.' His mouth slid lower, nibbling at the area where her neck met her shoulder. 'In fact, that's given me an idea.'

Katrina laughed. 'I can feel exactly what kind of an idea it's given you, and the answer is no. We can't right now.' To soften the blow, she turned in his arms, reached on to her tiptoes and pressed a kiss against his mouth. She'd forgotten how nice it was to touch him whenever she wanted to and kiss him whenever she felt like it. 'Our daughter needs feeding before she wakes the entire building.'

'You're right. You'd better attend to her before the neighbours call and complain. I'm going to have a shower.' Looking down at his body, he grimaced. 'I'd better make it a cold one.'

Katrina giggled.

Alex wagged a finger at her. 'You'll pay for that, young lady.'

'I'll look forward to it,' she said saucily.

Alex laughed.

Katrina was still smiling as she went in to the nursery. 'OK, missy, that will be enough out of you. Mamma's here to feed you.'

Reaching into the cot, she picked up her daughter and walked to the chair she reserved for feeding.

A couple of minutes later, Katrina looked down at her daughter suckling at her breast and realised that she felt happier than she had in a long, long time.

Even Samantha's birth, which should have been the most special, magical moment of her life, had been marred by the fact that Alex hadn't been there to share it with her.

For the first time, Katrina believed they had a future together. Before now she hadn't even dared to hope that it was even a possibility.

If there was one thing that could bridge the gap between them, it was their daughter. She was a unifying force that could just create a miracle.

'I think we're going to make it,' she whispered, stroking a hand down her daughter's back.

After dressing Samantha, Katrina went in search of Alex. The smell of frying bacon led her to the kitchen.

'I thought you said you couldn't cook,' she said, when she saw the feast he was preparing.

'Bacon and eggs isn't what I'd call *cooking*. All you have to do is shove them in the pan and make sure you get them out before they burn. Even I can manage that.' He turned and looked at Samantha. 'Good morning, Princess.'

Katrina put the bassinette down on the floor. 'Do you need a hand?'

'No. I have everything under control.'

Katrina watched Alex move confidently around the

kitchen. He had on the same worn denims he'd been wearing the previous evening, but this time he'd teamed them with a plain white T-shirt. Both clung in all the right places and Katrina couldn't stop her eyes from roaming over him.

'OK. We're ready,' he said, and put a plate piled high with food in front of her.

She laughed. 'I hope you don't expect me to eat all that.'

'Don't worry. I'll finish whatever you don't eat.' His eyes glinted. 'I happen to be starving this morning.'

Katrina flushed. She knew exactly what had given him such a healthy appetite.

Alex laughed. Then, obviously taking pity on her, he asked, 'So, how has your first week been?'

'After last night, how can I say that it's been anything but good?'

Alex grinned. It was a very boyish grin.

Like her, he seemed more relaxed. More at ease with the situation.

Last night they'd turned a corner. It wasn't just that they'd slept together; it went a lot deeper than that.

They'd addressed some important issues. Not only had they demolished a couple of stumbling blocks but they'd taken some positive steps forward.

For the time since she'd moved in, they really were a united team, working towards a common goal.

Katrina had to admit that it felt good.

'You're good for a man's ego.' The grin dropped from his face. 'But, seriously, how has it been? You have a new baby and a new home. You're going through some big adjustments. It would be quite normal for you to be feeling a little out of kilter.'

'I'm getting there. Settling into a routine has helped. But I must admit I feel as if I have too much time on my hands. I can hardly wait to get back to work.' She gave him an appealing look. 'Does that make me a bad mother?'

'Of course not,' Alex was quick to answer. 'But, speaking of your job, I'd like you to reconsider going back to work.'

Katrina just stared at him. 'Why?'

He shrugged. 'My mother had no choice but to work. She wasn't there when…' He raked a hand through his hair and around the back of his neck. 'Let's just say she wasn't always there when we needed her. I'd prefer it if Sam was your main priority.'

'Let's get something straight, Alex,' Katrina said, sitting up ramrod-straight. 'Sam is *always* my top priority. I can work and be a mother at the same time, you know. Just as *you* can work and be a father.'

'OK. Fair comment. But I'd really prefer one of us to be available all the time. At least until she's old enough to go to school. And, while I could be that person, it doesn't make sense financially.' He placed his hand over hers. 'I feel strongly about this. Please—will you at least think about it?'

Katrina unbent a little. At least he was asking her, not telling her. 'OK, I'll think about it. But I'm not promising anything,' she added quickly when she saw his smile. 'I really wouldn't know what to do with myself. I'm already struggling.'

His smile widened. 'Well, I might just have a solution for your boredom.'

Katrina grimaced as she cut into a crispy piece of bacon. 'Don't put it like that. It makes me sound as though I don't appreciate Sam, and I do. I love her to bits. She just doesn't completely fill my day.'

'You don't need to apologise. I completely understand. You're used to being busy; there's nothing wrong with that.'

'You said you might have a solution?' she asked hopefully.

He nodded. 'I do. In fact, I have a number of suggestions.'

'What are they?'

Alex gave her another of those boyish grins that made her heart turn over. 'I'm a big-shot executive, you know. I expect to be paid for my ideas.'

The look in his eyes made it perfectly clear exactly what kind of payment he was referring to.

Desire pooled low in her belly, her nipples tightening in the confines of her bra. 'Do you, now?'

His eyes glinted. 'Yes, I do.'

Katrina rose to her feet and went to brush past him. 'Well, I'd better go and get my purse. I'm sure I can spare twenty cents.'

Alex snagged her wrist and pulled her down onto his lap. 'Twenty cents? That's an outrage.'

'You're right.' Katrina nodded seriously. 'In the current financial climate, we should be watching our pennies. Let's make it ten cents instead.'

The tips of his fingers found the sides of her ribcage and tickled her.

Katrina writhed like an eel, her bottom grinding into his lap.

'Stop!' she gasped. 'I give up.'

Alex stopped wriggling his fingers and stared down

at her. 'You're going to have to pay for your insubordination, young lady. The price has just gone up. It's now going to cost you two kisses for each of my ideas'

She looked at him from under her lashes. In this mood, Alex was simply irresistible. 'I think I can manage that,' she murmured, her insides curling in anticipation.

His arms tightened around her. 'Well, pucker up, sweetheart. Here comes kiss number one.'

Katrina did as she was told and pursed her lips. His mouth landed softly on hers, lingered for just a moment and then retreated.

Her eyes blinked open.

'Now for kiss two,' he whispered huskily.

Her eyes fluttered closed again. This time his lips claimed her mouth with searing intensity. When he was done, he ran the tip of his tongue around the edge of her mouth before lifting his head.

'Just how many of these ideas do you have?' she whispered.

'A few.'

'Good,' she breathed.

Alex laughed. She could feel the rumble of his chest against her side.

He tapped her on the nose with the tip of his finger. 'OK. Pay attention now. Because I'm about to tell you about my first idea.'

'OK. I'm all ears.'

With his spare hand, Alex rubbed the side of his jaw. 'I've been thinking about this apartment.'

'What about it? It's gorgeous.' It was gorgeous— even if she did feel like she was living in a fancy hotel rather than a real home.

'But it's not exactly child-friendly, is it? It's OK for the moment. But as soon as Sam starts to walk it will be a disaster.'

Katrina looked through the open kitchen door at the miles of plush, cream carpet and the glass-topped tables and grimaced. 'You're right. In fact "disastrous" would be an understatement.'

'Which is why I'd suggest you start looking for a new house for us.'

Katrina struggled into a sitting position on his lap and stared him straight in the eye. 'Do you mean it?'

He nodded. 'I've been thinking about it ever since you moved in, but the time never seemed right to suggest it. I think it is now, don't you?'

The question was an acknowledgement of how much things had changed between them. Obviously Alex had been hanging back until their relationship was on a more stable footing. Now that they were both commit-ted, he'd put his foot on the accelerator and was ready to go full steam ahead.

She nodded.

'I want something with a yard for Sam to play in, and maybe a swimming pool,' Alex suggested thoughtfully.

Katrina remembered his tirade the day he'd learned he was Samantha's father; he'd mentioned that he'd grown up in a small apartment without a yard to play in.

'I think that's a wonderful idea. Have you got an area in mind?'

'I was thinking about somewhere on the north shore. What do you think?'

'That's fine. Apart from the yard and the pool, do you have any other requirements?'

Alex started rattling off a list of criteria that made her head spin. 'Hang on a minute; I need to write this down.'

Scrambling off his lap, Katrina dashed through to her bedroom, rooted around in her handbag for her notepad-cum-diary and returned to the kitchen.

Sitting back down in her seat, she scribbled down a couple of things, asked Alex to repeat several others and dutifully added them to the list. Luckily, they had similar tastes, and most of what he'd suggested matched her requirements. 'What about budget?'

He named a figure that took her breath away. 'Now you've lost me.'

He frowned. 'What do you mean?'

'I was thinking of the kind of house I grew up in, which was a two bedroomed semi-detached cottage with a garage and a small yard. You're talking about something altogether different.'

'Not really. Just something bigger.'

'And grander,' she said, trying to keep her tone even.

'You don't like grand?' he asked, raising an eyebrow.

How did she answer that? 'I guess I'm not used to it. I want a home that…' She shrugged, not sure how to put her feelings into words. 'Well, something that feel like a *home* rather than a showpiece.'

'Can't it be both?'

'I suppose so,' she said doubtfully.

'I know so.'

Katrina sighed and chewed on the end of her pen. 'Wherever we buy, it needs to be reasonably close to schools too.'

'Which brings me to my next point.' Alex beckoned her with a finger and a come-hither smile that made her heart go crazy. 'But not without my payment. Come here.'

Katrina rose to her feet, a tingle of excitement rippling through her. Instead of sitting in his lap, she bent from the waist and pressed her mouth against his. Alex fed his hands into the hair on either side of her head and took control of the kiss.

Slowly, he withdrew his mouth from hers. 'One,' he breathed. 'Two,' he said, and plundered her mouth again.

By the time he lifted his mouth from hers, Katrina's legs were trembling so badly she was in danger of falling down. She staggered backwards and collapsed in her seat.

Neither said anything for a moment. Silence filled with the beat of desire wrapped around them.

Alex was the first to break it. He cleared his throat before speaking. 'I want Sam to go to the best school we can afford. I don't know a lot about how this works, but I should imagine we might have to put her name down somewhere quite early. Why don't you do some research into our options? If you come up with a shortlist we can register our intentions with a couple of schools.'

Katrina, who had been educated more than adequately in a state school, opened her mouth to argue but just as quickly shut it again. From previous comments, it was clear Alex's experience had not been as good as hers. If he wanted to send Samantha to an expensive school, then who was she to argue?

She picked up her pen and tapped the end on the table. 'Maybe I should look at schools first. It might influence where we decide to live.'

'Good idea.'

She snapped her diary closed. 'Well, that ought to keep me busy for a while.'

'I haven't finished yet,' Alex said smoothly.

Her eyebrows shot towards her hairline. 'What else is there?'

He looked at her with a glint in his eyes.

Katrina couldn't help it; she laughed. She held up her hands in mock surrender. 'I know, I know. Kisses.'

She propped her elbows on the table and leaned forwards. Alex met her halfway.

This time when they kissed only their mouths touched.

But that was enough. More than enough. When it was over they both collapsed back into their seats.

Katrina felt dazed, as if she'd been plugged into an electrical outlet and the power switched on to full voltage. There were so many sensations racing through her system she half-expected her hair to stand on end before emitting fiery sparks.

Alex appeared similarly affected, although he was the first to recover.

He raked a hand through his hair. His eyes were such a dark blue they appeared almost black. 'OK. Now, where was I? Yes, that's right; I almost forgot. I have a couple of functions coming up. I'd like you to attend them with me.'

Katrina dragged in a deep breath and tried to concentrate. 'What kind of functions?'

'They're business dinners—which brings me to my last suggestion.'

Katrina went to stand up but his next words stopped her. 'No, don't get up. I'll collect my payment afterwards. In bed.'

Anticipation burned a hole in her stomach. Excitement made a pulse beat at the apex of her thighs.

'OK. What is it?' she asked breathlessly.

'We're going to need some kind of childcare if you're going to attend functions with me.'

The suggestion caught her off-guard. If felt as though a bucket of cold water had just been poured over her. A hollow formed inside her. Her breath hitched in the back of her throat.

'I've never been separated from Sam before,' she said doubtfully.

'It has to happen some time.'

Katrina stared at Sam, who was watching the brightly coloured butterfly mobile dangling over her head.

The thought of being separated from her baby for even a short time made her feel uncomfortable. Yet the last thing she wanted was turn into one of those over-protective mothers.

'It wouldn't be for very long,' Alex encouraged softly. 'Just a couple of hours to start with.'

'I know.' Her mouth twisted. 'I'm being silly.'

Alex shook his head. 'No, you're not. You're just being protective, which is what every mother should be. Never apologise for that. Never.'

He spoke so fervently that Katrina knew he had to be talking from personal experience. She wanted to ask what had happened to make him feel that way, but wasn't sure how to frame the question hovering on the tip of her tongue.

In the end she swallowed the words back. There was more than one way to skin a cat. She could ask the same question in a roundabout way. 'I don't like the idea of leaving Sam with strangers. Maybe your mother could look after her?'

Even before she'd finished speaking, Alex was shaking his head. 'I don't think so.'

'Why not? I'd much rather have her minded by a relative. I'd have thought you'd prefer that too.'

'In some instances relatives can be worse than strangers,' Alex said roughly.

'Oh.'

A void opened up inside her, filled with cold and whistling winds.

'Just what kind of family did he come from?' It was only when she saw the way Alex was staring at her that Katrina realised she'd asked the question out loud.

'Let's just say that being strong and protective weren't my mother's strong points,' Alex said in the same grim voice. 'When I was a kid I could have done with someone like you fighting in my corner. I admire you for the way you've fought for Sam every step of the way.'

A wedge of emotion formed in the back of her throat. It wasn't so much what Alex had said that made her feel sad but what he hadn't said. Instinct warned her that when he'd described his childhood as being lousy it had been an understatement.

'You haven't told your family about Sam, have you?' she asked quietly.

Alex couldn't hide his surprise. 'How did you know that?'

She shrugged. 'It was a simple matter of deduction. If you'd told your mother, she'd have been around here in a flash. After all, I'm presuming Sam is her first grandchild?'

'Yes, she is.'

Katrina squeezed her hands tightly together in front of her. 'Why didn't you tell them?'

She could tell from the look on Alex's face that this was a conversation he would prefer to avoid. 'As you've no doubt gathered, we're not close. What you don't know is that my family is actually a disaster.'

The look in his eyes chilled her to the bone. Her scalp contracted. Her stomach shrunk to the size of a pea.

Alex raked a hand through his hair and towards the back of his neck, got halfway through then stopped the action abruptly. 'I'll tell you the bare bones and then I don't want to talk about it again. OK?'

'OK.'

Her stomach shrunk some more until it felt in danger of disappearing altogether.

'My father was abusive.'

The world stilled and then tilted in on its axis. Her heart hammered.

'What…what do you mean by "abusive"?' She could hardly get the word out. Even the taste of it on her tongue was obscene.

His eyes didn't waver from hers. 'I won't go into details. Suffice to say that my brother and I were mistreated both emotionally and physically by him.'

Katrina gasped; she couldn't help it. Her hand crept protectively to the base of her throat. 'That's awful.'

She didn't think Alex even heard her. He barked out a harsh laugh that had no amusement in it. 'He always claimed that he hurt us for our own good, so that we'd grow up to be good and strong. You know? Character building. It was a lie, of course. He was just a sick bully who got what he deserved in the end.'

The hand at her throat inched higher. When he'd mentioned being bullied she'd never imagined that it had been at the hands of his own father. 'What…what happened to him?'

The eyes that met hers were as cold as chips of blue ice. 'I put him behind bars where he belongs.'

'He's in prison?'

Alex nodded. 'He received a thirty-five-year sentence. Frankly, I hope he never gets out.'

A shiver made its way up and down her spine. 'I'm sorry, Alex. I can't imagine what you must have gone through.'

'It was a long time ago,' he said dismissively. 'I kept hoping my mother would stop him, but she didn't.'

An invisible hand reached into her chest and twisted—hard. 'She was probably too scared.'

'That's what she said. One of the charities I sponsor is for the victims of domestic violence. I've heard a lot of stories over the years, so I know how easy it is for these situations to escalate. Mum was in an impossible position. I know that—with my head. But in my heart I've always found it difficult to forgive her.'

'I can understand that,' Katrina said softly. 'But not everyone is as strong as you. I'm sure she did her best in her own way.'

'Maybe.' His answer was clearly noncommittal.

'And your brother…?'

If she'd thought his expression had been grim until now, it was nothing to the bleakness that etched into every line of his face when she asked that question. 'I tried to protect him as best I could but it wasn't enough.'

Once again it was what Alex had left out that was revealing. No doubt by trying to protect his brother Alex had had to endure more himself.

'Michael couldn't cope,' Alex continued. 'He found his escape in drugs.'

Her heart contracted. 'Oh no. That's so sad.'

She remembered back to the conversation between Alex and Dr Kershew that day in his surgery. The doctor had told Alex that if there was anything he could do to help all he had to do was call. And Alex had replied that the first step was up to Michael. No doubt Michael Webber's drug addiction was what they'd been talking about.

'You've tried to help him, haven't you?' she asked.

Alex raked a hand through his hair and around the back of his neck again. He seemed to have aged during their conversation. 'Of course I've tried. He's my little brother. But Michael hates rehab and always refuses to go. Twice I've virtually kidnapped him when he's either been passed out or so high he didn't know what was going on around him. I've admitted him to the private clinic, but each time he's simply walked out.'

Katrina placed a hand on his arm. 'I'm sorry. That must be difficult for you.'

'It is.' He sounded weary. 'Every time I see him, I try and persuade him to get help, but he never listens.'

'Maybe he's just scared.'

'Maybe.' Alex splayed his hands wide and gave her a twisted smile that held not an ounce of humour. 'So, there you have it—the Webber family, warts and all.'

Katrina was silent for a long moment. It was difficult to know what to say that wasn't trivial or meaningless. 'Well, I can understand why you wouldn't want your mother looking after Sam, but I'd still like to meet her one day. And your brother.'

'One day.'

Katrina sighed. His response suggested that it wouldn't be any time soon. 'Which brings us back to childcare for Sam.'

He looked relieved that she'd changed the subject.

'Yes. Like you, I want to make sure Sam is looked after properly. I don't want to risk anything happening to her.' The acidic tone of his voice made it clear he was thinking of his childhood and what had happened to him. 'Which rules out babysitters. I don't want a parade of different people coming and going.'

'So, what do you suggest? It sounds to me as though we've ruled out just about everything.'

'Not quite.' Alex smiled in an obvious attempt to shake off the serious mood that had settled over them. 'I was thinking about a part-time nanny. Someone who is available for a set number of hours per week but flexible about when they'll be required. If we offer a generous salary, we should attract some excellent candidates.'

Katrina nodded thoughtfully. 'It sounds like our best bet. But I suspect it won't be easy to find the right person.'

'I know. We're both going to be picky. But there has to be someone out there who we'll be happy with.'

Katrina shrugged. 'Well, we won't know until we try, I suppose.'

'So, there you have it.' He gave her a pointed look. 'With that lot, you'll be too busy to think about going back to work.'

Katrina's smile dimmed a little. 'I don't know about that. They're all projects that won't last more than a month or two.'

'By then there will be other things, like decorating the new house.'

'Don't push, Alex. I've already said I'll think about it. OK?'

'OK.' His eyes glinted. 'Now, there's just the little matter of payment to take care of.' He held out his hand. 'Come here, woman.'

Katrina waved her hand at their half-empty plates. 'What about breakfast?'

Alex snagged her hand and pulled her towards him. 'Forget the food. I have another appetite that needs feeding.'

CHAPTER NINE

ON MONDAY morning Alex was getting dressed in the bedroom Katrina now shared with him when he heard her murmur, 'Good morning,' behind him.

He looked up and smiled then moved to the side of the bed. 'Good morning. Did you sleep well?'

She nodded. 'I did.'

'So did I. No doubt it's all that fresh air we got yesterday,' he said, referring to their trip to Centennial Park to feed the ducks. It was their daughter's first experience with the real variety, rather than the plastic version which shared her bathtime.

Alex leaned down and pressed a drugging kiss against her mouth. By the time he lifted his head they were both breathing heavily. 'If I didn't have an important meeting this morning, I'd join you. But unfortunately I can't.'

Katrina stretched, arching her back and then, in a movement Alex was sure was accidentally-on-purpose, let the sheet fall to her waist.

Alex threw back his head and laughed. 'Witch.' Then he reached down and cupped her breast, fingering the tip until it contracted into a hardened peak.

Katrina groaned in the back of her throat.

Why that sound should send his blood pressure sky-rocketing, Alex wasn't sure, but it did.

'Maybe I can be a little late,' he said huskily, rapidly undoing his tie and pulling it free from the collar, his shirt following. 'Or maybe a lot,' he groaned as he came down on the bed beside her. 'I have the feeling I'm going to be very, *very* late.'

What followed blew his mind. He reached a peak he didn't think it was possible to reach, so dizzyingly high that he felt lightheaded.

'Was there anyone else while you were away?' he demanded. He hadn't planned on asking the question, but suddenly he needed to know.

She pulled away from him just far enough to look into his face. 'You mean a man?'

He nodded.

He already knew that Peter Strauss, Katrina's erst-while landlord, wasn't a threat. The Royce Agency had furnished him with a report that indicated the man was on a six-month assignment interstate and had merely rented the apartment to Katrina at minimal rent rather than leave it vacant.

Katrina herself had let slip that Strauss was the brother of the friend she'd stayed with when she'd first disappeared.

But that didn't mean that there hadn't been some-body else.

'You have to be kidding! I felt sick for the first four months, and by then I was big and getting bigger every day. And besides...'

'Besides what?' he asked when she failed to continue.

She angled her chin. 'Besides, at the time I was still under the misapprehension that I loved you.'

Alex felt an emotion he didn't want to examine too closely twist his heart tight.

Katrina moved away and pulled the sheet up to her chin. 'But you can't say the same, can you? I saw the pictures in the paper.'

Her voice was flat, the look in her eyes even flatter.

Alex felt tension string his flesh tightly together. 'No. No, I can't.'

'Just how many women did you *enjoy yourself* with while I was away giving birth to your daughter?' she asked with the same kind of sting a bee would be proud of.

'There weren't as many as you think,' he said quietly.

There had been women, sure. But he'd soon realised that sleeping with them was a waste of time.

They hadn't satisfied him the way Katrina had.

They hadn't made his senses reach for the stars.

They hadn't made his heart— His heart what…?

His heart had nothing to do with this, Alex assured himself.

It was just sex. Fantastic sex, admittedly; so fantastic that it was difficult to compete with.

But apart from their daughter that was all there was between them.

The days and weeks rolled into one.

Katrina was run off her feet. She'd found a couple of houses that had potential, but she was determined to wait until she found one that met all of their requirements before showing Alex.

They had time. Although Samantha was growing at

a rate of knots, she wouldn't be walking for several months yet.

She'd also compiled a dossier on two schools she thought would be good for Samantha. After getting Alex's seal of approval, she'd sent letters off to both, requesting a full information-pack complete with application form.

The nanny issue had sorted itself out quite by accident. It turned out that Leslie, their current part-time housekeeper, wanted more hours, and after some discussion Katrina had offered her a live-in position as housekeeper-nanny.

On the home front things were pretty much wonderful. She and Alex were growing closer with every day that passed.

One day Alex came home from work with a huge, white glossy box tied with a gold ribbon. 'This is for you,' he said, handing it to her.

Katrina took it automatically. 'What is it?'

'Why don't you open it and find out?'

She placed the box on the glass-topped coffee table and carefully undid the bow. Removing the lid, she folded back the gold tissue-paper sitting on top.

She glanced at Alex when she was presented with black satin. Gently she picked it up. It was a short nightgown, trimmed with lace. One look told her that it was expensive.

'Every woman deserves beautiful nightwear,' Alex said huskily, gesturing between the garment and the box.

It was then Katrina noticed there was something else in the box. In fact there were several somethings—two more nightgowns, one in the most gorgeous ivory colour, and the other a pale lilac.

A lump formed in the back of her throat. 'I don't know what to say. I've never owned anything so beautiful.'

'"Thank you" might be a good place to start,' Alex said, and held out his arms.

Katrina rose to her feet and went into his embrace eagerly, rose onto the balls of her feet and offered him her mouth.

When he finally lifted his head they were both breathing heavily. 'I think we should retire to our bedroom and you can parade them for me.'

The glint of his eyes told her that he would do more than just look. Holding hands, they began walking down the corridor. 'I guess I can throw out my old trackie and T-shirt I usually sleep in,' Katrina said.

Alex came to an abrupt halt. 'No! Don't do that.'

Katrina turned to face him and was surprised to see colour striping his sculptured cheekbones. 'Why not?'

He gave her a rueful smile. 'I happen to think you look sexy as all hell in them.'

'You do?' She couldn't hide her surprise.

'I do.'

'Then why the nightgowns?'

'They're more for you than for me. I just wanted you to have something nice.'

Another lump formed in the back of her throat. It was a lovely gesture, and proved how thoughtful Alex could be.

There was just one thing wrong with that: she'd wanted to keep emotionally detached. But her reaction indicated it was too late for that.

* * *

One night Katrina woke to find she was alone in bed. With a frown, she was about to get up and investigate when she heard Alex's voice on the baby monitor.

Realising he was in the nursery, she subsided back against the pillow, listening curiously.

'Hello, Princess. What are you doing awake at this time of night? You should be asleep,' he said softly.

An indecipherable gurgle, barely loud enough for Katrina to hear, was his response.

She heard a rustling noise; it sounded as if Alex had picked Samantha up out of her cot.

'So you can't sleep either, huh? Neither can I. Maybe we should keep each other company for a while.'

The baby cooed, as if to say that it was a good idea.

'What woke you up, I wonder?' Alex said, keeping his voice low. 'You can't be hungry. You drank as much milk as a baby brontosaurus.' There was a pause, then, 'What did you say? Not as much as a brontosaurus, huh? OK. What about a tyrannosaurus rex? You're happy with that? Good.'

Katrina smiled.

In this mood, Alex could charm the bees from the trees.

'OK. That's settled—you're not awake because you're hungry. So what does that leave us with, Princess?' Alex murmured. 'Maybe you had a bad dream, like your daddy did? Is that it?'

The baby cooed.

Katrina, who was still listening, felt her smile slip a little.

'No. You look and sound far too happy to have had a nightmare. I bet I know what it is—you knew your daddy was having bad dreams so you woke up just so you could make me feel better.'

A wedge of emotion formed in the back of Katrina's throat.

'And do you know what? It's worked. How can I stay sad about those nasty things in my dreams when I have you around, huh?'

There was silence for a while.

Katrina knew she was eavesdropping on what was a private conversation—even if it was only one way—but she couldn't stop listening now. She waited with bated breath to hear what he said next.

She didn't have long to wait.

'Do you know something else? My father told me that when I had brats of my own I'd understand what he did to us. But he was wrong; I don't understand. I'll never understand. And you're not a brat. You're my princess.'

The wedge of emotion in Katrina's throat expanded until she could barely breathe.

She'd often woken in the middle of the night to find Alex not in their bed. She'd mentioned his restlessness to him several times, and Alex had admitted to the occasional nightmare about his childhood, but hadn't really wanted to discuss it. She'd always wondered what the nightmares had been about.

Now she knew.

With a shaky hand, she reached out and turned the monitor off.

She couldn't listen any more.

When Alex came in some time later, Katrina pretended to be asleep. She almost gave herself away when he pulled her into his arms, but she simply snuggled into him.

As she fell asleep in her lover's arms Katrina realised there was one positive to come out of what she'd heard—and that was that father and daughter were growing closer.

Despite the way everything was progressing so smoothly, Katrina wasn't entirely happy. She was aware of a low-grade discontent hovering just beneath the surface, like a toothache that just wouldn't go away.

This feeling came to a head on one particularly sunny Sunday when they put Samantha in her pram and drove to Bondi beach.

They were strolling along the promenade when it happened.

Because the weather was so nice, lots of other people were doing the same thing. Katrina found herself watching the other couples they passed.

No doubt she and Alex looked the same. No doubt with Samantha in her pram they looked just like all the other families.

But something was missing.

And that was when it hit her: somehow she'd fallen in love with Alex all over again.

She wasn't quite sure when it had happened. It wasn't as though it had hit her like a bolt of lightning. There had been no cymbals and drums, no choir of angels.

It had been a gradual thing that had crept up on her. It was there inside her, like a living thing.

She wanted to be like those other couples—in love, and loved in return.

But that was an impossibility, wasn't it?

What chance did she have of Alex falling in love with her when he didn't even believe in the emotion?

Alex liked and respected her. He was committed to her and their daughter. Surely that meant that he cared for her in his own way?

The more she thought about it, the more she was convinced that she was right.

Alex must feel something for her.

Otherwise how could he look at her with tenderness in his eyes? And how could he make love to her as if she was the most precious thing on earth?

Feeling marginally better, Katrina turned her attention to something else that had been bothering her.

It had niggled at the back of her mind for the last week but she couldn't quite put her finger on what was wrong.

Whatever it was, it was as elusive as the wind and as indefinable as the clouds rolling across the sky.

Katrina watched as another couple strolled towards them. The woman was pushing a pram; the man had a little boy of three or four sitting on his shoulders.

The little boy said something and tugged on his father's hair. The man laughed and reached a hand above his head, scooped the child into his arms and began tickling him.

Katrina stopped walking and stared.

There was something in the picture she was looking at that epitomised what it was that was bothering her. Still, she couldn't pin down exactly what it was.

Frustration imploded inside her. It was like a word sitting on the tip of your tongue that you just couldn't quite spit out.

She was sure that if she looked hard enough the answer would come to her, but it didn't.

'What is it?' Alex asked beside her.

Katrina gave herself a mental shake and forced a smile to her stiff lips. Whatever it was, it would come to her in its own good time. 'Nothing.'

Samantha chose that moment to start crying, saving Katrina from any further explanation, something she was thankful for.

Because, although she hadn't been able to figure out exactly what it was that was bothering her, she *had* drawn one conclusion. Whatever it was, it had something to do with Alex and Samantha's relationship.

And whatever it was it wasn't good.

Later that night Katrina woke to find she was alone in bed.

She made no move to get up and investigate. She was getting used to Alex's middle-of-the-night wanderings. No doubt another nightmare had woken him.

Sometimes he would go in to the nursery but as often as not Samantha was asleep and he would tiptoe out as quietly as he'd gone in.

Katrina was never able to go back to sleep during these times. Instead she lay there worrying about Alex—which was exactly what she was doing now.

Suddenly, she heard Alex's voice on the baby monitor.

'Hello, Princess. So you're awake tonight, are you?'

The baby let out a cry, barely loud enough for Katrina to hear.

She heard the familiar rustling sound of Alex picking Samantha up out of her cot.

'You're as pretty as your mother. Do you know that?'

Katrina's throat clogged with emotion.

Maybe he did care for her just a little bit. Maybe there *was* a chance he'd fall in love with her.

She heard Alex mutter something, but she couldn't make out what it was. She then heard a couple of sounds she couldn't decipher.

The next thing she knew, the bedroom door was flung back on its hinges. She jumped a foot in the air. 'What the…?' she gasped, bolting upright, her hand pressing against her chest. 'You scared me half to death!'

'Sorry.' He paused for a heartbeat then said in a voice she barely recognised, 'Sam's sick. We need to take her to the hospital.'

For the first time Katrina noticed that their daughter was cradled in his arms.

She blinked rapidly.

Her brain felt as if it was encased in fog, yet at the same time it was as clear as it had ever been.

Because suddenly what had been bothering her just smacked her across the face. Alex was never as relaxed with his daughter as the man at the beach had been with his son.

It was a subtle thing, which explained why it had been so difficult to pin down. But it was there.

He was never entirely at ease with her. It wasn't that he was tense, exactly, but he was never completely comfortable either.

Why?

Although she desperately wanted an answer to that question, now was not the time.

What Alex had just said cut through her thoughts like

the blade of a knife cutting through butter. 'What's wrong with her? Are you sure it's not just that she's teething?'

'No, it's more than that. I'll tell you as you get dressed. But we need to get moving. Now!'

The urgency in his voice spun Katrina into immediate action. She threw back the covers, hurried to the wardrobe and grabbed the first article of clothing that came to hand.

'Tell me,' she ordered as she pulled on her jeans.

'She has a fever. Her skin is blotchy. And she's not focussing properly.'

The list of symptoms made her freeze before she started to shake so hard she thought she might fall into a million pieces. 'What…what do you think is wrong with her?'

Alex shook his head, face grim. 'I don't know. But we need to get to the hospital as soon as possible.'

What followed was a nightmare.

They went immediately to the emergency department. As soon as they were inside, Alex said, 'We need a doctor. Right now!'

He possessed such an air of authority that a nurse immediately snapped to attention. After the briefest of examinations, she took Samantha and hurried out of the waiting area into the main emergency-room.

Alex and Katrina followed through the swing doors and watched as the nurse handed her charge over to a female doctor in her mid-forties. The conversation was brief. Although they were too far away to hear what was being said, their body language and the sense of urgency that surrounded them suggested the initial prognosis was not good.

A shaft of fear speared through Katrina's heart.

'You can't come in here,' the nurse said, spying them a moment later. 'You'll have to stay in the waiting room.'

Alex took Katrina's hand in his and squeezed it tight. The look he threw the nurse made her blink. 'We're not leaving.'

'But, sir—'

'We're staying here.' His tone brooked no argument; his face was hard and determined.

Alex and Katrina continued to hover in the background as Samantha was hooked up to an IV drip, and what appeared to be samples of blood were taken.

The longer they worked on her, the greater Katrina's fear became. 'If anything happens to Sam…' she muttered.

Alex wrapped an arm around her waist. 'Sam is going to be fine. The doctors know what they're doing.'

Katrina certainly hoped so.

Each minute ticked by with mind-numbing slowness. Neither she nor Alex moved an inch, nor did they speak. Katrina wasn't even sure they were breathing.

Eventually the female doctor hurried over to them. 'I'm Dr Niven. You are the child's parents?'

'We are.' It was Alex who replied, voice tense.

'What's her name?'

'Samantha. Sam.' Again, it was Alex who replied.

'OK. Well, we suspect Sam has meningitis.'

The word gouged at Katrina like hungry teeth until she felt as though she were bleeding inside. A moan escaped her strangled throat and her knees collapsed beneath her. If Alex hadn't been holding her, she would have fallen to the floor.

'Are you sure?' Alex asked, his voice reed-thin.

Dr Niven shook her head. 'No, we're not. We've put her on antibiotics just in case. And we've taken a sample of her spinal fluid for testing. We're going to rush the results through. We should know for certain in a couple of hours.'

'And if it *is* meningitis?' Alex asked.

Katrina's heart leapt into her throat. She knew what he was asking and wasn't sure she wanted to hear the answer.

'Then we'll continue with the antibiotics and monitor her progress. There's nothing more we can do.'

There's nothing more we can do.

Why did those words have a ring of finality to them?

Katrina swayed but didn't fall, Alex still holding her up.

'There has to be something I can do.' Alex was unable to hide his desperation. 'I can pay for the best specialist there is. Just tell me their name and I'll fly them in.'

'I'm sure you can. But it's not necessary. If it's meningitis, the best treatment is antibiotics.' The doctor patted his arm. 'That and lots of love, of course.'

Alex nodded then half-urged, half-carried Katrina across to Samantha's bed. He gently deposited her in a dull grey visitor's chair. Katrina felt like a rag doll with no power of her own to function.

She was aware of Alex pulling up a chair beside her but she didn't look at him; her entire focus was on their baby daughter.

Willing her to live.

Willing her to get better.

Alex stared at Samantha.

She looked lost in the adult-sized hospital bed with her little arm hooked up to the IV-drip.

They'd been waiting for what seemed like hours. A nurse came and went at regular intervals to check Samantha's temperature, blood pressure and whatever else the monitor she was attached to registered.

Every time he asked the same question: 'How is she?'

And every time the answer was the same: 'There's no change.'

Alex balled his hands into fists, his heart slamming against his ribcage. She looked so tiny and vulnerable. So young and defenceless.

A hollow formed in the pit of his stomach until it felt like a never-ending ravine filled with cold, whistling winds. Alex felt it pulling at him as if it was trying to suck the life out of him.

If Samantha died, Alex feared he'd disappear into the abyss for ever.

He couldn't lose Samantha. He couldn't let her die.

Fear beat on the inside of his skull with the force of a jackhammer.

Anxiety squeezed his heart with razor-sharp talons until he thought it might burst.

He wanted to jump to his feet and scream with rage. He wanted to howl at the gods for doing this to him.

He turned to Katrina. She looked shattered. Her face was pale and pinched, hands clenched so tightly together that her knuckles had turned white.

He placed a hand over her firmly woven fists. 'She'll be OK,' he said, imbuing his voice with a confidence he was far from feeling inside.

'If something happens to her…'

'*Nothing* is going to happen to her.' His eyes returned to Samantha who looked smaller and more fragile every time he looked at her. 'She's going to be OK. She *has* to be OK.'

Katrina was silent for a long moment and then she said quietly, 'You love her, don't you?'

His gut tightened. A lump the size and weight of a small bus formed in the back of his throat. 'Yes, I love her.'

It was there with every beat of his heart and every breath that he breathed.

Katrina turned her hands over and squeezed his tight.

Despite the gravity of the situation the corners of his mouth lifted. 'Aren't you going to say "I told you so"?'

She shook her head. 'No. I'm just glad…for both your sakes.'

So was Alex.

But as he looked at his gravely ill daughter Alex realised that he owed her some recompense.

He was a thief. A thief who had robbed Samantha of his heart. He'd spent time with her, done all the right things, but he'd been holding a part of himself back.

If Samantha died he would regret every minute he'd chosen not to give all of himself to her.

She had to live.

CHAPTER TEN

Six hours later they were still sitting there.

Still waiting.

Alex had never felt so helpless. Tension compressed his spine until it felt half its normal length.

Katrina sat as still as a statue beside him.

Alex did the exact opposite. He sat forwards. Then backwards. Then forwards again. Rested his head in his hands. Raked his hands through his hair and around the back of his neck.

Finally, he'd had enough.

He jumped to his feet, hands clenched tightly at his sides. 'I can't stand this! I have to find out what's going on.'

Katrina didn't answer him. She didn't look capable of it.

The look on her face gutted him. Swallowing hard, Alex gave her shoulder a reassuring squeeze before striding to the nurses' station, where he demanded to see the doctor.

'I want answers!' he said, when Dr Niven finally appeared.

The look she gave him was measured and calm. 'I know you do. So do I. But we have to wait while pathology runs the tests. It shouldn't be too long now.'

Alex shoved his hands deep into his pockets. He knew he was being unreasonable but he couldn't help it. 'I just—'

The doctor placed a hand on his arm. 'I know. You don't have to explain.'

'Alex…?'

The voice came from behind him.

Alex spun on his heel. He blinked. Then blinked again. He couldn't believe what he was seeing.

Because standing in front of him were his mother and brother.

'Mum. Michael. What on earth are you doing here?'

Audrey Webber raised a brow, hands folded in front of her thickened waistline. 'We're here to support you, of course.'

'I don't understand.' Alex shook his head, as if the action could clear his confusion. 'How did you even know I was here?'

This time it was Michael who answered. 'It was on the news. They said your daughter had been admitted to hospital. Is it true? Do you have a daughter?'

Alex nodded. Someone must have recognised him and leaked the story to the press.

What a terrible way for his family to have found out. He opened his mouth to apologise but his mother got in first.

'Why didn't you tell us?' She held up a hand. 'No, don't answer that. It's not important right now. How is she?'

'She's—'

'Alex.'

This time it was Katrina's voice saying his name. Alex froze. For a heartbeat he didn't move. Then he spun towards the doorway.

'What's happened?' He had to force the words past the constriction in his throat. 'Is she worse?' he asked, not at all sure he wanted to know the answer.

Even before she spoke Alex noticed Katrina's shaky smile. 'Sam's started to respond to the treatment. The doctor is with her now.'

The relief was so powerful that his insides sagged. 'Thank God for that!' He turned to his mother and brother. 'I have to go, but I'll be back as soon as I can.'

Audrey pointed to the row of grey visitors' chairs similar to the ones he and Katrina had been sitting on for so many hours. 'You go and do what you have to do. Michael and I will wait here.'

Emotion rose up inside him like a tidal wave. Sweeping an arm around each of them he pulled them close. 'Thank you,' he said in a choked voice. 'It means a lot to me that you're here.'

He meant every word. His mother's support in particular went straight to his heart, and he found himself blinking back tears as he strode to Katrina's side.

He held her hand tightly as they approached the doctor.

'The diagnosis of meningitis has been confirmed,' Dr Niven said. 'That's the bad news. The good news is that the antibiotics have started to do their job. Sam's vital signs are improving.'

'How long before she's out of danger?' Alex asked. Although Samantha's response to the antibiotics was fantastic news, he didn't want to count his blessings too soon.

'Another twelve hours should do it.'

Alex nodded.

'I notice you have other family who have arrived. Please keep the visitors to two at a time.' The doctor placed a hand on Alex's arm. 'You saved your daughter's life with your quick action. It would have been too late if you'd left it to morning,' she said before departing.

'Oh, Alex,' Katrina said 'If you hadn't…'

He didn't want Katrina thinking about what might have happened. He didn't want to go there himself.

'But I did,' he reassured her quickly.

And he always would.

The thought, which had ridden immediately on the back of the first, almost knocked the legs out from under him.

He felt as if he'd driven smack-bang into a brick wall at high speed. 'Shattered' would be an understatement.

He reeled backwards.

Katrina caught his arm and guided him towards a seat. 'Alex! What is it?'

For a minute, he couldn't speak. He couldn't even breathe. The sound of his blood pounding at his temples was deafening.

'Should I get the doctor?' Katrina asked worriedly beside him.

'No.' He grabbed her arm. 'Just give me a minute.'

She nodded and held his hand.

He dragged in a breath. Then another. And slowly his heartbeat returned to normal.

He flung himself against the rigid back of the chair. 'God, I've been such a fool!'

Katrina shook her head, green eyes clearly confused. 'I don't understand.'

'I know you don't.' He looked at the bed then back at Katrina. 'I was petrified I was going to hurt her.'

She gasped, her body jerking against his side. Her eyes narrowed on his face. 'What on earth are you talking about?'

'My father's blood runs through my veins. Something made him into a monster. I kept on thinking: what's to say the same thing can't happen to me?'

Katrina shook her head vehemently, her grip on his hand so tight her nails dug in to his flesh. 'It wouldn't happen.'

'I know that now. But for a long time I thought it could.'

Her eyes flashed. 'Is that why you had the vasectomy?'

Alex nodded. 'My father was always telling me how much alike we were. Taunting me with it. And it's true; we're similar in lots of ways. I grew up believing that I'd turn out just like him.'

'That's abuse in its own right,' Katrina said thoughtfully. 'But, still, a vasectomy was a rather drastic measure to take when there was absolutely no evidence to support your theory,' she said with a frown.

His gut twisted tight. And then again, even tighter. 'There was evidence. Or, at least, I thought there was.'

'Tell me.'

Alex ran a hand over his face. 'Back then I was full of rage over what my father was doing to us. One day at school, my best friend said something I didn't like. To this day, I can't even remember what it was. I punched him in the face—so hard that I broke his nose.'

'Oh, Alex,' she said, her voice drenched with sadness.

Alex didn't want her sympathy. But he did want her understanding. 'But do you know what the worst thing was?'

She shook her head.

'The worst thing was that on one level I enjoyed it. Oh, I was sorry that I'd hurt Jason, because we were mates and he was one of the few people who made my life bearable. But on another level it felt good—hitting him got rid of some of the pent-up anger. And suddenly I saw my father's face when he hit me and I wondered whether I had the same look on my face when I hit Jason. And I thought: it's *really* happening. I'm turning out exactly like my father. That was the day I decided to have the vasectomy. It seemed to be the only way to break the cycle.'

'And that's why you've been holding a part of yourself back with Sam during the last month,' Katrina murmured as if she were speaking to herself.

Alex frowned. 'I admit I've been cautious. And now you can understand why. But I didn't think it was noticeable.'

'It wasn't entirely. I sensed something wasn't quite right, but I couldn't figure out what it was. Until tonight.'

He raised an eyebrow.

'When you carried Sam into our bedroom I suddenly realised you were never entirely at ease with her. Not the way you should be. After what you've just told me, my guess is that you were being over-cautious.'

Alex frowned again and then shook his head. 'You could be right. I'm a fool.'

He didn't believe in fate. He preferred to believe that a man could shape his own destiny. So why had he been stupid enough to believe that genetics could override his true nature?

'I'm not going to disagree with you,' she said, once again wielding the words as if they were a plank of wood she was hitting around his head.

The corners of his mouth turned up. 'Little Miss Confrontation strikes again, does she?'

'You'd better believe it. I can understand why you might have thought you could turn out like your father in the beginning. You were in an untenable situation. But, later, you should have known there wasn't a chance of it happening.'

'You sound very sure.'

'That's because I am. I know *you*.' She tilted her head to one side. 'Tell me something.'

His eyes narrowed on her face. 'If I can.'

She waited for a moment before asking softly, 'Did you try to take some of your brother's beatings for him?'

Alex gasped. He couldn't help it. 'How did you know that?'

'You mentioned that you'd tried to protect him. I simply guessed the rest.' She raised her eyebrows. 'Do you really think a man who's prepared to do that would ever hurt anyone, let alone a defenceless child?'

Alex shook his head. 'You're a lot wiser than me.'

'No. You've just been a bit too harsh with yourself; I believe that's a common trait of high achievers.' She nodded towards the doorway. 'I think you may have been a bit harsh with your mother, too. What say you introduce us?'

Alex clasped her hand in his and led her out to the

waiting area. On the way he sent up a silent prayer of thanks.

Not just because Samantha was on the mend. But also for giving him Katrina.

Once he'd only seen her beauty, but now he could see her strength and intelligence.

Alex admired her more and more with every day that passed. If he had chosen a mother for his child, he could not have chosen more perfectly.

His two girls.

His two *special* girls.

How could a man get so lucky?

For the next twelve days they kept a constant vigil at Samantha's bedside, taking it in turns to eat, shower and sleep.

On the third day, Alex found himself alone with his mother in the hospital cafeteria, where they had queued to buy coffees to take back upstairs.

That morning Samantha had been pronounced out of danger and at Alex's insistence had been moved into her own private room.

'I meant what I said the other day,' Alex said. 'I really appreciate you being here for me.'

Audrey's eyes—the same eyes that Alex, Michael and Samantha had all inherited—met his. 'Like I wasn't before? Is that what you're saying?'

Alex shifted uncomfortably. 'Mum...'

She laid a hand on his arm. 'It's OK, Alex. I know what you think, and I understand. But just remember that your memories are those of a young, frightened boy, and an angry and just-as-frightened teenager.'

Alex took her arm and led her to an empty table. Pulling out one of the inevitably grey plastic chairs that dotted the public areas of the hospital he motioned for her to sit down.

When they were both seated, he said, 'Tell me.'

Alex wasn't sure why he was prepared to listen to his mother's version of events after so many years.

Maybe it was because Samantha's illness had reminded him that life was short.

Maybe it was because he'd made such a terrible mistake when Katrina had told him she was pregnant and he was prepared to accept he might have made a similar mistake with his mother.

And maybe it was because realising he was nothing like his father had somehow had a cathartic effect. It certainly felt as if a void had opened up between him and the past. The memories were still there, but they couldn't hurt him any more.

They talked for over an hour. When they finally left the cafeteria, Alex felt they'd taken the first tentative steps towards putting the past behind them.

On the eighth day, Alex found himself alone with Michael at Samantha's bedside.

Just that morning Samantha had given them her first smile since falling ill. Katrina had cried; Alex had felt like joining her.

Michael gestured to his niece with a bony hand. 'Why didn't you tell us about her, bro?'

Alex shook his head. 'I'm not sure. I guess I didn't want to taint her with our past.'

Michael punched him on the arm. 'Hey, aren't you the one who keeps on telling me the past is in the past and that we should leave it there and move on?'

Alex nodded gravely. 'I am. I guess I'm not good at taking my own advice.'

Then, without planning on doing it, Alex found himself admitting to Michael what he had so far only admitted to himself and Katrina—that he had been terrified of turning out like their father.

Michael's reaction was to laugh his head off. When he finally managed to speak, he said, 'You're as screwed up as I am.'

Looking at his brother long and hard, Alex shook his head. 'I'm not any more. What about you?'

They both knew Alex was referring to Michael's drug addiction.

For the first time since the conversation started, Michael looked away. 'It's not that easy, bro.'

'I know it's not. But promise me you'll think about it.'

Michael nodded.

It wasn't a very enthusiastic nod, but it was still the first time Michael had agreed to consider getting help. Although he knew there was still a long way to go, Alex knew this was a hugely positive step forward. He punched his brother on the arm. 'Good man.'

Just then Katrina came in and shooed Michael out.

A feeling of peace settled over Alex. Katrina was his rock. He didn't know how he would have got through this ordeal without her at his side.

In fact, he didn't know what he would do without her, full stop.

On the thirteenth day, Samantha was well enough to go home.

The morning after their return from the hospital, Katrina woke slowly.

It was a pleasant change to have slept in a real bed. For almost two weeks she'd slept in chairs or spare hospital-beds. Once or twice she'd even slept cradled in Alex's arms.

Even before she opened sleep-drenched eyes she was frowning.

Where was Alex?

She knew he wasn't beside her. She didn't need to look; she could feel his absence. They normally slept wrapped in each other's arms—quite literally—legs entangled, her head in the crook of his shoulder. His hands holding her close.

Pulling on her robe, Katrina padded out of the bedroom to investigate.

She found Alex lying on the sofa with Samantha sprawled on his chest. Having recently discovered her own hands, the baby was taking great delight in trying to poke a finger in her father's eye.

Seeing the two of them like this made Katrina's heart melt in her chest.

The barriers between father and daughter had finally come tumbling down.

Alex was no longer hanging back; the distance she'd felt between them no longer existed.

This was what she'd wanted from day one—for Alex to be a father to his daughter.

And what a wonderful father he was. Gentle and caring, and at the same time strong and protective.

There was only one thing that could make life even more perfect. And that was if Alex loved her.

Once she'd thought that was an impossibility. Now there was room for hope.

Alex had claimed not to believe in love, but since then he'd admitted to loving his daughter. Surely that meant there was a chance he could learn to love her too?

Remembering how Alex had acted while they were at the hospital, Katrina was sure there was.

He had been her rock. Supportive. Encouraging. He'd been there to cling to when she'd needed it. And he'd been there to pep her up when she was feeling down.

He obviously cared about her. Wasn't it possible that his feelings could develop into love?

Katrina certainly hoped so.

She was about to tiptoe away when Alex spotted her. He was relaxed and smiling. 'Good morning.'

Katrina smiled back. 'Good morning.' She gestured to the baby. 'I wondered why it was so quiet.'

Alex grinned. 'Sam woke around six, but you were out for the count so I decided to let you sleep. She's been fed, she's been changed and we've just been playing.'

Katrina smothered a laugh. 'Have you, now?'

'We have. She's very clever, aren't you, Princess?'

Samantha's answer was to smile and gurgle her complete agreement.

'Well, since you have everything under control, I might as well go and have a shower.'

'No. Don't do that.' Alex swung his legs to the floor and sat up. The smile dropped from his face. 'I want to talk to you about something.'

'You sound serious.'

'I am.' He patted the cushion beside him. 'Come and sit down.'

Katrina did as he asked. 'OK. Shoot.'

She wasn't quite sure what she was expecting, but it certainly wasn't what came next.

'I think we should get married.'

Katrina just stared at him.

Her insides stilled at the same time as her heart took off at a gallop.

Licking her lips and dragging in a breath, she said, 'Say that again.'

He didn't hesitate. 'You heard me—I think we ought to get married.'

The breath locked tight in her lungs. She'd heard him right. 'Why?' she asked.

It was the question that stood out amongst all the other thoughts tumbling through her brain.

'Why?' he repeated. He was clearly stunned that she hadn't thrown herself into his arms with an immediate acceptance. 'Isn't marriage the final step in becoming a family? Isn't it a commitment Sam deserves from us?'

His answer felt like a guillotine blade falling from a great height, cutting her heart in two.

She wanted to howl with the pain of it. Alex wanted to marry her because of Samantha, *not* because he loved her.

She pleated the edge of her robe with unsteady fingers, unable and unwilling to look him in the eye for fear he'd see how devastated she was. 'I can't think about that just yet. I can't think about anything. I just want to enjoy having Sam home for a few days.'

He frowned and wrapped an arm around her shoulders. 'I'm sorry. I didn't mean to rush you. I know how stressful the last couple of weeks have been.' He gave her a rather sheepish smile. 'Sam's illness has made me face up to myself. There are a few things I want to do differently from now on, and top of the list is formalising our relationship.'

Katrina suppressed a wince.

There was a huge difference between 'formalising our relationship' and 'I love you'.

The two might as well have been on different planets.

'I understand,' she said, reaching for Samantha.

The problem was that she understood all too well.

Her hopes and dreams lay like dust at her feet.

The big question now was what was she going to do about it?

That night Katrina lay awake for hours.

For a while she just stared at the ceiling. Later, she rolled on her side, propped her head on her raised elbow and watched Alex sleep.

Moonlight streamed in through the windows. It added a silvery sheen to his dark hair and cast shadows on the sculptured lines of his face.

Her heart clenched hard. She kept trying to tell herself that nothing had changed, but it had. It had changed the minute she'd realised she loved Alex. She just hadn't realised it at the time; Samantha's illness had distracted her.

But Alex's proposal had hit her around the face and made her confront the reality of the situation head-on.

Could she stay with Alex—marry him—knowing that she loved him but he didn't love her?

Already the pain of it was eating her up inside. What would years of that do to her?

If she was deeply unhappy, what would that do to Samantha?

Those questions plagued Katrina for the rest of the night. They went around and around in her head until she was dizzy with them.

In the end, she decided it was time to be brave. It was time to be Little Miss Confrontation again and tell Alex how she felt about him.

Yes, she was opening herself up to being hurt again, but it was a risk she had to take. Because only once she knew exactly what Alex felt for her could she decide what to do.

She might just have to sweep the dust of her dreams into the rubbish bin, or she might be able to breathe new life into the dreams themselves.

CHAPTER ELEVEN

ALEX was gone when she woke up. Not just from the bed but from the apartment. She found a note propped next to the kettle telling her he'd decided to let her sleep and that he would try to come home early.

Although his concern was touching, Katrina was disappointed. Now that she'd decided to tell Alex how she felt about him, she could hardly wait to get on with it. But it looked like she had no choice but to wait until he came home.

Mid-morning, Katrina was playing with Samantha on the carpet in the lounge when the phone rang.

She lifted the hands-free receiver to her ear. 'Hello?'

'Could I speak to Alex Webber, please?' an efficient female voice asked.

'I'm afraid he's not here. Can I take a message?'

There was a momentary pause. 'Is that you, Katrina?'

Katrina frowned. She didn't recognise the voice. 'Yes. Who is this?'

'It's Tracey from Dr Kershew's office. How are you? And how is Samantha? We were sorry to hear she'd been in hospital.'

Katrina smiled. 'Yes, it's me, Tracey. I'm fine, and so is Sam. Thank goodness!'

'That's great. Anyway, on to the reason for my call.'

'Certainly. You wanted me to pass on a message to Alex?'

'Yes, please. I was just calling to tell him we've arranged for him to have his vasectomy redone, as he requested. The appointment is scheduled for eleven a.m. on the twenty-eighth of next month at the Royal North Shore Hospital.'

Katrina pressed a hand to her chest.

'Katrina, did you hear me?'

She drew in a deep breath. 'Yes, I heard you; I'm just looking for a piece of paper and a pen so I can write the date down. I'm not sure Alex will be able to make it then.'

By the time she finished with him, he probably wouldn't need the procedure—she might very well take care of it herself with the bluntest instrument she could find!

'If he can't, that's OK. Just get back to me and I'll change the appointment.'

'Fine.'

Katrina didn't say any more. She couldn't. She pressed the button to end the call before the phone dropped from her nerveless fingers.

A vasectomy. She couldn't believe it.

Jumping to her feet, she scooped up her daughter and began to pace, her mind spinning. Thoughts tumbled one over the other like a piece of paper caught in a force-ten gale.

She'd decided to tell Alex that she loved him, but what was the point now?

The answer came back with soul-stripping speed: there was none. She'd told Alex she wanted more children. If he'd been even the teeniest, tiniest bit in love with her, then he wouldn't have arranged to have his vasectomy redone.

The question now was, could she stay?

She felt as if her heart had been ripped to shreds and then dunked in a vat of acid. Years of feeling like that would be intolerable. But what was the alternative? If she didn't stay it meant taking Samantha away from her father.

The bond between father and daughter was as strong as between mother and daughter.

Samantha would miss Alex.

And Alex…

She put trembling fingers to her lips. Alex might not have fallen in love with her but he *had* fallen in love with his daughter. Separating them now would be cruel.

Katrina sank down on the carpet as if the weight of the world was on her shoulders.

How long she remained there, she didn't know.

It could have been minutes or it could have been hours. Her mind was so numb that time didn't seem to have meaning any more.

It was only when Samantha began to cry that she finally moved. Choking back a sob, Katrina raced through to the bedroom. Placing Samantha carefully in the middle of the king-sized bed, she put two pillows on either side of her so the baby couldn't roll off, then went into her old bedroom and pulled her suitcase out of the closet.

Blinking back tears, she returned to the master bedroom and began flinging her clothes willy-nilly into the open suitcase.

The future seemed untenable.

She'd told Alex once that she wasn't good mistress-material. It appeared she wasn't good unloved-wife material either.

Alex frowned as he closed the front door behind him.

The apartment felt different. How, he wasn't quite sure, but it did.

Maybe it was because Katrina wasn't in the lounge as she usually was when he came home.

'Katrina?' he called.

There was no answer. His voice seemed to echo off the walls. A frisson of unease slid down his spine.

A quick search of the apartment showed no sign of either Katrina or Samantha.

They could, of course, have gone for a walk. But somehow Alex didn't think so.

Gut instinct warned him that something else was going on here.

He went back to the bedroom. This time he looked more closely. The frisson of unease settled uncomfortably at the base of his spine and remained there, pricking at him.

The clothes he'd bought Katrina were hanging in the closet, but her toiletries and her own clothes were missing.

He hurried through to the nursery.

Here the difference was even more noticeable. Nappies, wipes, powder—all gone.

But it was the absence of Samantha's pink teddy bear that was the real clincher. Samantha loved that bear; it slept beside her every night.

Alex sank down on a chair.

Only then did he notice the envelope sitting on top of the chest of drawers with his name on it.

He jumped to his feet and tore it open.

The envelope contained a single sheet of paper covered with Katrina's neat hand writing.

Dear Alex,

I'm sorry to spring this on you, but I knew if I told you face to face you'd try and talk me out of it or insist that I leave Sam with you. You've commented several times about how much Sam's illness has changed things for you. Well, it's changed things for me too. Although we're both agreed that giving Sam a proper family is the right thing to do, I just don't know whether I can do it. You said you weren't prepared to sign up for a life of celibacy. Well, I'm not sure I can sign up for a loveless marriage. Please don't worry about Sam. I will take good care of her. I will be in contact soon.
Katrina.

Alex crumpled the note in his clenched fist.

They'd gone. Disappeared. Katrina had packed up their belongings and left. His heart started pounding until he could feel the blood pumping at his temples.

The smell of baby powder lingering in the room seemed to mock him. So too did the yellow rubber-duck that Alex was now such an expert at making quacking noises for.

Where had they gone?

And how on earth was he going to find her?

He'd told Royce to cancel the man tailing Katrina weeks ago. It hadn't seemed necessary any more.

He hoped it wasn't a decision he was going to live to regret.

Katrina had disappeared once before. He remembered her telling him that she wasn't a fan of credit cards; it was her use of cash that had made it so difficult to track her down last time.

If she did the same this time…

Pulling out his mobile phone, he called the agency and filled Royce in. 'I don't care how much it costs. Find them.'

As he hung up, his insides turned to ice. Ice that seemed to saturate every particle of his being until it felt as though he'd never be warm again.

Fear sliced through him until it felt as if he was being skinned alive.

One thought ran through his head, clearer than any other, chilling him to the bone.

What if he never found them?

Two days later Alex was in the middle of his monthly board meeting. He was trying and failing to concentrate on the various presentations.

All he could think about was Katrina and Samantha—and the action he'd taken overnight to flush them out of wherever it was they were hiding.

Suddenly, the double doors to the boardroom were thrown forcefully open. The handles hit the wall with a crash, the sound so loud he stopped speaking mid sentence.

All eyes, including his, turned in that direction.

Katrina was standing in the open doorway, caramel hair swirling around her shoulders.

She looked magnificent.

She also looked angry.

Her cat-like green eyes were spitting emerald fire, fury striping her razor-sharp cheekbones a bright, burning red. Alex suspected one look would be enough to set the long boardroom table on fire.

'Out!' she instructed, her eyes never leaving Alex's face.

The board looked in his direction for guidance. From the look on their faces, they clearly expected him to tell Katrina to wait outside until the meeting was over. They knew he allowed nothing to interfere with these monthly gatherings.

What they didn't realise was that the Webber Investment Bank was no longer the most important thing in Alex's life.

His girls were.

His two special girls.

They were the centre of his world. The epicentre of his existence.

'Please leave,' he told the board. His voice was calm but he was anything but inside; tension was tying his muscles into such tight knots it felt as though he'd swallowed a ships anchor. 'I'll let you know when we'll reconvene.'

With much shuffling of paper and curious looks, the five men and two women picked up their belongings and made their way to the door.

As soon as they were alone, Alex rose to his feet and stalked across the room to Katrina. To give her her due, she didn't back away from him.

He stopped in front of her, so close they were

almost touching. He could smell the scent of her perfume and could see the little specks of golden-brown in cat-like green eyes that were focussed challengingly on him.

'Where have you been?' he demanded, resisting the urge to shake her until her teeth rattled.

Her chin angled upwards. 'Away.'

His hands clenched into fists. 'Away *where*?'

'It doesn't matter.'

Fury strung his flesh tightly together. 'It matters one hell of a damned lot when you take my daughter away without my permission and without telling me where you were going!'

She tossed her head, sending an invisible cloud of her scent into the air. 'I left you a note.'

He gritted his teeth. 'That's not good enough. Not by a long shot. Where is she?'

'She's right outside. Justine is looking after her.'

Relief washed through him, unravelling the tension that had hardened his insides.

'I could kill you for taking her,' he said.

'Is that why you announced to the world that Sam and I were missing?' she demanded, her eyes spitting chips of cold, green ice at him. 'I couldn't believe it when I saw our photos plastered all over the TV and newspapers.'

'Yes,' Alex hissed. 'You seem to be an expert at disappearing. I wasn't going to take the chance I'd never see my daughter again.'

She frowned. 'I told you in my note that I'd be in contact soon.'

'Forgive me, but *soon* just wasn't good enough.

Going to the press guaranteed me a result. The Royce Agency has already received floods of phone calls with possible sightings. If you hadn't turned up here this morning, it would only have been a matter of time before I tracked you down.'

She tossed her head again. 'Well, it worked. I came back. So, what do we do now?'

It was a good question.

Alex knew exactly what he wanted.

He just wasn't sure of his chances of getting it.

'That's entirely up to you. You either come back to me so that we provide Sam with the family she deserves, or we sort this out in court. Your choice.'

Alex imbued every word with as much determination as he could muster.

Samantha was Katrina's weak point. The threat of taking her daughter away from her had worked before. He was counting on it working again.

He could barely breathe as he waited for her answer.

Tension drew his shoulders up towards his ears and shrunk his stomach until it felt as though it had turned inside out.

The anger seemed to drain out of her. The eyes she turned on him were sad and filled with pain. 'I'm sorry, but I just can't do it. I can't sign up to a loveless relationship for the rest of my life.'

Her words were like an arrow piercing his heart. Although he was bleeding inside, Alex tried not to show it.

His mind grappled to find a solution, but there wasn't one.

If there was a way to make Katrina love him, then he

didn't know what it was. He wasn't a magician; he couldn't conjure something up out of thin air.

'I can't help you with that.' Alex could barely get the words out. 'You can't force feelings that just aren't there.'

Katrina flinched. Then she seemed to shrink in front of his eyes. Her shoulders sagged. Her head dropped. 'I can't. I'm sorry. My lawyer will be in contact with you to arrange joint custody. Goodbye, Alex.'

She turned on her heel and stalked to the door.

Something inside him twisted tight, so tight he expected it to snap.

'You can't leave,' he said in a voice he hardly recognised as his own.

But it was already too late. She'd gone.

Alex stared after her.

He couldn't breathe. He couldn't move. He couldn't even blink as her words penetrated deep into his soul.

An invisible hand gripped his heart.

His chest felt so tight he half-expected to hear his ribs crack under the pressure.

It couldn't be too late. It just couldn't. He wouldn't accept that it was over.

He loved her.

He'd been forced to admit the truth when he'd found her gone.

Gone. Katrina.

The words finally connected in his numbed brain.

She'd run out on him again!

With a curse, Alex sprang towards the door, yanked it open and began sprinting down the corridor towards the lift. Stabbing the down button, he barely contained his impatience until the door opened.

Every time the lift attempted to stop he pressed the closed button.

On the ground floor, Alex headed directly for David. He was only halfway across the vast foyer when the security guard spotted him and pointed upstairs.

Alex stopped then completed the distance more slowly, not sure if he was reading the guard's unspoken message correctly.

'She went back upstairs,' David said with a beaming smile. 'She got halfway across the foyer and then seemed to change her mind about leaving. Turned around and got straight back in the lift.'

His heart turned over, then did it again.

When she'd left he'd feared she'd given up.

On him. And them. And a future together.

Her return upstairs gave him a sliver of hope.

Alex thumped David on the back and grinned. 'Remind me to invite you to the wedding!'

'What do you mean, he's not here?' Katrina demanded. 'He was here two minutes ago.'

Justine nodded. 'I know. I think he went chasing after you.'

Her heart turned over in her chest. 'He did?'

Again, Justine nodded. 'Well, he ran out of here as if the building was on fire only a couple of minutes after you left.'

'Oh.'

Her heart flipped again. When Alex had let her walk away, she'd thought he'd given up.

On himself. On her. And on the possibility of them having a future together.

Surely the fact he'd gone chasing after her meant he hadn't given up?

The thought made her legs give way beneath her and she sank down on the visitor's chair on the opposite side of Justine's desk.

At that particular moment the door to Justine's office flew open. Without looking, Katrina knew who it was. She could sense Alex. It was as if his presence somehow changed the air particles between them, creating an invisible string that joined them together.

Katrina turned her head. Although she moved at normal speed, it felt as if she were moving in slow motion.

Alex stood in the doorway, staring at her with an odd look on his face.

Katrina stared back.

Neither said anything.

She sensed rather than saw Justine looking back and forth between them. After a moment, the other woman rose to her feet and cleared her throat. 'I think I'll give you guys some privacy.'

Katrina heard her but barely registered a word she said.

'You came back,' Alex breathed when the door closed.

Katrina nodded, hands clenched tightly together in her lap. 'I should never have left in the first place.'

She'd been halfway across the foyer before she'd realised that.

She'd been convinced that she couldn't live with Alex knowing that he didn't love her.

But saying goodbye had almost killed her.

She'd stopped in the middle of the vast foyer with tears stinging the back of her eyes.

And as she'd stood there she'd realised there was something worse—much, much worse—than living with the knowledge that Alex didn't love her. And that was being without him altogether.

She needed him whether he loved her or not.

His face was all planes and angles. 'Why not?'

'Because it's time I told you the truth.'

'And what truth is that?'

Katrina dragged in a deep breath for courage and flattened her spine against the back of the chair. Then she stared him straight in the eye. 'I love you.'

Alex gasped. 'Say that again.' His voice was strangled; his eyes locked on her face.

Undecided whether his reaction was good or bad, Katrina said it again.

Pleasure swept through him, bright and sweet.

Accepting Samantha into his life had enabled him to put the past behind him. As a result, he'd achieved the sort of peace he hadn't known existed. But the joy he felt now lifted his spirit, his soul, to another dimension.

A dimension where the light seemed brighter and the air smelled sweeter.

He smiled a big wide smile and watched Katrina blink.

Then he crossed the room in a couple of strides, grabbed her hands in his and pulled her to her feet, straight into his arms.

He didn't waste time talking. Instead, he claimed her mouth with his, telling her without words exactly how he felt about her.

Only when he knew they either had to stop or find somewhere more private did Alex lift his head. He rested his forehead against hers. 'You've made me the happiest man alive.'

'Have I?' she whispered.

He nodded and lifted his head so that he could look her in the eyes. He picked up her hands in his. 'Will you marry me?'

She tried to pull her hands away, but Alex wouldn't let her. She shook her head. 'No. I'll live with you, but I won't marry you.'

Alex frowned.

Had he misheard her a moment ago?

He was sure he'd heard Katrina say that she loved him. So what was the problem?

'Why not?' he demanded.

She shrugged. 'If I ever get married, it will be for the right reasons.'

Alex wondered if there was something wrong with the connection between his ears and his brain, because what Katrina was saying to him just didn't make sense. 'And what reasons would those be?'

If she wanted the moon, he would try to get it for her.

The stars? No problem.

He would create miracles if that was what it took to have Katrina as his wife.

She angled her chin. 'Well, it certainly won't be because you feel obliged to do the right thing for our daughter.'

He cupped the side of her face. 'And is that the reason you think I asked?'

She nodded.

'Well, it's not.'

'Then why?'

He smiled, filling it with the intensity of the emotions teeming inside him. 'I asked because I love you.'

She gasped. 'No, you don't.'

'I do.' He smoothed the soft silkiness of her skin with his fingers. 'I think I've always loved you.'

She shook her head. 'I don't believe that!'

'Well, you should.' His mouth twisted. 'I seem to be very good at self-deception.'

She frowned. 'I don't understand.'

'Do you remember when you first came back? You burst into the board room like you did today.'

'What has—?'

He held up a hand. 'Wait. Let me finish. Do you remember I commented that you'd disappeared without a trace?'

She nodded. 'I remember. I made some crack about the TV show.'

'That's right. You did. I was glad you didn't give what I'd said too much thought, otherwise you might have realised what it meant.'

She frowned again, clearly puzzled. 'And what does it mean?'

Alex dragged in a breath. 'It means I had a private investigator searching for you. Not just in Sydney, but anywhere and everywhere.' He paused. 'I was desperate to find you.'

Her mouth twisted. 'That's only because I was pregnant.'

'Was it?' He recaptured her hands and squeezed them even more tightly. 'Don't forget, at the time I was convinced I wasn't the father.'

He felt her body jerk through their connecting hands as the importance of his words hit home.

'So, why were you looking for me then?' she asked, her voice little more than a whisper.

'That's the question, isn't it? I tried not to think about that too much. I didn't like the implication. I had all kinds of excuses, but the truth is that I was missing you like crazy.'

Her eyes glowed. 'Like crazy, huh? I like that.'

He pulled her to him and wrapped his arms around her waist. 'You do, do you?'

'Uh-huh.' Her face grew serious. 'You still don't have to marry me if you don't want to. Or have any more children.'

'I know I don't,' Alex replied with his usual arrogance. 'But I want the world to know that I love you and our daughter, and the best way to do that is to put a ring on your finger.' He put her away from him. 'And I *do* want more children.'

Her brow wrinkled. 'But you've arranged to have your vasectomy redone. Why would you do that if you want more children?'

Alex frowned and held her at arm's length. 'Who told you that?'

Katrina told him about the phone call from the doctor's office.

His frown cleared. 'I asked Dr Kershew to arrange the operation weeks ago,' Alex explained dismissively. 'It was just after I'd received the DNA test results. I was in a panic when I spoke to him. Maybe that's why he took so long to get back to me. To be honest, I'd completely forgotten I'd even mentioned it to him. Now that

I have my head straight, I'd love to have more children. A round dozen sounds like a good number.'

Katrina sputtered. 'I always said you were an over-achiever. Would you settle for half a dozen?'

His face grew serious. 'I'll settle for anything you want. I just want to make you happy. Do you know what I want to do right now?'

She shook her head.

'I want to take Sam and go home. I want to hold you both in my arms and tell you how much I love you. And then I want to take you to bed and start working on a brother or sister for her. What do you say?'

She took the hand he held out to her and squeezed it tight. And then she smiled. It was the most beautiful smile in the world. 'I'd like that. But I want you to know that, if all I ever have is you and Sam, I'll still be the happiest woman in the world.'

4_ST_6

MILLS & BOON®

Exciting new titles
coming next month

With over 100 new titles available every month,
find out what exciting romances
lie ahead next month.

Visit
www.millsandboon.co.uk/comingsoon
to find out more!